ONLY WITH YOU

KYRA LENNON

Copyright

Dedication

"Lie only become truth if person wants to believe it" - Mr Miyagi, Karate Kid.

To anyone who has ever been told you're something you're not.
To anyone who has ever felt looked down on, unworthy, or dealt with people spreading misinformation about you.
You will always be better than those who talk about you.
You owe nobody an explanation.

Trigger Warnings

Only With You covers topics such as anxiety, mentions of self-harm, a character pregnancy, and mentions of emotional and domestic abuse. Please proceed with caution.

Contents

1.	Chapter 1	1
2.	Chapter 2	3
3.	Chapter 3	10
4.	Chapter 4	22
5.	Chapter 5	31
6.	Chapter 6	39
7.	Chapter 7	51
8.	Chapter 8	57
9.	Chapter 9	61
10.	Chapter 10	65
11.	Chapter 11	72
12.	Chapter 12	79
13.	Chapter 13	91
14.	Chapter 14	95
15.	Chapter 15	107
16.	Chapter 16	115
17.	Chapter 17	127

18. Chapter 18   139

19. Chapter 19   150

20. Chapter 20   162

21. Chapter 21   175

22. Chapter 22   179

23. Chapter 23   195

24. Chapter 24   203

25. Chapter 25   209

26. Chapter 26   220

27. Chapter 27   228

28. Chapter 28   235

29. Chapter 29   240

30. Chapter 30   251

31. Chapter 31   258

32. Chapter 32   263

33. Chapter 33   270

34. Chapter 34   280

35. Chapter 35   286

36. Chapter 36   289

37. Chapter 37   299

38. Chapter 38   303

39. Chapter 39   314

40. Chapter 40   319

41. Epilogue   327

Acknowledgements   344

Other Books by Kyra Lennon   346

About The Author   347

Chapter 1

Cal

I RUBBED MY HAND across my face, my overgrowth of stubble grazing my fingers. I could smell the alcohol on my breath, and as I slowly regained consciousness, a dull ache crept across my forehead, worsening with each blink of my eyes. My mouth tasted like an old, dirty sock; dry and stale.

Where the fuck am I?

I wasn't in my bedroom. Wasn't even on a bed.

My eyes darted around the room I was in. The furnishings told me I was at Guy's. Where I'd crashed out on the sofa after seven solid hours of sinking beer after beer.

Guy and I were just two miserable bachelors now. Two grown-ass men who'd taken turns getting pissed over the state our lives were in. Last night just happened to be my turn.

Guy had watched Aiden for me, keeping his own head clear so I could allow myself one night to wallow in my misery.

A misery of my own making.

Shannen.

The pain in my head combined with the ache in my chest, and I swallowed down the urge to roar out the agony that had settled within me.

Hence the drinking. I'd just about managed to avoid it when I thought I'd lost her before, but now? I had nothing left to lose. Not with her.

With her...?

I'd already lost.

Shannen

48 HOURS EARLIER

"Why is it always raining?" Aiden whined.

He knelt up on his chair, facing the window and looking through the glass at the downpour outside. It was the first day of half term, and the weather was... unsurprising. There seemed to be some weird universal law that said as soon as kids are on a school holiday, the heavens must open. Still, it was only February, so it was to be expected. I just wished it could have waited for a day when we didn't have plans with friends.

"British weather, kid," Donovan said with a laugh.

Aiden frowned, making the rest of us around the table smile.

Cal, Aiden, and I had met up with Nova and Donovan in Dawlish Warren, a small seaside resort on the edge of Dawlish in Devon, and Gaby had joined us too. We'd intended to go for a walk and maybe play football with Aiden on the green, but no sooner had we got out of the car, relentless raindrops pounded on us, and we'd had to dash to the Boathouse pub, getting drenched in the process since there was limited cover on the way. Unfortunately, the rain showed no signs of slowing, so our afternoon would probably be cut short. Until then, though, we'd settled ourselves at a table near the doors at the back of the Boathouse.

"What do you want to eat, Aiden?" Cal asked him, dragging a menu across the table towards him.

Aiden remained staring through the window, chasing the raindrops on the pane with his finger. "Is there a chow mein?"

A ripple of laughter drifted around the table. "Not in here, sweetheart," I told him. "Sit down so you can choose something." I gently put my hand on his arm, and he turned himself around to sit down. At his other side, Cal looked at me as if I'd just performed some kind of miracle.

I gazed at him curiously, and he said, "If I'd asked him to do that, there would have been hell to pay."

Aiden had been grouchy because of the small change in plans. He'd been promised a full afternoon outside with us, but as Cal had explained, we couldn't do much about the weather. When Aiden was grumpy, he was far less inclined to do as he was told. I had a feeling that being with Nova, Donovan, and Gaby made him slightly better behaved, though. After all, he was out in public with three of the teachers from his school. I hoped nobody from work or any of the parents saw us. It wasn't common knowledge that I was dating the father of a child in my class, let alone that said child now semi-regularly spent time with other members of the staff of Oakwood Lane Primary School too. Although there were no rules against it, there was still a part of me that wondered how it would be viewed. Whether people would think Aiden might be shown better treatment than the other children because of my relationship with Cal. That wasn't the case, of course, but the possible perception concerned me sometimes. However, I figured on such a horrible day and away from home, we'd be safe from any potential witnesses.

"Is there a burger?" Aiden asked, breaking me from my thoughts.

"Yes," Gaby told him from her place across the table. "Well, a cheeseburger."

Aiden grinned and bounced in his seat. "Can I have a cheeseburger, please?"

"Yes," Cal said, sliding the menu slightly towards me so I could pick something.

Before I could look, Aiden pulled it back towards him again and said, "Are there desserts?"

"Only if you sit still," Cal teased, and Aiden immediately stopped wiggling, resting his hands on the table and sitting up straight.

"See, he listens to you," I said, smiling.

"Sometimes." Cal smiled back at me, and for a second, everything and everyone else around us vanished.

It had been twenty-four hours since my dad had surprised me by showing up at my flat. Forty-eight hours since Cal and I had been dangerously close to letting everything we'd built slip away. Since I'd told Jade and Scott to go to hell.

It had been a wild few days, but at last, everything felt... settled.

After meeting Cal and spending a short time with us, my dad had done a complete one-eighty on his feelings about my dating him. Well, maybe not a full one-eighty. I could tell his doubts about Cal weren't totally gone, but he had agreed to give him a chance. Perhaps he had seen how genuine Cal was. It didn't really matter what had swayed him, all that mattered was that nothing was hanging over our heads now. No judgemental friends. No concerned parents.

We were free to just be. Free to be the way most couples are when things are new.

Once we'd all decided what we wanted to eat, Cal and I went to the bar to order for everyone.

We ate together, chatting easily, and Aiden behaved like an absolute angel. By the time we were finished, the rain had stopped, and although the grass was too wet to play on without getting covered in mud, we decided we could still take a walk around the path by the sea wall. The bottoms of my and Cal's jeans were still a little wet, and Aiden's tracksuit bottoms were also damp around the ankles. With that in mind, we decided a puddle splash since we were going home soon wouldn't hurt.

Gaby was more than happy to join in, and while Nova and Donovan walked behind us, laughing at our antics, Cal, Aiden, Gaby, and I chased each other along the path, jumping in puddles to soak each other. Aiden's giggles and squeals were a joy to hear, and Cal was the most relaxed I'd ever seen him. It was like offloading everything from his past and my accepting it had taken a weight off his shoulders. Even though the two of us always had fun together and Cal was happy around me, something had shifted within him. Like he was free to fully let go. He looked at me with even more... something. The L word was still unuttered by him, even though I had told him twice now. But I didn't doubt that he felt it. Now more than ever, it seemed like it was only a matter of time before he said it, but

I wouldn't rush him or stress over it. We were together, no pressure on us, and that meant more than anything to me.

Aiden screeched with shock and delight as Cal took a run up behind him and splashed down into a huge puddle, covering Aiden and himself in rainwater.

"Gotcha," Cal said, winking at him.

Aiden gave a fake glare before laughing and throwing his arms around Cal's soaked legs. "I will get you back!" As Aiden let go of Cal, he pushed him, making Cal lose his balance, and I grabbed his arm to steady him. Aiden giggled as he ran away, and Gaby followed, also laughing while I wound my arms around Cal's waist.

"Having fun?" I asked, looking up at him.

He grinned, his deep brown eyes softening on me as they always did. "I am." He pressed a gentle kiss to my nose. "I'm glad we came out."

"Me too."

"Get a room," Donovan teased as he and Nova caught up with us.

Cal mouthed, "Piss off," at him, and they both laughed, Donovan clapping him on the shoulder as he walked by.

Considering how little time they'd known each other, they'd really connected. Donovan was a great guy, and I was sad he was leaving to go back to work in a couple of days, but he said he'd be back for Easter for a couple of weeks, so I hoped we could all hang out again then.

Cal pulled me in tighter. "I wish we could just go back to mine, take off our wet clothes, and warm up in a hot bath."

There was no mistaking how he intended for us to ensure the bath remained hot, and the thought made my stomach flutter.

I grinned up at him as a memory flickered through my mind. "I recall the day after we met, you mentioned us having a bath together."

"And we still haven't." Cal's hands tightened on my hips. "Next time we get a night to ourselves, we're doing that." He lowered his head and brushed a kiss loaded with promise to my lips.

I hope there's no law against being this happy. If there is, I'm so screwed.

I deepened the kiss, my arms winding around his neck.

I would never get enough of the way his lips alternated between feathering lightly against mine and then pressing harder, a constant dance that caused the flutters in my stomach to move downwards, making me press my thighs together and move my hips against his, hating that we were in public.

As our lips parted, albeit reluctantly, he grinned wickedly, and I let out a frustrated moan and a chuckle as I dropped my arms from around him so we could keep walking. He took my hand as we followed our friends. Aiden and Gaby had run all the way along the path and were splashing each other close to where the Go-Karts and mini golf were. Nova and Donovan were also hand in hand a fair way in front of us.

"It's going to be a while before we get some time alone," I said. "But at least we'll get to see each other a lot this week."

"Yeah." Cal sighed.

"Don't sound so excited about it," I teased, and he laughed, looking down at me.

"I like that we'll get to spend time together, but I'm just... I feel bad for asking you to watch Aiden so much."

One of the major side effects of Guy and Helen breaking up was that Aiden's childcare had abruptly halted. Helen had taken half-term week off work to help out, but now she was gone, Cal had been left with no time to figure out who would take care of Aiden while he was at work. Guy had already arranged to let Cal have a couple of days off so Helen didn't have to have Aiden for the whole week, but from Wednesday, they had a large job on and Guy needed him back. I'd offered to look after Aiden because, firstly, there was literally nobody else and I didn't want him to have to scrabble around trying to find a childminder last minute. But mostly because I wanted to. Cal and I had leapt over some huge hurdles together, and since I'd had Aiden for the night over the weekend—or would have if Cal hadn't come back—I figured we were in a good enough place that I could do this for him. Spending time with Aiden was fun for me. I loved seeing the changes in him, so helping Cal by watching Aiden seemed the logical solution, even if only for the short term.

Aiden hadn't yet been told that Helen wouldn't be around anymore. It was a conversation Cal didn't want to have with him. Not until he was totally sure she really wasn't coming back. From all he'd told me about what Guy had said, it didn't seem likely that she'd return. I hadn't spoken to him myself yet, but I wasn't certain he even wanted her back now. Either way, though, it would be hard for Aiden to know that the woman who had been there for him since he'd gone back to live with Cal would no longer be in his life. I'd floated the idea of her still being able to see Aiden, but Cal was adamant that wasn't going to happen. She'd really upset Aiden the last time she'd seen him, and although Cal knew Helen would never have truly meant to hurt him, he didn't want her around him anymore. So, he'd have to figure out a long-term plan for Aiden as soon as possible.

"You didn't ask," I pointed out. "I offered. I can easily keep him entertained while you're at work."

"And you're sure you don't mind staying at my place for a few days?" The worry in his gaze warmed me; he didn't take anything about us for granted. He really was different to anyone I'd ever been involved with. With them, everything was just... expected. With Cal, I was *asked,* and it only cemented for me that being with him was right.

I laughed out loud. "I get to spend three days with you both. It sounds great to me."

He smiled down at me. "You won't be saying that when Aiden's having a tantrum."

"You know I can handle those," I said. "Plus, he's been so good lately. He's doing really well at home and at school."

"I know. I just... Helen was always going on about how I was dumping Aiden on her. I don't want you to feel like that's what I'm doing."

As much as I had tried to create some kind of friendship with Helen, it had always been a lost cause when she refused to have any respect for Cal. He might not have truly cared what she thought about him, but her words had still left scars on him, and they made themselves known every time he doubted himself.

"Cal, you have to work, and this week, I don't. You're not dumping him anywhere. I'm watching your son because you are my man and I want to make your life easier."

His smile widened, and he squeezed my hand. "I'm your man, huh?"

"Yup." I smiled back at him, my heart swelling at the way he looked at me. "All mine."

"I really like hearing you say that."

"Well, get used to it. You. Are. My. Man."

He let go of my hand and slung his arm around my shoulder, pulling me close to him again. "And you are my woman. I'm going to take you out somewhere there are no chicken nuggets on the menu as soon as I can."

Laughing, I said, "That sounds good to me!"

We caught up with Nova and Donovan, and the four of us walked together, chatting as we finally reached Aiden and Gaby, whose bottom halves were soaked again from where they'd been splashing in any puddles they could find.

"Miss Davis is so fun!" Aiden giggled, jumping up and down.

Gaby grinned at him. "You're fun too, Aiden. I haven't had such a good time in ages!"

"Do we have to go home yet? I want to stay and play!"

He looked up at Cal hopefully, and Cal said, "Sorry, bud. We need to get home and get dried off."

Aiden pouted, and Gaby said, "I'm sure I'll see you again before you go back to school. Your dad's right. You need to go home and warm up so you don't catch a cold."

"When I got a cold before, Helen made me soup and we played games and watched movies all day."

Cal and I exchanged a look, both of us knowing how hard it was going to be to tell him he wouldn't see Helen anymore. Given Aiden's fears over losing people from his life, it wouldn't be easy.

"That's a pretty good way to spend a day," Gaby said. "But it's much better not to get sick. Maybe if you're really good, Shannen can take you into Exeter later this week and we'll go and get a hot chocolate and a cake."

Speaking straight to his heart.

Aiden's face lit up, and he looked up at me with wide eyes. "Can we?"

I nodded, smiling. "If you're good."

He smiled brighter, and I chuckled. We hadn't actually spoken to him yet about the arrangements for the week, but from his enthusiasm, he was probably going to be okay spending some extra time with me. He looked up at Gaby with adoring eyes, and Cal and I grinned at each other, pretty sure we were witnessing his first crush.

Chapter 3

Cal

EVERYTHING IS GOOD.

My life hadn't been a total shitshow for a good few years. Since getting Aiden back, things had improved, but it wasn't until I had my own place, had Shannen, that things took off a little bit more.

Telling her everything about me, about the things I'd done, hadn't been easy. Not just telling her but facing it again myself. The things I'd had to explain were things I kept locked away, and letting it out... it was a lot. Admitting my shame and thinking Shannen would never be able to get over it was the toughest thing I'd ever faced because no one other than my family had ever meant as much to me as she did.

Even though she still wanted to be with me, the one thing that played on my mind was her saying that the things I told her had scared her. I hated that she'd had that feeling about me because I would never do anything to harm her. But I also understood *why* it scared her. My life and hers were so different. Her upbringing had seen her protected from the kinds of things I'd experienced. She'd been raised with the upper-middle classes, gone to private schools, and mixed with people who had money. She hadn't known people who struggled to pay their bills. People whose parents worked sixty-plus hours so their kids could eat. She wasn't oblivious to the existence of those issues, she just hadn't grown up around them. Her parents were happy. Her world was safe, and mine had been unstable—and that was putting it mildly. Still, she had the kind of compassion inside her of a person who'd seen and experienced more than she had. Her lack of judgement and trust in her instincts were why she allowed me a space in her life, even amongst those flickers of doubt.

It was crazy, but like she'd said to me... it worked. And I wanted it to work.

It would work.

Shannen was the reason I hated myself a bit less. The reason I smiled more. And I had just had an afternoon with people who were becoming new friends. Even a few months ago, it never would have occurred to me to have anything more than a job, a place to live, Aiden, and Guy. I hadn't wanted a relationship, and I never thought I would. But now I had it, I was going to protect it with everything I had.

Even if I still didn't fully believe I deserved it. Even though those voices in my head taunted me.

As the six of us headed for the car park, chatting on the way, Aiden holding my hand, I was probably the happiest I'd been in years. Since way before Aiden. Maybe even since I was a child.

"You up for some drinks when I'm back at Easter?" Donovan asked from behind me.

Turning my head to look at him, I said, "Yeah, for sure. How long will you be back next time?"

He smiled, and Nova beamed beside him, her eyes lighting up. "I get two weeks for Easter, so plenty of time to hang out."

"We should definitely arrange some kind of day out," Nova said. "Maybe we could go to the zoo."

"Can we?" Aiden asked, jumping instead of walking. "I've never been to the zoo before!"

I tried to fend off a wave of guilt. Just another thing on my list of failures. I'd taken care of Aiden, but I was only now seeing how much difference it made to spend real time with him. Not simply watching TV or playing together, but actually doing things like my parents had once done with me.

"We can do that," I promised.

"We could have a picnic," Shannen added, and Aiden squealed.

"Yes! I want a picnic!"

"Easy, tiger," I said with a laugh. "It's still a few months away yet."

"We should take him to Crealy too," Shannen said. "He'd love it."

11

Another internal flinch. Fuck. I was surrounded by great places to take a child, and I mostly took him to the local park. Shannen moved closer to me and wrapped her arm around my waist as if she knew that I was thinking.

"Plenty of time," she said quietly, so only I could hear.

"What's Crealy?" Aiden asked curiously.

As Shannen explained that Crealy was a theme park with rides and attractions, my eyes narrowed slightly as my gaze caught something up ahead. We were getting closer to Shannen's car, and I noticed there was a police car parked next to hers. Instinctively, my palms grew sweaty, even though there was no reason for it. It was probably that someone had tried to nick something from the huge shop by the pub and the police had been called to deal with it, but even so many years later from any wrongdoing, the sight of a police car made me anxious.

Shannen must have noticed my hand getting hot in hers, and she looked up at me. "You okay?"

I nodded towards the police car, and when she looked, she joked, "I hope I didn't get caught speeding on the way here."

I smiled, trying to relax. Clearly, she didn't feel any kind of concern. Maybe they had just parked next to her and I was being paranoid.

We stopped a short distance from Shannen's car to say our goodbyes to Nova and Donovan, but the second we stopped walking, the doors of the police car opened. Two uniformed officers approached us, not walking with any speed or urgency, but their eyes were fixed on me.

What the fuck?

"Callum Lewis?" the tall male officer asked as they got closer. The other cop was a woman, who looked like the older of the two and was probably slightly senior to the younger man.

I instantly stiffened, and the group fell silent, turning towards the police, who had stopped beside us.

I nodded, waiting to see what they would say next.

The female officer said, "I'm Constable Wood, and this is Constable Williamson." She gestured to her colleague.

Shannen glanced up at me again, questions in her eyes that I couldn't answer.

"Mr Lewis," Constable Wood began. "We've been looking for you in connection with a report of domestic abuse."

I blinked, sure I must have misheard. Because of the shit from my past that had recently been brought to light, I'd assumed it would have to be about that. Attacking the man who had killed my mum and brother was the worst thing I'd ever done. Although, I wasn't sure how it could have been about that either. Edward Firth had been dead for years and it was unlikely a random witness would have crawled out of the woodwork after all this time that could link me to his attack.

But a domestic abuse accusation was even less likely since I had never done that.

I could feel everyone's eyes on me, and I hated it. The people around me, all except Shannen and Aiden, still didn't know me well. But they did know a bit about my past, and until that moment, none of them had judged me for it. But now? With police officers coming to find me when I was having an afternoon out, they had to already be re-thinking their connections with me.

How the hell did the police even know where to find me? It wasn't like I was in a place I went to regularly. *Why would they have thought to look for me in Dawlish Warren?*

Still unable to look at anyone, I kept my focus on Constable Wood. "What?"

"A Miss Katie Young came to us very late last night with the claims, and we need you to come into the station so we can ask you some questions."

The words around me dulled to a hum as I tried to understand what had just been said. Katie was Aiden's mum, who I'd never laid a hand on in a violent way. I'd barely laid a hand on her in any kind of way. We were in a relationship out of convenience more than anything. Any sex we had was when we both had an itch to scratch. Most of the time, we just lived side by side, taking care of Aiden together. Any other communication between us was minimal.

Why the fuck would she report me for something that had never happened when I hadn't been a part of her life for so long? Why would she come back now? Where the hell had she even been? And if she was around, why was her first instinct to make up a lie about me instead of wanting to see her son?

Was *that* why? Was she trying to discredit me to get him back?

My throat closed over as questions pounded at my brain, and Aiden's little hand squeezed mine. It had taken me so long to get my relationship with him to a good place, and the idea of Katie trying to take him back from me now made me sick to my stomach.

Shit. I really didn't need him to see this, and as if Shannen had had the same thought, she moved in front of us and held her hand out to Aiden.

"Aiden, let's go and play in the arcade for a bit."

Aiden's grip on my hand tightened, his dark brown gaze full of determination. "No. I want to stay here."

I glanced down at Shannen, trying not to think about all the sets of eyes on me. They had to be judging me now. They knew about my temper and what I'd done to Edward, so of course they were going to think I'd done something to Katie too.

When my eyes met hers, I flinched because where I'd only ever seen her trust in me, for a second, uncertainty flashed across her face.

She knows what you're capable of. It's not such a stretch to think that you'd hit a woman.

The thought that she doubted me about this slashed at my insides. When we'd had our talk at the weekend, I'd questioned her fear of me. Hated that she felt it because if she feared me even for a moment, that worry might never fully go away for her. I'd believed her when she said she wasn't afraid of who I was now. Let her make me think we would be okay because she understood me. She knew the things I'd done weren't the me I was now.

She'd heard what I said to her dad, and *he'd* seemed to believe me too.

I was still stewing over it because that was what I did. It wasn't until she'd looked at me with that hint of mistrust, though, that I'd seriously considered her doubt in me might be lingering.

I blinked, and when my focus cleared, Shannen's expression was the way it always was. Supportive. Trusting.

Did I imagine it?

I didn't have time to deal with the thoughts and fears that had started to press down on me. I needed to get Aiden away and find out what this was about.

I crouched down so I was at his level. "Listen, buddy, I need to talk to these police officers for a few minutes. Why don't you and Gaby go and play for a bit, and then we can go home."

As much as I thought Shannen might be questioning my innocence, I still wanted her next to me.

Aiden's eyes were wide, full of doubt and confusion. "I want to go home now."

Me too, kid. Me too. I was just grateful he didn't know what 'domestic abuse' meant. Or at least I hoped he didn't.

"Soon," I told him. Taking a deep breath, I looked up at Gaby, hoping I wouldn't see the same doubt on her face too. She offered me an understanding smile. "Please can you take him?"

She nodded. "How about we go and get an ice cream?" Gaby said, smiling at Aiden.

He glanced between me, Gaby, and Shannen, and I said, "Go with Gaby, mate."

Donovan stepped over to us and said, "We'll come too. Let's see what ice cream flavours they have."

Aiden still didn't look convinced, but he took Gaby's hand, and he, Donovan, and Nova began to walk across the car park to the small kiosk that sold snacks and drinks. I could hear Donovan talking to Aiden as they stepped away. Shannen stayed at my side, though I noted she wasn't touching me. Her posture was rigid as if she was in shock.

I turned my attention back to the officers, who had been patient while I handled Aiden.

"What exactly am I being accused of?" I asked, trying not to show any kind of nervousness.

"We'd like you to come to the station to answer some questions," Officer Wood said, completely sidestepping what I'd asked.

"And if I don't?" I hadn't done anything wrong, but confrontation with authority made me defensive. I was aware my sharp tone probably wasn't helping, but the words flew out of me unchecked.

"Cal," Shannen said gently, and I looked down at her. Her blue eyes were begging me to stay calm. "It's probably a good idea to go with them."

I stared at her. Once again, our difference in backgrounds was clear. Where she came from, everyone does as they're told. Almost to a ridiculous degree. But me? I wouldn't go anywhere with the police unless I had to.

"You're not under arrest," Constable Williamson said. "But a serious allegation was made against you. It would be far easier if you came with us now."

"Or what?" I asked, taking a step towards him, and Shannen moved in front of me as both officers stepped back.

"Hey," she said, while I continued to glare at the police over her shoulder. "Look at me."

I didn't want to look at her. I still saw the echo of doubt in her eyes, and I didn't like that it had been there. Didn't like that I'd been confronted by the police, especially in front of my son and people who were still getting to know me.

More than anything, I was afraid about what Katie had told them and whether it could lead to her taking Aiden from me.

"Cal," Shannen said again, resting her hands on my shoulders. Her touch drew my attention, though it didn't feel like it usually did. Didn't calm me because I was too consumed with the need to defend myself. I finally dropped my gaze to her, my jaw clenched. "Don't make this harder, okay?"

"I haven't done anything wrong," I snapped, her gentle tone bothering me when I felt as if my life was about to fall apart. Again. "Whatever she's told them, it's all fucking lies!"

"You need to calm down," she said, almost in a whisper so the police officers wouldn't hear her.

But I didn't want to calm down. I didn't handle fear well. Fear was a sign of weakness, and I couldn't show that. If I did, they would think I had something to hide.

And I didn't. Every horrible thing I'd ever done had already been laid out. There was nothing left now.

Shannen moved her hands from my shoulders and down my arms to link her fingers with mine. My eyes fell to the place our hands joined, and a surge of emotion shot through me. A different kind of panic. The kind that made me think I might lose this. Lose her if she didn't trust me anymore.

"Do you believe her?" I asked, my voice colder than I meant it to be.

There was the tiniest hesitation that sent a pulse of anger into my veins, but she shook her head. "I don't," she said, and I knew she meant it. But I couldn't stop myself circling back around to the fact that she had felt scared when she found out how badly I'd hurt Edward. Hearing this on top... how could I even blame her for having questions?

But she should have known me better.

"Mr Lewis," Officer Wood said, shaking me out of my increasing concerns. "The sooner you come with us, the sooner we can get this cleared up."

Cleared up? I'd just been accused of domestic violence. There was probably no evidence Katie could have manufactured at this point, but that didn't mean I would get away with anything, or that it would be 'cleared up'. This was her word against mine, and if it came to a court case, I'd never make it. I'd never be able to control my anger, and any jury would think I was guilty.

I glanced down at Shannen again, her eyes glistening with tears, and it tore at my fucking heart. Showed me that I hadn't lost her to her worries about whether I was a woman beater. She still cared. Still wanted me.

But how much more could I put her through? How much more of my shit could she take?

"Can you please watch Aiden for me?" I asked her, trying to keep my focus on what was real and not whatever my mind was trying to lead me to, and she nodded.

"Yes, of course."

With a sigh, I gave a single nod in return and turned to the officers again. "Fine. I'll come with you."

Shannen squeezed my hands before letting them go and stepping aside.

Constable Wood took a step forward, unclipping his handcuffs from his belt and brandishing them towards me.

I held my hands up and reared back. "What are you doing?" Flashbacks of the last time I was in handcuffs raced through my mind.

Edward. Fear. Panic. Trapped.

As if she'd noticed my anxiety, Shannen looked at the officers and said, "Please. Is this really necessary?"

"It's just a precaution," Constable Williamson said calmly.

"But I'm not being arrested and I've agreed to come with you." I took another small step back, tension weaving its way through my body

"And you've also already shown signs of aggression," Constable Wood said, confidently moving into my space and slapping the cuffs on my wrists as if I was scum. That was how he looked at me. How it made me feel.

Tension made way for shame and humiliation, and I fought with my instinct to bodycheck this dickhead police officer onto his ass. Due to the shitty weather, there weren't as many people around as there might usually have been, but we were far from alone. People driving into the car park turned their heads to watch, and the few who passed on foot lowered their heads, but I could feel them watching me once they'd walked by.

The last time I'd been arrested, it was at my home, and arrests happened in that area regularly. Now, I was out in the open, with a woman I'd only just managed to keep hold of, whose father had only recently agreed to give me a chance. When he heard about this, everything would go backwards. He'd want me out of her life, and Shannen would be torn in two again.

Or maybe she wouldn't. Maybe this public embarrassment would be the thing that finally pushed her over the edge.

And I could still lose Aiden too.

I could be left with nothing.

"Fuck this!" I spat, my frustration spilling from my lips as I felt the debris of my world crumbling around me, beating at every part of me.

"Callum," Shannen said, the use of my full name drawing my attention, but not enough to stop the anger coursing through my veins.

"I haven't done anything, Shan," I said. "I haven't done anything!"

She placed her hand on my arm again, her gorgeous blue gaze begging me. "Take it easy," she said softly. "Please."

I knew she was trying to help me, but I hated her seeing this. Seeing me in handcuffs, questioning what I was truly capable of.

Because just when I'd had the tiniest belief that we had something real, Katie had come along to ruin it.

I shrugged Shannen off, catching the surprise and hurt at my move as her eyes widened, and the tears that hadn't yet spilled brimmed to the surface again.

Before I could do or say anything else, Officer Wood took my arm. "Okay, Mr Lewis. Let's go."

The four of us headed across the car park, and as we passed the ice cream kiosk, I was glad Aiden wasn't looking my way.

Gaby had her eyes on me, but I kept my gaze straight ahead. I wouldn't look down, wouldn't show how shameful it felt to be paraded across a car park in handcuffs, but my insides burned with it. Shannen was still beside me, and even though I refused to look at her, I could feel her upset. At the situation, and at my behaviour.

This is what happens. This is why you stay away from people.

The words spun around in my mind, and while they rang less true than they used to, I could feel the doubt winning.

You promised you wouldn't hurt her, but you did. Not physically, sure, but my shitty attitude and dismissal of her comfort had hurt her.

But her wondering even for a second if I was capable of domestic abuse had hurt me too.

From behind me, I heard someone shout, "Aiden, wait!"

Shannen and I both turned to see Aiden running at us, Gaby behind him, trying to catch him.

Aiden reached us in no time, and he threw his arms around my legs. Looking up at the officers with defiance in his eyes, he said, "Don't take him away from me!"

Tears stung my eyes, and I couldn't even put my arms around him because my hands were bound. "Aiden," I began, trying to keep my voice even. "I need you to stay with Shannen, okay? I'll be home really soon."

"NO!" he shouted, holding on tighter, his face pressed against my legs. "You're coming home with us!"

I wanted to say something more, to try to assure him I wouldn't be long, but I didn't know that. I didn't know what was going to happen. I glanced at Shannen, and her eyes still shone with unshed tears. For me. For Aiden. For how insane all this was.

Because less than ten minutes ago, we'd been getting ready to go back to my place. To spend the afternoon together because that was where we were happiest.

Now, it had been blown out of the water. Her pain was almost tangible, and even amongst my resentment, I wanted to ease it. Wished there was something I could do to take it away from her. Because now, all I could see was her belief in me, and it messed with my head.

It messed with my head because I understood her confusion, and that colliding with my anger made me want to growl out the frustration building up in my chest.

Gaby reached us, and she fixed her eyes on me. "Go with them. Stay calm. Say nothing." She turned her attention to the officers. "Take him in, but don't expect to get anything out of him until his solicitor arrives."

My face creased in confusion. I didn't *have* a solicitor. Shannen's expression mirrored mine, and my head was starting to spin with the amount of stuff swirling around in it. Most prominently was the feeling of Aiden's tears soaking through my jeans and cracking my heart even more.

"Trust me," Gaby said. "Someone will be with you as soon as possible."

"We need to get going," Officer Williamson said, not giving me a chance to respond to Gaby. I hoped whoever she was sending would be quick because I wanted this over with.

"Okay, just give me a second with my son," I said. I wanted to kneel, but he was clinging on too hard, and I couldn't use my hands to untangle him. "Aiden, listen to me. I need you to go with Shannen, okay? She's going to look after you until I get back."

"No," he mumbled. "No, no, no. Don't leave me."

Tilting my head back, I tried to stay in control of myself, of my feelings. I wanted to hug him, and I hated that I couldn't.

Shannen lowered down to his level and placed a gentle hand on his back. "Sweetheart, I promise you, he isn't leaving you. He will be home really soon. The police just need to take him to the police station to ask him some questions and then he'll be back."

She glanced up at me, letting me know she really believed that, even if I didn't. I knew they could hold me for twenty-four hours, and they would probably max that out if they could.

What if they didn't let me go at all?

The fact was, I had done nothing wrong, but I was still being carted off like a criminal. What was to stop them keeping me there for longer than twenty-four hours if I said the wrong thing? If I lost control?

You are *a criminal. You might not have done anything to Katie, but this has been a long time coming.*

Aiden clung to me, and I took a breath and said, "Shan, take him. Please."

She nodded, trying to prise his arms from around me, but he gripped tighter, and the tears I'd held back spilled over. I couldn't wipe them away, just had to let them fall as my boy fought to remain attached to me.

"Aiden, come with me, baby," Shannen said gently, but I heard the tremor in her voice, letting me know she'd seen my tears.

Another stab deep in my gut.

Aiden screamed as she finally managed to tug him away from me, but she held on to his arms as he struggled to get free. With a quick shift, she hoisted him up from the ground and onto her hip, tears rolling down both their cheeks as the officers led me away.

All I could hear were Aiden's screams of, "NO! Come back! Bring him back!" and I knew Shannen would be able to calm him down, but his pain cut through me.

My breathing was ragged, and I heard Constable Williamson saying something to me, but I had no idea what it was. My chest ached with each step I took away from Aiden and Shannen because his screams and pleas followed me, torturing me.

"DAD!"

My heart stopped, and so did my feet. Officer Wood tried to tug me onwards, but I whipped around, making him lose his grip on me. Shannen's eyes were wide, and Aiden was leaning forward as if trying to reach for me.

Dad.

I hadn't heard that word from him since he'd first learned to talk. I'd been waiting. Waiting impatiently and wondering if he would ever call me that again. I knew things were better between us. That we were closer and things were the best they had ever been. But I wasn't sure if he would ever push over that last barrier.

But he did it. When I needed it the most.

I took a couple of steps back towards him, so I could kiss him goodbye and hope he knew how much I loved him.

Even if I still couldn't say it.

I'd barely got anywhere before I was grabbed. "No, you don't," Officer Wood said, dragging me back. I turned my head, but I was yanked again before I could speak. Constable Williamson had opened the back door of the police car, and I was shoved inside, the door slamming, leaving me staring at my son through the window, his screams ripping at my heart.

I dropped my head back on the seat, a weird mix of relief and terror rolling through me.

Aiden had finally called me Dad. But now... I couldn't enjoy it. Couldn't bask in that feeling because all I could think about was what would happen to me next.

As the police car began to move, slowly passing by the people I'd been having such a good time with, I saw Aiden clinging onto Shannen, his head buried into her shoulder, and the look of sheer devastation on her face as she watched us drive away.

Chapter 4

Shannen

AIDEN'S TEARS SOAKED INTO my shoulder as mine dripped into his hair. We'd already gotten drenched once today, so a stream of tears wasn't going to make too much difference.

"Shh," I soothed, gently stroking his hair. "It's okay, sweetheart. It's okay."

He didn't answer, but he tightened his arms around my neck, and I wished more than anything that I could take his worries away. Having him close to me was the only thing stopping me from totally falling apart because... what the hell had just happened? One minute, we were having a discussion about our plans for the week and for the Easter holidays, and the next, Cal was being taken away by the police.

For questioning.

About domestic abuse. On his ex. Aiden's mum.

From what Cal had told me, she hadn't been in the picture since Aiden was a year old. He'd told me, on the very few occasions she'd come up in conversation, that their relationship wasn't a real one. They weren't a proper couple who enjoyed each other's company. They were two people who had made a child together and decided to try and make it work to raise that child.

And he'd always sworn to me that he would never hurt a woman.

I'd believed him.

Do you still?

Yes. God, yes. Deep down inside me, I believed it. Not only because it was what I needed to believe, but because I *knew* him. The man I'd shared so much of myself with was not a monster. He wasn't someone who was luring me into a false sense of security, only to ruin my life. He was real. Honest.

But the moment the officer had said what Cal was being arrested for, it was like someone stole the air from my lungs. I couldn't breathe. Couldn't think past the shock.

He's got a temper. You know that. You know what he's done in the past.

That moment of doubt... I knew Cal had spotted it. His entire body had turned rigid, and I hated that I'd let it show. Hated that I'd even thought it.

The timing was awful. Just when things were finally able to move forward between us with no more secrets, this happened.

If it was true, why would he have left it out when he's shown me every other frightening side of himself?

Because him beating up a man who was responsible for the deaths of his family, while horrifying, doesn't hold the same concerns for me as admitting he'd hit Katie would have.

Sure, his violent streak *had* worried me. Made me consider whether I was safe. But lashing out at a woman he was in a relationship with was something he was adamant he would never do, so if he *had*... what would I even do with that information?

All I wanted to do was be at home, doing my best to comfort Aiden while I tried to figure out what I was feeling.

Aiden had called Cal *Dad*. It should have been the most beautiful moment. In spite of the situation, it still kind of was. Because the look on Cal's face had made my heart swell and break at the same time. I knew how much it meant to him, and when he'd tried to come back, to be close to Aiden and then been pulled away again, my whole body had weakened with the unfairness of it. I just hoped Aiden saying the magic word would help Cal. Carry him through the questioning he was about to endure.

"Shannen?"

Gaby's voice broke me from my thoughts, and I shook my head. My cheeks were sticky from drying tears and damp from the fresh tears that still fell. Her face was full of concern, and she wrapped her arms around

23

Aiden and me. The move triggered a sob to spill from me, and Gaby said, "Don't worry. I'll sort this out."

Her words reminded me of what she'd said to Cal a short time ago about how someone would be with him as soon as possible.

"What do you mean?" I asked as we separated. "You said something about a solicitor."

She smiled reassuringly. "My brother is a solicitor. I've just called him and he's going now. He'll meet Cal at the police station."

She must have made that call while I was lost in my thoughts. "Is that even... I mean... is he able to get there so fast?"

Gaby nodded. "When *I* ask, he will be there. He owes me a favour."

"And this is how you used it?" I asked. "Must have been some debt he got himself in."

Going out to deal with a person with little to no information to work with was a lot for Gaby to ask. Especially when she had even less idea of whether Cal had actually done anything wrong.

I hoped I didn't sound ungrateful; I wasn't. Just amazed by how quickly she'd jumped in to help out. Amazed, but not surprised. Gaby was a great friend to have, always there when anyone needed her. And man, did we need her.

My sister, Sadie, was also a solicitor and she was always so busy that she couldn't just run if someone needed her out of the blue. She, however, was not the kind of solicitor that would have been helpful to Cal. She was a corporate solicitor, but even if criminal law was her thing, I didn't think it wise to involve her given the sensitivity of the matter and that she was too close to me to look at him objectively.

Oh, God. I couldn't let my dad hear about Cal's arrest. At least until we had some idea of what was going on. We'd only just got his blessing. I didn't need him taking it back already.

Before I could say anything more, I felt a gentle hand on my back and turned to see Nova behind me, Donovan at her side.

"Are you okay?" she asked, then shook her head. "Stupid question, but if there's anything we can do, let us know."

I gave her a soft smile. "Thank you. I think... I need to get home. Well, not home to my place, but I'll probably call Guy and see if Aiden and I can wait at his house."

The last thing Guy needed was more crap news after his split with Helen, but he had to know what was happening. Plus, I figured Aiden would be better there than at mine. At least he had toys and changes of clothes there. I wasn't sure how long Cal would be, but if he did need to spend the night somewhere, it would be easier for him to be in a more familiar place.

Thank God we'd brought my car since we'd picked Gaby up. I wouldn't have been able to drive Cal's van back.

"Okay," Nova said. "We'll go home too, but please can you call us later when you know what's going on?"

"Sure." I nodded.

Aiden was still crying against me, and I put my hand in his hair again, gently stroking. He was starting to feel heavy in my arms, and I'd need to put him down soon.

Donovan lightly ruffled Aiden's hair, offering me a reassuring smile. "This will be okay, Shannen. It will."

As much as I wished that were true, an uneasiness had settled in the pit of my stomach, just like it had the day Cal had text me to tell me he needed to talk. The day all of his skeletons were released from his closet. It wasn't that I believed Cal was guilty, more that I had a bone-deep fear that he couldn't take much more. Not while his head was still wrecked from dealing with all he'd recently re-lived.

After saying their goodbyes, Nova and Donovan headed across the car park, leaving me and Aiden with Gaby, my brain still foggy.

"Come on," Gaby said, placing her arm around my back. "Let's get out of here."

We walked the few steps to my car, and I asked Gaby to take the key out of my bag and unlock the doors for me. She opened the back door, and I carefully leaned down to put Aiden into his car seat. As I tried to slide my arms from around him, he clung more tightly.

"Don't let me go," he said quietly.

My heart fluttered and ached simultaneously. I didn't want to let him go either, but I couldn't drive with him wrapped around my neck like a monkey.

"Aiden, it's okay," I said gently. "I promise I won't leave you, but I need you to let go of me for two minutes so I can talk to you. I'm going to stay right beside you."

He sniffled and nodded, loosening his grip until he finally dropped his arms from around me. My neck was warm and sticky from his tears, and I relished the cool air licking at my skin as I knelt by the car door.

"Is Cal going to jail?" Aiden asked, his eyes lowered.

Back to Cal already. I hoped that was merely a slip and not that he'd become so instantly afraid that Cal was going to leave him again that he was disassociating. There was no way to tell what was going on inside his head, but he was a worrier. His trust in Cal had been right on the edge of being cemented before this happened.

"No," I told him, taking his hand. "He's only gone to the police station to answer some questions."

"But they put handcuffs on him. On TV shows, they only put bad people in handcuffs."

I couldn't fault his logic. In a bid to teach kids right from wrong, they were taught that if you did something bad, then the police would take you away and lock you in jail. And he was too young to know that sometimes, mistakes were made, or that even good people sometimes had to answer questions from the police. It was the handcuffs that had prompted his question more than anything, though, and I had to fix it before he tried to answer the questions for himself and reached the wrong conclusions.

"Your dad isn't bad, sweetheart," I told him. "I promise he has just gone because he needs to explain something to the police officers."

"And then he'll come home?"

I nodded. "Yeah, he'll come home. It may not be until tomorrow because he needs someone to come and help him answer the questions, but he *will* be home."

That might have been the worst explanation I could have given, but I'd never had to explain the legal system to a five-year-old before, and with my head all over the place, that was the best I could do.

"Will you look after me?" Aiden asked, his voice now dropping to almost a whisper, and I squeezed his hand.

"If you want me to, but we're going to Guy's house a bit later because I don't have a key to your apartment, and there are toys for you to play with at Guy's."

"But will you stay?"

I nodded, the tremble of his chin causing my voice to croak. "Yes. If it's okay with Guy, I will stay."

26

"And Helen," he mumbled, and my heart sank further. I didn't want to be the one to tell him the truth about that situation. It wasn't my place. Instead, I chose not to respond to that part.

I straightened up, securing Aiden in his seat. "We're going to leave in just a few minutes, okay? Gaby will stay with you while I call Guy." I kissed the top of his head, an overwhelming feeling of love and heartbreak for him washing over me.

As I stepped back from the door, I looked at Gaby, and she nodded without me even having to ask. I mouthed, 'thank you' to her before taking my phone from my bag and walking to the edge of the car park to phone Guy. There was no guarantee he would answer right away because he'd be working, but I hoped he did because how the hell was I meant to explain what had just occurred via voicemail? I wasn't sure I would be able to put it into words anyway.

"Jesus Christ," I mumbled to myself as I scrolled through my contacts to find Guy's number.

It rang once. Twice. Three times. Four. I had never had a reason to call him before, so I didn't know how long he usually took to pick up, but on the sixth ring, I was about to give up when I heard him say, "Hello?"

His tone was confused because usually, if Cal needed anything, he'd call himself. Guy had to know something wasn't right.

"Hey," I said, heaving out a breath.

"Shannen? Is everything okay?"

Nope. It was about the furthest from okay it had ever been.

Trying to keep my voice from breaking, trying to prevent the tears from spilling over again, I said, "Erm... I... We were.... I'm at Dawlish Warren. We were about to come home when the police approached us. They said..." I paused, the words lodging in my throat.

"Shannen, take it easy. What's happened?"

"They..." I swallowed hard. "They took Cal to the station for questioning because... they said Katie has accused him of domestic abuse."

The words tasted bitter on my tongue, and I lost the ability to hold my tears in any longer.

This was so messed up. The two of us hadn't been able to catch a break since the day we met, and just when we had, it was snatched away again.

"What the fuck?" Guy said. "Katie?"

"Yup."

27

"But... why the hell would she say that now?"

"I don't know," I said, letting out another sigh. "Guy, my head is pounding, Aiden has only just calmed down, and I... I can't even think straight."

There was a pause. "Shannen, I know you've had to handle a lot from Cal lately. I know that. But he did not lay a hand on Katie. There's no way."

His fierce defence would usually have warmed me, but my head was a mess. All I could manage was, "Can you really know that for sure?"

Another pause. "For sure? No. I don't mean to sound like a dick by not believing a claim of domestic abuse, but I just don't see any way he would have done anything to her. He's done a lot of things, Shannen, but that is something he would never be able to come back from."

Some of the pressure in my chest eased at his words. What Guy was saying was something I believed too, but everything had happened so fast that I hadn't been able to override my worry with logic.

"Then why would she come out of the woodwork now?" I asked, putting a voice to the one question I couldn't shift. "Why if it wasn't true? What would she gain?"

"I don't know. I mean... unless she wants to get Aiden back and she thinks this would help her cause."

My blood ran cold at that thought. If she tried to take Aiden away from Cal, he would never survive it. Could that really be the reason, though? She hadn't sent so much as a birthday card in the time she'd been gone, so what would make her want him now?

"Guy, something doesn't feel right," I said. "If this was a simple case of asking him to come in for questioning, why did they come all the way down here to get him? How did they know where to even find him? The only people who knew we would be here today were you, the people who were here, and my mum. So... how?"

That thought had only just hurtled into my mind and fallen directly from my mouth. Maybe Guy's reassurance had freed up some space for other thoughts to filter through. And now it had taken hold, it took over everything.

Cal and I had never been to Dawlish Warren together before. I wasn't sure if Cal went often, but I didn't. I hadn't been down there in a few years, so it wasn't an obvious place to look for us, and yet the police car had pulled up right next to mine. Cal wasn't under arrest, so why would they need to find him so urgently that they had to come to us while we were out? Why not just call around to his place later?

The more I gave that thought some space to grow, the weirder it was. Unless...

No. There was no way Scott could have somehow found out where we were via my mum, was there? I'd told Mum we were giving Gaby a lift, but I couldn't envision any way she would be involved in giving Scott information about where I was. She certainly wouldn't have wanted public humiliation for me.

But something deep inside me told me something was not right about this. Something more than just my desire for Cal to be innocent.

"How was Cal when they took him in?" Guy asked.

"Confrontational, which probably didn't help."

Guy hissed out a curse under his breath. "Yeah, he doesn't handle accusations well, more so if they aren't true. So, what happens now?"

"Well, my friend Gaby was here when it all happened. As it turns out, her brother is a solicitor, and she has sent him out to advise Cal."

Gratitude for her fast response swept through me, knocking away a little of my fear. She didn't have to do that, especially not for someone she barely knew and had really only met properly once.

"Thank fuck," Guy said. "Please thank her from me. If left alone, he'd *actually* get himself arrested."

From the way Cal had squared up to the police, I knew Guy was right. Cal could control his temper, but if he felt cornered, he lashed out like a wounded animal.

"What time do you finish work?" I asked. "I was thinking it might be better for me to come to yours with Aiden. He asked me to stay with him until Cal gets back, though. Would that be okay?"

"Of course. I've got about an hour to go, so I'll be home in about an hour and a half. Maybe go back to yours and have a cuppa, then swing around to mine after."

"Okay, thanks. Guy, I..." I paused. I meant to tell him what Aiden had said about Helen, but then I realised I hadn't actually checked in with him. They'd only split up two days ago.

"What is it?" Guy asked patiently.

"I... Sorry. I just dropped all this on you and I haven't even asked how you're doing."

Guy let out a long breath. "Under the circumstances, I understand why, but thank you for thinking of it. I'm... okay, I guess. It still isn't really sinking in."

"I can imagine. Have you heard from Helen?"

"No. I didn't expect to. She said she'll be over on Wednesday night for her stuff, so we'll probably talk a bit more then."

I wanted to ask more, to see how he was feeling and maybe offer a friendly ear, but I was very aware that I'd left Gaby with an upset Aiden, and I wanted to get back to him.

"Aiden was asking about Helen," I said hesitantly. "I don't know what to say to him. I don't think I should be the one to explain anything."

"Cal was going to do it before he brought Aiden over next, but now..." he trailed off. "I'll talk to him if he brings her up, but hopefully, he won't. He doesn't need any more bad news today, but I also don't want to lie to him."

That somewhat answered my question about whether he thought the two of them might get back together. If there was even the slightest chance in his mind, he could have just told Aiden she'd gone away for a couple of days, or she was working late. But this suggested he wasn't expecting her to come back permanently.

"Okay," I said. I wasn't sure on the best course of action, but it also wasn't my place to make decisions on what was best for Aiden. Guy had way more right than I did, so I'd let him take the lead on this.

"I'd better go if I want to finish on time, but Shannen, don't drive until you've calmed down. I don't need to hear you've been in an accident on top of everything else."

His words of concern eased another bit of the stress inside me. We got on well, we had from the start, but it was nice to feel support from him.

"I promise," I told him. "Thank you. I'll see you soon."

Chapter 5

Shannen

Two hours felt like both forever and no time at all. We got back to Exeter, had a cup of tea at my place, and dried off like Guy suggested. We went to Guy's about thirty minutes after he said he was home to give him a chance to shower and change. I'd asked him if it was okay if Gaby came with us because she had a direct line to her brother, who would have the fastest information on how things were going with Cal, and he agreed.

And while that all seemed to go quickly, I felt like Cal had been missing from my side for days.

I hated that he was taken away so abruptly after such a great day. Hated that he missed out on that special moment with Aiden.

Hated that he'd felt my doubt.

I wanted to see him. Be with him. Tell him I trusted him. Believed him. Because I did.

I just hoped he already knew it.

As we approached Guy's door, Aiden ran ahead and knocked while Gaby and I followed him up the path to the steps. Guy only took a moment to answer.

He was dressed in a pair of old, faded blue jeans and a white T-shirt that hugged his muscles, and he smiled as he looked down at Aiden.

Aiden had been quiet the whole way back to Exeter. He'd just sat down, drawing some pictures while we were at my flat. I'd tried to see if he wanted to talk, but he'd shaken his head when I tried to engage him in conversation. He'd had a shock, seeing his father being taken away like that, but I hoped once we were at Guy's, he'd open up.

Guy bent down to scoop Aiden up into his arms, then turned his attention to us. He let us inside before pulling me into the hug with Aiden.

"You okay?" he asked, and I nodded against his chest.

Stepping back after a moment, I said, "Guy, this is my friend, Gaby. Her brother is the one who is helping Cal."

Guy looked at her with a level of familiarity. "Hi. It's nice to meet you. I've seen you at the school when I've picked up Aiden." His gaze swept up and down her, probably thinking how different she looked in casual clothes rather than her schoolteacher attire, offering her a smile.

Gaby nodded, clearing her throat. "You too. Thanks for letting me gate-crash."

Guy chuckled, his smile slightly breaking through the stress that had been written through his features. "The more, the merrier."

"Where's Helen?" Aiden asked, lifting his head to look at Guy.

Guy stiffened, his smile fading as quickly as it had appeared. He took a moment as if bracing himself, then said, "She's at work, mate."

I shot him a sympathetic smile as he lowered Aiden to the ground. He said he wasn't going to lie, but I understood how difficult that conversation was going to be. Perhaps he'd thought better of placing anything more on Aiden's already heavily burdened shoulders. If I was honest, I thought it was better to hold off until there was less going on.

"Oh, okay," Aiden said. "Can I go and play in my room?"

Smiling gently, Guy said, "Course you can," and Aiden ran off up the stairs.

"I love that he still calls it his room," I said, watching until Aiden had disappeared from sight.

"Me too. Has he been okay this afternoon?"

"Quiet." I sighed. "He cried himself out, I think. I want him to have some time to himself, but I also don't think he should be left alone for too long. He's still upset, but he's not saying much."

"Hmm, wonder where he gets that from."

It was my turn to chuckle. Like father, like son was more than just a phrase where those two were concerned.

"How are you doing?" I asked, though I glanced at Gaby, hoping she didn't feel too left out of the conversation. She smiled to let me know she was fine.

Guy rubbed at his forehead and shrugged. "I'm... yeah." He let out a weak laugh, and I reached out and took his hand.

"I'm sorry, Guy," I told him. "I really am."

With another sigh, he said, "Thanks. It feels so bloody empty in the house without her here, but things hadn't been right for a long time. Since I've had time to think, I've realised how long things had been off. I still love her, and that will take a while to fade, but honestly... quiet as it is around here, it's also a relief not to have to tiptoe around her all the time." Guy glanced at Gaby too. "Sorry if that made me sound like a prick. It's a long story."

With a shake of her head, Gaby said, "No judgement here. I am the queen of bad relationships." Her eyes dropped to the floor briefly before she bounced back to her usual self. "You guys probably have some things to talk about so I'm going to see if I can reach my brother and find out if there are any updates. Is it okay if I..." she trailed off, indicating to the kitchen.

"Yeah, sure," Guy said. "We'll go and sit in the living room, but... don't hide in the kitchen the whole time. Come and join us when you're ready."

He'd clearly felt her slight unease at being the newcomer in this scenario. It was an odd change as, not so long ago, it had been me standing awkwardly in the hallway.

"I will."

Gaby went into the kitchen, and I followed Guy into the living room. We both sat down on the sofa, and I looked around. It *did* feel weird without Helen around, although in a strangely positive way. In spite of the tension of the current situation, somehow, it felt easier to breathe. I hadn't realised how much of my energy was sucked out when she was in the room. Even though I didn't have a problem with her personally, she had an ability to create uneasiness, and now she was gone, it had eased. Some of the floral displays that had sat in the corners of the room had vanished too, leaving empty spaces where they used to sit. It didn't look like something was missing, though. It looked like even the lounge had a freer feeling to it.

As if he knew what I was thinking, Guy said, "I always hated those flowers."

33

A small laugh escaped me, but I didn't comment on the decor. Instead, I said, "Should we check on Aiden?"

"Yeah, in a bit. I just want to make sure you're okay. How are you feeling? Really?"

That was a pretty loaded question. A plethora of emotions had rushed through me, none of them settling for long before another took over. Drawing in a deep breath, I said, "I'm pissed off that our day was ruined by this. I'm confused about why Katie would report Cal now. I hate that Cal was carted off in front of our friends, and that Aiden called him Dad for the first time and he couldn't even enjoy it because he was dragged away."

Guy blinked. "What?"

I smiled softly, the memory warming me a little. "He did it without thinking. Aiden saw Cal was being taken away, and he just screamed it out."

"Wow," Guy said, leaning back. "I wish I'd seen that."

"It wasn't all good. There was a moment where Cal looked so relieved to have heard that word from him, but then he was pulled away and he looked like someone had ripped his heart out." With a sigh, I said, "I wish the timing had been better. And that none of the last few hours happened. I don't know what the hell I'd have done if Gaby hadn't been there to get someone to help Cal. I don't think he would have been able to keep his cool on his own."

Guy gave a slow nod. "I've been thinking about what you said, and I don't get why the police were *so* desperate to speak to him that they came to find him either. This is not a time sensitive thing. If Katie said Cal did something to her years ago, she probably didn't have any proof, and also, he's not a threat to her now because he had no idea she was even in the area. So, waiting a couple of hours for him to get home surely couldn't have hurt."

"Exactly. I feel like..." I hadn't had time to think it all the way through, but I couldn't help thinking Scott had a hand in this somehow. Once Katie rocked up at the police station, if he was there and heard Cal had been reported for something, he would have gone out of his way to get him pulled in. I just couldn't figure out how anyone had known where to find us. "Do you not think it's a bit coincidental that this happened the same weekend Cal told me about his past? More specifically, the same weekend his existence caused me to step away from my former best friend, who happens to be engaged to the man who couldn't nail Cal for his past crime."

"Well, the fact that your former best friend is engaged to the man who arrested Cal years ago is a pretty big coincidence anyway, so it's not impossible that another one happened."

He had a point. What were the chances that I would date a man Scott had arrested? He'd arrested a lot of people in his time, and the likelihood of me even *meeting* one of them was slim, let alone being in a relationship with one.

But I couldn't shift the feeling that something didn't make add up about this.

Or maybe I was just walking on a dangerously thin tightrope, with paranoia on one side and denial on the other.

"I miss him," I said. "I've been apart from him for a lot longer than this, but I miss him." An ache ran through me as I, again, thought about what we should have been doing. About our afternoon together at my place or Cal's. Now, all I could think about was how Cal was handling whatever he was being told at the police station. Whether he was staying calm or losing his shit.

Whether he was remembering my fleeting moment of mistrust.

"The questioning shouldn't take too long, Shannen. Especially not with a solicitor there."

I was about to answer when I heard footsteps, and then Aiden wandered into the room. Without a word, he sat down beside me then climbed onto my lap, cuddling in tight against me and curling himself into a ball.

I cast a look at Guy as my heart filled with warmth, and he smiled at me. I wrapped my arms around Aiden, and he shuffled as if trying to get even closer to me. Like he needed to feel safe.

"Do you want to talk about anything, sweetheart?" I asked softly.

He shook his head against me, then after a moment, he said, "Is my dad coming home soon?"

God, why was this day such a mess of emotions? The pain of Cal being taken away, to the happiness at hearing Aiden say 'Dad', to the worry and guilt that continued to hang over me. It was too much. Too extreme.

"I don't know," I told him honestly. "I think it will still be a while yet. What do you want to do while we wait?"

"Nothing," he mumbled. "Just sit with you."

"Okay." I gently stroked his hair, running my fingers through the soft strands, hoping to comfort him. "We can do that."

"Do you want a drink?" Guy asked me.

"Coffee would be amazing." Vodka would also have been amazing, but I had to drive and keep an eye on Aiden.

With a nod, Guy stood up, leaving Aiden and me alone.

"Shannen?" Aiden said quietly.

"Yes?"

"If my daddy goes to prison, who will I live with?"

Bless his sweet little heart. It sucked that he was too young to understand what was going on, but it didn't surprise me that this had crossed his mind. If Cal wasn't in the picture, where *would* he go? Back to his foster family? To Guy? Or would he have to go back to his mum since she was around all of a sudden?

The very idea made me shudder. She might have been his mother, but where had she been all this time?

Moreover, if Cal was violent, why would she have left her child with him?

That thought hadn't occurred to me before. I didn't have time to analyse the answers, though. Not when Aiden needed me.

"Your dad isn't going to prison," I told him. While I couldn't be one hundred percent certain of that, I was still relatively sure because I couldn't envision what kind of evidence Katie might have been able to present. I wasn't sure if she would even *need* any evidence. I didn't know if the police could just arrest people with no proof of anything and hope they confessed.

I was way out of my depth. Not for the first time with Cal. I couldn't even guess what went on inside a police station. I didn't watch crime-related TV shows often enough to know how their procedures worked. Criminal activity had simply never been a part of my life.

"But what if he does?" Aiden pressed, sounding more fearful this time. "Who would look after me?"

My heart ached because he was looking to me for answers I didn't have. If Katie was looking to get him back, would she be able to just take him because she was his mother, or would there be a getting-to-know-you plan beforehand? And if so, would he have to go into foster care because he had no other blood relatives?

My head began to pound with the questions. Not just Aiden's, but my own too.

I hadn't been prepared for this. Wasn't sure how to reassure him.

"I don't know, sweetheart," I told him. "It isn't going to happen, but if it did, then I promise you I would make sure you're somewhere safe."

He leaned back a little to look up at me, his dark eyes shining with tears. "I liked living with Angela and Simon. They were nice to me. But I would like to live with Guy and Helen or with you."

This kid was going to kill me. One minute, my heart was breaking, the next it was melting. Often, it was doing both of those things at the same time. I hated that Aiden had already been through so much in his five years. If he had to get used to living with a different foster family than Angela and Simon, or even if he had to go with his own mother, it would mess with his head more.

And he still didn't know Helen wouldn't be around anymore.

"And we would love to have you," I told him, stroking his hair again. "But your dad will be home, and he'll keep on looking after you."

He nodded, snuggling against me again. I wished I had more solid answers for him. The truth was, if it came to it, I would have happily been the one to take care of him, but I doubted it would be possible because of my job. Aiden had become such a huge part of my life now, the idea of not having him around made me feel ill.

I turned my head as I heard soft footsteps approach, and Gaby entered the room, putting her phone into her pocket. I raised a hopeful eyebrow, praying she had some news.

"My brother is with Cal at the station now," she said. "Cal hasn't been questioned yet, and Gavin has asked that I don't call him again because he's going over everything with Cal shortly."

"Any word on how Cal is?" I asked.

She shook her head. "I got the feeling he didn't want to go into that because Cal was in the room, but he is in good hands, Shannen. Don't ever tell him I said this, but my brother is great at what he does."

I laughed as she cringed at her words, but I could see the pride on her face. She hadn't really talked much about her family, and I felt bad that I didn't know much about her life outside of work other than her dating disasters. I knew a lot about *her*, what she liked and disliked, but I hadn't got any information on where she came from. This probably wasn't the right time to ask either.

"So, now we wait, I guess," I said with a sigh.

She nodded. "Yup. I was thinking, though, after we've had a drink, instead of sitting around watching the clock, why don't we go out and do something fun? It's not too late. We could go bowling."

Looking down at Aiden, I said, "What do you think? You want to go out?"

"I want to play with my Lego," he answered. "But I want you to help me."

I glanced at Gaby and smiled, and she laughed lightly. "Okay," I told him. "We'll have to ask Guy if he wants to help too."

"He likes Lego," Aiden said. "He'll want to."

I wasn't sure how much it would help take our minds off things, but I was willing to give anything a go. Anything to stop my mind from wondering if Cal was staying calm, if he would answer the questions the police had for him.

And mostly, if my life was about to take another dramatic turn.

Chapter 6

Cal

TEN HOURS. I WAS at the police station for ten hours. Being asked the same questions over and over until I was ready to lose my shit. If Gaby's brother, Gavin, hadn't showed up, I would have spent the night in a cell for, at the very least, hurling abuse at a police officer.

It wasn't the first time I'd been taken in for questioning, but the last time, I'd been strangely calm about it. Fear had gripped me internally because I didn't want to go to jail, but if I had, I would have deserved it.

This time, though, the accusations were unfounded, and I'd grown increasingly angry as the day went on.

Katie had told the police that when we were together, I hit her regularly. Starting with the occasional slap and eventually resulting in an attack that left her covered in bruises, and that was the day she left me.

Funny, since she'd had no trouble packing her bags and skipping away, leaving Aiden behind.

I barely touched her in any way, let alone violently, so to say she had been black and blue when she walked out was ridiculous. I didn't have it in me to hit a woman, no matter how pissed off I was, and some days, Katie had pushed my temper to its limits. I'd never even raised my hand to her, let alone slapped her with it.

Gavin had spoken to me before the questioning started and asked me about the allegations. I told him what the situation was with her, and he believed me when I told him I'd never hit Katie. He was a good guy, calm but serious, and his influence had helped somewhat to keep my outbursts in check while I was being interviewed.

When I was finally released pending further investigation, I was exhausted. Exhausted and pissed off.

I knew Shannen was at Guy's with Aiden because Gavin had told me so after Gaby called him. Guy had confirmed that Shannen and Aiden were sleeping over at his place when I rang him for a lift home. Both had gone to bed, but Shannen had got up again because she couldn't sleep.

And I didn't know how to feel about that. About her being at Guy's, waiting for me.

Because I saw something in Shannen's eyes earlier that I didn't like. Something I'd only recently allowed myself to believe I was never going to see from her because she trusted me.

Doubt.

A flicker of it danced across her gaze at the words 'domestic abuse', and as much as I told myself I'd imagined it, I knew I hadn't.

And it messed with my head.

I understood her doubt. I'd waited for it the whole time I'd known her. But it still made me feel like shit to know that she'd considered there was truth to Katie's accusation.

Shannen had been the best thing to walk into my life... ever. Every single second I was with her, especially at first, I'd been edgy, just waiting for her to figure me out. To push me to tell her the truth about where my family was and what I'd done. And she never did. She was patient, and she had given me the benefit of the doubt over and over. She'd even risked upsetting her own family for me, not to mention ditching that bitch she used to call a best friend.

I still didn't think I deserved it. Deserved *her*.

Yet when I'd seen that moment of questioning cross her gaze, it fucking hurt. Even if you half expect something, when it happens, it's still like being kicked in the gut.

Through the endless circle of questions I'd had to answer that day, I couldn't stop seeing that one moment when Shannen had looked at me as if she wasn't sure who I was. By the time the police let me go, it had eaten me up from the inside.

Although Gavin had offered me a ride, I didn't want to take up any more of his time. I wasn't sure how the hell I was going to pay whatever rate solicitors charged as it was.

Guy arrived within ten minutes of my call, helped by the fact there was less traffic on the road at just after half past two in the morning.

When I got into his car, I huffed out a sigh and dropped my head back against the headrest. From the corner of my eye, I could see Guy had turned his head to look at me, making no move to drive out of the police station car park yet.

I'd already explained to him what had happened, that there was a chance I might get called in for more questioning, so I wasn't sure what he was waiting for me to say.

"Do you want to go home and I'll bring Aiden over in the morning, or do you want to go back to mine to see Shannen?" Guy asked.

I wanted both. To go home and be on my own, *and* to see Shannen. I wanted to give my boy a goodnight kiss because he had been on my mind all day too.

He'd called me Dad, and I hadn't been able to get to him to enjoy the moment I'd waited for for so long. Hearing him shout out to me, hearing his cries, was the worst thing. I knew Shannen would make him feel better, but being unable to be with him felt shitty.

"What did Shannen say to you?" I asked.

She must have said something to him. Something that questioned my innocence. Or she'd noticed that I saw her doubts and talked to him about it because, usually, he wouldn't have had to ask what I wanted. He would have known I would want to be wherever Shannen was.

"About what?" Guy asked.

"Me. About me being questioned. Does she believe me?" I braced myself for his response. "Or does she believe I hit Katie?"

"She believes you," Guy said, and I finally turned my head to look at him. The car was dark, but I could still see his expression clearly. A look I'd seen on his face a million times before when he was sick of my shit.

"Really?"

Guy shook his head. "Cal, don't. Do not push her away because you've already made an assumption about how she feels, or because you're projecting how you feel about yourself onto her. She's been worried sick all day. Aiden has been stuck to her side most of the time, but once he'd gone to bed, I got a pretty good idea of how she really feels. And she...” Guy trailed off, his eyes dimming like he'd said more than he meant to.

"What?" I asked, staring at him.

"It's not my place. I shouldn't have said anything."

I could see from his expression that he wished he'd kept his mouth shut. Guilt was etched on his face because he hated to betray someone's trust, but something had started to tumble out because he was pissed off with me and he couldn't take it back.

"Well, you did," I said. "What is it?"

He sighed, scrubbing his hands over his face. "One of the parents of a kid in Aiden's year saw what happened at Dawlish Warren. They saw you being taken away by the police. They contacted the school via their social media page, and the headteacher called Shannen to ask what was going on."

My eyes widened before panic shot through me. Shannen had had enough threats to her job lately; she didn't need this on top. "What did they say?"

Shaking his head again, Guy said, "You need to talk to Shannen about that. But... Cal, do not freak out over it because Shannen isn't."

I wasn't in the mood to be called out. He was right about me freaking out and about making assumptions, but I didn't want to hear it. Self-destruct was my default, and I was way too far gone to listen to reason. If someone had seen me get carted away in a police car and the school's head had been contacted, that couldn't mean anything good.

You need to get away from her before you hurt her any more.

I'd had too much time to think, and the reminder of what a mess I was had been pounding at my skull since the moment I was picked up that afternoon.

I *should* have asked Guy to take me to my flat so I could try to get my thoughts straight.

But that wasn't the decision I made.

There was tension in the car on the way back to Guy's, as if he could feel the storm brewing inside me.

If Shannen had been unsure of the truth about what I'd done to Katie, that made her sensible. Blindly believing someone without taking a moment to consider the possibilities was not a good idea, and she was way too cautious and logical to just accept my word. Anyone in her position, with someone like me, would have looked at the whole picture before reaching a conclusion.

Yet I was still pissed off about it. All it did was cement the idea that she deserved better.

Not a word was spoken between Guy and me, not even as we parked outside his house. The tension in me was affecting him, and as we entered Guy's place, he said, "Do not fuck this up, Cal. I mean it."

Instead of answering, I walked in ahead of him and went straight upstairs to see Aiden.

His room was dark, and I quietly stepped inside. He looked so peaceful. Probably drained from crying so much and tired from the amount of energy he'd burned jumping in puddles and running around earlier.

Quietly walking over to him, I didn't sit down. Instead, I stood by the bed and gently stroked his hair.

"See you in the morning, buddy," I whispered before placing a light kiss on his cheek and leaving his room again.

I could easily have stayed there with him. Sat on the edge of the bed and hidden. From my thoughts, from Shannen, and from Guy, who had predicted my mood with annoying accuracy.

But I couldn't.

Because I also needed to have Shannen in my arms. I needed her body against mine, even amongst my anger.

On the way down the stairs, I could hear Guy and Shannen talking quietly in the living room, though I couldn't hear what they were saying. Wasn't sure if I wanted to know. I was exhausted and on edge, and I couldn't stop the nagging voice telling me that now was not the time to have any kind of conversation because my head was not in the right place.

I took off my jacket and hung it on the coat rack, then took off my shoes. As I entered the living room, Guy was heading for the door. As he passed me, he gave me a warning look before he said, "I'm off to bed. See you in the morning."

I nodded once, letting him know I understood what he wasn't saying. To stay no matter what happened with Shannen and be there for Aiden in the morning instead of leaving to lick my wounds.

Once he'd gone, I stepped further into the room, where Shannen was standing between the coffee table and the sofa. She must have gone back to hers when it got late and I wasn't back yet because she was wearing her grey and pink stripy pyjama bottoms with a grey vest top. Her hair was tied back in a ponytail, and she looked knackered. Her face was pale, and dark circles had begun to form under her eyes. It wasn't just that, though. Her shoulders were slightly slumped, like she knew exactly where this conversation was going, and the knot inside my stomach tightened.

"Hey," she said quietly.

I kept my eyes fixed on her, and I felt like shit. There she was, my woman, who'd been waiting for me all day, and I didn't know what to say to her.

"Are you all right?" she asked, but she didn't make a move towards me.

"Yeah. I'm all right."

I wanted her in my arms. I wanted to hold onto her and feel her close to me because that was the only thing that ever brought me back from wherever my mind took me.

But I was hurt too. Hurt that she doubted me, even if I understood why.

"Cal, I..." she began, but then stopped and looked down, letting out a frustrated sigh.

And that was when I gave in. I crossed the room towards her and slipped my arms around her waist. She flung her arms around me, holding me so tight it was almost painful, but I didn't want her to let go.

She looked up at me, tears making her eyes glisten. Deep in her gaze, I could see her guilt. That she had been torturing herself about her moment of uncertainty all day.

After another moment of holding her, I let go of her waist, took her hand, and led her to the couch. I sat down in the middle, then l lifted my legs and lay down on my side. I tugged Shannen's hand, beckoning for her to join me, and she did, lying on her side too, facing me. I wrapped her up in my arms, keeping her close to me, and she tucked one arm between us, the other winding around my back.

For ages, we just lay there together, not speaking, listening to the ticking of the clock on the wall.

"I didn't do it, Shan," I said eventually. "I didn't do anything to her."

"I know," she mumbled. "I know you didn't. I just... I didn't, and I still don't understand why she would have made a claim against you after so long. I thought for a second... if it wasn't true..."

She trailed off, and I said, "It's a lot of effort to go to for nothing."

"Yeah. A lot. But then I thought that if you had done it, why would she have left Aiden with you? Wouldn't she have wanted to protect him from you if you were violent?" She shuffled closer to me, holding me tighter as if trying to show me how sorry she was, and I kissed the top of her head.

"I mean... I know I can't say much since Aiden was taken from me, but she stopped showing interest in him the moment he learned to walk. I don't know if she ever really cared about him."

"Any ideas why she did this?"

My chest jolted as the possibility that she might want Aiden back shot through me. "Not really. But if she's decided she wants to take Aiden now, I really might hurt her."

I couldn't imagine what life would be like without him. I could not be a weekend dad to him after raising him by myself for so long. Even when he wasn't living with me, I was the one who went to see him. I was the one who got myself sorted out so I could take him home. She didn't come back or even check in.

"There's no way," Shannen said. "No way would anyone allow her to take him. She might want to see him, though."

Even that made me feel ill. If Katie wanted in, she would have to earn it the way I did.

"She made a false accusation against me. I think I'm within my rights to want my son kept away from a liar, even if she is his mum."

I had no idea where I stood legally, but morally, she was screwed.

"Do you know where she is?" Shannen asked. "Is she still around?"

"I don't know. Nobody said anything about that. I just had to keep on answering the same questions until they were satisfied with what I told them. Gavin made it easier. He kept me calm."

She nodded. "I'm glad. It was a good thing Gaby was with us."

"Yeah. It was."

As we fell into another silence, my thoughts moved to what Guy had told me in the car. Shannen hadn't offered the information yet and I didn't want to drop Guy in it, but I also didn't want to be left wondering what had been said to her by her headteacher. Something obviously had because Guy had told me it wasn't his place to tell me.

"Shan, Guy let something slip in the car," I began, and she stiffened in my arms. "He didn't mean to," I added quickly. "He was telling me how much of a prick I am, and it slipped out."

"What did he say?"

I still couldn't see her face properly as she was tucked in against my chest, her head nestled below my chin, but her tone was a little off, like she didn't want to tell me about it because she knew what my reaction would be. And that unsettled me further.

"Just that someone from school saw me being taken away and spoke to the headteacher, and she called you."

Blowing out a breath, Shannen said, "Yeah, that's pretty much it. It was a parent of one of the kids in Gaby's class. She saw almost all of what happened, including the way you spoke to the police officers."

She ran a hand slowly up my back, so slowly that I almost couldn't feel it moving, and I knew she was trying to keep me calm, but fear had already begun to trickle into my veins. Not for myself, but for her. For what the result of that phone call had been. I was sure she hadn't lost her job because she wouldn't have been so calm if that were the case. But something must have come from it.

"Okay..." I said, prompting her to continue.

"The parent was concerned about my involvement with you... a person who was, as far as she was concerned, being arrested," Shannen answered, keeping her voice steady. "I explained the situation as best as I could, and Iris, the headteacher, told me not to worry and that she would tell the parent a misunderstanding had occurred."

"A misunderstanding? *You* told her it was a misunderstanding?" If Shannen had really thought I'd done something wrong, she wouldn't have tried to protect me. She'd told me so the first time she saw me lose my temper.

"I told her what happened. That you were approached, accused of domestic abuse, and taken in for questioning, but it didn't make any sense to me because you are not abusive. She said she wouldn't disclose the reason for you being questioned, just that you were helping the police with their enquiries and it would be cleared up in due course."

I'd spent the entire day being pissed off because she had a second of doubt in me, while she'd told her boss that I was falsely accused of something based on nothing but trust. Because she actually believed in me. Even after everything she'd learned about me, she believed I would never lay a hand on a woman, even though back then, I was a waster. A person I was ashamed to have ever been. I'd lost my child because I couldn't look after myself, so it wasn't a stretch to believe I could have hit Katie.

But Shannen *didn't* believe it.

"And that was the end of it?" I asked. "That explanation was just accepted?"

"I don't know. I haven't heard anything more about it, but hopefully."

What if it wasn't, though? What if they pushed for more information? What if that parent told another parent, and another, and another? The story would get retold in different ways, and eventually, I would be made out to be a criminal, and Shannen's judgement and suitability as a teacher would be questioned. Even though I hadn't done anything, Shannen could still face a backlash because of gossip.

"Stop it," she whispered. "I love you."

I moved my hand up her back and into her soft hair. It was all bunched up, but I ran my fingers through the messy curls. "How do you always know what I'm thinking?"

"Your thoughts are noisy," she said, her voice still super soft. "Your body gets tense, and even though you aren't saying anything, I know how you think. And I know you're still wondering why I questioned whether or not you were capable of domestic abuse."

"I know why you questioned it. It's the same reason you were scared when I told you about Edward. You do know me, Shan, better than anyone. Yeah, it pissed me off that you doubted whether I did it, but it pisses me off more that I know how much being with me is making your life harder, and that I won't let you go because I'm selfish."

I felt her sigh rush through her whole body, and she let go of me, then tugged at my wrists to loosen my grip on her so she could move. She carefully rolled off the sofa and got to her feet.

"It pisses you off that you won't let me go?" she asked. "Why do you keep doing this, Cal? We just got over the 'I'm not good enough' thing, and now you're getting angry with yourself for being with me? How does that even work? Do you want this or not?" She gestured between us, and I felt like the world's biggest prick.

Because of course I wanted her. I wanted her like I'd never wanted anything in my life.

But I also couldn't silence the things inside my head that told me she would always be above me. Better. I would never be enough for her. I'd come a long way since I'd been with her, but I had a whole lifetime of demons wrestling around in my head, and eight weeks wasn't long enough to get rid of them all. Especially not when they'd all been exposed to her.

Released from that box in my mind where I'd left them to fester for so long.

It was me. All of the problems were because of me, but whenever she confronted me, as much as I wanted to let her know that I wanted her, I always said something dickish. Something I didn't mean.

Shaking my head, tiredness washing over me, I said, "I didn't get over the not being good enough thing, Shan. That's not something I can just get over. I'm still trying to deal with you knowing so much about me."

Her face twisted with confusion. "But this morning, we were happy. *You* were happy! Weren't you?"

Pulling myself into a sitting position, I said, "I was happy. But that doesn't mean all of the shit goes away. I'm still processing it. Still trying to deal with what I did. Just because you know, doesn't mean I don't still blame myself for the things I screwed up. I killed my mum and my brother, I almost killed Edward, and I made him feel so shitty for what he did that he killed himself. Those are facts."

"They are not facts," Shannen said through gritted teeth.

"Why? Because you really believe it, or because you don't want to believe you could be stupid enough to sleep with someone who has killed people?"

There he is. My inner arsehole had been dormant for a while, and just when she needed me not to be that guy... I was.

Instead of marching across the space and punching me in the face, she just shook her head, a tear falling down her cheek as she turned away from me.

The worst part was her eyes. I wished I hadn't looked into them before she turned. She wasn't only crying because I'd hurt her with my words, she was crying because of the things I was saying about myself. I saw it, etched way into those blue depths. It was like she knew I was drowning and she couldn't reach me.

But she had. She had reached me time and time again, yet I kept cutting the rope. Kept letting go of the lifeline she offered me so I didn't end up dragging her under with me.

I was doing it for her. Doing it for myself.

Doing it because I didn't know how to do anything else.

"I've been here all day, Cal," she said quietly. "I've been with Aiden. Today, right here in this room, he sat on my lap and asked me what would happen to him if you went to jail. And I didn't know what to tell him.

The only thing I knew was that I wanted to be the one to take care of him, even though that is very unlikely to be possible." She paused, still facing away from me. "All the time, you say you don't know how to do things. Don't know how to be a dad, or to talk about feelings, or be the person I need you to be. The truth is, nobody knows what they're doing most of the time. We just do the best we can in the moment. And sometimes it's wrong. Sometimes we mess it up. But we keep trying. Right now, though, I don't know if that's what you want. If you want to keep trying with me.

"Today, I messed up by doubting you. I hate that you saw that second when I panicked. But it *was* only a second. After that, I spent the whole day worrying that you'd stew on that and you'd forget how good things were this morning." She sighed. "I'm tired, Cal. This past weekend has been exhausting, and I thought we were in a better place than this. I thought things were moving forward."

Each word hit me like a bullet in the chest. I got it. I knew what she was saying, and I wanted to make it better. Wanted to be able to tell her I was happy. That being with her was the only thing that made any sense.

But being with me was hurting her. It had caused rifts in her friendships, in her family, with her work. I didn't want that for her.

"I'm sorry," I said quietly. "I'm sorry."

"I don't want apologies, Cal." She slowly turned to face me, her cheeks streaked with tears, sending another sharp pain through my chest. "I just want you to be with me. I want you to understand that I want all of you. Every bit. And that just because there was a moment when I freaked out, it doesn't change how I feel about you. How I think you feel about me too."

I love her.

I loved her so fucking much it made me ache. It made my stomach churn and my entire body feel like it might explode from holding it in. I wasn't even sure how I recognised it because I had never felt anything like it before. It made me happy and afraid and excited and sick and protective and vulnerable, and all of those feelings happened at once every time I even thought about her. And when I was with her? When I looked at her?

I was hers. Completely hers.

I looked into her eyes, hoping she could hear me telling her the words I couldn't say. The words I wanted to say but couldn't because... since the moment she said them to me, everything had gone wrong.

Yeah, keep telling yourself that. It wasn't the words that were the problem, it was the stuff you withheld from her that led to everything blowing up.

That thought didn't make me feel better. However I looked at it, I continued to be a fuck-up who was ruining her life.

In her blue eyes, I could see that she understood. I could see everything she had said to me and more, like it was coursing through every inch of her body. Every inch of her goddamn soul.

I meant something to her, and I believed it, but why couldn't I *accept* it?

Why couldn't I just let her love me without throwing it back at her like she was the problem?

Shannen

IT HAD BEEN A long, long day.

Time had dragged, and I'd spent every second of it worrying. Worrying that maybe Cal wouldn't be released. That Aiden's fears might become a reality. That I didn't even know exactly what Cal had been accused of or if there was any semblance of truth to it. I didn't believe he would have lashed out at Katie, but what if she had used something relatively harmless and turned it into more? What if she had tried to attack him and he'd pushed her back? What if he'd accidentally hurt her...

And then the guilt. Was I now a woman who didn't believe other women? Was I a woman making excuses for her man because she refused to look at the truth?

But it didn't matter how I looked at it. I couldn't see any way Cal would have hurt Katie, not even at his lowest point. I wasn't just viewing it as someone who was in love with him. I was looking at it as someone who had witnessed his devastation over what he'd done to Edward. As someone who genuinely believed he'd killed his mum and brother. The guilt he carried around over all of it. He wasn't faking that. And if he still felt so ashamed of that, he would never be able to forgive himself for hitting a woman. He would have confessed because he was done with keeping stuff from me. He had been actively trying to push me away when he told me everything he'd done, and domestic abuse would have successfully done the job. But he hadn't told me about it because it hadn't happened.

All of those thoughts had pounded at my brain until I was exhausted. I'd just wanted to crawl into bed and sleep, but when I tried, the noise still wouldn't silence.

Every single part of the day's events had made my mind a mess. Drained me. Stripped away what was left of my composure, leaving me standing in front of Cal feeling frustrated, and sorry, and desperate with the need to stop him from ruining this when we'd just turned a corner.

In his eyes, I saw everything he felt. Little flashes of fear, regret, panic, shame, and underneath all of it?

Love.

It should have been reassuring. Should have given me something to hold onto, but even deeper beyond that, defeat shone bright and I wanted it gone.

Why couldn't he hear me? Why couldn't he see how hard I wanted to fight for us even though his own fight seemed to be slipping away with every second we stood there?

I mattered to him, I knew that. But now it felt like, for him, it wasn't enough.

Without a word, I slowly walked towards him, chasing away the physical space between us until we were mere inches apart. My heart clenched as I trailed my gaze across his beautiful face. His dark, melted chocolate eyes. His stubbled jaw that was thicker than usual now. His perfect full lips, and the tiny scar on his chin. The scent of him. That combination of leather and coffee and his cologne. Every part of me knew deep down in my soul that he was mine. That he was the man I was supposed to be with.

And that he was preparing to walk away.

It was right there in his rigid stance. In his refusal to look me in the eye now we were so close.

Instead of speaking, I placed my hands on his chest, feeling the warmth of his body and stepping in closer. I slid my hands up to his shoulders, then around to the back of his neck. He still didn't move, but I saw his throat bob as he swallowed down his emotions.

Lifting up onto my tiptoes, I lightly kissed his cheek, his jaw ticking beneath my lips.

"Cal," I whispered against his face. He tensed, and I trailed my lips along his jaw until I reached his mouth.

I felt his intake of breath, the way the tightness in his neck eased as I stroked my thumbs softly up and down. A low growl rumbled from his chest as his hands landed on my waist. Not over my clothes, but underneath my pyjama top and straight onto my skin. When he kissed me back, it wasn't soft and slow, it was hard and deep as his fingers dug into my sides. His tongue slipped into my mouth and I wanted to cry out with how good it felt to have him right there with me. To feel him against me, his lips on mine, his fingers on my skin.

All too soon, though, he pulled away from the kiss and dropped his head back. I could feel the hammering of his heart, and as he lowered his head to look at me again, his eyes were heavy with regret. "I... Shan..."

My eyes prickled as his sparkled with tears, and I shook my head. "Don't," I said through gritted teeth. "Please."

He drew in a deep breath, and I could feel him shaking in my arms. His gaze fixed over my head, and I moved my hands to his chest and tugged at his shirt, my fists lightly clenching at the material as his hands slipped down to my hips.

Shaking my head again as my tears fell, I said, "No, Cal. If you're going to say it, then you say it to my fucking face."

The only sign he'd heard me was in his slight flinch because I hardly ever swore. But he didn't move his head. Not to look at me or turn away, and the frustration and hurt bubbled over.

I slammed my palms against his chest, but he still didn't move. Still kept his hands on my hips as a tear dripped down his cheek. I knew he was hurting. Knew his heart was breaking apart inside his chest the same way mine was, but he was the one who was pulling away from me. He was the one who'd shut down, and I couldn't reach him. Not with words or kisses or by trying to make him talk. I was on the outside. He'd put me there, and I'd given him the out he needed from this relationship when he'd seen that flash of mistrust in my eyes.

It didn't matter that I'd fought for him. That I would always fight for him. He didn't want me to. Not because he didn't want *me*, but because he was sick of needing to be fought for. And it tore at my insides because I understood why. I got it, but I didn't want it. I wanted him to fight for *us*. I needed him to tell me he understood where my doubts had come

from, that he was willing to stand with me and make this work because...
otherwise, what was the point in all we'd been through? To let it go now
was a waste of what we'd faced.

He was tired. I was too.

But while he was ready to put our relationship to bed, I wanted to push
through the night until the sun came up again so we could walk into the
next day and all of the ones that followed together.

Suddenly, the sensation of his hands on my skin was too much. But I
knew once I stepped away, I'd never feel that again, and my tears fell harder.

I wanted to lash out, to make him say something. But he was trembling,
like the indecision I saw in his eyes was ripping him in half. He wanted the
pain to end, but he didn't want to let me go.

And I wanted to make it easy for him, but I couldn't.

"I deserve more than this," I said, my voice cracking as I put my hands on
his wrists and pushed him away from me, turning my back on him because
I couldn't look at him. Couldn't have him so close and not have him be
mine.

"That's what I've been trying to tell you all along." His voice was stripped
of emotion, and I rounded on him, my frustrations spilling out again.

"No. I'm not talking about this fucked-up idea you have that I'm better
than you," I said, tears still raining down my cheeks. "I'm talking about this,
right now. We have been through so much, and you can't even look at me
long enough to end this. If that's what you want, Cal, you're going to look
me in the eye and say the words because I have not come this far with you
to be dismissed like I don't matter."

I watched as his jaw clenched, his anger simmering on the surface as his
eyes flicked to me.

"You matter, Shannen. You matter in a way nobody has mattered to me
in a long fucking time."

Throwing my hands up, I said, "Then what is happening here? Why are
you doing this?"

Right then, he could have told me I was wrong. That I'd made an
assumption and he wasn't trying to extract himself from my life. But we
both knew exactly what he was doing. Why he was cold, even though he
didn't mean it. Even though he didn't want this to end either.

"Because I can't..." he bit the words out, then stopped himself from
finishing the sentence.

"What, Cal?" I took a step towards him, angrily wiping at my tears with the back of my hand. "What can't you do?"

He flew at me, his hands gripping my shoulders, his eyes blazing with pain and rage. "I can't love you, okay!" he shouted, the words hitting me like bullets, piercing through my flesh and penetrating right through to my soul. "I can't let myself because everything I touch turns to shit! Me and you, Shan... I want it, but we have been disaster after disaster and it doesn't matter how much I try to get away from my past, it follows me everywhere!"

His fingertips crushed into my shoulders, bruising me the way his words had. His voice was raised as he yelled at me, but the only thing I felt was the crushing ache in my heart. I wasn't scared of him. Wasn't scared to shout back. The only reason I didn't was because I was choking on my own tears and because I didn't want Aiden being woken up by us arguing.

Drawing in a shaky breath, I said, "You think that will stop just by us not being together? It's your past, Cal. You can't change it or hide from it."

With one last hard squeeze of my shoulders, he let me go and turned away, and the stab of rejection began to eat away at me. Nibbling at my flesh, burrowing inside me and seeping into my bones until it overwhelmed me. I felt like I was internally screaming, pleading with him not to let us go. To hold on with me and push through this next battle like we'd got through all of the others.

As he stood there with his back to me, he felt a million miles away. I could touch him physically. I could walk over there and wrap my arms around him, feel the familiar press of his body against mine. Breathe in his scent, touch his stubbled jaw, and kiss those lips that had taken me to heaven and back more times than I could count, but his brain had disengaged. He'd put his heart on ice and swiftly built up the walls I'd knocked down. He was a fortress, protecting himself from my words and my affection.

He wanted it, but he didn't want it enough.

And feeling his pain on top of my own was killing me.

"This morning," I began, pausing to swallow the lump in my throat, "you wanted this. You wanted me."

He nodded, still not looking at me. "This morning, you weren't afraid of me."

"I'm not afraid of you now," I said quietly. "I've never been afraid of you. The only thing I'm afraid of is losing you. And I am, aren't I?" The last words were almost a whisper.

He didn't answer, but I watched as he slumped over, pressing the heels of his hands over his eyes for a moment before finally facing me. His eyes still glistened, and in them, there was so much conflict. So much torture.

My legs weakened, trembling as I waited for him to do the one thing I'd asked of him.

Waited for him to break both of our hearts.

He sniffed, then breathed in deeply, his lips parting to speak, but no words came out. I swallowed, trying to keep any further signs of devastation from showing on my face, but it was too late for me. I couldn't stop the tears, but I also couldn't beg him to reconsider anymore. Wouldn't.

His entire body was shaking as his gaze moved across my face, from my eyes to my lips, and back to my eyes. "I can't do this anymore, Shan. I can't be with you. I know you trust me. I know you believe me. But I can't stop thinking about the way you looked at me. Like you didn't know me. I'm afraid to lose you, but I'm afraid to let you stay. It's just... it's easier this way."

His eyes shifted down to the floor and I watched as a tear fell from his eyes all the way down to the carpet at his feet.

Because he's lying. This wasn't easier. Maybe for him, but not for me. Not dealing with his feelings was *his* comfort zone. He was hurting himself like he always did because it was easier for him to punish himself than to face things. Safer because, in that self-made prison he'd built in his head, he could torture himself over and over. He didn't have to push through the hard times to get somewhere better because he still didn't believe he deserved better.

Understanding, though, didn't stop the bitter laugh that spilled from me. "Your idea of easy is very different to mine," I said. "Because falling in love with you is the easiest thing I've ever done. Pretending I'm okay with this is going to be the hardest."

Chapter 8

Shannen

I DIDN'T GIVE HIM a chance to speak. Didn't even look at him. I lowered my head and walked past him, out of the lounge and up the stairs to the room I was supposed to be sleeping in—what used to be Cal's bedroom—my body feeling heavier with every step. My entire frame was trembling as I tried to hold in the sobs threatening to escape. Tears still dripped down my cheeks, but what I wanted to do was cry out from the pain in my heart that had now weaved through every limb.

When I reached the bedroom, I closed the door and took off my vest top, opening the overnight bag I'd brought over and pulling my clothes out. I threw my top on first, then took off my pyjama trousers and put my jeans back on. I didn't care about how scruffily I was dressed. I was only getting into my car and driving home anyway. Well, I would as soon as I could see straight. I couldn't stay. Cal would need somewhere to sleep, and I sure as hell wasn't going to be sharing a bed with him anymore.

The thought shot another ache through me. Sleeping beside him, waking up wrapped in his arms had become my safe place. The place where I was happiest. Being shrouded in his scent, his safety, the familiar feel of his body against mine. I thought... I thought he was home.

I sank back onto the bed, not even finishing packing my nightclothes into my bag. Leaning forward, I placed my head in my hands and finally squeaked out a sob.

This wasn't how this was supposed to go. Cal and I... we'd cleared a whole bunch of hurdles in our short time together. We'd stumbled, crashed, and picked ourselves back up over and over, but the race... it was done now. After overcoming so many things, this was what it had come down to.

An end that had broken us both.

I knew this wasn't easy for him either, but he hadn't been prepared to fight for us, and that... it hurt like nothing I'd ever felt before. I'd had breakups in the past. Some of them had been my decision, some of them not. Every one had been sad in its own way, but even my hardest breakup didn't feel like this. Didn't feel like my skin was too tight, like I couldn't breathe.

Like I didn't want to feel anything again.

A soft knock on the door made me jump and look up. "Shannen?"

Guy.

I blew out a breath, trying to brush my tears away with my sleeve. "Come in." My voice cracked and there was no way he wouldn't have heard it.

He opened the door, still fully dressed, probably because he knew what would happen. I could feel my lower lip trembling, that sting in my eyes and nose, and when I looked at him, another sob ripped out of me. Guy rushed over to me after quietly closing the door and sat down beside me, bundling me into his side and holding me tight as if he could stop me from falling apart. I clung to him, my tears seeping into his T-shirt and my shoulders shaking with the force of my crying.

He didn't need to ask. He knew as well as I had that this was how the day would end. If not guaranteed, it had always been a high possibility because Cal had been battling with his issues since the day we met. I'd just hoped that he would allow us to push on. To have a future that wasn't riddled with his secrets and insecurities. I'd trusted him. Trusted that we could get through anything. Believed that if I loved him enough, he could let the last few walls around his heart fall away and let me all the way in. But I'd let him down by doubting him, and he'd used that and his belief that he was trying to protect me as an excuse to put an end to us. No matter what I said, he didn't understand that I would have fought until my last breath to be with him. That he would always be my choice, but *his* choice was to hurt himself by pushing me away.

"I'm sorry," Guy said softly into my hair as he gently rubbed my arm. "I'm sorry."

His voice broke a little, and I wanted to speak, but my mouth was dry, my emotions pouring out of me too fast to control.

"I told him, Shannen. I told him not to fuck this up."

My stomach ached with the intensity of my grief until I felt sick, and still my tears continued to soak into Guy's shoulder, unable to get a grip on the agony that surged through me.

"It was all for nothing," I choked out. "Everything we went through... it was for nothing."

Guy held me tighter. "I know. I know how you feel."

And he absolutely did. Because while I was falling apart, he was too. I'd been with Cal such a short time compared to his almost eight years with Helen, but it was the same thing for him. All that time with her, only for it to end up the way it did. Both of them alone. Both of them never getting what they'd wanted so badly.

"Sorry," I said, trying again to wipe my eyes. "You don't need this on top of what you're already going through."

"I don't," Guy agreed, his voice hard. "But you don't have anything to apologise for. This is all Cal and his stupid insecurity shit."

I nodded against his chest, words failing me again. I wanted to say more. To say that while I agreed, I knew Cal hadn't broken things off because he didn't want me. He did; he'd even said so. The fact didn't make it better or worse because the outcome was still the same. It still meant he'd cut me off and I was going to be healing from this for way longer than the time we'd been together.

"He's a fucking idiot," Guy said. "He knows you're the best thing that ever happened to him and he's going to regret this."

"You let Helen go. Do you regret that?"

"Not the same thing, darlin'. She walked away, and I didn't stop her because I was tired of the way she treated me and the way she made me feel every damn day. I miss her, but it needed to be over. You and Cal... you two make sense. Even if it seems like you shouldn't."

"You and Helen made sense once."

He nodded. "Sure we did. But the truth is, when Cal and Aiden lived here, they were holding us together. They gave us a focus to distract us

59

from the fact that we weren't okay. We should have ended long ago." With a sigh, he said, "Anyway, don't change the subject."

"The subject is the same." Tiredness washed over me, my voice suddenly sounding as hollow as Cal's had. "We've both been left behind, Guy. Now you have to deal with your break-up and mine."

And somehow, I think handling Cal will be a lot harder than the aftermath of Helen.

"Cal won't be getting much sympathy from me," Guy said. "Not from the breakup side of things anyway. He's just walked away from something he won't ever find again. And that's his own fault."

The reminder of what I'd lost pounded into me again, and I closed my eyes, breathing slowly for a minute, hoping it would ease. But it didn't. Of course it didn't. This was a wide-open wound that had only just appeared; it wasn't going anywhere for a while.

At that moment, it didn't feel like it would ever leave.

How was it possible that someone could have such a huge impact on me after such a short time? How could I have fallen for someone so quickly and so hard?

Warmth and agony filled me simultaneously as I remembered the first time I saw him. The cocky swagger and the cheeky smile. The glint in his eyes, the way I'd watched his lips as he spoke and wondered what it would feel like to kiss them. I'd been so different then. I'd lived another three or four lives since then; from the woman who'd been certain Cal was a fling, to the woman who wanted to give this unusual pairing a try, to the woman who had had her dirty side unleashed and developed the confidence to tell Jade and Scott they'd meddled in my life for the last time to... this. Now. It was all too much. Entirely too fast.

A loud smashing sound from downstairs shook Guy and me from the sombre silence we'd been in, and Guy jumped up, swearing under his breath as my heart sped up. What the hell had caused that smash?

When another one sounded, Guy said, "Stay here. If Aiden wakes up, please take care of him."

I didn't have a chance to respond before he was out the door and his footsteps thundered down the stairs.

Chapter 9

Cal

Fucking. Useless. Arsehole.

I was exactly what my father said I would be.

Nothing.

Just when I'd almost had it all, I'd lost it. No, not lost it. I'd shoved it away.

I'd broken her.

The only thing I could see was the devastation on her face, and all I could hear was her voice begging me not to end it. The final words she said to me circled in my head until I needed a release. Needed a way to stop the noise of my thoughts, reminding me what a piece of shit I was.

A plate with a few breadcrumbs on it rested on the coffee table, and I picked it up and launched it at the wall so hard that it shattered, the pieces falling to the carpet, but it wasn't enough. There was too much rage in me to keep it contained, and I picked up the mug that had been beside the plate and flung it at the wall too. Another crash.

Still not enough. I grabbed the TV remote, my arm up, ready to hurl it when I heard Guy snarl, "Are you fucking kidding me right now?"

His voice brought a sense of clarity for a second, but I was already coiled, ready to throw something. Instead of destroying the TV, I shot the remote at the wall in the same place as the plate and mug, watching as it bust in half and hit the floor before I let out a roar of anger, tugging at my hair as I sank onto the couch.

"Are you done?" Guy snapped.

His tone didn't help my mood. Not when I knew everything he was about to say was going to be truths I didn't want to hear.

"Back off," I said sharply.

"Back off?" His tone was as harsh as mine, and the only reason he hadn't yelled was because Aiden and Shannen were upstairs. "You're down here smashing up my shit and you think I'll back off?"

He was still behind me, probably still in the doorway; I hadn't turned around to check.

"What is wrong with you?" he said coldly. "If I hadn't just seen Shannen, I would not have believed you really fucked this up. You got through everything you were worried about with her, only to piss it all away now."

I hadn't expected his support over this. *I* didn't even believe in the decision I'd just made, but in that moment with her, when I should have been working through how I felt with her, all I could see was us a year down the line, Shannen hating me because being with me had left her with nothing. And I couldn't do it. I couldn't let her resent me.

She resents you now, you prick.

God, I'd messed up. I wasn't proud of a single thing I'd done since the police had appeared, apart from holding back from punching one of them. I'd let myself get caught up in thinking Shannen was done with me, in thinking that this would be the final straw. That this one more thing on top of all the others would mean the end. But I was the one who'd made that decision. I was the one who had pulled the plug.

I'd seen her tears. Heard her words. I could feel how much I was hurting her, but I couldn't stop it. I'd made the decision the second I saw her doubt me, even though it wasn't fair.

"Is she..." I began, not sure what I was trying to ask. *Is she okay?* Of course she wasn't okay. And I knew she hadn't left because only one set of footsteps came down the stairs. I could have gone up to her. Got off the couch, stopped feeling sorry for myself, and taken my words back, but it was too late. She'd trusted me not to hurt her. The woman who'd told me I made her feel safe, and I'd just... let her go. Not even let her go. I'd forced her away. There was nothing I could do to change it now because I'd severed every bit of faith she had in me.

"She's devastated, Cal."

Well, that makes two of us.

Tugging harder at my hair, I growled in sheer frustration before getting to my feet again, too much coursing through me to allow me to sit still. "Guy, I need you to... please, just go to her, okay? I can't talk about it. I don't want to talk about it. So... take care of her."

Even though I wasn't looking at him, I felt a drop in the tension. Turning, I raised my head. Guy remained in the doorway, his jaw clenched, but something in his expression told me that even though he was pissed off with what I'd done, he wasn't going to make me feel worse than I already did. I didn't think that was possible anyway.

"She wants to go home," Guy said quietly. "But I don't think she should drive in the state she's in."

Closing my eyes, I immediately opened them again when an image of her crying tormented me. Seeing her cry, especially because of me, had almost killed me, and I never wanted to see it again. Knowing she was up there, sitting on my old bed, hurting, was killing me, but the idea of her driving when she was so upset made my chest tighten and my legs buckle.

Mum. Luca.

My hand shot to my chest as the ache there became so intense that I had to lean back against the wall.

My mum had left our house upset, and she and my brother had lost their lives because of it. Because they were trying to escape an angry, fucked-up man.

If anything happened to her because of me...

My eyes closed again, and after a couple of seconds, I felt Guy's hands on my shoulders. "Cal, relax," he said gently. "I won't let her leave tonight. I won't. She can sleep upstairs, and you can sleep down here or in Aiden's room."

I nodded, glad I didn't have to explain my freak-out to him. He hadn't said what he said to trigger me, but he knew why it had made me panic.

"You're an idiot," he said, his hands still on my shoulders, "but you're giving yourself a hard enough time. Calm down and get some sleep. I'll make sure Shannen stays."

I nodded again, knowing there was no way I was getting any sleep. Not with the way I felt and knowing Shannen was upstairs.

I also wouldn't be able to relax in case she tried to sneak out. I needed her to rest, to calm down before she drove anywhere, and I'd give up my own sleep to make sure that happened.

Guy patted my shoulder before heading back upstairs, leaving me alone again.

I dropped my head back, staring up at the ceiling, wishing I could just go up there. To be the one sitting with Shannen, holding her. Not that she'd accept any comfort from me now. I mean, what the hell even were we? I'd ended it. She wasn't going to want to be around me for any reason now, and I didn't think I could be friends with her after being more.

"Fuck."

I spoke the word aloud, that rippling of anger and irritation bubbling up again.

For lack of other options, I sighed and walked over to the remains of the broken plate and mug, and the two halves of remote and the batteries that had fallen out of it. If I just focused on something mundane, I could keep the rage and self-hatred away.

Just for a little while.

By the time I'd picked up and disposed of as much as I could without having to get the hoover out, the voices in my head telling me I'd screwed up were getting louder. However, I was surer that Shannen wasn't going to try to leave. If she was going to, she would have done it by now. At least that was one less thing to worry about.

Throwing myself back down on the sofa, I heaved out a breath.

She was upstairs. One floor away. The room she was in was directly above where I sat. I *could* go up there. Talk to her. Tell her I'd made a mistake.

But as much as I didn't want to break up with her, I couldn't get my head straight enough to believe I could make it work with her now.

Chapter 10

Shannen

"SHANNEN."

I heard the quiet voice, and at first, I wasn't sure if I was dreaming. It wasn't until I felt a tiny hand on the top of my arm gently shaking me that I fluttered my eyes open. I blinked a few times, and the blurry image of Aiden appeared in front of me.

My head ached as if I'd been on a drinking binge, and it took me a second to realise where I was and why I felt like crap.

"Why isn't my dad back yet?"

His voice cracked and his chin wobbled, a tear falling down his cheek. Pushing the impending approach of my own misery aside, I shuffled back a bit and sat up slightly, beckoning for Aiden to sit down on the bed in his blue Toy Story pyjamas.

"He's not at the police station anymore, sweetheart," I told him, my voice croaky and my throat dry. "I don't know if he's downstairs or at your place."

I also didn't know what time it was. There was some light coming in from outside, so I guessed it was morning, likely pretty early as it was still a little dark.

"Why isn't he with you?"

My heart twinged. Of course this was where he thought Cal would be. If he was home, he would usually be beside me. This was Cal's room at Guy's house.

But he wasn't beside me. Never would be beside me again now.

My own eyes filled with tears, but I tried my best to force them away. He didn't need to see me upset. And once again, we were in a position where Aiden needed something explained to him, but I wasn't the right person to fill him in.

"He couldn't sleep," I said, hating that I was lying to him.

Aiden nodded and then shuffled further onto the bed, closer to me. "Is he still in trouble?"

"No," I told him, with a shake of my head. "He answered the questions he needed to answer and everything is okay now."

He nodded again, but he still looked sad, and there was nothing I could do about it. I didn't want to ask what he needed because if I did, then I would probably break down too. What *I* needed to do was get up and get out of there, so I could go home and sort through the mess circling around in my head.

Shifting myself slowly to sit up fully, I said, "Let's go downstairs and see if we can find him."

Honestly, the last thing I wanted was to see Cal, not when I was barely conscious and hadn't had a second to figure out how I felt. I took a moment to properly put my PJs into my bag; I'd just left them hanging out and fallen asleep in my clothes after a long WhatsApp session with Gaby and Nova to catch them up on what was happening. Once my stuff was zipped away, I stood and retrieved my phone from the bedside table. It was only twenty past seven, but I guessed Guy would be up as he would be going to work. Cal still had another day off, but Guy might have woken him if he was moving around and getting ready.

I slipped my phone into my jeans pocket, picked up my bag, and then turned to Aiden, who was still sitting on the bed. Poor kid. He looked as if he didn't believe Cal was really back, but there was something else lurking in the depths of his dark eyes, and my heart ached again.

"What's wrong, sweetheart?" I asked, not meaning for the affectionate term to slip out so easily. I needed to switch back. Be more like his teacher and less like a... friend? I wasn't sure exactly how Aiden viewed me outside of school. I just knew that the bond we'd formed away from the classroom was about to reach an abrupt end.

"Helen isn't here."

My brow furrowed. Guy had told him that Helen was at work last night, explaining her absence for the evening, but how did he know she wasn't home now?

Before I could speak, Aiden said, "She didn't come home. When she worked at night when we lived here, she came home before I went to bed. But she didn't come home last night. I forgot because I was really tired, but when I woke up, I remembered."

I closed my eyes, the sadness in his voice triggering my pain again. It made me hate what was happening even more because he'd had the best stability and balance since he and Cal had got their own place. He'd had more time with Cal and still got plenty of time with the two other important people in his life. Aiden and I had become close, but losing Helen was going to hit way harder than me no longer being around. At least he would still see me at school.

Although, that wasn't necessarily a good thing either. This was precisely why Cal had wanted to keep our relationship from Aiden, but that hadn't panned out as we'd expected when Aiden had seen us together before we meant him to. I hadn't foreseen us going to crap like this either. Until the day before, I thought we were actually going to make it.

Naive after such a short time? Probably. But maybe not. Because I'd never experienced anything like being with Cal. Nothing had even come close, even with the man I'd been sure at the time I'd marry. The connection was different with Cal. It had felt like there was something deeper between us, beyond the surface stuff, that would see us through anything.

With a sigh to hold in another deluge of tears, I reached out for Aiden's hand. "Come on. Let's go and see if we can find your dad and Guy."

Aiden jumped down from the bed and took my hand, and the two of us walked silently from the room and downstairs. I could hear deep voices from the kitchen, but I chose not to listen to whatever conversation was going on. I really wasn't ready to see Cal, but for Aiden's sake, I'd have to suck it up and say goodbye before I could escape.

We entered the kitchen, and Aiden's eyes widened when he saw Cal. He threw himself into Cal's arms, and the relief on Cal's face made my heart lighten a little. Guy sat at the other side of the kitchen table, dark circles under his eyes and his hair a mess. He wore a scruffy white T-shirt and grey sweatpants. Cal was in the same clothes he'd been wearing the day before, so I figured he'd crashed out the same way I had.

"You're really here," Aiden said as Cal hoisted him up onto his lap.

"Yup. Just like I told you I would be." Cal smiled at him, and my stomach clenched as I saw the brightness in his eyes.

My man. That smile.

The love I had for him, for both of them, was suddenly without a place to go. I couldn't hug him, kiss him, say the words that scared the hell out of him, even though I knew he felt it too. We were done, and I had to carry around the weight of everything I felt until it slowly eased away over time.

I just... I couldn't envision that time ever coming. My heart held tiny patches of space for all the people I'd ever loved, whether romantically or platonically. It was covered in the fragments of them that had seeped into my soul. Even if things ended badly, or if we no longer talked, they left a mark. But Cal? The space he occupied was huge. I still didn't understand how it had happened after a matter of weeks, but the impact he'd had on me wasn't dependent on time. It was the changes he'd made in me, the way he'd made me view things differently, the way he'd confirmed to me what I wanted, not just in a relationship but in my life. That I could be happy with someone who didn't have some high-powered job and ludicrous expectations of me. He was the, albeit complex, kind of man I'd always wanted.

A lump rose in my throat, and I swallowed, even though my throat was closing over. I wanted to tell them I was leaving, but I was certain I'd choke if I tried.

Cal hadn't even looked at me yet, his focus on Aiden, and I needed to keep it that way. I couldn't deal with looking into those gorgeous eyes knowing, to him, I wasn't worth fighting for.

As I was about to turn, Guy caught my eye, a feeling of sheer grief and understanding passing between us. We were both in the same position, both of us hurting over our failed relationships. I knew Cal was too, but he was the one who did this to us. Guy and I hadn't had much of a choice. Decisions were made for us, and we had to get on board. The only difference was, Guy would eventually be okay with Helen's decision.

I blinked away the tears that had formed and offered him a weak smile before turning away.

"Shannen!" Aiden's voice sliced at my insides. I wouldn't have left without saying goodbye; I needed to put my shoes on before I could leave anyway. I just needed a minute to pull myself together.

I turned back around, trying to block Cal from my view while I focused on Aiden. Difficult when he was sitting on Cal's lap, but I refused to meet his eye.

"I have to go home," I said, trying to keep my voice even. I hoped I was fooling him because I wasn't fooling anyone else, least of all myself.

"But you haven't had breakfast yet. Can we make pancakes like we did before?"

A tear fell before I could blink it away, and when Aiden saw it, he slipped off Cal's lap and wrapped his arms around my legs. There was confusion on his face, like he knew something was very wrong, but he didn't know what. He had to be able to feel the charged atmosphere because it was oppressive as hell to me.

I ruffled his hair. "No pancakes today, Aiden," I said gently.

"Tomorrow?" he asked, his cheek pressed against my legs.

My body began to shake, everything pressing down on me again. I hadn't had enough sleep, and if I didn't calm down, I'd be stuck there forever. Guy had told me the night before that Cal wouldn't let me drive home while I was upset, something that had triggered another bout of sobbing. Even separated, he was still looking out for me, and I both appreciated it and resented it. If he wanted me safe, he needed to *keep* me safe the way he always had.

I really needed to get out, but I felt frozen, and I still hadn't given Aiden an answer. Instead, I loosened his arms from around me and crouched down in front of him, pulling him against me for a hug. I needed it as much as he did.

"I'll see you soon, okay?" I told him. "Be good for your dad."

I began to pull back and his brown eyes, so like his dad's, met mine, tears in them. "You're not coming back."

It wasn't a question, and all I could do was shake my head, brushing my own tears away before reaching over to gently swipe his away too. The sadness in his gaze turned back to confusion, and the flickers of anger I knew so well began to spark.

"Baby," I said softly, my hands lightly on his wet cheeks, "remember what you need to do when you feel angry?"

Aiden nodded, his jaw tight, the resemblance to Cal's actions when he was trying to control his rage uncanny. Cal and I had worked hard with Aiden to help him control his temper by asking him to sit down with someone and talk about how he was feeling instead of running away to fume privately or break things. It was working, and I wanted to stay with him and help him through this, but how could I? He didn't even know the extent of how many of his core people were being ripped away from him. I wasn't *really* one of them, but I had added an extra layer of stability for him in that he knew me and saw me as an adult he could trust.

Or he did.

I hadn't noticed Guy stand up and approach, and he took one of Aiden's hands. Aiden looked up at him, and Guy said, "Let's talk, buddy. Come on."

I knew he wanted to help, and I offered a grateful smile, but I really didn't want to be alone with Cal.

As Guy and Aiden left the room, I turned to follow them as far as the hallway so I could get my shoes, but Cal's voice halted me.

"Shan."

Just my name falling from his lips made me squeeze my eyes shut, knowing this might actually be the last time I heard it. I couldn't bring myself to turn to look at him, but I also couldn't make my feet walk away.

I need you to let me go.

I couldn't handle any more emotion. I wasn't even sure what might come out of my mouth if I spoke to him. I'd barely been awake for twenty minutes. My head was pounding, my throat was dry, I was dehydrated from crying, and my entire body felt like I'd been dipped in cement. I wanted to move, but every limb weighed more than usual, every inch of me filled with exhaustion and hurt.

"I can't talk to you right now," I said, the break in my voice now way too familiar as the feeling of needing his arms around me threatened to drown me.

Want his warmth. Want his comfort. Want his safety.

"Okay," he said quietly. "But can you please text me to let me know you got home okay?"

I owed him nothing. Not peace of mind. Not even a damn text. But I knew why he'd asked, and in spite of everything, I wouldn't let him stew over my safety.

"I will," I said. "But I think... I just... I don't know if I can..." My words failed me as I tried to articulate what I meant.

"You don't want to hear from me once you've let me know."

The coldness in his tone pissed me off and damaged me at the same time. He had no right to be mad that I didn't want to talk to him. What did he think breaking up meant?

But I also knew the reasons. This sucked for him too. But he was still the one who did it.

"Yeah," I said. "That's probably for the best. For now, at least."

I paused for a moment, waiting in case there was anything else he wanted to say. When he remained silent, the sob I tried to swallow came out as a breathy gasp as I walked away.

 Chapter 11

Shannen

I COULDN'T REMEMBER A more miserable week in my entire existence. Half term was supposed be full of fun, friends, and happiness. Instead of the time I'd expected to have with Cal and Aiden, and Nova and Gaby, my main company had been Ben and Jerry, with the occasional visit from Mr Kipling and Aunt Bessie.

I'd seen my girls, of course. They'd come to me the day after Cal and I split, had dragged me out for lunch and then stayed overnight for the kind of sleepover the three of us had had at Nova's just before Christmas. This one was way less joyful. I cried, I laughed, and all three of us drank more than usual, but having them be there for me meant everything.

Unlike Jade. I thought cutting her out of my life meant I'd never have to deal with her again. But after I told my parents why Cal and I were no longer together, word clearly got around. I didn't think my parents would have told Jade's mum all the details, just that he and I were over. Jade had seen fit to send me a message saying:

> If you'd only listened to me, you'd never have had the humiliation of being dumped by a no-body. Not sure why you're even sad about it, but you made your choice. Hope you're happy being a social outcast.

Dramatic, petty bitch.

The truth was, hardly anyone in my family's circles knew anything about Cal. It had all happened so fast, and as my mum promised, she told Judith to keep her mouth shut and that Jade and Scott should do the same. I didn't care who knew, but my mum wouldn't risk anyone badmouthing me, and I appreciated her support.

I was so ready to go back to work the following Monday. I'd had enough of wallowing. Of eating junk food and wandering around my flat, looking like a slob. I needed to get back into the classroom and put some structure back into my life. The only cloud on an otherwise brighter horizon was seeing Aiden because I wasn't sure how he would respond to me. The potential for seeing Cal at the end of the school day made me edgy too. I hadn't heard from him since I'd text him when I got home as promised. I'd spoken to Guy twice via text. He'd wanted to check how I was, and I returned the favour a few days later. He told me Helen had gone to the house to pick up some more stuff and then arranged for a van to take whatever else was hers that she couldn't fit in her car over the weekend. Aiden had not handled it well, so I was prepared for the possibility he would not be the same little boy I'd been getting to know. On the plus side, though, Guy mentioned that the police had informed Cal he was no longer needed for questioning. He didn't give any further details about why it had all ended as quickly as it started, why the whole thing had been dropped, and I didn't ask. Perhaps Katie had withdrawn the claim. Though, that made even less sense to me than anything else, because why cause so much chaos if only to take it back almost immediately after? I was glad Cal had been cleared, but at the same time, it brought with it another layer of stress and sadness. All of this, the pain, the breakup... it was over nothing. Not, nothing, because Cal had obviously seen my moment of doubt as a betrayal, but had she not gone to the police, it would never have happened.

I wasn't even sure if there was anyone to blame at that point. Was it my mistrust, his insecurity, or her? They were all vital pieces in the puzzle of this disaster, and overthinking it wasn't going to change a thing.

Decisions were made, and now, we had to live with them.

The first thing that happened when I arrived at work on Monday morning was being called in to see Iris, the school's headteacher. I'd dropped my things off in my classroom and headed for her office.

She smiled kindly at me as she leaned on the edge of her desk, her hair neatly secured in a bun at the back of her head. I'd half expected to be called in as I'd let her know that Cal and I were no longer together, though I wasn't sure exactly what she was going to say.

"Morning, Shannen."

"Morning. How was half term for you?" I asked with a smile in return.

"Oh, you know. Just another week, really. Spent some time with my daughter and the grandchildren, caught up on some reading. How are you doing?"

Her eyes were empathetic, as they always were, and I sighed deeply, unwilling to let my emotions drown me, at least not until I got home again.

"I'm okay," I told her, even though it wasn't the absolute truth. I'd pulled myself together because I had a job to do, but my insides still ached like they'd been crushed, and my heart had a huge chunk missing. The chunk I'd left behind in Guy's kitchen the week before. "I spent some time with Gaby and Nova, went to see my sister and my nephew. Spent a lot of time thinking."

My sister, Sadie, was way out of the loop when it came to my relationship status. My mum had mentioned to her that I was seeing someone, but Sadie and I hadn't seen each other in the entire time I'd been with Cal. It wasn't that we weren't close, it was more that life whizzed by so fast. We communicated mostly in memes that made each other laugh and saw what the other was up to on social media, but the reality of two women who worked, one while raising a child and having a husband, meant that we simply didn't get to see each other as much as we liked.

"I presume you and Mr Lewis are still separated?" she asked gently.

"That's the polite way of putting it," I said. "I think obliterated would be a better choice of word."

It hurt. Every time I thought about it, which was roughly equal to the number of times I breathed, it hurt. I'd spent so much time going over and over everything during the past few days, trying to figure out if I could have changed anything. Trying to figure out if there was something I could have done differently. The only thing I could have done was not let my panic show on my face, even if it was only fleetingly. But even that... I knew it was the trigger for him, and I regretted it with every inch of my soul. However, even if that hadn't happened, his being taken in for questioning had allowed him time to think about how unworthy he was of being with me. I would always find the thought process ridiculous, but for him, it was real. And I couldn't fix that for him. I'd told him repeatedly that I loved him, that he was all I wanted. I thought he was coming to accept it, but his arrest had knocked him off his axis again.

I wanted him back. I wished with everything inside me that we could change the way things were, but I couldn't make him hear me. It had been eating away at me, but I wasn't the one who could fix it. And the feeling he might always cling to his fears meant we were done.

"I'm sorry," Iris said, placing her hand lightly on my arm. "I know he means a lot to you."

I nodded, unable to do anything more for fear the floodgates would open again.

"The parent who reached out with her concerns..." she began. "I told her the whole thing was just a misunderstanding, and that regardless, you and Mr Lewis have now parted ways. She accepted it, but other parents do know." Pausing, she sighed. "I think it would be best if you let Hannah bring the children in and see them out for a few days until things have calmed down. You haven't done anything wrong, but I know how some of the parents can be. You don't need to be dealing with any mutterings or judgements at the moment."

With a sigh I said, "Maybe just for today. I don't want to hide, and I have nothing to hide from, but I need today to get my head in the game."

"Okay. If you're sure."

"I am," I told her, even though I wasn't certain it was true. I knew my job was safe because my personal life was nobody else's business, plus, Cal and I were over, so any concerns would be irrelevant anyway. But people talking about me and questioning my ethics bothered me. They could say whatever they wanted about me, but any doubts over my teaching abilities and whether the children were safe around me was upsetting and unfair, especially when I'd had nothing but good feedback so far.

Iris smiled softly. "It will get easier."

"It better because feeling like this all the time is taking it out of me and I hate it. I just want things to feel normal again."

"I understand. I'm behind you one hundred percent, Shannen. If I hear any remarks about you that are untoward, any playground gossip, I will ensure it's dealt with. The children here need to be kept safe, but so do my staff. I won't have anyone speaking badly about you."

For the first time in what felt like forever, I gave a genuine smile. I couldn't have asked for a better principal. "I really appreciate that, Iris."

She smiled back at me. "It's no problem. Now, let's hope for a nice easy start to this half of the term."

Apparently, that was too much to ask.

When Hannah, my classroom assistant, led the children into my class, I tried hard not to look for Aiden, but I couldn't help it. I needed to gauge his mood, and it took less than ten seconds to realise that teaching him was going to be rough. He looked... withdrawn, but with an underlying hint of angriness. I recognised the look well. It was the one he had when he was upset but trying to pretend he wasn't, disguising it with a scowl that spelled trouble. He refused to look at me as he walked in, and I wondered what Cal had told him about us. I didn't think he would have blamed the breakup on me, but it was quite clear Aiden wasn't happy about it.

That made two of us.

The only thing I could do was continue as normal, and that was what I tried to do. Most of the kids seemed glad to be back, and I wanted the first day in to be fairly easy, so I'd kept the day's lessons on the more creative side rather than trying to get them to focus on anything more complex.

A bit before lunch, I split the class into two halves, with me keeping an eye on one half and Hannah watching the other as they played a memory game. We'd placed a plate on the table in the middle of each group with some items on, and we had the kids close their eyes while we took one or two items away to see if they could remember what was missing. I kept Aiden in my group because he'd refused to interact with me for most of the morning, and I didn't want to make him feel like I was pushing him aside by putting him on the other side of the room from me.

In hindsight, it wouldn't have mattered. He was itching for a fight, and he got it when he said, after two rounds of guessing, "This game is stupid," and swiped the plate across the table at speed towards me. Luckily, it didn't hit the floor because I stopped it, but the items on the plate slid off and scattered across the table. The other kids jumped back, and instead of settling, Aiden picked up the apple and held it up in the air like he was about to throw it across the room.

"Aiden," I said firmly, but he glared at me and launched the apple hard. It flew through the air and landed on the small, carpeted area in the corner where the bookshelves were.

Normally, I would have handled the situation much more quickly, but the way he was staring at me pierced holes in my already fragile heart. It was as if I'd somehow betrayed him, and I inhaled sharply, trying to control the waves of pain rippling through me. Instead of giving him a proper warning to sit down and get back to the game, I walked around the table towards him.

"Come with me, please."

"Make me."

My eyes widened at his coldness and his words, even though I saw right through it. I could feel the other children watching, so I turned back to them and smiled brightly, though I wasn't sure I was fooling anyone. "Avery," I said to one of the most well-behaved children in the room, "please can you help everyone to pick everything up for me and then you can go and join Miss Taylor at the other table."

Avery nodded enthusiastically. "Come on, everyone," she said. "Let's help Miss Morgan!"

The others immediately began scrabbling to put the misplaced items back into the middle of the table, all except Aiden, who stomped off to the corner where he'd thrown the piece of fruit. I went to Hannah's table; her group was still enthusiastically playing the game. They hadn't noticed the apple soaring across the room because they were behind us, and I whispered to her that I needed to deal with Aiden.

She offered a sympathetic smile before I crossed the classroom, where Aiden was standing in front of one of the bookcases. As I reached him, he started pulling books off the shelves and onto the floor, the scowl still set on his face. He was practically snarling with each title he flung, and I said sharply, "That's enough, Aiden."

He took the next book and opened it up, tearing out the pages and throwing them over his shoulder. I couldn't stop the first handful, but as he went to grab some more, I took the book from him. He instantly reached for another, but I slipped around in front of him, blocking him. He stared at me, his frustration growing and my heart aching. Slowly, I crouched down so I was at eye level with him. This time, I didn't say anything, just waited for him to calm down.

He was too far gone, though. Aiden took a few steps back to pick up one of the books he'd discarded on the carpet, and before I could blink, he launched it right at my head, the corner hitting the side of my right eye.

I gasped and tears filled my eyes, from shock more than pain. It hurt because it had caught the bone, but it was my heart that hurt the most.

The little boy who'd come to mean so much to me had just thrown something at my head.

He was angry and confused by what had been happening in his life, but there was no excusing his behaviour. No other child in the class would have got away with that, and as I blinked to focus on him, I saw the tiniest flicker of regret in his eyes, but he was still so wound up. Standing up, I said, "Wait there."

Instead of listening to me, he ran for the classroom door and out into the corridor. My heart shot into my throat, and I rushed out after him, not sure where he was going. Luckily for me, he ran straight into Iris, and she gently put her hands on his shoulders to steady him.

"Aiden, where are you going?" she asked him, not taking her eyes off him.

"Away from her!" he shouted, pointing at me.

Iris looked from him to me, and seeing the tears brimming in my eyes, she said, "What happened?"

The side of my eye was sore, and I wondered if there was a mark.

"I threw a book at her!" Aiden snapped, and Iris's eyes widened. I nodded in confirmation, wanting to find some words, but I wasn't even sure what to say. He was a child who still wasn't great at expressing his feelings, but he also couldn't be led to believe that what he just did was okay.

"Go back to your class, Miss Morgan," Iris said. "I'll take care of Aiden."

I hesitated for a moment, though I wasn't sure why. He'd already shown he wasn't going to listen to me. I couldn't deal with him with things the way they were. With him mad at me and everything so raw. With another nod, I turned and went back into my classroom.

Chapter 12

Cal

I HUNG UP THE phone with a growl, muttering a curse under my breath. I was up to my ears in painting the bedroom of an old woman whose house we'd been hired to totally redecorate while she was on holiday. The job was slow going as it was, and the last thing I needed was a call from the Oakwood Lane Primary School headmistress, asking me to go in and see her at the end of the day.

"Everything okay, mate?" Luke said from the other side of the room. He was carefully dealing with the window frames while I worked the walls. We didn't usually work two to a room, but we were already a bit behind, so he was helping me out.

"I need to call Guy," I said. "That was the school. Aiden's in trouble." I held in the word 'again'. It had been a couple of months since I'd last been called in, and I'd been half-expecting it because his behaviour lately had been awful.

The day I had to explain to him that Shannen and I had split up, followed by Guy telling him Helen wasn't going to be coming back either had triggered a meltdown that hadn't really ended. Aiden had thrown a lot more stuff around than I had. He'd trashed his room at Guy's, thankfully breaking very little, and the screams of sheer rage coming from him must have had the neighbours thinking he was being murdered. That tantrum had blown through fairly quickly, but the peace between rounds had been

79

pretty short too. When I took him home, he got worse. I hadn't been much use at first. I'd been just as miserable since Shannen left Guy's that day, and as hard as I'd tried to be there for Aiden and wanted to help him deal with his feelings, I wasn't dealing with my own. Guy tried too, but since Helen was gone as well, Aiden wasn't a big fan of either of us.

And he'd immediately reverted to calling me Cal again, which didn't help my mood.

All the things Shannen had helped me to do with him, like trying to get him to talk about his feelings, didn't work anymore. About the only thing that helped was taking him out to the park to play football or burn off some energy on the swings and climbing frames. Even then, he was aggressive and grouchy. Those had been his main two moods, and I hoped having the structure of a school day might help him.

And it might have if Shannen wasn't his teacher.

I wondered if she'd asked the principal to deal with whatever had happened because, last time, it was Shannen who called me in. I doubted she wanted to see me, so she'd probably handed the problem to someone else.

Or he'd done something *really* bad.

"On day one of term?" Luke asked with a knowing chuckle. He had kids of his own and his eldest son had been in his fair share of trouble too.

"Yup." I sighed. "I'm going to need to knock off early. Guy was meant to pick Aiden up today, but I'll have to go instead."

Luke raised his brow. "Good luck with that."

Without Helen around to help with Aiden, Guy and I had rearranged our entire work days. Now, I'd finish work early on Wednesdays and Fridays to collect Aiden, and Guy would do business admin stuff in the afternoons and pick Aiden up on the other days. It meant he couldn't help us on jobs as much, but it was the only way we could make things work until I made other arrangements. With me having to leave early, it meant Guy might have to get his overalls on and cover for me. He wouldn't mind under the circumstances, but I hated that I'd lose another few hours pay on top of the days I'd had to take off over half term.

The whole rest of the day, I stewed over what Aiden might have done and worried about whether or not I would bump into Shannen. I wanted to see her. Even just from a distance, but at the same time, it was better if I didn't.

I'd hurt both of us, but I was used to hurting myself. Hurting Shannen was new and only increased my loathing for myself. Until I could stop being such a self-destructive prick, I was no good to her. The only thing I'd managed to do for myself was stop drinking after the one bender Guy had allowed me.

The part of it all that grated on me the most was hearing from the police that there would be no further questions for me. That Katie had dropped the allegations.

So, what the hell was the point in it all? Why make an accusation, only to drop it again?

If it had happened at any other time than right after I'd confessed what a bastard I used to be, maybe Shannen wouldn't have doubted me. We'd have been fine. She'd accepted my past, but hearing that on top? A couple of weeks down the line, a month, maybe things would have been different.

But if I was honest with myself, my decision to split from her had less to do with her doubts and more to do with myself. There was still too much shit spinning around in my mind. Too many truths that I'd released all at once, and even though I really had believed Shannen and I would make it, the way I saw myself was still an obstacle I couldn't fully overcome.

I got to the school just as the teachers were letting the kids out. I looked around for Shannen, but instead of seeing her ushering the children into the playground, her classroom assistant was doing the job instead.

As I walked by the waiting parents, I was aware of some people turning in my direction, their eyes following me.

Oh, yeah. One of the parents here saw me being carted away by the police.

I hadn't forgotten exactly, but it hadn't been on the top of my list of worries about coming to the school. Now, though, when I could feel their gazes following me, I wondered if the person who'd raised the issue was amongst them.

"Is that him?"

I paused on hearing the loud whisper as I passed, turning my head to look behind me where two women were huddled close together, looking at me. One was roughly in her forties, and the other barely looked older than twenty. I wasn't sure if they were both parents of kids in the school or if they'd simply come together to pick someone up. Either way, my glare in their direction caught the attention of a couple of other mums and dads gathered around.

The younger woman at least had it in her to look embarrassed. The older of the pair eyed me like she thought I was scum. "What did you do that got you arrested?" she asked, not keeping her voice low and attracting the attention of a few more people.

With a long, slow sigh, I turned all the way around to face them. She squared up to me as if she wanted a fight, and the mood I was in, she was lucky she didn't get one. In the past, I might have been more tempted to argue my case, but I needed to get to my son.

Before I could speak, she went on, "I hope you don't think sleeping with a teacher will keep your son out of trouble. If I had my way, she'd be sacked for getting involved with a criminal."

My body turned rigid, and I'd never had to work harder not to snap. I was not a criminal—at least not of this particular crime—and the woman's feelings about Shannen made my fists clench so hard it was going to leave marks on my palms. I wasn't sure if she was the person who had seen me at Dawlish Warren, but she'd clearly become the spokesperson for the parents. It was only the first fucking day back. Did they all gather to discuss it in the playground that morning, or had they been creating drama on social media all week?

"Firstly," I said, "not a single thing about what you just said is any of your business. But so we're clear, Miss Morgan and I are no longer seeing each other, so you can calm yourself down and stop talking shit about her. Secondly, call me a criminal again and I'll be speaking to my solicitor." Without another word, I turned and continued on my way.

Technically, I still didn't *have* a solicitor, but I did know one now. I wouldn't be spending money fighting to defend my name because it wasn't worth it, but that woman didn't know that. Somehow, I doubted this would be the end of the gossip, but at least they knew they didn't need to worry about Shannen. Not that they ever did, but people are stupid. Any sniff of a story and they're all over it.

I wasn't sure where Aiden was, but I made my way into the reception area and approached the young woman at the desk.

I was about to tell her why I was there when the door to Mrs Braithwaite's office opened, and she smiled gently at me from the doorway.

Not the greeting I was expecting.

"Mr Lewis, please come in," she said.

With a deep breath, I walked past the reception desk and to Mrs Braith-waite's office. She let me inside, and I was half-expecting Aiden to be in there with her. When he wasn't, I said, "Where's Aiden?"

The older woman said, "At the moment, he's in the classroom with Miss Morgan, but once Miss Taylor has seen the children out, she will take over."

"Will Sha... Miss Morgan be joining us?"

She shook her head. "No. Although, if you wish to speak to her after we're done, she is willing to do so."

I felt my brow furrow. What the hell had happened here?

"Let's sit down, shall we?" Mrs Braithwaite said.

I nodded, and she rounded her desk and sat behind it, while I took the seat in front.

"There was an incident today in Miss Morgan's classroom," she began. "Miss Morgan was playing a memory game with her class and Aiden decided he didn't want to play."

She paused, and I winced, waiting for the rest of the story.

"There was a plate on the table with items on for the class to memorise, and Aiden pushed the plate across the table towards Miss Morgan, disrupting the game. He then threw an apple across the classroom. When Miss Morgan went to speak to him after he stormed across the classroom, he was throwing books all over the carpet and ripping some up too. He threw one at Miss Morgan and it hit her in the face."

My entire body stiffened. He might have seen me throw things, but he'd never seen me throw something at another person.

"Was it an accident?" I asked, bracing myself.

"Aiden confessed that he threw it at her on purpose."

My jaw tightened and I wanted to get to Aiden and give him the telling off of his life. I'd never shown him it was okay to hurt people. Around Shannen, he'd only seen kindness, and I was certain he never saw Guy laying a hand on Helen. He had witnessed Helen being a bitch to Guy and me, but to my knowledge, she'd never physically hurt anyone, so what he did had to have been a product of his anger and not something he learned. Not that that made it any better. It was bad enough when I saw signs of my father in myself; I certainly didn't want to see it in my son.

"Is Shannen okay?" I asked, trying to keep it together.

"She's fine. She's got a small bruise beside her eye, but nothing that will do any permanent damage."

I crossed my arms, waiting for what was coming next because she didn't call me here only to tell me Aiden had a meltdown. He'd hurt his teacher and trashed schoolbooks, so there had to be some comeback for that.

"Mr Lewis, I understand that your relationship with Miss Morgan has come to an end recently, and that Aiden has also had some large changes in his life and routine over half term," Mrs Braithwaite said. "A certain amount of allowance will be given because of that. However, he deliberately hurt a member of staff and was, for a short time, unmanageable today, so there will be consequences. Aiden will lose lunchtimes and playtimes this week, and he'll be kept inside with a member of staff."

That sounded more than fair to me. Maybe even a bit less than he deserved considering the damage he'd done. I just nodded, and Mrs Braithwaite continued, "I'd like to ask you, though... considering the current circumstances between you and Miss Morgan, if you think it might be better if Aiden were moved to a different class. I've spoken to Miss Morgan, and she says she'd prefer you to make the decision because you know him best. She is happy to keep him, but her concern is whether Aiden will find it hard to be around her at the moment."

Dropping my head back, I sighed. Shannen, I knew, only wanted what was best for him, and if he could move to another class—Gaby's class since she was the other teacher for his year—it might be easier on him. But he also already felt like he'd been abandoned. Both by Shannen and Helen, and even though I'd explained that their leaving had nothing to do with him, he felt the rejection. He didn't remember his own mum, and then Helen and Shannen, the only female figures he spent a lot of time with, had vanished too, almost at the same time.

"I don't know," I said after a moment or two. When I levelled my gaze on Mrs Braithwaite, I added, "Does this decision have to be made today? I think he needs to stay where he is or he's going to think Shannen doesn't want him in her class anymore. But I also don't want her to have to worry that he's going to kick off all the time either."

"Maybe you can have a talk with him and see how he feels. If he makes the decision, then it might be easier."

I nodded. "Yeah. Maybe."

Mrs Braithwaite watched me for another moment, then said, "Mr Lewis, I understand that the past week has not been easy for you. Is there any way I can support you?"

There was only understanding in her eyes, but her words made my hackles rise. People of authority wanting to 'help' usually meant they thought something was wrong and they were going to get other people involved. I was damn sure I wasn't going to lose Aiden again, not now.

"We're fine," I said sharply. "Thanks." I added that only because I didn't want her to think I was rude as well as out of control. She had no idea how hard I'd had to work to make sure everything was covered now Aiden and I were more or less on our own. Without Guy, I'd have been screwed, but between us, we were just about managing.

"I'm not trying to interfere," she said gently. "And I'm not in any way concerned for Aiden's safety, but I do want to ensure that you both feel supported. Aiden has made huge progress since he started at this school, and I don't want to see it slip away because things at home have been a bit shaky."

I stared at her, looking for deception, but I saw none. Shannen had always said what a great person the school's headteacher was. My gut told me she really was only trying to help, and I let go of some of the tension in my body.

"I think he just needs some time," she went on. "But if things get difficult, you are welcome to call any time and we can have a chat about ways we can help. I actually already have an idea or two in mind."

I raised my eyebrows. I couldn't fault her dedication. I wasn't sure if she was being so helpful because Shannen was involved, or if she went this hard for all the children in her school, but I had been wrong to assume she was trying to take me down. She really seemed to care, and I appreciated it.

"I'm open to ideas," I said, offering her my first smile since I'd arrived, even if it was only a small one.

"Well, I understand that you might be struggling with childcare at the moment," she said. "We have a breakfast club here which begins at half past seven during term time. It costs four pounds fifty per day, so if you need to start work earlier because you're having to finish earlier, that could be an option."

I vaguely remembered Shannen mentioning it when we'd realised I'd need some extra help with Aiden, and it hadn't seemed like a terrible idea, I just hadn't looked into it.

"The other thing is, as you know, Aiden really likes drawing. We have an after-school art club he could join too. Although, there is art involved in breakfast club. I think any activities you can enrol him in would be helpful to keep his mind occupied."

"He's got a really short attention span at the moment," I said. "He wants to do things, and then after half an hour, he wants to do something else. He isn't usually like it, though, so it's probably more because he's upset. I think art club would be good, and maybe breakfast club too. I will talk to him and also to my boss to see if earlier starts could be something I could do. It would be better to spend more time with Aiden after school than before, when he was barely awake and hardly registering my presence anyway."

"Let me know what you decide," Mrs Braithwaite said. "I think more than anything, Aiden is going to need as much stability as you can give him, especially in the short term. Whatever routine you decide on for him, try to ensure it stays as steady as possible. It's very difficult when a parent goes through a breakup, and Aiden has lost two people who were important to him. But also..." She paused, leaning forward slightly. "I think you would benefit from giving yourself a break. I won't speak on your relationship with Miss Morgan, but I will say that single parenting is hard. You are doing a good job."

I snorted. "Really? You called me in because my kid threw a book at a teacher. Doesn't sound like good parenting to me."

She smiled that kind smile again. "Whatever difficulties you've had, Mr Lewis, Aiden has changed in a very good way during the months he's been here. Today was a blip, and I'm sure you'll find your way through it as you have everything else. It's okay to say you need help, though. As I said, if there is anything we can do at the school to make life easier, we will do it. Aiden is a very intelligent boy who just needs to feel secure again. I have no doubt you will be able to do that for him."

This stranger had more faith in me than I did. It made me wonder what Shannen had told her about me. It can't have been anything bad if she believed I was doing a good job of raising Aiden.

Fuck. Shannen. I needed to know if she was okay.

"Please could I see Shannen?" I asked, my voice suddenly croaky, and I swallowed.

Mrs Braithwaite nodded. "You can. If you wait here, I'll get her to come to you and I'll stay with Aiden in the classroom with Miss Taylor."

I nodded as she stood and walked around the desk. As she passed me, she paused and rested her hand on my shoulder. "This will all resolve itself. I guarantee it."

She left the office, and I thought over her words. I wasn't sure how anything could possibly be resolved at this point. I'd pissed my relationship with Shannen away and emotionally wounded my son. What could I do to change that?

Just admit you messed everything up and get her back.

But how the hell was I supposed to do that? After hurting her so badly, how could I say, 'Wait, sorry, I changed my mind'? That was almost as much of a dick move as breaking up with her in the first place. The damage was done.

Shannen always talked about how she hated it when I said I didn't deserve her. But I *didn't*. I couldn't. Even less so now I'd done this to her. And my son had attacked her in her own classroom. It just highlighted the differences between us even more. She was educated, intelligent, beautiful, and kind. I was a screw-up, and until I stopped being that, I would never be worthy of her.

And I hadn't thought of myself any other way since I was fourteen.

Okay, maybe there were moments lately when I'd started to shift it. To see that maybe I deserved something more. But every time she said she loved me, something else came along to screw me over. Jade and Scott, Shannen's dad, the police, Katie. I'd pushed through the first few things with a fight, but I'd done it because I wanted to be with Shannen. Wanted to allow myself to believe I could have a life with someone, a life that gave Aiden a better childhood than I had. But something continued to take from me, to have a laugh at my expense and my trust that things could be better.

The door opened, shattering my thoughts, and I turned my head as Shannen tentatively entered the office. Once the door was closed, she leaned back against it, one hand still on the handle as if she wasn't sure whether she wanted to be there. She hadn't met my eye yet, and the need to go to her and pull her into my arms filled every inch of my body until it ached.

Slowly, I stood up and faced her, keeping my distance despite my instincts.

And she still didn't look at me.

Instead, I took the time to study her. She wore a knee-length black skirt, with black tights and low-heeled black ankle boots. A thin pale blue jumper covered her top half, and her black curly hair was tied back in a low ponytail. Finally, my gaze landed on her face. Sure enough, there was a small bruise at the side of her eye, and I flinched just looking at it.

I knew she could feel my eyes on her because her chest began to rise and fall a bit more rapidly, and her jaw tensed like she was trying to hold in her emotions. As I looked at her eyes again, I saw them glisten, and my chest... that weird fluttery feeling I used to get every time she smiled at me appeared for just a moment before it turned into a pain so intense that I drew in a sharp breath.

It caught her attention, and she finally raised her head slightly, letting go of the door handle and straightening up. This time, our eyes locked.

"Are you okay?" I asked, my voice cracking a little.

She nodded, her gaze dropping to the floor again. "Yeah."

Look at me. I need you to look at me.

Against my better judgement, when she still refused to meet my eye, I crossed the small space and planted myself directly in front of her. I could practically hear her heart beating when I was standing so close to her, and every instinct screamed at me to hold her and kiss her and make this nightmare end. To bring her back into my life and deal with my own shit so I could be with her again.

But dealing with my own shit while I was with her hadn't worked out so well. Not for long, anyway.

From the corner of my eye, I saw her hand move from her side slowly, with hesitation, before dropping down again. Her entire body seemed to sag, and I took a small step back. She wanted to touch me, but she didn't. This time, I felt her watching me. Could feel her gaze trying to work out how I was feeling, sending every bit of her love to wrap around me like the hug I so badly wanted to give her. The fact that I could feel so much emotion from her after all I'd done made me take another step backwards. It wasn't because I didn't want it. I always wanted it. But it was hard to feel it when I knew I'd broken her heart.

"Cal, I... we need to figure out what to do about Aiden, but I just want to..." Her words trailed off, and she shook her head with a sigh.

Seeing her like this was a physical and mental torture I didn't know how to stop. She'd never hidden how she felt from me, and I'd always liked that about her, but now, I wished she could shut it off because it was like a knife twisting deep in my gut. That she was struggling to be around me, that she was battling her internal agony made me want to run, but I couldn't. Wouldn't.

"I'm sorry about what he did," I told her. "I'm sorry."

"I know. And he's apologised too. Kind of." She shrugged. "He's angry, and I get it."

But it still hurts. Those were the unspoken words written all over her face.

"I will make sure he understands how wrong he was to do that," I promised her. Again, the idea that he had the same tendencies as me, but more my dad, ripped through me, and she saw the exact moment my body tensed because her features softened slightly.

"It *was* wrong," she said. "And I know you'll handle it. But he needs some time to deal with everything."

"Yeah, but he can't go around throwing books at you and disrupting everyone else in the class." The bubbles of frustration inside me amped up, and I turned away from her, landing a soft kick at the chair I'd been sitting on. It jumped forward only slightly, and I wanted to kick it harder. To watch it fly across the room and shatter against the wall.

Catching myself before I slipped into a spiral I couldn't get out of, I pulled in a deep breath through my nose and let it out slowly.

"Do you think he would be better in Gaby's class?" Shannen asked.

"Do you want him gone?"

The bitterness in my voice wasn't intended, but it was out there, weaved into my words.

There was a long moment of silence, and eventually, she said, "It's hard having him in my class now you and I..." Another pause. "I want what is best for *him*, Cal. He's come such a long way, and I don't want him to go backwards because of all this. If he wants to be in my class, then I'm happy for him to stay. But if it's too hard for him, then he can go to Gaby's class instead. I don't want him to struggle, so see what he wants to do."

Turning back around to face her again, I said, "I don't want him to feel like you don't want him."

The glisten of tears was back in her eyes again. "I know. But he also doesn't like me very much right now."

89

Unspoken questions lingered in her eyes, and I said, "I didn't make our breakup your fault."

"What *did* you tell him?"

"Just that we won't be seeing each other anymore."

She closed her eyes and shook her head. "That's not enough information. Especially if Guy said the same thing about Helen. He's going to think that people can just leave out of nowhere with no warning."

Which is what his mother did, and what he thought I did when he was taken away from me. That was probably why he'd screamed so much when the police took me away. Why he thought I might not come back. My son had attachment issues, and when the few people who had been in his life kept vanishing, it only made them worse.

"What did you want me to say to him, Shannen?" I snapped, annoyance ripping through me again. It wasn't even annoyance at her, it was at myself. "That you didn't trust me? That you left because you believed I'd slapped his mother?"

Her lips pursed, and she took in a deep breath. The anguish on her face caused my insides to shrivel, adding to the ache already coursing through me. I was being a dick, but I couldn't stop myself from lashing out.

"This was a mistake," she said, her voice colder than I'd ever heard it. Her expression, her eyes still glistening with her pain, told me she didn't feel cold towards me; she was protecting herself the way I was, but it still cut deep. "Please talk to Aiden about what he wants, but even if he stays in my class, I think it's better if you deal with Mrs Braithwaite if there are any other behavioural issues. I will refer any concerns to her from now on as it's clear that you and I are unable to be near each other at the moment."

Shannen took a long breath, lowering her gaze as she turned to the door.

"Shan."

That one word from my mouth made her stiffen, and she turned her head to look over her shoulder at me. The issue was, I didn't even know what I wanted to say, I just didn't want her to go yet. Didn't want the last words we said to be angry ones, even though we both were.

When I didn't speak, she said, "I hate this, Cal. I hate it. But I can't be around you. It's too hard."

Before I could find any words to reply, she walked out of the office, leaving me alone.

Chapter 13

Shannen

AFTER WORK DRINKS WAS not quite what I'd had in mind for my first day back after half term, but with the day I'd had, Gaby and Nova had both instructed me not to go home after my unexpected school meeting with Cal. Instead, I was told to meet them at The Prospect Inn, a pub on the Quay. I didn't have the heart to tell them that the Quay was just another place that reminded me of Cal, but most things did now. At least he and I had never been to this particular pub together, which was something.

On the drive over there, my mind whirled with the events of the day. Aiden throwing a book at me hadn't been on my after-half-term bingo card. I'd gone in expecting him to be either quiet or disruptive. I hadn't expected the violence, but I wasn't entirely shocked either. Throwing was something Cal did when he was frustrated, though never at people. As confused as Aiden must have been with recent events, it wasn't surprising he'd responded to me the way he had. It wasn't okay, and the school had made his punishments clear. I hoped Cal would also talk to him, but I had no idea what he would say to him. I didn't know what to say to him either, but it wasn't on me to deal with his behaviour anywhere other than in the classroom, and that was being dealt with.

Cal, though. Seeing him had caused pain I hadn't known was possible. One look at him, his thick black hair, those deep, chocolatey eyes, his utterly kissable lips on a face that continued to show up every night in my dreams. Being unable to touch him, to hold him. That was a new kind of torture, and the only way I could handle it was by avoiding eye contact as much as possible and trying to pretend I wasn't crippled by the agony of the distance between us.

I'd missed people before. Been separated from people I cared about. People I loved. But being apart from Cal was slowly killing me. When he'd snarled out harsh words in Iris's office, it made it marginally easier because at least then I could tell myself that was the real him, and his dark, angry side was something I didn't want in my life. The truth was, that anger was a hangover from the days when he'd lived drunk on his rage, on his torment. Sometimes, snippets of it slipped through, but it was something I'd tried my hardest to help him heal. Even though it wasn't my place because they were his wounds to tend to, being by his side as he slowly fixed them was something I'd been happy to do. He didn't *need* me, but I couldn't help but worry about how he would handle things now, when it was just him and Aiden. Guy would still support him, but he had his own stuff to deal with.

Before I could begin bawling over my steering wheel, I pushed thoughts of him aside, turning up the volume on the radio to drown out the noise in my head.

When I entered the pub, Nova and Gaby were already sitting at a small table close to the bar. Since we were all driving, they both had soft drinks, and there was a glass of what looked like lemonade in the space where I would sit.

"There she is," Nova said with a smile as I approached and sat down.

My friends watched me with concern, and for a moment, I wondered exactly how I looked. I felt exhausted. Not just from the day, but from the aftermath of a breakup I hadn't seen coming. One I didn't want. When I'd looked at myself in the mirror before I went to work, I still looked like me. Miss Morgan, schoolteacher and professional. My eyes, though, gave me away. I hadn't been able to bring myself to check my reflection before I got out of the car, but I felt dishevelled. Not in my clothing, but I felt like my hair was falling out of its ponytail and that the tiredness was etched into my face.

"We should have met at mine," I said, eyeing my glass of lemonade. "I need wine. Lots of it."

Gaby laughed softly. "And if we didn't have work in the morning, we'd join you. Maybe we can have a blowout at the weekend."

I smiled, though it wasn't as genuine as they deserved. "I have my mum's birthday dinner on Saturday. Otherwise, I would take you up on that."

Nova reached over and placed her hand on mine on the table. "Was seeing him that bad?"

My eyes flicked up to look at her. "You know how I felt the morning after we broke up?" She nodded. "It was like that. But worse because I was at work, and I couldn't just lose it right there in the classroom. Not when anyone could have seen me and further questioned whether or not I'm fit for my job."

"What did he say to you?" Gaby asked as I reached for my glass to take a sip.

"He apologised, but it ended as it always does. With him snapping at me. God," I said, running a hand across my forehead. "I'm a mess. I don't think I've ever felt less in control of my life."

"Give yourself a break," Gaby said. "This is new. It's not as if you've been stuck in the same place for a year. This has all only just happened and you've been through a lot with him. You don't wake up the morning after a tornado has ripped through your life and find your house has been magically rebuilt. It takes time."

"It feels like forever," I said. "I feel like I've been without him forever. I can't believe this time last week, everything was great. But more than that, why can't I just shut up about it? It's like... talking is all I have left of him now. I need to let it go. Let him go because he isn't coming back. And maybe I can't have him back."

"Can't have or don't want?" Gaby asked with a raised eyebrow.

A groan escaped my lips. "Both?" The word came out as a question, and I shook my head. "What I want is for us not to have ever got to this point. But we did. And I just... I can't see a way back. He thinks I don't trust him and there isn't any way I can fix that. The doubt is in his head. And while he understands why, I still hurt him, and he hurt me back. So, although I miss him and I wish there was a way he could forgive me, he's so hung up on his own mistakes that I don't think he can forgive himself either. We both messed up, and now we have to live with the decisions we made."

"Shannen, I..." Nova began, but words failed her, and her eyes filled with sadness. Although minimal, she and Donovan had spent more time with me and Cal than Gaby had, and we'd been starting to form a strong quartet. Donovan was lovely, and I loved seeing Cal make a new friend in him. Although they could still be friends via the powers of social media, I wondered if Cal would cut that off too. "I hate that this happened."

"Me too. I just don't think there's a whole lot I can do about it. All I can really do is hope things calm down so Aiden doesn't feel so unsettled and abandoned."

It was a lot to ask of a kid who'd already faced so much disruption in his five years. To not feel like people kept leaving him. I only hoped in time he'd come to trust me again, as his teacher if nothing else.

Chapter 14

Cal

Hearing that my son had lost his temper and deliberately hurt Shannen caused a deep, burning rage inside me. I had never hit Aiden, and I never would, but in the moment when I walked into the classroom and he glared at me with defiance, I could understand the instinct to lash out from frustration. The disrespect was clear in the depths of his eyes; a glimmer of my father edging into his innocent gaze, making me shudder. He was five years old. I should not have been able to say I could see even a hint of that cold-hearted arsehole in him.

But of course I would. Because I had it in me too. I'd just learned how to control it. Mostly.

And *I* was *not* my father. I would never use my fists to 'teach Aiden a lesson'. Even the concept of a light smack didn't work for me. Had we been at home and not accompanied by the school's headteacher, I would have exploded at him. Still not right, but I was so fucking angry with him. I was in no mood for the calm conversation I was supposed to have.

I will not raise a child who thinks it's okay to hurt people.

I just didn't know how to firmly ensure he understood that.

After thanking Mrs Braithwaite for watching Aiden while I talked to Shannen, I swept him out of there and into the car park. He stomped every step, and as we got to the van, he turned to me and said, "I'm not sorry."

The simmering rage crept higher at his words, and I had never had to fight harder to keep control. My child was trying to goad me, and I wasn't having it. That was the only way I could keep him in check; by not letting him rile me the way I used to.

He stared up at me beside the passenger side door, and I said, "You're not sorry, huh?"

"Nope."

I breathed in slowly through my nose and let it out through my mouth. "That's fine. When we get home, you can sit quietly and think about that, but there will be no video games and no iPad until you've explained to me why you threw a book at your teacher."

He shrugged; he had the attitude of a spoilt teenager, and before I rammed my fist into my work van, I unlocked the door and hauled Aiden up into his car seat, securing him before closing the door and walking to the driver's side.

The second I was buckled in, Aiden let out a loud sound that was somewhere between a scream and a cry before tugging at his seatbelt as if it were strangling him. Moving quickly, I unclipped my own seatbelt before moving across to the middle seat and freeing Aiden from his before he broke it. Once he was free, he slammed his clenched fists down on his legs over and over as tears spilled from his eyes.

"I'm bad! I'm bad!" He shouted the words over and over, his face turning red with his sobs and the force he was using to thump himself.

The words tore at me. In that moment, he was the physical version of what had lived inside me for years. A little boy who was always told how useless he was, how pathetic and pointless, so that when I actually did something terrible, my inner voice did what Aiden was doing. I had an internal meltdown that felt like hands punching at my insides.

Without thinking about it, I slid him from his car seat and onto my lap. He wriggled and fought for a moment, but when I kept my arms tight around him, he stopped and shouted out again. No words, just a cry of frustration.

"Aiden, it's okay," I said gently into the top of his head, even though neither of us was okay at all. We were falling apart and unable to handle it.

"No! I did a bad thing!"

I didn't know what to say to that because it was the truth. Telling him he hadn't wouldn't help, I just didn't know what the right words were.

Useless parent. Useless on your own.

"I want to go to Shannen's house!"

His words were spoken at a slightly lower volume, but I wasn't going to be able to make that happen for him either. There was no way, under the circumstances, I could go to her place, not even for an apology. If that was what he was offering.

"We can't, buddy," I told him. "But you can talk to her tomorrow at school."

"I don't want her to be mad at me until tomorrow."

"I understand." *Man, do I understand.* "But Shannen isn't... we can't just go and see her whenever we want to anymore."

"I hurt her, though. I need to say sorry."

"She told me you already said sorry earlier."

"But I didn't mean it then!"

That feeling inside me that made me hate myself surged through me again. Maybe she was right and I didn't give him enough information about our break-up, so he'd drawn his own conclusions. Truthfully, he didn't like me much at the moment either, but I was the one who deserved the brunt of his upset.

"Why were you angry with Shannen?" I asked quietly.

"Because she left us. She just went home and didn't come back."

Closing my eyes, I sighed. "I know. But... it's... Shannen didn't choose to leave us. I asked her to."

Aiden looked up at me, confusion heavy in his eyes. This was not a situation I could explain to him. He was too young, but he needed *something* from me. Some kind of explanation.

"Ask her to come back," he said.

"It's not that easy, buddy," I told him. "I... made her feel bad. And I didn't mean to."

Yes, you did. In the moment, that was exactly what you meant to do.

"But you said if we say sorry to people then it makes it better. So, you can say sorry to her."

"Some things are too hard to forgive."

Aiden still looked confused, a tiny wrinkle on his smooth forehead. At five years old, there was no way he could understand how I felt, why I'd made the decisions I had. I didn't totally understand why. Not beyond self-sabotage and irrational rage.

"Will she forgive me?"

"Yes, buddy. She will."

Aiden shrugged as if he didn't believe me. "Can we go to the park?"

My instinct was to tell him we could, to get some fresh air and let him unwind. But he'd still done something he shouldn't have, and I couldn't just forgo the consequences because he was upset.

Or could I? Was I being too hard on him?

I'd thought being a single parent when Aiden was a baby was rough, but at least then he didn't ask me questions I couldn't answer. Now, I was winging it. I had to make these decisions on my own.

"We need to go home," I said. "What you did today was wrong, Aiden, and so we're not just going to go to the park and forget about it."

He nodded sadly. "Okay."

I wanted to take it all away, to tell him he was forgiven and not change anything for him, but at the same time, I refused to allow his cute face and sad eyes to sway me, but I would be more lenient since he'd admitted he was sorry.

"No video games for a week," I told him. "And you will say sorry to Shannen tomorrow when you go to school."

"Can I draw her a picture when we get home?"

I nodded. "Yeah. You can."

Once I'd taken Aiden home, he'd gone straight over to the dining table to make a card for Shannen while I started making food. It had been a while since I'd made a lasagne, and it was something simple that didn't require much thought, so it seemed like the best option. I sent Guy a text to ask him if he wanted to join us as an apology for cutting out on work early and making him finish off my job. Plus, I was pretty sure he was living on sandwiches and Pot Noodles since Helen left. It wasn't that he couldn't cook, he just hadn't felt like it, and if I didn't have Aiden to think about, I'd probably have done the same.

Aiden was pretty quiet through dinner, and I still felt horrible about what he'd done, so I wasn't the greatest company either. Even Guy couldn't cheer Aiden up, when usually, he was good at that. At around six, Guy must have sensed I needed a break, so he 'reminded' me I needed some milk and suggested I go to the shop while he watched Aiden. There was an almost-full four-pint bottle in the fridge, but Aiden wouldn't check.

I shot out of the apartment like my arse was on fire, desperate for some fresh air. Some days, when Aiden was on edge, it was hard to breathe. It felt like it used to in the times before Shannen. Like everything was too much. It sounded stupid because it wasn't as if Shannen had ever been like a parent to Aiden; we hadn't been together for long enough, but having her there... that additional support was enough. I hadn't wanted to rely on Guy over the past week because of everything he was going through, and aside from that first couple of days after Shannen left, I'd gone back to just... surviving. I'd tried hard to use the techniques Shannen taught me with Aiden, but they didn't always work if I was as wound up as he was. And I had been.

What Aiden had done that day was proof I needed to get myself together. I had to be better, had to get my head straight because if I couldn't control my own feelings, I couldn't help Aiden with his, and I would have done just about anything to ensure I never saw even a hint of real malice in his eyes. He shouldn't have to ever feel that angry.

But he did, and that was because of his upbringing, the number of people in his life who had left him. He needed reassurance. Patience. Neither were things I was good at, but I needed to try.

I had to stop my own fears about people leaving affecting him too.

I let out a huff, my breath visible in the cold air. It was still early days, I knew, but the ache of missing Shannen hadn't changed since the day she left. I was pretty sure it wouldn't leave anytime soon, and it only got worse after seeing her. I'd needed it. To be in the same room as her, but at the same time, it had been torture not to touch her, kiss her, even hold her hand.

"Cal?"

The quiet voice stopped me in my tracks, and without even realising how far I'd gone, I'd sped my way almost to the small corner shop that was a couple of streets away. I was just at the entrance to the park I usually took Aiden to, and there, standing by the gate, was Katie.

I had to be fucking dreaming. The stress and lack of sleep were making me see things. I blinked a couple of times, but when I stopped, she was still there.

God, she was a mess. She wore a pair of grey leggings and a too-big black coat over the top. Her brown hair was limp around her once-pretty face.

She was the same age as me, but she looked older. If she hadn't recently tried to get me locked up, I might have felt sorry for her.

As I stared, the familiar stirrings of anger trickled through me.

The last time I saw her, she'd begged me to take Aiden out of the flat so she could get some sleep. He'd been restless overnight, and none of us had had much rest. She was lying on the bed, and she'd smiled gratefully at me for agreeing to her request. She'd been getting lazy with Aiden over the last few weeks, doing less and less for him, but never did I think when I got home, she'd be gone. Packed up some of her shit and walked out. That one move had led to my downfall with Aiden. If she'd only said she needed a break, then maybe things would have been different. Maybe I would never have lost him.

I never missed her because I never wanted to be with her. All I'd wanted was for her to help me raise the child we'd created.

And now, there she was. Just a week after she'd made another attempt at ruining my life. Pretty successfully too.

"You have thirty seconds to get out of my way," I said as she stepped in front of me.

Fear filled her eyes, probably from my stone-cold glare, but she shook her head, standing her ground. "I need a bit more than thirty seconds."

"How are you even here? Is this just a weird coincidence, or did you know I live around here?"

She grimaced. "A bit of both. I found out where Aiden's school is and guessed you probably lived nearby somewhere. I've been coming out at night, looking for you and hoping I might see you, but I'd just about given up. If I didn't see you by tomorrow night, I was leaving anyway."

"Why were you looking for me? And why the hell did you think I would want to talk to you after what you did?" My voice rose slightly, and her eyes dimmed as she lowered her gaze to the ground.

"That's *why* I wanted to find you," she said quietly, but desperation tinged her words. "To explain."

"Explain?" I snarled, taking a step towards her. "You know I never laid a hand on you, and you lied to the police so I got handcuffed and taken away in front of my son, my friends, and a load of strangers! What explanation is there for that except that you're a fucking mess?"

"That's why I did it, Cal!" she snapped, looking up at me. "Because I'm a mess! Look at me!" She gestured to her oversized clothes and flicked her greasy hair. Tears filled her eyes. "I know you're angry with me, and I deserve every bit of it, but I need to tell you what you need to know and then get out of here before he finds me and makes me pay."

I felt my brows dip despite my growing rage. "Before who finds you?"

She drew in a deep breath, then paused, looking around. There was nobody nearby aside from the occasional passing car, but she grabbed my arm and pulled me through the gate into the park so we were away from the road. She didn't stop dragging me until we were hidden under the cover of some trees, far enough from the nearest streetlight that we wouldn't be seen.

"What's going on, Katie?" I asked, my fury slowly being replaced by an unsettled feeling deep in my gut.

Katie let out a long, slow breath. "Cal, when I left you... you know how things were. It was hard, but I never meant to stay away forever. I was going to just take a break and come back so I could be a better mum to Aiden, but I..." she paused, shame taking over her features. "I was selfish. I went to stay with a friend in Taunton, just for a few days I thought, but..."

"You didn't even leave a note, Katie," I said pointedly. "You never called. You never even sent a text."

She shook her head. "I know. I just... in my head, I was coming back, but I was so messed up. Maybe I knew deep down that I didn't want to, and I... it was all too much. I wasn't ready to do what it took to be a mother, and me and you, we didn't belong together either. I was drinking, Cal. Even back then, I was drinking, and once I left, I felt free to do what I wanted. Before I knew what had even happened, I was having wine for breakfast and whiskey for dessert. I partied so hard that I ended up in hospital, and by the time I knew I needed help, nobody was left. I just kept stumbling from shitty person to shitty person and getting used and fucked over, and... I just wanted it to stop. I *want* it to stop."

Her words tumbled out like she'd been holding them in for years, and maybe she had. She looked truly terrible. Not just physically, but there was nothing left in her eyes, no spark of light like she used to have. Considering how much she said she drank, she didn't smell like alcohol, but she did have that drawn look heavy drinkers have. It had aged her.

But I wasn't sure if I felt bad for her. A couple of wrong choices, and I could have been in the same position as her, yet I backtracked. I didn't let my demons swallow me forever. Even when I was alone and at my weakest, I wanted to get my son back, but her? She didn't check in a single time.

"And how exactly does this relate to you reporting me to the police?" I asked, my voice still cold.

Heaving in another deep breath, she said, "A few weeks ago, I got a call from an anonymous number. The man who called me asked me if I knew you, and he was asking all kinds of questions about what you were like, if you'd ever done anything to hurt me, and I told him the truth. That you never had, and that the reasons I left were nothing to do with you. He didn't seem very pleased with my answers, and he said he knew you, that you had been in trouble a long time ago and did something that you got away with."

The unsettled feeling I had a moment ago was growing at a crazy rate, and it crawled from my stomach through my whole body, sneaking through my veins and bubbling, simmering, waiting for her next words.

"I didn't know what the hell he was talking about," she went on. "His voice was really... threatening. I got scared and told him I was going to hang up, but he said he had an offer for me, and if I knew what was good for me, I'd take it." She paused, looking up at me with a pleading gaze. Tears sat unshed in her eyes. "He said he knew where I was. That he knew I needed help. I don't know if he was guessing, or if he really knew, but... I do need help. I'm in so much debt, and I hate the mess I'm in. He told me if I went to the police and said you hurt me, he'd give me five grand, and I could use it to get out of trouble."

Five grand. *Five fucking grand?*

"And so, what..." I said. "You just took the money without a second thought for what it might cause?"

"No!" she said, stepping towards me, desperation in her voice. "I said I wouldn't do it, that I wouldn't lie, but he... he told me that Aiden wasn't safe with you. That he'd been taken away from you because you were a drunk but you'd got him back. He made it sound like you were as fucked-up as me, and he said that Aiden would be better off with people who could look after him properly. He told me that if I said you were dangerous, I could save Aiden from getting hurt."

"Like you ever gave a shit!" I snapped, turning away from her for a moment and running my hands through my hair. "You left him and never came back! Are you telling me you suddenly cared about him because a stranger told you a story?"

"I always cared!" she shouted, the tears now falling from her eyes. "I cared, but I... I was gone for so long, I was afraid you wouldn't let me see Aiden. I thought he was safe with you until I was told he was taken away from you. He got me so confused, Cal! He made me think Aiden wasn't safe with you, and that you were a psycho, and I... I needed the money."

She turned away from me, pacing, then stopping and pulling at her hair in frustration.

She was pathetic. She'd gone from simply being self-centered to an all-out trainwreck. She said she always cared about Aiden, but she walked out on him without a word, and if she thought she was coming back in a few days, she *would* have called. She could have phoned me any time to find out how he was, and even though I called her for days... weeks, she never answered. She abandoned him.

But then... maybe if Aiden's foster parents hadn't helped me, I'd have drunk until the only thing I lived on was booze. Until I became nothing but skin and bone and debt. Maybe I could have been like her.

But you didn't. You're not like her.

"Did you get it?" I asked, her back still to me. "Did you get the money?"

"Some of it. I asked for half of it upfront, and the rest was to be given once I made the statement." She let out a dark chuckle before turning to look at me again. "And you know what? He didn't pay me the rest of the money and called me naive for thinking he would. Then he mocked me. Told me Aiden was fine, but he had some other things I could do for him and he'd help me get Aiden back. I told him to go fuck himself and retracted my statement, but Cal..." She rushed back towards me again. "He is determined to get you into trouble. And that's why I was looking for you. To apologise and to tell you to be careful. Please don't do anything that will put you at risk because I am in no position to look after a child, and I don't want Aiden to be taken from you. I'm sorry about what I did to you, I really am, but I'm scared. For myself and for what he's trying to do to you."

Tears were now raining down her cheeks.

What she had done had damaged me. Me, Aiden, and Shannen because we'd all fallen apart with her allegation. I would never agree that there was any reason good enough to make a false accusation against someone, but...

I paused in my thoughts. *He* had got into her head?

While I had a strong suspicion I knew who she meant—because who else had that much money to throw around?—I wondered if she knew who she'd been dealing with, and I needed confirmation.

"Katie, do you know who gave you the money?" I asked.

She nodded. "His name was Scott McCalden. A police officer. A high-up one, he said. I met him one time, so he could give me the money. In cash. That's why I'm scared. He told me that because of his job, he'll always be able to find me if he really wants to."

Fucking ballsy dickhead. Didn't even pretend to be somebody else. But then, why would he? With the word of a superintendent against a woman reliant on alcohol to get through the day, which one would be believed if she told someone what he'd done?

Why did he want me in jail badly enough that he'd pay someone to accuse me of something, though?

Or was this not to do with me at all anymore? He had to know that with nothing to back up what Katie said, no proof of me hurting anyone before, and her subsequently disappearing after retracting her statement, the main damage he could have caused was between Shannen and me.

And that was exactly what happened.

I'd played right into the bastard's hands by letting Shannen go, and for what? Did he really only want to hurt Shannen? Or *was* it both of us?

Either way, the burn of fury was fully surging inside me now; the kind of rage that made me want to do *something*. Something cruel. Something I might not get away with but would happily do time for if it meant that prick could never hurt anyone again.

"You know him?" Katie asked.

I nodded, my mind growing darker. "Yeah. I know him. And I'm going to make sure he never forgets me before I shove him into an early grave."

"No," Katie said, reaching out and grabbing my leather jacket. "You can't touch him. He wants a reason to put you behind bars. Don't give him one."

By the time I've finished with him, he won't be able to speak to anyone ever again. The monsters in my head rampaged, envisioning me pummelling his smug face until there was nothing left but blood and bone. For everything he'd helped me lose. For the pain and suffering my son and Shannen were both going through because of what his actions caused.

But still... when it came down to it, I was the one who'd made the decisions that had hurt everyone. He'd simply loaded the gun, but I'd pulled the trigger.

"What are you going to do now?" I asked Katie, her hands still clutching my jacket. I needed to know, for my own sanity, and to keep my mind from thoughts of kicking the shit out of Scott.

She sighed, letting go of me to wipe her eyes. "I'm going back to Taunton. That's where I've spent most of my time. Some of the money will clear a bit of the debt, but I need rehab, Cal. I need to find somewhere that will take me and keep me until I kick this habit so I don't die before I'm thirty-five."

"And what about Aiden?" I asked through slightly gritted teeth. I wanted her away from him, didn't want to look at her after what she did. But I also knew I had no real right to keep him away from her, especially if she was clean and sober.

She shook her head, her tears falling harder as she finally let go of my jacket and stepped back. "He's yours. He doesn't know me. One day, if he wants to find me, I'd be open to that. But I don't want him to know me like this, and I don't want to disrupt his life. Please, just take care of him."

She let out a sob, burying her face in her hands, and a small part of me cracked. All the time she was gone, all the years she wasn't part of Aiden's life, I was so angry with her. For leaving me alone with him to struggle, while I'd thought she was away somewhere living a good life, free of responsibilities. She had been free of responsibilities, but it wasn't fun for her. Maybe for a while, but now she was an empty shell. She'd given up her child to saddle herself with debt and addiction.

For everything else she was, she was still the mother of my child. It may have been in name more than anything else, but my son was part of her, and that meant, no matter whether I liked it or not, she was a part of me too.

Taking a small step forward, I rested my hands on her shoulders. She jumped, surprised by the move before looking up at me. "Get yourself sorted out," I said gently. "Get sober, get your debts cleared, and start over. Move away from anything that was bad for you. You can't live like this anymore. Use that money and just... get better."

She nodded, resting one hand over mine and squeezing gently. "I will. And thank you. For not losing your shit and for letting me explain."

I shrugged.

Offering me a small smile, she said, "I'm going to leave now. I'll get the next train out of here and make things right."

"Be careful, Katie," I said.

She nodded. "I will. I really am sorry, Cal. I can see now that everything he said was a lie." She trailed her eyes up and down my body for longer than I was comfortable with. "You look good. I'm sorry I doubted you."

For a second, a glimpse of the old Katie shone through. The flirty girl who had made me laugh with her cheeky words and pretty smile. Not that it did anything for me now. All she had ever been for me was a bit of fun that had got out of hand when I'd got her pregnant.

I didn't regret it, though. Hard as things had been, I didn't regret Aiden.

With a sigh, I said, "Apology accepted. But if McCalden ever tries to get in touch with you again, don't trust a single word he says. Hang up and change your number because nothing he has to say to you will be anything good."

Katie nodded. "I promise. Thank you for taking care of Aiden. If he ever asks about me... let him know that I might not have been around, but I think about him every single day."

She stared at me for a moment, her lower lip trembling before she turned and walked away so I couldn't see the tears I was sure were falling now.

I watched her until she disappeared into the darkness, my heart pounding and my head overloaded with everything I'd heard.

Chapter 15

Cal

I DIDN'T GET THE milk.

Instead, I made my way back home on autopilot, Katie's words circling around my head. When I walked into my flat, Aiden ran at me as if I'd been gone for hours. Somehow, with all I'd learned in such a short time, it felt that way to me too. I glanced at Guy, who was sitting at the dining table, where Aiden had been before he charged at me. The table was covered in coloured pens and paper.

Aiden wrapped his arms around my legs, a piece of paper clutched in one hand. "I finished Shannen's card," he said, squeezing me tight.

Needing him close, I lifted him up and into my arms, and he circled his around my neck, the paper tickling the hair on the back of my head as he flapped it around. I kissed the top of Aiden's head, and said, "Let me see, then."

He beamed at me and let go of me with one hand to pass me his creation. He'd folded over a piece of A4 paper, and on the front, he'd drawn a picture of the Brave Little Toaster and Kirby, the vacuum cleaner from the same movie. There was a speech bubble over Kirby's head that said, "Im sorree." The bubble over the toaster's head said "Frenz foreva." He'd also coloured the characters in, and a lump formed in my throat. Having seen the film approximately seven hundred times since Shannen had introduced Aiden to it, I knew that Toaster and Kirby had a turbulent relationship. They

107

butted heads all the time, but they were always there for each other in the end. I wasn't sure if Aiden had truly understood the significance of the two characters he'd drawn or if he'd just picked any two because he knew the movie was something Shannen loved. Either way, pride filled me that he'd gone to so much effort. He was young, and there were lots of things he didn't understand, but he did seem to know that while an apology was usually enough to fix most things, doing a bit extra would make things better faster. One-handed, I opened up the card, and inside, Aiden had scrawled: Sorree I hurted you. Can we b frenz like towster and kurbee. From Aiden.

I guess he did know the significance.

"That's great, buddy," I told him, handing the card back to him and giving him another squeeze before lowering him back down to his feet. "Shannen will love it."

He nodded. "I will give it to her as soon as I get to school."

"Sounds good. Now, can you go and put your PJs on? I'll be in in a bit to read you a story."

"Okay!" He ran around the sofa and placed his card for Shannen carefully on the coffee table before zooming past me to his bedroom. "Don't be long, Dad!"

In spite of the chaos in my head, a smile slipped through. He didn't call me Dad every time, but when he did, it was the best word in the world. It had always been a negative one when related to my own father, but hearing it from Aiden's mouth was a small reminder of how far the two of us had come. It meant even more after my recent chat with Katie. One day, I knew he would ask me about her, but until he did, I was a bit closer to feeling like I was enough.

I sighed as Aiden left the room, and Guy said, "You feeling better?"

I shook my head. " I need to talk to you, but I also need to make sure Aiden doesn't hear."

Guy's mouth turned down into a frown. "What's up?"

Taking a quick look over my shoulder to make sure Aiden was definitely gone, I walked further into the living room towards where Guy was sitting, facing me. "I saw Katie," I told him in a low voice. "And now I don't know what the fuck to do."

Guy's eyes widened. "She's still around?"

"Not for long. She said she's leaving tonight, but..." I trailed off and blew out a breath, shaking my head. "I found out some things, and I don't know what to do with them."

Getting to his feet, Guy gave me a supportive slap on the arm. "I'll put the kettle on, and you go and see to Aiden."

Within twenty minutes, I was back from putting Aiden to bed, and Guy and I sat at the dining table, mugs of tea in front of us. In the time I'd been gone, the things Katie had told me had continued to spin around in my head. I'd believed every word, which maybe made me a bit stupid, but there was no way she would have come back here unprompted, not after all this time. She didn't come to take Aiden from me... probably. No. I was sure of that. There was enough left of the girl I used to hang out with that I trusted her word on that. Even though she and I weren't compatible, she wasn't a horrible person; not really. She had no reason to lie. No reason to risk her safety by hanging around to tell me what she knew.

But what if it was part of a bigger set-up? She'd told me not to go after Scott, but she *knew* I had a temper. There was always the chance that I would fly off the handle no matter what, especially if I felt threatened. And I did. That prick wanted to make me suffer, and while I would never disagree that I probably deserved it for the things I'd got away with, Shannen, Aiden, and even Katie didn't.

"I'm gonna need you to say some words," Guy said after a while.

I'd been staring into the distance while my thoughts chased each other around, and I shook my head, focusing on him. He looked tired as fuck, and I said, "Sorry. I really... if you want to go home, we can talk about this tomorrow."

He snorted out a laugh. "Are you serious? Do you think I'm going to go home without knowing what the hell happened tonight? And this afternoon. You still haven't filled me in on what Aiden did."

I sighed. "I didn't want to explain it all with Aiden here." Leaning an elbow on the table, exhaustion rushing through me as I rubbed my forehead, I said, "He threw a book at Shannen and it whacked her in the eye." I didn't feel the need to add details of the rest of his meltdown in the classroom and how he'd also been ripping up books. The violence was what bothered me more than anything. With as bad as Aiden felt about it, I was surprised he hadn't told Guy about it himself.

"What?" Guy's eyebrows rose. "Shit. Is she okay?"

I nodded. "Yeah. I saw her. I asked to speak to her."

"How was that?" A slight grimace crossed his face.

Guy knew I'd had no contact with Shannen since she left his house a week ago, though he'd told me he'd checked in with her a couple of times. He'd actually asked me if I minded if he texted her because he was worried about her, and I knew she was worried about him too. A small part of me hated it because I couldn't be the one talking to her, but I also knew Guy and Shannen had become pretty good friends, and I didn't want them to lose that because of a decision I made. Plus, it meant I could ask Guy how she was doing without having to lose my mind trying to guess if she was okay.

"It was shit," I told him, huffing out another sigh. "Being near her but not being able to touch her was shit. And seeing the bruise Aiden gave her was even worse. I felt terrible about it. I still do, even though she accepted my apology. She looks... well, like you and me. Tired, and sad, and pissed off with everything."

Guy nodded. "Yeah. I can imagine. Were you with her for long?"

"Nah." I lifted my head and wrapped my hands around my cup. "She couldn't wait to get away, and I was a cock, the way I always am when things are hard with her. I just wish I could change it."

Guy wrapped his fingers around the handle of his mug but kept his eyes on me. "She'd have you back in a second, Cal. All you have to do is talk to her."

"I can't talk to her," I said through gritted teeth, tightening my grip on my cup and letting the heat burn my hands. I needed to let go, but the pain gave me something else to focus on. "Every time, my words come out wrong. And every time, it reminds me that I can't be with her when my head's in such a mess. I just... I miss her and I don't know how to get into a place where I'm not going to keep ruining it."

Finally giving in to the stinging sensation from the heat of my cup, I moved my hands away, rubbing them together. My palms were red and sore, but I knew they'd calm down quickly enough. Unlike my racing thoughts.

Guy shook his head. "Cal, you know she's been understanding of everything you've thrown at her before. She would be again."

I nodded. "Yeah, I know, but I don't want her to *have* to be understanding."

I wasn't sure how long it would take, or if she would even want me once—and if—I ever got it together, but she deserved more than the damaged version of me that I kept giving her.

With an understanding nod, Guy said, "So... Katie?"

"Yeah. Seeing her wasn't in my plans for today. Or ever."

I took a moment to centre myself after the conversation about Shannen before explaining everything Katie had told me. About where she came from, where she'd been, and what Scott had done to get her to report me. Guy sat quietly through it all, not saying a word, just taking it all in. Repeating it back to him sounded insane.

"I..." Guy began, then paused and sighed. "I don't even know what to say. I mean... what the hell are you supposed to say to all that?"

I let out a short laugh. "I don't know. I don't think I've really understood it all yet myself."

"Do you believe what she said? That Scott bribed her to make that accusation against you?"

"Yeah. Because she wouldn't have known anything about him otherwise. Other than Shannen and you, nobody else knows about what happened with Edward, so Scott had to have contacted her. It doesn't surprise me at all that he tried to pay her off to do him a favour. And I get why she did it. You should have seen her." The memory of how unwell she looked, how desperate she sounded, clawed at me. "She looked... old. She might be homeless for all I know. I didn't get many details from her other than Taunton is where she's been and where she's going back to." I didn't even know where she'd been staying while she was in Exeter, but I guessed she could have used some of the money Scott gave her to stay in a hotel. Although, if she had, she probably would have been cleaner.

"So, all of this... it was because of Scott?"

"Yeah," I said. "All because of Scott."

This was a deliberate act meant to cause maximum damage. At worst, it could have resulted in Katie taking Aiden—I assumed it was Scott who had told her where Aiden's school was. What was to stop her from snatching him in a split second when nobody was keeping an eye on him? I could have lost him *and* Shannen. With a less understanding person running the school, Shannen could have been in trouble for being with me. The damage Scott had already managed to inflict was bad enough, but knowing he could have further obliterated my life caused my anger to resurface.

I could understand him hating that I'd got away with the horrible thing I did when I was younger, but it was eleven years ago. Time doesn't fix it, but I had never done anything like it since. No run-ins with the law. Not even a fucking speeding ticket to my name. So, why was he hellbent on ruining everything I'd struggled to build?

"I want to kill that smug bastard," I growled, one fist clenching on the table. "What the hell is his problem?"

"You," Guy replied. "You are his problem. He probably hadn't thought about you in years until you had the audacity to rock up, dating his woman's best friend. You slipped through his fingers when he tried to arrest you, and to see you doing well, with someone he considered above you, pissed him off. He's taken every opportunity to take you down, *and* he got to hurt Shannen in the process. The man's a spoilt little shit with more money than he knows what to do with, so he uses it to get what he wants. And sometimes it works."

Was this really partly about Shannen? Some kind of revenge for her walking away from Jade? Or was Guy right; I was the target, but upsetting Shannen was a bonus?

"You need to tell her," Guy said, interrupting my thoughts. "You need to tell Shannen that he was behind this."

Did I? Because the only thing I could see telling her achieving would be causing her more stress.

"What good would it do?" I asked him, looking him in the eye. "How would it help her to know? He was behind me getting taken in for questioning but I still... I was the one who pushed her away."

He raised his eyebrows slowly as if he was thinking it through. After a minute, he said, "It might not help her. But she deserves to know."

"I think it would hurt her more. Okay, she would know for sure that I hadn't hit Katie and that I was set up, but I'm pretty sure she knows I didn't do it anyway. Other than that, though, it would just be another way Scott tried to screw her over. One more thing for her to be angry about. And with her family's closeness to his fiancée's family, it could only make things more uncomfortable, whether she confronts it or not."

Guy rubbed a hand over his face and sighed. "Maybe. But then *you* have to hold all of the anger."

I shrugged. "What else is new? You can't tell her either, Guy. Just pretend you don't know."

"I don't want to be the one to break that news to her, mate. But if she finds out you knew, I don't know how she'll feel about that."

Dropping my head back with a sigh, I said, "Yeah, she probably wouldn't be happy I've kept it from her, but if we don't tell her, how else would she find out? Scott isn't going to confess, and even if he did, he doesn't know that I know the truth."

Unless Katie actually is planning to fuck me over...

Could she have faked being worried about me? Did she mean everything she said about Aiden, or was she just trying to get me to trust her so she could run back to Scott? Was she really baiting me so I'd lay into him and he'd finally have a reason to lock me up? Maybe he'd offered her more money for it.

"What are you thinking?" Guy asked, and I realised I hadn't spoken for a few minutes.

Shaking my head, I said, "I'm just trying to figure out what all this shit means, and if I should expect more of it. Scott went to Katie because it was the easiest way to attack me without doing it himself, which he wouldn't do because he'd never get his own hands dirty. What if she's messing with me? What if she was lying to me for him and he's just waiting for me to react?" I leaned on the table, pushing myself to stand because I felt like insects were crawling under my skin, and I needed to get rid of the sensation before I snapped. As I began to pace, I went on, "I feel like I'm losing my mind."

"Calm down," Guy said, getting to his feet and standing in front of me, his hands on my shoulders to still me. "If Scott is trying to provoke a reaction from you, then don't give him one."

Shrugging out of Guy's hold, I said, "I want to hurt him. I want to kill him for everything he's done, but he just gets away with it! And I know..." I began to pace again, "I know I got away with what I did, but I have paid for it so hard by having to live with it. But him? He screws with people's lives then goes home to his fancy house with his fancy fiancée, all because he wears a uniform and has money." With my last words, I threw myself back onto the sofa, scrubbing my face with my hands.

It was only now fully sinking in just how far Scott's hate for me had gone. How extreme he'd been simply to make my life a misery. Was he satisfied now he'd ripped Shannen and me apart, or would he keep going until I snapped?

113

"Cal, come on," Guy said. "You need to keep it together. Now more than ever. If Katie was telling the truth and she's leaving, there is nothing left he can throw at you. If he could have nailed you for Edward's attack, he would have. Don't let him get to you. You've come too far to let that twat take it away."

He was right. As much as I wanted to find Scott and break every single bone in his body, I couldn't. I'd worked too hard to get on track for him to take the wheel and steer me off course any further, especially when I was more than capable of doing that for myself.

Throwing my head back again, I said, "I miss her so fucking much."

I didn't need to elaborate.

That feeling of insects beneath my flesh came back with the thought, just like it always did if I allowed myself to think for too long. Shannen was always on my mind. All the time. But when I really let myself get caught up in it, it was a pain like I hadn't felt since my mum and brother died. A bone-deep agony that wouldn't let up, and it only got worse because I knew she felt it too. The same hurt. The same sense of missing something.

"I know, buddy." Guy dropped onto the sofa beside me. "I know you do."

Chapter 16

Shannen

EARLIER IN THE WEEK, when Gaby had offered a weekend blowout, I should have known better than to think she'd accept my raincheck. I genuinely did have my mum's birthday dinner coming up on Saturday night, but as Gaby pointed out, that meant I was free on Friday.

With Nova still a little downhearted since Donovan left, Gaby had taken it upon herself to organise something she said would guarantee to put a smile on our faces.

And that was how I found myself standing outside the Bridal Loft in Exeter's city centre at seven o'clock on Friday night.

Nova had pointed out that taking a newly single woman to an event at a wedding dress shop was perhaps not a great idea, but Gaby argued that what we were doing was not about weddings per se. It was about girls getting together and having a good time. The Bridal Loft had created something called Bride For a Night, for women—and men who were up for it—to have a pamper evening and get their hair and makeup done, try on wedding dresses, drink, and have a mini photoshoot. The concept was genius, inspired by an episode of *Friends*, apparently, and in spite of my recent break-up, I was looking forward to it.

Even if it did bring back memories of being there with Jade when she was wedding dress shopping.

I headed up the stairs to the Bridal Loft, thinking how right Gaby was that I *needed* this. Needed a pick-me-up after a turbulent week. Thankfully, the bruise Aiden had given me at school had almost completely disappeared, and the bit that was left was easily covered with makeup.

Aiden had come in the morning after 'the incident', clutching a card he'd made for me to apologise. When he handed it to me, I'd almost cried on seeing the effort he'd gone to. Not only had he chosen to use characters from my favourite childhood film, but he'd clearly taken a lot of care with his colouring in as it was so neat. Plus, the words he'd used had hit me right in the heart, and I'd wanted to bundle him up and give him a huge hug. Because we were in the classroom, the best I could do was tell him I accepted his apology and ruffle his hair.

He'd behaved fairly well for the rest of the week, and he was forming a new friendship with a trio who all went to breakfast club—which Aiden had now joined. It seemed that having some people he was eager to get along with had made him less disruptive. Before, he used to float between various children, but he had never formed an attachment. It was almost as if nobody wanted to keep him around for too long because he was so volatile. It was early days, but it was good to see him beginning to make a connection with the same few people instead of drifting but never fully appearing to fit in.

Aside from the stuff with Aiden, I'd been informed by Iris that some of the parents were continuing to press for information about whether I was still with Cal. I had no idea why it was so interesting to them as they had been told numerous times by the school's headteacher that Cal had merely been taken to the police station for questioning and there was no wrongdoing on his part. Perhaps gossip was the only interesting thing going on in their lives, but I was tired of the judgemental looks thrown my way when I was in the playground. Not a single person had confronted me, and unless they did, I wasn't going to engage with them.

The bell above the door to the Bridal Loft tinkled as I opened it. Gaby and Nova were already inside, standing near the front counter, talking to the owners, Tegan and Emma. Tegan had long brown hair tied back in a neat high ponytail. She wore a knee-length deep blue dress with a lace bodice and sleeves. Emma had shoulder-length shiny blonde hair and the cutest face with rounded cheeks that made her look like a porcelain doll. Her slim but curvy figure was accentuated by the black shift dress she wore. They were both so elegant, and while I knew I didn't exactly look horrendous, I was looking forward to being glammed up.

Everyone greeted me warmly, and Tegan said, "Hi! I know you. You were here a few weeks ago with your friend, weren't you? You're Shannen, right?"

I flinched inwardly at the word *friend* but nodded with a smile. "Yes. Well remembered."

"Tegan is really good with names," Emma said, smiling sheepishly. "Me... not so much."

I chuckled. "I imagine you meet a lot of people. It would be almost impossible to remember everyone."

Emma nodded. "We do try, but between regular customers and Bride For a Night, it's a lot." She reached for a glass of champagne from a tray on the counter and handed it to me. "Now you're here, let's get started!"

After thanking her, I took a sip of the drink. The taste was fantastic, the bubbles giving me a little shiver of excitement as they shot through my system. Gaby and Nova both caught my eye, and we exchanged smiles.

"Okay, let's go through and see where the magic happens!" Tegan said, and she and Emma led us across the shop and through an archway, where another room was attached; the place where the changing cubicles were.

The area where the sofas sat now had white balloons all around it, and on the table in the middle of the seating was a selection of finger foods, slightly fancier than the ones that had been set up when I'd been with Jade and our mums. A bucket with champagne on ice was next to the food, and I grinned as I took it in.

There were two other ladies waiting for us by the sofas, each of them with a trolley of makeup and hair supplies beside them, and a man was sitting at the back end of the room, examining something on his camera.

When Emma had given our names to the others in the room, she pointed to each of them in turn. First, the young girl with incredible coils of black hair that bounced around her beautiful face. She had super high cheekbones and full lips that beamed brightly at us. "This is Fiona," Emma said. "She's going to do your makeup." She then turned to a tall and very slim older-looking woman with short, light brown hair that was flecked with grey. "This is Belinda, and she'll be doing your hair." Finally, she pointed to the man with the camera. "That's Cameron, who doesn't usually work here, but our photographer is ill, so he's stepped in. He's also Tegan's husband."

We all said our hellos and waved to Cameron, and Tegan said, "Okay, who wants to get made up first?"

Gaby's mischievous grin formed, and she wiggled her eyebrows at me. "You," she said. "Get in that chair!"

I rolled my eyes but laughed as I stepped towards Fi. "I guess it's me."

Fi's smile widened. "Okay, let's do this!"

Gaby encouraged Nova into the chair to get her hair done, and Emma said, "Gaby, why don't you take a look at the dresses we have available while you're waiting? You can pick a few out ready to try on if you want."

With another grin, she said, "Try and stop me!"

We all laughed as she walked across to the long rail of dresses available for us to wear.

It was an extremely surreal experience, but so far removed from the time I was there with Jade that it was easy for me to cast that memory aside and focus on the time with my friends. Music began to play—cheesy pop tunes that had us all singing along. It was so easy to see why Bride For a Night had gone down a storm. Not everyone would have or even want a wedding, but almost everyone had thought about it. Rather than run around *Muriel's Wedding*-style pretending to have a fiancé in order to try on bride's dresses, this allowed people to live out a dream, and it was so much fun that it didn't matter that it wasn't real. A part of me had worried that it would be a little depressing; what it actually was was an upmarket fancy dress evening, and I loved it.

"I've never done anything like this before," Nova said once all of our hair and makeup was done and we were browsing the wedding dresses available to us.

She looked beautiful; we all did. Nova's hair was down, straightened, but with a few delicate curls around her face. It really suited her. She had soft features that didn't require much makeup; too much and it would have looked too heavy on her. She had gone simply for foundation, a hint of bronze on her cheeks, and a soft pink lipstick. Gaby's usually straight blonde hair had been curled, and it bounced around her shoulders. She'd opted for some false lashes, but not too thick, a brown smoky eye that made her blue eyes pop, slightly heavier bronzer on her cheeks, and her naturally pink lips had been enhanced with a thin layer of lip gloss. My makeup was somewhere between Gaby's and Nova's. I'd chosen a dark red lipstick that I instantly fell in love with, a lengthening mascara on my eyelashes, and the subtlest hint of pink blush that gave my skin a healthy glow. My dark curls were left loose, but with a small section from the sides pinned at the back of my head so it didn't fall in front of my eyes.

"How come?" Gaby asked, taking a dress from the rail to examine it.

Nova shrugged. "I don't know. I never really had the kind of friends who dressed up to go on nights out." She paused thoughtfully. "I never really went on nights out, come to think of it."

"Not even when you were at uni?" I asked, watching Gaby as she carefully considered the gown in her hands. There was a sparkle in her eyes as she looked it up and down.

Nova shuffled further along the rail, shaking her head. "No. We mostly did quieter things, like evenings in the pub."

"That's why you have me in your life." Gaby finally tore her eyes from the dress and winked, making Nova and me laugh.

Out of the three of us, Nova and I were definitely the most alike. In everything, I was the middle ground; not as quiet as Nova, but not as wild as Gaby. Somehow, we'd all begun to balance each other out. Nova was coming out of her shell more under Gaby's influence, as was I to a degree, and in turn, Gaby was somewhat calmer with me and Nova around.

Only somewhat, though.

"I'm grateful," Nova said seriously, resting a hand on the rail of dresses. "Since the end of last year, spending more time with both of you and meeting Donovan... I hadn't realised what an old woman I'd become." She giggled, shaking her head slightly. "I wasn't unhappy before. I just think I got so comfortable that anything beyond family and work life was passing me by."

Nodding, I said, "I hear that. Putting all of my focus on my career meant I wasn't really doing anything else. If Gabs hadn't encouraged me to go out now and again, I'd still be spending every spare second I have thinking about lesson plans, along with my regular weekly lunches with Jade and visiting my parents and sister."

Gaby's eyes squinted slightly like she was in pain. "I probably owe you an apology. If I hadn't encouraged you to go out and get your fanny tickled, you wouldn't be in this position right now."

There was a beat where the three of us looked at each before we all exploded into laughter.

Life had been so intense lately. The mention of *that night,* when Gaby and I went to my local—the night I'd met Cal—could have brought back the constant cloud of sadness I'd been living under, but her choice of words had forced it to breeze on by. The fact was, in spite of all the heartache, I wouldn't have taken back a second of it. I wouldn't have made a single different choice, even if I could have.

As the laughter subsided, Nova moved closer to me and wrapped an arm around my shoulders. "Come on. Let's go and get one of these dresses on so we can get our photo taken before Gaby can lower the tone any further!"

"I may not have many uses," Gaby said, "but lowering the tone is definitely one of them!"

When she grinned, I said, "Don't underestimate yourself. You are a legend, and one day, your grandchildren will be telling their friends all about their crazy Granny Gaby."

Her smile dropped a little, her eyes dimming before she said, "Nah. With my dating record, a family is not on the cards for me." With another grin, she hoisted up the dress she'd been holding and added, "Right, I'm getting this beauty on! It's the one, I can feel it!"

As she swept away to one of the changing cubicles, I turned to Nova, wondering if I'd imagined Gaby's momentary change in mood. "Did you see that?" I asked her quietly.

Nova raised a brow. "The sad look?" she said, equally as quietly. "Yeah."

"Do you know what it was about?" Although no major discussion had been had about the evening's choice of activity, I'd seen it as a bit of harmless fun that would take my mind off all the crap I'd been dealing with lately. But what if it was something more for Gaby? Was it some kind of wish fulfillment for something she believed she might never have? Her bad luck with men was not a secret, but she never seemed as if it bothered her to be single. Of course, I hadn't known her for as long as Nova had.

"I'm not sure," Nova replied. "She's approaching thirty-five soon, though. She mentioned to me the other day that while turning thirty didn't bother her, thirty-five somehow seems like a bigger deal. But she didn't say anything about thinking she would never have a family."

"Do you think we should talk to her about it?"

With a head shake, Nova said, "No. In my experience, Gaby will only talk when she's ready. But I suspect we might need to be on hand if she needs us in the lead-up to her birthday."

As the two of us went back to browsing through the dresses, I was struck the same way as before by how on-the-surface my knowledge of Gaby was. I could have easily reeled off that she loved going to the gym, a wild night out at a pub or club, and that she wouldn't be seen dead in anything pink or overly girly, yet she had an obsession with buying new dresses and shoes. I could list her favourite TV shows and movies, but I didn't know if she'd always lived in Exeter, and I hadn't known she had a brother until she called him to help Cal.

"Oh my God," Gaby's voice called from her cubicle. "Not to toot my own horn or anything, but if anyone saw me walking down the aisle in this, they'd want to sack off the vows and skip to the honeymoon immediately!"

Nova and I cackled at her words; she sounded so certain. I could imagine her wide smile as she looked herself up and down. The funny thing was, although she was gorgeous, she was not arrogant at all, so the self-praise was alien coming from her lips.

"Also, can someone come in here and help me do up the back? I don't want to give you an eyeful of my titties when I come out from behind the curtain!"

We all laughed again, including the staff, and Tegan said, "I'm on my way!" As she scurried past us, giggling, she said, "I'm so glad you ladies came in tonight!"

She slipped behind the curtain, and Gaby said, "Sorry, Tegan. I sometimes forget where I am, and things just fall out of my mouth. I think it's a side-effect of working with kids and having to watch what I say most of the day. Once I'm out of there, everything I've locked away falls out."

"Honestly," Tegan said, "it's fine. We're here to have a good time, so don't censor yourself on our behalf."

I tuned out of their conversation as my eyes fell on a wedding dress that looked like the kind of meringue-style nightmare I would never want in real life, but the diamante detail on the bodice had me mesmerised. I was absolutely certain I would look more fairy godmother than demure bride in it, but it wasn't as if it would be for my actual wedding. I took it off the hanger, struggling to get it out due to the huge skirt.

"That's pretty," Nova said, and I saw she had also made a selection.

I smiled. "Shall we?" I suggested and nodded towards the cubicles. Nova linked her free arm through mine. "We shall!"

We spent our time at Bride For a Night drinking champagne, eating fancy food, and having our photos taken, as well as laughing with Tegan and Emma. Fi and Belinda left after their jobs were done, but Cameron, the photographer, was a lot of fun. He confessed to missing spending as much time at the events as he used to. It was clear how happy he and Tegan were, though, and there was such a great vibe there. We took plenty of photos on our phones, not that we would share them publicly. Nova, Gaby, and I all used social media, but as teachers, we were very aware that what we did could be seen and analysed, as I had found out since being with Cal.

"I can't believe the night is almost over," I said with a dramatic sigh, leaning back against one of the sofas and taking my last sip of champagne. I'd had more glasses than I'd intended to, and if I had any more, I was sure the room would start to blur and spin.

Nova and I had already changed back into the clothes we'd arrived in, but Gaby was unwilling to remove her dress until the last minute. All three of us were finishing our drinks, and Cameron, Tegan, and Emma had told us to take our time while they tidied up around us.

"This was a great idea, Gaby," Nova agreed, reaching over for a cucumber sandwich. "Can we do this every weekend?"

"Maybe not every weekend." Gaby stroked the skirt of her dress lovingly. She looked super reluctant to part with it. "But I definitely think we should come back and do it again sometime."

"Maybe for your hen party, Nova," I teased, and her cheeks flushed.

"Please. I met Donovan in December and it's only February!" The coy smile on her face told me she had thought about it, though. It was clear Donovan was besotted with her, so I was sure a wedding was going to be a part of their future.

"We all made rather lovely brides," I said. "I can't wait to see the photos!"

"Me too," Gaby added. "Those bad boys will be worthy of framing."

I didn't have any photos at home of friends. I supposed that perhaps, subconsciously, that was a sign I was already distancing myself from Jade. I had photos with her on my phone, but nothing that proclaimed our friendship in my home. I loved the idea of framing the memories made at Bride For a Night and hanging them on my living room wall so I could always remember it. It felt like Gaby, Nova, and I had done more than have a simple night out. We'd let loose, been silly together, and the seeds of a lifelong friendship had been sown amongst it all. You don't try on wedding dresses with just anyone, after all.

Getting to her feet suddenly, Gaby said, "Tegan, can I have this dress?"

There was a collective pause in the room.

Tegan was collecting some empty plates from the table when Gaby asked the question, and she halted and turned to Gaby. "It's a company policy that we don't agree to any sales when customers have been drinking."

"That makes perfect sense," Gaby said, "but I've only had two glasses of champagne. It's these two reprobates that have drunk you dry." She pointed to Nova and me, and we laughed, but Nova nodded.

"Strange but true," she agreed.

Tegan let out a small chuckle. She knew Gaby wasn't lying as Gaby had asked for soft drinks after her first couple of glasses of alcohol because she didn't want to go to the gym in the morning with a hangover.

"Well," Tegan began, "I suppose you could buy it, but do you want to sleep on it first? I can make sure it's kept aside for you, but I don't want you to make a spur of the moment purchase and regret it in the morning."

Gaby pursed her lips as if thinking over Tegan's words, but then she shook her head. "I'd like to take it now, if that's okay."

Nova and I side-eyed each other, grins of apprehension on our faces over whether she was really going to do this. It was totally the kind of sponta-neous thing she *would* do, and as she'd pointed out, it wasn't because she was under the influence.

She turned to us, eyes wide. "You think this is a bad idea?"

"Not bad," I said. "Just curious why you're so attached to the dress."

With an uncharacteristic giggle, she said, "When I was little, I went to my cousin's wedding. I was about seven or eight, I think, and she had a dress exactly like this. I remember watching her all day and thinking she looked like a princess, and that if I ever got married, I wanted a dress that was the same." She turned to Tegan again and added, "It probably sounds stupid, but it felt... magical somehow. It made me believe in fairytales, and I've never seen a dress so similar to it." As if embarrassed that she'd been so openly soppy, she flashed her cheeky grin again and said, "Plus, I look hot in it and I want to wear it to every party I ever go to!"

I watched Tegan's expression soften. She'd clearly seen the vulnerability behind Gaby's words, and she said, "I was also captivated by weddings at a young age." She gestured around the room. "Hence the career choice. If you are absolutely certain you want to do this, have a chat with Emma and she will sort you out."

Gaby beamed. "Just to be clear, you are agreeing to sell me this dress, yes?"

Laughing, Tegan said, "Yes."

"Thank fuck." With the confirmation, Gaby turned back to the table and filled two glasses with champagne, sinking them both down immediately and triggering another round of giggles. "Emma, bill me, woman!"

Emma was howling with laughter as she took Gaby's hand and led her through the archway to the other side of the shop.

"Is she always like this?" Tegan asked us, grinning.

"Always," Nova told her. "And we have another few hours of this since we're all staying at Shannen's tonight!"

"Not gonna lie, I kind of wish I could join you." Tegan was still chuckling as she walked away to take the plates out to the back room.

"What just happened?" I said, my mind reeling from Gaby's quick decision to do some shopping.

"I'm not sure, but I have a feeling we should go and see what she's doing so she doesn't add a veil and shoes to her purchase!"

Mock alarm crossed our faces and we both hurried to get up, laughing as we bumped against each other in our haste to save Gaby's bank balance from further damage.

"Would you like me to help you out of the dress so we can box it up for you?" Emma was asking as we reached the counter.

Gaby shook her head. "I'm only getting in a taxi, so I'll keep it on and change into my PJs when I get to Shannen's. Might as well see this out until the very end of the night at this point!"

"I suspect there will be an additional photoshoot when we get home," I whispered to Nova, picturing Gaby strategically positioning herself in random places around my flat like beside the coffee machine or sprawling across my bed.

"I heard that," Gaby said with a snort as she used her bank card to pay for her dress. I had no idea how much it had cost. My understanding was that any dresses used for Bride For a Night were long-time clearance dresses, and occasionally, some that brides had donated because they no longer wanted to keep them. Even so, it was still an upmarket boutique, so I doubted it would have been cheap. It was one hell of an impulse buy, especially if it would only be for fancy dress parties. That was another thing I knew about Gaby, though. She took any opportunity she could to dress up.

"Was I wrong, though?" I challenged, and Gaby shook her head.

"Nope. Selfies will be taken in the car park, in the lift, in the bathroom mirror, and... definitely one with a gigantic coffee and some snacks."

"Please send them over to us when you're done." Emma giggled as she handed Gaby a receipt, which she tucked into her cleavage since she had no pockets.

"Will do." Gaby winked at her.

"I'll go and see if I can find us a cab," Nova said, heading back into the other room where she'd left her bag. I was torn between going with her and staring at my crazy friend. Where she stood, surrounded by other wedding dresses, she looked perfectly in place. Once we left the premises, though, she was going to look like she'd run away from her big day with two drunk bridesmaids in tow.

We made small talk for a few minutes, until Nova wandered back to us, clutching her phone in her hand. "I've called three different cab companies, but they have nothing available for over an hour, and any apps I usually use have hiked the prices up due to it being a 'high demand' time. Even split three ways, I'm not paying forty quid for a ten-minute ride."

"Crap," I said. If two of us weren't tipsy, I'd have begged Gaby to change so we could walk back, even though it would have taken over half an hour. "We can't stay here for an hour. These guys want to go home."

"We could wait in a pub," Nova suggested.

"Is there anyone who could come and pick you up?" Emma asked as Tegan and Cameron joined us.

Immediately, my mind leapt to Cal because... of course it would. I suspected that even though we weren't together, he'd probably have come to get us, but I didn't want to ask. I didn't want to see him when I was drunk because alcohol made me either emotional or horny, and I didn't need to be either of those things around him. Plus, Aiden would be in bed by now, so he wouldn't actually be able to leave.

"I guess I could ask Guy," I said hesitantly. I didn't want to rely on him either, but I also wasn't sure what other options we had besides waiting around or walking all the way back to my place.

"Would he mind?" Nova asked, looking hopeful.

"I don't know. But it never hurts to ask."

Chapter 17

Cal

"AIDEN, HURRY UP WITH those chicken nuggets," I said, watching as he dipped the one he was holding into first barbecue sauce, then sweet and sour.

He looked up at me and grinned mischievously, and in spite of how much I needed to get him home, I couldn't help smiling back.

Although technically, Aiden was still being punished for what he did at school, he'd apologised to Shannen and been on his best behaviour for the rest of the week. He'd taken to breakfast club well, and he came home telling me about his new friends, Avery, Aria, and Maxwell, who were all in his class. I wasn't sure if it was because of those new friendships, but he'd been rewarded with a whole load of stickers for good work in class and good behaviour, which, even on his best weeks, was rare. He understood that some of his privileges were still revoked for a few more days, but I also wanted him to know that I had seen the good as well as the bad.

As a way to celebrate his change in behaviour, Guy and I had taken him to Paignton Pier late on Friday afternoon. We'd only planned to spend an hour there, but several intense games of air hockey, plus the usual two pence push machines, claw machines, and a walk to the end of the pier to admire the view meant we ended up staying for just over two hours. By the time we got back to Exeter, it was after nine p.m, and Guy had the bright idea of stopping into McDonald's before we went home. Aiden was so excited to be staying out later than his bedtime that my request to use the drive-thru was shot down.

Looking back, it probably wasn't a good idea to fill Aiden with Coke and chicken nuggets before bedtime, but it *was* the weekend, and it felt good to do something different for a couple of hours. Something that broke up the never-ending feeling of being pissed off every hour of the day.

"You have to be the only kid who doesn't insist on a Happy Meal and goes straight for the biggest box of nuggets," Guy said to him, laughing as he wiped his hands on a napkin after finishing his burger.

"The toy was a *book*," Aiden said, his face wrinkling with disgust. "I don't want to read when I go to McDonald's!"

"Kid's got a point," I said, chuckling as he continued to dunk his nuggets in both sauces before eating them. It wasn't like he hadn't been fed before we went out, and he'd had some chips while we were at the pier too.

The sound of Guy's phone ringing caught my attention, and he reached into his coat pocket to pull it out. His brow furrowed. "It's Shannen."

It was getting close to ten, and as far as I knew, she didn't usually call him. They only communicated through text messages. "Are you going to answer?"

He nodded and pressed the button, lifting the phone to his ear. "Hello?"

I could only hear his side of the conversation, and I followed it closely, trying to figure out what she wanted.

"It's okay," he said. "What's up?... I'm out, but I'm not drinking... Okay..." He paused, glancing at me and then Aiden, who was now slurping at his Coke. "Well, I can, but I'm with Cal and Aiden, so I'd need to drop them at home first... Yeah, we went to Paignton and time got away from us... No, it's fine, but you'll have to give me twenty minutes or so to get home and then back to you... Shannen, it's fine. I don't mind at all... Okay. Yeah... See you in a bit. Bye."

He clicked to end the call and slipped his phone back in his pocket.

"What was that about?" I asked, trying to not sound like a jealous prick. I wasn't jealous that they'd stayed in contact, but she clearly needed something, so why didn't she call me?

Because you broke up with her. Why would she?

Obviously, that was the answer, but I didn't have to like it.

"Shannen is out with her friends, and they're drunk and need a lift home," Guy said, smirking slightly. "I said I would swing around and pick them up, but there isn't enough room in my car unless I take you and Aiden home first."

I raised an eyebrow. "Yeah, that's not happening." I wasn't sure how it would work, but if there was a chance I could see Shannen, then I was going to take it. Just the thought made my heart bang against my ribcage and my palms begin to sweat. I was reacting like a junkie preparing for his next hit, but that was how it felt to me. I hadn't seen her in days, and even just a glance would do. "Where are they?"

"She said the Bridal Loft. They've been at that Bride For a Night thing that was all over the news a while back. I said I'd pick them up. I can't leave them there."

"I'm not suggesting you leave them there. I'm suggesting you take Gaby and Nova home and then take Aiden back to mine. I'll get Shannen home."

I said the words without thinking them through properly. There was no way she was going to let me take her home, but in that moment, it was all I wanted to do. Guy said she was drunk, and even though I wasn't sure how drunk, or even how she was when she was pissed, I wanted to be the one to take care of her.

"I'm not certain that's the best idea," Guy said carefully. "I mean, she might go for it, but if she doesn't..."

When he trailed off, I knew what he meant. I would feel way worse than I already did if she refused to stay with me. As quickly as it had sped up, my heart rate dropped at the thought.

"I'm finished!" Aiden said, wiping his dip-covered fingers on a napkin and grinning at me with barbecue sauce around his lips.

"Good timing," I said, picking up another napkin and wiping Aiden's mouth with it. "We have to go home."

"Cal," Guy said as I began shoving the empty food packets onto the tray. "Let me take you home first. It'll be better that way."

I glanced up at him, and I could see from the way he was looking at me that he was only trying to save me from another awkward as fuck interaction with Shannen, but... I needed to see her. Even if only for a minute.

"Take me to her, please."

Blowing out a breath, Guy's eyes locked with mine. He knew I wouldn't back down, and I could see from the way he was looking at me that he understood, even if he thought it was a bad idea. "Fine."

Within ten minutes, we were pulling up outside the Bridal Loft, and there she was. She had her arms wrapped around herself to fend off the cold, but even though she was shivering, she looked amazing. Her hair was done differently, and she had makeup on that made her natural beauty even more obvious. Her cheeks were glowing, and her eyes seemed to sparkle as she glanced at her phone.

My chest ached to look at her, but Guy's laugh distracted me. "What the fuck?" he said.

I shifted my focus to him for a second, confused. He was staring out the car window. Following his gaze, my brows rose. I'd been so focused on Shannen that I hadn't really noticed her friends. More specifically, Gaby, who was wearing a wedding dress and swaying the skirt around her as the three of them walked towards us.

"Is Miss Davis getting married?" Aiden asked from the back seat. I turned to look at him, and his eyes were glued to her. A pout formed on his lips.

I'd forgotten how Aiden had followed her around with puppy dog eyes the day we'd gone to Dawlish Warren. "No, buddy. She's not getting married. I don't think." At five years old, I was not prepared for him to have crushes yet, especially not on one of his teachers.

"Why is she wearing that dress?"

"Good question," Guy said, his eyes fixated on her before he shook his head. "How am I meant to fit her in here in that?"

Shannen had always described Gaby as 'quirky'. Going for a night out and returning home in a wedding dress definitely proved the point.

"No idea, mate," I said, unclipping my seatbelt and opening the passenger door. Before I got out, I turned to Aiden. "You and Guy are going to take Nova and Gaby home, okay? I'm going to make sure Shannen gets home safely, and then I'll be home to put you to bed."

Aiden nodded, his eyes still on Gaby, and I chuckled, pretty sure he wasn't listening to anything I said. I turned to Guy to see if he'd noticed, but his eyes were also on Gaby, an amused grin on his face.

All three girls looked incredible, but Gaby's dress had clearly gained most of the attention. Understandably, since she was standing on a random street in the cold when she looked like she should have been at a wedding reception.

Guy and I got out of the car, and when Shannen saw me, she drew in a sharp breath, probably because she hadn't expected me to be here.

"Good evening, ladies," Guy said, laughing as Nova stumbled in her high heels and knocked Gaby slightly off-balance. He reached out to steady her, and she grimaced, her cheeks reddening as she held onto his arm while Nova righted herself.

"Sorry," Gaby said, looking up at him. "Thank you for coming to rescue us."

I tuned their conversation out as my eyes fell back on Shannen. She was staring at me, and I could see the same need I was feeling pulling her towards me too, but she didn't move, and neither did I. I wanted to. But there was something else in her eyes, almost a warning for me to stay back. Not because she didn't want to be near me, but because she did.

Gaby and Nova's laughs pulled my attention from Shannen for a second, and I heard Nova say, "Okay, we need to get Gaby home before she gets into any more trouble!"

Gaby was still holding onto Guy's arm, although she didn't look drunk or like she needed to be holding onto him anymore, and she said, "She's not wrong. I just made the best impulse buy ever, but I should get this baby home before I get it dirty." She stroked her hands over the skirt as if to ensure it wasn't damaged. "We're going to Shannen's, but I don't think we'll all fit in your car at once." She eyed Guy's blue Audi Q5, and when she spotted Aiden in the back seat, she smiled. "Ooh, my buddy's here!"

Guy shook his head, laughing as she rushed to open the back door and clambered in, fighting with her dress on the way. I ducked down to see through the window as Aiden grinned brightly while Gaby chatted to him.

"Okay, how do you want to do this?" Guy asked, looking between Shannen and me.

Shannen glanced at me then Nova, who shrugged.

"I can stay here with Shannen if you want to take Nova and Gaby first," I said before any other suggestion could be made. She might reject it, but I wanted to put it out there.

Nova turned to Shannen. "It's up to you," she said, then she offered me a kind smile. I wouldn't have minded staying behind with Nova, but every one of us knew my preference, and Shannen let out a small sigh.

"You go with Gaby," she said to Nova. "I can wait here with Cal."

Something inside me seemed to sag with relief. Shannen didn't look excited by the idea of staying with me, but at the same time, I could still feel that thing that kept drawing us together. It was like, no matter what was going on between us and however much we were meant to stay apart, we couldn't stop the pull.

I was grateful when Nova headed straight for the car, lightly touching my arm as she passed without giving Shannen a chance to change her mind.

"Wait," Shannen said, and Nova stopped and whirled around. Shannen walked over to her, dipping her hand into her bag and pulling out her keys. "You'll need these. The main door code is 2293." Singling out a key, she said, "And this is the key to my flat."

"2293," Nova repeated, taking the keys from Shannen. "Got it. See you in a bit!"

Nova ducked into the car, and Guy got into the driver's side. "I'll be back for you as soon as I can," he called.

As they pulled away, Aiden didn't even turn his head because he was too engrossed in talking to Gaby, but Nova and Guy waved as they drove off, leaving Shannen and me standing on the pavement, shivering on the dark, lamplit street.

I took a small step towards her, and she took a couple of steps back towards the wall as if she didn't want to be in the way if anyone passed. The street was empty; it was more of a side street that didn't see much foot traffic at night because everything around there was closed. I kept the distance she'd created, and now we were alone, I wasn't sure if staying with her was the best idea. What would we even say?

At the very least, Guy would be twenty minutes, but if he hit any traffic, it could be thirty minutes plus before he got back. Could I really just stand in silence with her for that long?

You could tell her about Katie.

The thought had crossed my mind a few times over the last couple of days. I wondered if I should let her know that Scott was involved in everything that had happened to us, but I kept circling back to the same thing. That it wouldn't change anything, other than making her angrier than she already was. And what if Jade knew about it too? Shannen had had her mind messed with enough lately. To know Scott had been fucking with her life again wouldn't help her. It was bad enough that I'd been dealing with it. Since I'd spoken to Katie, I didn't know if I felt better or worse. What she'd done to get money had helped to blow my life to pieces. I would never forgive that, but desperation can make people do stupid

132

things. I had beaten a man half to death out of rage, so I was in no position to judge.

The fact was, I could have chased the what-ifs around until I went insane, but nothing would alter where we were now. Nothing we'd already done could be taken back.

"I'm sorry if my call ruined your evening," Shannen said after a while. "I didn't realise you would all be out tonight."

I shrugged. "It's okay. We were trying to get Aiden out of McDonald's anyway. He was taking his time with his massive box of chicken nuggets."

She smiled. "Yeah, that doesn't surprise me." After a short pause, she added, "He's had a great week, Cal. I mean, Monday aside. He's loving going to breakfast club and he's been much better in class."

"Yeah, I guessed that from the number of stickers he came home with. He's not... sometimes, at home, things aren't okay, but it's been better than I expected."

Aside from debating whether to tell Shannen about Katie, I'd thought about talking to Aiden about her. He'd never really asked about his mum. Never pushed a conversation. I thought with him being at school, it might have come up again by now, but since he hadn't got close to any other children in his class, maybe it hadn't crossed his mind. Perhaps he thought the dysfunctional family he had was normal. He'd seen movies where there were mums, dads, brothers, and sisters, but he'd also seen movies where animals and kitchen appliances could talk, so I guessed he didn't necessarily see any reality in what he watched. I knew one day that conversation would come, and I'd never fully figured out what I would say. It seemed to me that after Katie left, Aiden had never crossed her mind, but what she'd said suggested I was wrong. She could have been lying, but I didn't think she was. I wanted to be able to tell him that, even though she wasn't in his life, that didn't mean she'd forgotten about him or didn't care about him, but I'd also have to figure out how to make him understand that she wasn't coming back. That was another concern. Although Katie was the first woman to leave his life, he didn't remember her. With him also losing Helen and Shannen, I was worried that he'd develop an idea that women never stayed because that was all he knew. He was still just learning whether he could fully trust *me*. So, I chose to let it go for the time being and handle his current meltdowns before giving him a reason to have new ones.

Shannen nodded. "He's not one hundred percent happy right now, but with everything that's happened lately, I would be surprised if he was. Avery and Aria especially are a good influence on him, though. I think Avery has got a bit of a thing for him."

I laughed. "Well, Avery is going to be disappointed because Aiden has only got eyes for Gaby. He was almost crying when he saw her wearing a wedding dress."

"Oh, no!" Shannen covered her mouth with her hands, but a laugh still escaped. "Poor Aiden. I'm sure Gaby will be quick to tell him she isn't getting married anytime soon."

"Why *did* she buy a wedding dress?" I asked, taking the smallest step towards her. I wasn't sure she'd even noticed, but the sound of her laugh and seeing her smile had made me need to be closer to her. I wanted to be next to her, have her in my arms, but I also didn't want to break this moment of normal between us.

"Well," Shannen said, straightening up a little. "First and foremost, Gaby is a nutcase... in the best possible way. But she seemed really attached to it and she said it was similar to the wedding dress her cousin wore when she was little. I don't think she's planning to get married in it herself, more that it reminded her of something she loved." She paused and chuckled. "I don't know if Guy is equipped to handle her. I should have warned him."

"Nah, he'll be fine. I haven't seen him smile that much in a while. He needed the laugh."

"I think we all did," Shannen said, her own smile dropping slightly, and she lowered her head with a sigh, leaning her back against the shop's wall again.

Just like that, the comfortable vibe vanished, and awkwardness crept around us instead. I'd hoped the easy conversation would last for longer, but I should have known better.

I shouldn't have been so selfish in wanting to be near her. I should have just let Guy take me and Aiden home so as not to screw up her night.

"I'm sorry," I said quietly.

Without me offering an explanation, she seemed to understand what I meant, and she nodded.

"I get it. I..." She trailed off, then looked up at me. "When Nova said there were no cabs, you were the first person I thought of, but I... it just..." A frustrated huff left her before she stood up straight again, rubbing her forehead. "I wanted to see you too, but it's... I've been drinking, and I miss you, and I didn't think it..." Her voice croaked on the last words.

Without thinking, I closed the space between us and pulled her into my arms, holding her tight, one hand on her back and the other in her hair. For a moment, she clung to me, and I breathed her in. Her warmth, her scent, the way she felt so right pressed against me.

I pulled back from her a bit so I could look at her face, my hand moving to the back of her neck.

"Shan," I whispered, my voice gruff with the emotion I was trying to keep down.

Her eyes explored my face slowly, like she hadn't seen me in forever and was trying to familiarise herself again. When her gaze dropped to my lips, her tongue slipping out to moisten hers, my breath caught in my throat. She slid her arms from around me, slipping them inside my leather jacket to circle my back again.

I'd never wanted to kiss someone as much as I wanted to kiss her in that moment.

You gave her up. You gave her up.

Whenever I was near her, I found it so hard not to touch her. She'd turned my whole world upside down in the best way, and I couldn't make my feelings for her stop.

I didn't believe in many things, but I fully believed she was mine.

Except she isn't. Not anymore.

But I couldn't let her go.

"Cal," she murmured, tilting her head back slightly, her lips an offering as her eyes half closed.

My dick immediately jumped to attention as her light breaths fanned across my cheek. I began to lean in, her mouth a fraction from mine.

I could almost taste her.

"How drunk are you?" I asked huskily.

She pressed her hips against mine, her eyes widening a little as she felt my hard cock pushing against her. "Not drunk enough that I think this is a good idea, but just drunk enough that I want it anyway."

My dick twitched as lust filled her gaze.

Not so long ago, she had stopped me from fucking her in my van. Now, she was offering herself to me... where? There was nowhere else for us to go but right there against the hair salon beneath the Bridal Loft.

But it was a quiet street. Nobody had passed us since Guy and the others left, and there was no sign of anyone nearby.

Her breaths grew heavier as she waited for my answer, and I couldn't take my eyes off her lips. They were dark red, and the colour made her look sexier than ever, emphasising their fullness more.

I could almost feel them wrapped around my dick.

"Cal, please," she breathed. "I need this."

Yeah, I needed it too. So bad I was worried my dick was going to rip itself out of my jeans.

"What if you regret it?" I asked, desperate to do the right thing, even though, in my head, I was already inside her.

"I've never regretted in an orgasm, Cal."

If I wasn't so turned on, I would have laughed at the un-Shannen-like words.

"I can still walk in a straight line," she said, moving her hands down to my ass. "You saw me. Please. I need you."

In her eyes, I could read her thoughts so clearly. How much she wanted me, how much she missed me, how cheated she felt by the way things ended. She was asking me to give her the only thing I *could* give her now. Asking me to distract us both from the pain.

She'd been drinking, but she wasn't drunk.

She was able speak in full sentences, hold herself up, and most importantly, she'd given me her full consent.

Twice.

Using the hand at the back of her neck to draw her closer to me, I kissed her gorgeous red lips, and my other hand moved between us, flicking open the buttons on her coat so I could get to her skin. Her tongue pushed into my mouth, and she gasped as my cold hand dipped inside her coat and moved underneath her top, grazing her waist lightly.

I wished more than anything we were somewhere I could have her completely naked, kiss the parts of her body that drove her crazy. I wanted her moaning as my tongue teased her nipples, to feel her writhing underneath me.

My fingers found the cup of her bra, and popped one of her tits out, making her cry out as I ran my fingers across her soft skin before tweaking her hardened bud between my thumb and finger.

She kissed me harder, her hands moving to the front of my jeans and unzipping them. I could feel her shaking as she manoeuvered my clothes to get her hands on my dick. My jeans were slipping down, but I didn't care because as her fingers curled around my length, nothing else mattered.

She moved her hand up and down firmly but slowly, and I growled at the sensation. I dropped my hand from the back of her neck and reached into the inside pocket of my jacket for my wallet. The hand that had been tormenting her nipple pinched it hard one more time, causing her to whimper before I withdrew it so I could locate a condom. While I was doing that, she hitched up the knee-length skirt she'd been wearing and shimmied her knickers all the way down her legs.

I was dangerously close to flinging the condom away and shoving myself inside her, but I didn't need to take any more risks. *This* was risky enough.

She backed up against the wall, a cry slipping out of her when her bare arse hit the cold stone behind her. My body stayed as close to hers as I could get it while I made sure we were protected, and the second I was ready, I lifted her leg, securing it around my hip, and then sank into her warmth.

She wound her arms around my neck, holding on tight as I pounded into her, one hand in her hair, the other holding her leg up.

"Yes," she mumbled against me, rocking her hips against mine. Her eyes were closed, her cheeks flushed as she began to gasp. "Yes, Cal."

I would never, ever got tired of making her come, and I dropped the hand that was in her hair down to her clit, massaging it for a moment before pinching it sharply so she let out a feral cry that made me shoot my load inside her as her walls spasmed around me dick.

She wrapped her arms tightly around me, and for a moment or two, we just stood there, holding each other up as our bodies came down from the high.

That was not a good idea for either of us, yet somehow, we needed it. The hurt was still there on both sides, threatening to choke us with its intensity, but I wanted to hold her, to make her feel less alone, and I needed her to do the same for me.

When Shannen began to shiver, I knew it was over. Time to let her go again. I kissed the top of her head and gently released her from my hold. Her arms slowly dropped. Staying close to her, I shielded her body with mine as we both straightened ourselves up, and I tied a knot in the condom and flung it in a nearby bin. I was worried when I looked at her that her eyes would be full of embarrassment, maybe even shame for begging me to fuck her in a city side street. She was a good girl. This was beneath her.

I didn't see any of that, though. Her cheeks were still glowing, but she looked... satisfied, even though the hurt from the disaster we'd become began to shine through.

I wanted to say something, but I didn't know what the words were. Didn't know what would make the moment better or worse, or if there was anything that wouldn't disturb the delicate limbo we were stuck in.

"Just so you know," she said quietly. "In case you're worried... I don't regret that. I won't."

I nodded slowly, for once accepting her words as truth and not trying to second guess them.

Not dragging her into my arms to hold her one more time was the hardest thing I'd ever done.

No.

In reality, the truth was, that was nowhere near the hardest thing I'd ever done.

That honour would always go to letting her go the first time.

Chapter 18

Shannen

I NEVER USUALLY DREADED going to my parents' house, but I was about to see them for the first time since I'd pretty much begged them to give Cal a chance, and barely two weeks later, I was walking back in there having broken up with him. I knew they would be relieved, in spite of them both offering to make an effort when they eventually met him, and I wasn't sure how I felt about that. A part of me was embarrassed that I'd fought so hard for someone who had let me go, but a bigger part of me knew they were family, and they would feel for what I was going through, even if they hadn't fully approved.

It was my mum's birthday, and the family usually got together with her closest friends on that day to either have dinner at their place or go out for a meal. Mum had opted to host at her place this year, and I would get to see my sister, brother-in-law, and nephew for the second time in two weeks, which was pretty unusual. I couldn't wait. I was less enthused about seeing Judith and her husband, Hugh. Mum had asked me if it was still okay for her to invite Judith, and while I didn't particularly want to see her, she was still my mum's best friend. I could hardly dictate who did and didn't come to her house for her birthday. Jade and Scott, however, had been uninvited. That was also not my decision, but my mum was still so disgusted by Scott going to my workplace to tell Iris his 'concerns' about my relationship that she couldn't stand to look at him, nor was she enamoured by the idea of seeing Jade.

I'd had a brilliant night with Gaby and Nova the night before, and the partying continued well after we got back to my flat.

Once I'd cleaned up after doing the most uncharacteristic thing I'd ever done.

After having sex with Cal outside the Bridal Loft, I was glad I wasn't going back to an empty home. Drinking and then screwing someone you miss so much that it's killing you can never end well. I was slightly mortified that I'd had sex in public, so I tried hard to block that part of the equation out. The cold, the possibility of being caught... none of it entered my head. All I'd wanted was a break from the unending misery of missing him.

When he held me so tightly, every part of him telling me he still felt the same way he always had, it took everything in me not to beg him to give us another chance. Except nothing had changed. Something was still broken between us. The trust on both sides was still shattered, and neither of us was over it, not really.

I'd told Nova and Gaby what had happened, and neither of them was surprised; aside from the public aspect of it. Instead of letting me dwell on it, though, they'd poured more drinks down my throat, and we'd put on music and danced like we were in a club until we crashed out somewhere around three in the morning.

I arrived at my parents' house mid-afternoon on Saturday. Everyone else would be arriving around five, but I'd been invited to stay the night since there would be drinking involved; not that I'd be having many. Judith and Hugh would usually have also been invited to stay, but with the potential for tension, they'd chosen to spend the night in a hotel, and my sister and her husband didn't drink anyway, so they would be going home so as not to interrupt their son's routine too much.

When I got there, I knew my mum wanted to have a face to face conversation about how I was doing and get the full details about what had happened with Cal. I'd kept the information pretty light when we'd spoken on the phone because I'd been too upset to dig into it. Thankfully, my sister and her family arrived about forty-five minutes after me, so there was no opportunity for me to be interrogated. I still wasn't ready to talk about it properly. It was bad enough that Cal was on my mind all the time, more so after seeing him. There was no end to the ache I felt from our separation. I felt... empty. Able to go about my daily tasks as normal, but it was like something was fundamentally missing from me.

My nephew, Alexander, took up most of my attention until everyone else arrived. I was sitting on the floor with Sadie and Alexander when Judith and Hugh walked in. Even though we were dressed on the smarter end of smart-casual clothing—both Sadie and I wore our best blue jeans, mine paired with an off-shoulder white jumper with a black bow on the left side of the neckline, and Sadie's with a dark grey jumper with gold buttons on the cuffs—nothing was going to stop me playing with my nephew. We were doing a jigsaw with large pieces on my mum's glass coffee table, and the first words out of Judith's mouth were, "Oh my goodness... the fingerprints on that glass."

Sadie and I exchanged an eye roll. Our backs were to her as we sat side by side, Alexander on the other side, and Sadie raised her eyebrows as if to say, "And so it begins." She tucked her shoulder-length brown hair behind her ear, and we continued to help Alexander put the pieces together.

"For goodness' sake," my mum said with an amused tone. "The glass will clean."

In the interests of politeness, Sadie and I turned and said hello as her footsteps, followed by Hugh's, softly padded against the plush carpet, but we quickly went back to what we were doing. Her smile was as fake as ours, and Hugh was as meek as ever. I always felt bad for him. From what I understood, Judith had snagged him because his family came from money, and he would one day—and since had—inherit a multi-million-pound PR agency, but he himself was... bland. Rich, yes, but Judith was the one who wore the trousers, and I'd never spied much in the way of a personality from him.

I heard them settle on the sofa a little bit behind us, and my parents busied themselves fussing around, offering them drinks. Dinner was going to be served around six; the smells coming through from the kitchen where the caterers were working made my stomach rumble. Oftentimes, Mum would prepare dinner herself, but she'd told me this year she preferred to get some people in to do it for her. I wasn't sure what they were making, but I wished the next sixty minutes away. Once we were eating, I felt sure Judith would be too busy to bother me, but while we weren't doing much, I was going to be on edge, waiting for some comment about my love life, or maybe even about Jade.

"Shannen, can I get you a drink?" Mum asked, and I nodded.

"A coffee would be great." I turned around to offer her a smile.

"Sadie?" Mum said, turning her attention to my sister.

"I'm okay, thanks, Mum." She had a cooling cup of tea beside her.

Although Sadie and I were playing with Alexander, I could hear Judith making small talk with Sadie's husband, Stefan, and everything about her grated on me. She was so freaking nosy. She could never just ask someone how work was going. She had to also ask if they'd bagged any new clients or if they were on track to reach their financial goals. It was no surprise Jade was so preoccupied with money. Scott earned a decent wage, but she would never have settled for him if he didn't have the backup of a family fortune too. It made me eternally grateful that my parents hadn't brought Sadie and me up to value money over relationships. We understood its importance, but it didn't rule us.

"It must be time for you to expand your family again soon," Judith said, raising her voice deliberately to catch Sadie's attention.

My mum chose that moment to come in with the drinks, and it wasn't a moment too soon. It was so inappropriate to ask people about their plans for 'expanding their family'. It wasn't like she and Hugh had popped out a lot of kids. They only had Jade, though from what I understood, Judith had wanted more but had been unable to make it happen. I felt bad for her in that respect, but she more than anyone knew it wasn't always possible for everyone to have more than one child.

"We're in no rush," Stefan said politely. "We have our hands full with work and this one." I assumed he'd gestured in our direction.

"Oh, please. There's no point in hanging around, and Sadie isn't getting any younger."

"I'm twenty-nine, Judith," Sadie said, without glancing back. "Not eighty-nine."

"Of course, darling, but you never know what might happen. You don't want to leave it too long."

Sadie made an irritated face that made me snort before she turned around to look at Judith. "We'll be fine," she said. "If we have another, we have another, but we're also happy with what we have."

Bored of his puzzle, Alexander walked around the table and slipped in between Sadie and me. He then plonked himself into my lap. I had to shuffle back from the table a bit, and I turned as I did, no longer able to keep my back to the rest of the room. I was aware it had been impolite not to have turned around sooner, but I was in no rush to look at Judith.

"Honestly, kids these days," Judith went on. She looked at my mum. "Back in our day, we were encouraged to have children. We didn't have to work a traditional job."

"Speak for yourself," my mum said. "And we're not *that* old!"

She was right. She was fifty-two. I was the same age now as she was when she had me, and she had also worked, even though she didn't have to since my dad had a good job. My maternal grandparents raised my mum the same way my parents raised me. They were wealthy, but they were hard workers. Even though our circles kind of encouraged an old-fashioned lifestyle for women, it had never been what Sadie or I wanted.

Having had enough of the conversation, I prompted Alexander to stand, twisted myself onto my knees, and stood up. "Come on, little one. Let's go and play out in the garden for a bit."

"Yeah!" he cheered, smiling at me, the dimples in his cheeks showing.

"You coming, Sadie?" I asked, and she nodded, getting to her feet too. It was a little cold outside still, but I could tell she would have taken any excuse to get out of that room.

Honestly, if this was the way the rest of the evening was going to go, I was already wishing for bedtime.

Thankfully, the meal went smoothly. I was positioned far away from Judith and Hugh, and we ate a fantastic dinner of prawn cocktail for the starter, a main meal of beef wellington, and tiramisu for dessert. I drank a touch more wine than I planned to. I wasn't even slightly tipsy, but I'd definitely had enough that I didn't feel as edgy and uncomfortable as I had when I'd arrived.

Conversation remained polite while we ate, but once we'd all retired to the living room for coffee, I could feel Judith eyeing me across the room. I was sitting beside my mum, my dad at her side. Sadie and Stefan were on the middle sofa, with Alexander in between them, flicking through the pages of a magazine as if he could read it, and Judith and Hugh were on the sofa directly across from my parents and me.

Jade's wedding had become the topic of conversation, and on instinct, I'd zoned out. I didn't want to hear about my former friend and her husband-to-be. It was still so raw to me. Jade had never been someone who would keep quiet about something if she didn't approve, but usually, once she'd had her say, she was done aside from an occasional snide remark. Something about Cal had really irked her, but most of her feelings about him were down to straight-up snobbery. And Scott... well, he'd always been self-obsessed, self-serving, and smug. The only thing I had ever been able to give him credit for was that he seemed to really love Jade. If he'd shown any sign of using her in any way, I would have spoken up, but his feelings appeared genuine, even though nothing else about him was.

"... and finding a new maid of honour has been very hard for her. Being let down at this late stage has caused no end of stress."

Wanting to switch from the coffee to chug another glass of red wine, I shuffled very slightly in my seat. I couldn't even pretend not to have heard as Judith's voice was loud in the enclosed space. I didn't speak, though. She wasn't talking to me, so I wouldn't answer.

"Well, I'm sure she'll find someone suitable," my mum said. "It's not as if she has a shortage of bridesmaids. How is everything going with the catering?"

Mum's attempt to change the direction of the conversation was disregarded as Judith went on, "It's not that simple, though. Jade wanted her oldest friend to be a part of her big day. She's very upset."

I bit the inside of my cheek to stop myself from snapping. It was what Judith wanted, and I refused to give it to her. I didn't care if it made me look cold; I wouldn't give her the satisfaction. The truth was, some part of myself had said goodbye to the girl Jade used to be a long time ago. While I had cared for her, and I still would never wish for her to come to any harm, my grieving for our friendship had been happening slowly for years, so when it finally ended, there was a strange peace to it. Not that it didn't hurt at all; it did. But ultimately, it was better for me to not have her negativity and fakery in my space.

"Perhaps she ought to have thought about that before letting her fiancé throw Shannen under a bus."

Sadie bit the words out in an uncharacteristically sharp tone; it was something Judith naturally brought out in people. My sister's protectiveness of me eased some of the pressure in my chest. Although she wasn't looking at me, I sent a grateful smile her way. Her eyes were locked on Judith.

Judith fixed her with a hard stare in return. "If Shannen picked her boyfriends with more care, Scott wouldn't have had to get involved."

"Shannen's relationship had absolutely nothing to do with her job," Sadie said. "Scott went to her workplace solely to try to make her look bad, and it didn't because there was no criminal record. An arrest is not proof of guilt."

Sadie was aware that Cal was guilty of the crime he was arrested for, but factually, she was right. Cal didn't have a record, and Scott *was* only trying to cause trouble.

"Regardless," Sadie went on, "your daughter and that piece of crap she's about to marry deliberately tried to cause trouble for Shannen. A good friend would have stood up and told their husband-to-be to back off, but Jade is so obsessed with how things look and what people think, she forgot the life-long friendship that she is apparently so sad about losing. I'm sorry, but I don't buy it. If she didn't want to lose Shannen, she should have at least warned her about what Scott was going to do. This situation is all of her own making."

I wanted to dart across the room and hug the hell out of my sister. We were close, in spite of how little time we got to spend together, but I still hadn't expected her to defend me so hard.

"Sadie," my dad warned, and I glanced at him, as did my mum. He kept his eyes on Sadie. "Let's try to keep things polite. It's your mum's birthday."

"I'll be polite if she is." The petulant tone was unlike her as she shot a poisonous glare at Judith.

Standing, I said, "Sadie, can you help me in the kitchen for a sec? I'm sure everyone could use a top-up of their coffee."

She nodded and stood up too, and we walked out of the living room and down the hallway. Instead of going to the kitchen, I tugged her into my dad's home office and wrapped her up in my arms.

"Thank you," I said, holding her tight. "That meant a lot."

"Of course." She squeezed me in return. "That bitch has been dying to get that out of her system all night. I'm impressed she waited so long."

I chuckled as we stepped apart. "Me too. I don't want to be rude, but she makes it so hard to be civil with that judgy stare."

"I know. I didn't want to make a scene, but I also wasn't going to let her keep talking about Jade as if you've ruined her life by getting her out of yours. She's always been a nasty piece of work. Always acting like she's better than everyone. I hate what she and Scott did to you, but I'm glad she's gone."

I blinked at her a few times. "Really?"

"One hundred percent. Shannen, she was frequently vile to you. Nice on the surface, but everything she says has a bite to it. I think the last time she looked at you with any kind of genuine fondness or respect was at your high school prom. Once you left for uni, the only thing she wanted to talk about was herself. Anytime you talked about what you were doing, she was barely listening, waiting until it was her turn, and she's been bloody unbearable since she met Scott. I'll be glad when this wedding is over. If I hadn't already said we'd go out of family loyalty, I wouldn't be there."

My eyes were wide with surprise at her diatribe. Not so much because I was shocked that Sadie was aware of how Jade was, it was more that I'd never even seen her roll her eyes at anything Jade had said or done. Judith... well, she'd always been a pain, someone we tolerated out of respect for my mum, but we'd often exchanged exasperated glances when she was in the room. I thought Sadie believed Jade was at least tolerable. "I didn't... I didn't know you felt that way."

Sadie shrugged. "I guess I didn't think my opinion of her was something you needed to hear. She was your friend, and you were happy."

"I thought I was. I'd just somehow accepted the way she was. But when I started my job and I met some of the women there, I remembered what it was like to have friends who aren't self-obsessed. Then I met Cal. I got so sick of Jade's lack of respect for my choices. I wanted to keep her in my life, but she made it so hard. The night she met Cal was just... I was ashamed she was my friend with the way she acted towards him. And what Scott did... there was no coming back from that."

An ache rushed through me at the reminder of what a disaster everything had been lately. Sadie pulled me into a hug as a tear dripped from my eye.

"I'm sorry, Shannen," she said. "I know I didn't get to meet Cal, but when Mum told me you'd met someone, she said she thought he was special because of the way you talked about him. I hate that it didn't work out."

"Me too," I said quietly. "I miss him so much."

It shot through me then. Every ounce of grief and pain and regret. Cal and I had only been apart for a short time, so I knew it would hurt for a while yet, but I was so tired. I'd been carrying it all around, trying to hold it together when I was sure it was obvious I was falling apart.

"Is there really no chance of you working things out?" Sadie asked gently. "If you miss him this much..."

"No," I interrupted. *In spite of what last night said about our feelings.* "The truth is, being in a relationship scared him, and he'd been trying to push me away the whole time we were together. It wasn't that he didn't want to be with me. I know he did. But somewhere in his head, he was just waiting for something to prove that people always screw him over. And I'm angry that he let that happen, and angry with myself for letting him see my doubts in that one second. Because that was all it took to ruin it."

"Oh, Shannen. From what you told me about him, it sounds like he's got some issues to work through. Maybe in time, things will be different."

"Maybe. But as much as I want him back, it still hurts that he didn't fight for me. For what we had."

That was what it always came back to.

With a sigh, I pulled back from our embrace, and my hand hit the edge of my dad's desk, scattering some pieces of paper on the floor. I wiped my eyes before we both bent to pick them up.

"I saw how you were when you broke up with Matthew," Sadie said as we gathered piles of paperwork. "You were hurt, but that was mostly because you realised what a phenomenal waste of time the relationship had been. This, though... it feels different. Like it's not over."

As I stood, I said, "It's not over for me. The relationship is over, but I haven't... I still love him, and I can't see that changing. With Matthew... even though I thought I'd marry him one day, when it ended, I was done. That's how it's been in all my relationships. But not with Cal."

Sadie straightened up too. "What the two of you had was fast, and it sounds intense. If you feel that strongly about him, though, don't give up on him yet."

With a sad smile, I said, "I wasn't the one who gave up, Sadie."

I turned to place the pile of documents I'd collected back on the desk when I realised there was a chequebook at the top of the stack.

Only my father would still use cheques.

I wasn't sure I even owned a chequebook anymore. The front cover was folded back so well that it hadn't unflipped when it hit the floor, and the little stub at the side had been scribbled on.

S-KY. £5000.

I had no idea what S-KY represented, but five grand was a lot of money to pay out. I didn't think most businesses bothered with cheques since bank transfers were so easy to do now.

"Shannen?"

Placing the pile of stuff down on the desk, I shook my head and looked up at Sadie. "Sorry, what did you say?"

Sadie put her gathered papers on top of mine. "I was saying that things will work out how they're supposed to. I don't recommend waiting around forever for Cal to figure out what he wants, but I don't think you should let it go yet."

Before I could answer, the two of us jumped at the sound of my dad's voice as he stood in the doorway. "What are you doing in here?" he asked, a deep crease across his forehead.

"Hiding," Sadie replied. "Has that wench left yet?"

My dad tried but failed to hide a smile. "Not yet, but it probably won't be long. Alexander is dropping off, though, so Stefan said you might want to head back soon."

She nodded, and I could almost see her brain flick back into mum mode. "Right. I'll go and start getting our things together." Before she left the office she said, "I'll come and say goodbye before we go, but think about what I said."

"I will," I told her, then sighed as she walked out, leaving me with Dad.

"Are you okay?" he asked, a hint of something I couldn't pinpoint in his voice. I guessed that since he'd never been keen on my being with Cal, even though he'd given us the go-ahead eventually, he wasn't sure how to talk to me about the break-up. He knew I was fully aware of his distaste for the man I'd chosen, but he was also my father and didn't want to see me suffering.

"Yeah," I told him, but the crack in my voice gave me away, and I closed my eyes as my tears fell again. Within seconds, my dad's arms were around me, and even though he didn't say anything, for the first time in a while, I felt safe in the arms of the one man who would never let me down.

Chapter 19

Cal

TWO MONTHS LATER

I fist-pumped the air as I watched Aiden sink his fifth and winning penalty, and cheers erupted around the playground for him. He jumped up and down in his Newcastle United football kit—Guy's choice—and the grin on his face as he looked at me gave me a feeling I'd never experienced before.

Pride.

I was always proud of the things Aiden achieved, but this was something else. My boy had been going to football club at school, and he'd joined a nearby Under-7s team a couple of months ago too. Turned out, he was pretty good at it, and his successful penalty shoot-out at the school's May Day Fair had just proved it.

I wasn't the only one celebrating Aiden's win. His two new best friends, Aria and Avery, were jumping up and down and cheering for him, and their mum, Evie, was clapping too with a big smile on her face. His other friend, Maxwell, was the one he was up against in the shoot-out, and although Max looked a bit disappointed, he high-fived Aiden as they walked over to their football teacher, Mr Carr. Mr Carr presented Aiden with a small medal that he placed around his neck, and Maxwell was given a certificate, then they both ran over to us.

I smiled at Evie as the kids all jumped around, hugging and celebrating.

"Could they be any cuter?" Evie asked, grinning.

"I don't think so," I replied.

Any other watching parents and kids began to file back into the school's main hall, where a bunch of stalls was set up with various things for sale.

"Dad, look!" Aiden said, holding his medal out to me, a huge smile on his face. "I won!"

"Yeah, you did." I knelt down to take a closer look. It was a simple gold-coloured medallion with a football on it, hanging on a red, white, and blue striped ribbon, but it was the first thing Aiden had ever won. "You did great, buddy!"

He called me dad all the time now, and every time, it was a reminder of how far we'd come. Moving into our own place had been the start of it, but as bits of our world had slipped away, it had only made us closer. He didn't fight me as much as he used to, and I guessed that was because he finally felt like I wasn't going anywhere. That I wasn't going to leave him, or he wouldn't be taken away by strangers again. That trust had taken more than a year to build, but we'd only been able to do it fully when we'd left the additional safety of Guy's house. It wasn't always easy. In fact, a lot of the time, it was still hard when he shut down and used his temper to let me know how he felt, but I was learning how to get him to talk to me, and he was learning it was okay to say when he was angry or sad. Adjusting to life without Helen and Shannen had been rough, and he still missed Shannen being around because he told me so often, but putting his focus into football was making a big difference. The running around to take him to and from football practice was worth it to see him this happy.

Aiden flung his arms around me, and I held him tight. "Can I have a cake now?" he asked, and I laughed as he pulled away.

"Yeah. Let's go inside with everyone else."

As I straightened up, the small group of friends rushed across the playground towards the doors to the hall, and Evie said, "It's a shame Ash couldn't be here. He'd have loved this." She rested her hand on her large baby bump as we began to follow them.

"He would have," I said, smiling.

Ash was Evie's husband, and also a big football fan. Aiden had been to their house a few times and always came back talking about how cool Ash was. Ash loved raising girls, but they were into princesses and dancing, so he got to have a kick about when Aiden went to theirs.

It was strange. After years of just coping, I now had something that resembled a decent life. Aiden was happy, doing better at school, and he had friends. In turn, that meant I had started to spend time with people other than Guy and the people I worked with. I wouldn't have said I was close to Ash and Evie, but it was good to have other allies within the school to counteract the bitchy mums who still stared at me like I was a psychopath every time they saw me.

I'd also spoken to Donovan a few times. He'd sometimes text me to check in, and we'd had a couple of phone calls too. I hadn't seen him when he'd been back at Easter, but we were making plans to meet next time he was back in the country.

Work was good. My flat was good.

While a lot of things were better... I still wasn't with Shannen. Still missed her as much as I did the day she left. I'd hardly seen her, other than at school, since the night at the Bridal Loft. There was always a pause, like everything stopped when our eyes met, but it passed, and we carried on as we were.

I didn't know if it was still as difficult for her as it was for me. I knew she and Guy still talked, but I never asked him for information on what she was doing, if she was seeing anyone. I wouldn't have been able to handle it if she was. And I never asked him if she asked about me, even though it killed me not to know.

I'd thrown every bit of energy and strength I had left into making sure Aiden felt safe. Into making sure that he wasn't confused about who was picking him up on which days and that things wouldn't change as often because of my work. He'd lost a lot in so many different ways, and while I was used to losing people, I didn't want him to have to get used to it. The day I had seen an image of my father in him scared me. It wasn't a flash of the good man I once knew, it was a glimpse at the angry man who wanted everyone around him to suffer because he was, and I refused to raise a kid who went the same way.

The noise of the school hall interrupted my thoughts, and I looked around to see where Aiden was. It was no surprise that he and his friends had made a beeline for the cake stall. It was three tables long, and there was already a crowd around it. Evie and I approached, rounding up our kids. I was somewhat taking responsibility for Maxwell since his parents still hadn't arrived. They were usually late to collect him due to whatever their jobs were. His mum often came rushing in, dressed in a suit and heels, and his dad, when he came, was also always well-dressed.

"I want a chocolate cupcake," Aiden said, jumping up and down, his medal bouncing against his chest.

I was about to tell him we needed to get in the queue when my phone began to vibrate in my pocket. I pulled it out and saw an unfamiliar number on the screen. That wasn't unusual since sometimes the people I was working for took my number in case they needed something, or someone had been given my number if they needed some painting and decorating work done.

Looking down at Aiden, I said, "Wait in the queue. I just need to answer this. Stay near Evie, okay?"

Aiden nodded, and I answered the phone as I walked quickly across the hall to the exit so I'd be able to hear better. "Hello?"

"Hi, is that Cal?"

The voice was female and sounded a little unsure. It wasn't a voice I recognised, though.

"Yeah," I said. "Who is this?"

"Hi, my name is Caroline Long. I'm calling from Phoenix Grove Rehabilitation Centre in Bristol. I have a Katie Young here, and she has given me permission to contact you and inform you of her situation."

I paused for a second, unsure whether I'd misheard. I hadn't seen or heard from Katie since February, when she'd dragged me into the park to tell me about what she'd done. I'd thought about her now and again, wondering if she was really sorting her life out or if she'd carried on drinking the way she had been before, and I guessed this answered one of those questions.

"Okay," I said. "Is she all right?"

"She is," Caroline answered. "She's been with us for four weeks, and she will be leaving us tomorrow. We had to take a contact name and number when we admitted her here, and she gave us yours with the instruction that we could only contact you if something happened to her. Now, though, she is getting ready to leave and she needs someone to collect her since she doesn't have any transport of her own."

Several thoughts entered my mind at once, but the first to leave my mouth was, "How did she get there in the first place?"

"She got a bus to Bristol, and then a taxi to our facility. While she is fully detoxed, she is very nervous about leaving here alone. She explained to us that she's worried about someone coming after her."

Scott. I wondered if he'd tried to find her since she'd gone against him by taking back her allegations about me, or if it was just something she was considering as an option since he'd gone to so much trouble to bribe her in the first place. She'd also mentioned debts, though. I had no idea who she owed money to, but since Scott hadn't paid her the amount she'd been expecting and she'd been in rehab for a month, she couldn't have paid off everything she needed to. God only knew what kind of people could be looking for her.

"Was she not able to call me herself?" I asked.

"She came in without a mobile phone. The only thing she had was your number written on a piece of paper. We did offer for her to use the phone here to call you herself, but she... I think she was afraid you'd say no."

For someone who had never really known me, she'd got that right. If Katie had called me herself, I *would* probably have said no. Was she that low on friends that I was the only person she could reach out to?

I'd had a while to process what she did, and I'd decided that, even in desperation, it was a shitty move to accuse me of something just to get money. I didn't wish her any harm. In fact, I hoped she sorted herself out, but I didn't want a part in it.

"Did she tell you who I am to her?" I asked. "Because I should be her last resort. Does she not have anyone else she can ask?"

"I'm afraid I can't discuss anything she's disclosed regarding her relationships with other people, but, yes, she did explain who you are."

Blowing out a breath, I wasn't sure what to tell her. If I refused to take her wherever she needed to go, couldn't she get a bus like she did on the way there? She'd got herself *to* the facility, so couldn't she find her way back? What difference would it make if I picked her up or not anyway? If Scott, or anyone, was trying to find her, that would still be true once I dropped her off. I sure as shit wasn't staying around to keep an eye on her.

If she hadn't bumped into me that night a few months ago, she would never have considered calling me for help.

"You don't have to make a decision right now," Caroline said. "If you want to think about it, I can call you back later."

"Where does she need me to take her?" I asked. "Where does she live?"

"Her home is in Taunton."

So, she was telling the truth about that.

I still had a million questions, mostly about why she'd asked me for help and whether she expected anything more than that.

Like to actually stay in touch and eventually see Aiden again.

That familiar shudder rushed through me at the idea that she might try to take him. She was his mum, and apparently sober now, but the thought of her wanting him back didn't feel good.

"Okay," I said, "Can you ask her to call me tonight? You can't answer the questions I need answers to, so I need to speak to her."

"And if she refuses?"

"Then she'll have to find her own way home."

I hung up before anything more could be said, stuffing my phone into my pocket with a sigh of frustration.

I used to wonder a lot about what would happen if Katie made a return. What she might want, what she would be like. But the more time went on, the less I thought she'd ever come back. And my guess was, if Scott hadn't found her, she probably never would have. She'd told me she thought about Aiden all the time, but it wasn't enough for her to call me and ask how he was, let alone come and see him. What brought her back was the offer of money. And even though she felt bad about it, she still did it. So, why was she now asking me for favours when the thing she did fucked up large parts of my and Aiden's life?

Maybe she did only need a lift home. But did that mean I had to do it?

If it was only a lift, *could* I just do it and then leave and never hear from her again?

I'd have to ask Guy to watch Aiden for me because there was no way I could take him if I went for her.

Are you really considering this?

Shaking my head, I held in the growl that was trying to crawl up my throat because there were other people wandering around; some parents and kids leaving, and some parents just showing up. Even though it was ages ago, there were still people who seemed to have something against me based on the rumours that had circled around about my 'arrest', so I needed to keep my temper under wraps.

"Cal?"

I'd zoned out while trying to control my temper and hadn't seen Shannen approach, but her voice pulled me back to reality.

There was a look of concern on her face, but she also seemed... nervous wasn't the right word, but she somehow didn't look right. Her face was a bit pale, and while she had been tense around me since we split a lot of the time, there was something else that I couldn't quite put my finger on. Even with all of that being true, though, the sight of her still made me want to pull her into my arms and hold her. Kiss her. Take her home.

It never fucking stopped. I missed her all the time, and when I saw her, it made everything harder. Made me remember how much I'd messed up, and how much better she was without me.

But she didn't look better. She looked tired.

That doesn't have anything to do with you, you narcissistic prick. She's probably seeing someone else by now. Probably being kept awake by some other man who doesn't stress her out half as much as you did.

That thought didn't help, and when I felt her hand gently touch my arm, I shrugged her off before I could stop myself.

Her concern turned to hurt in a second, and she took a step back. "Sorry," she said. "I just... you seemed upset, but... never mind." She looked around as if remembering where we were, and that us touching each other in any way in the school playground wasn't a good idea.

Her blue eyes dimmed as she began to turn away, but I reached out, not to hold onto her, just lightly brushing her hand to make her stop. And she did.

We hadn't had a proper conversation in ten weeks. That was two weeks more than we were in a relationship. Should it have really still been so fucking painful?

And why did I even stop her? I couldn't tell her why I was pissed off without explaining the other stuff about Katie, which would then lead into Scott being involved, and even if I wanted to go into it, this wasn't the time or place.

"Shan, I..." I began, and her body visibly reacted at my use of the name only I used for her. She jolted slightly, like hearing it for the first time in so long had made her shiver, and she turned towards me again, less tension in her frame. "Sorry. I... I had a weird phone call. Are you okay?"

She nodded a bit too quickly, and swallowing hard, she said, "Yeah. I'm okay."

My eyes narrowed slightly. "You sure?"

When she only nodded again, I knew she was lying, but I wasn't sure why. When I'd had the thought that she was seeing someone, I hadn't really believed it, but maybe she was. Was that why she was acting so strange around me? If she was with someone else, though, would she still be looking at me like she cared?

Knowing I couldn't push it right then, I said, "Aiden won the penalty shoot-out. He got a medal."

Her face brightened into a smile, more of her discomfort falling away as her shoulders relaxed. "Aww, I'm so pleased for him! I'll congratulate him when I see him."

"He's inside with Aria, Avery, and Max. They're waiting to get cakes."

"Of course they are," Shannen said with a chuckle. "Are you coming back in? I have a stall to get back to."

Our eyes connected fully, and when she smiled softly, it took everything I had not to grab her and pull her against me. But everything was still too much of a mess for me to do that, and I also didn't know what was making her so edgy. It didn't feel like the usual edginess she had when we were near each other, the kind where I felt how much she still wanted me but knew she was staying back to protect herself. Something was different. But her smile also told me that the connection between us was still there, and that had to be enough.

"Yeah," I said, and we started to head towards the doors to the hall. "I don't want Evie to get stuck having to pay for everything."

When Shannen laughed again, she said, "She's lovely. I met her and her husband at the first parents' evening we had. I'm really glad Aiden's made some friends."

"Me too. Breakfast club has been good for him."

"It must have helped you out too, with getting around work and making sure you can pick him up after school."

I nodded. "Yeah. It's taken a while to get used to everything now Helen isn't around, but her not being there makes going to Guy's a lot nicer."

Shannen bit her lip like she was trying to conceal a smile as we re-entered the hall. She had tried to be friends with Helen, but Helen was a bitch, pure and simple. As much as Shannen wanted to get to know her, Helen had made it almost impossible. Shannen hated that Guy had gone through a break-up, but she also understood that life was better for everyone without having to navigate Helen's rage.

The noise of the hall put a stop to any further conversation, and Aiden ran over to us with a chocolate cupcake in his hand. "Look what Evie got me!" he said, grinning.

I searched her out, and she was still standing close to the cake tables, Aria, Avery, and Maxwell all eating baked goods too. Shit. I'd have to get the treats next time to even things out. She smiled as if to say, 'don't worry about it,' and I mouthed, 'thank you' to her before turning my attention back to Aiden and Shannen.

"Look what I won!" he said to her, pointing to the medal around his neck.

The pride on Shannen's face as she smiled at him almost knocked me on my ass because as much as I wasn't sure how she felt about me now, she still had all the time in the world for my boy, and it wasn't just because she was his teacher. That was part of it, but the bond the two of them had was still intact.

"Aiden, that's brilliant," she told him. "I'm so proud of you!"

His cheeks reddened as he grinned. "I'm going to be as good at football as Alexander Isak and Anthony Gordon!"

Shannen side-eyed me, clearly not knowing who they were, and I laughed.

"Newcastle United," I informed her. "Guy has got him hooked."

She raised an eyebrow. "They are both traitors to their local team," she teased.

I was about to answer when Mr Carr appeared behind Shannen, placing his hands on her shoulders.

"Can you give me a hand with the raffle in a sec?" he asked. "We're going to draw it soon."

She turned her head to look at him, their faces way too close for my liking. My body stiffened as I pushed down the urge to drag him away from her and smack him in the mouth for touching her.

Mr Carr was one of the only other teachers I regularly had contact with because of football club, and I'd never had a problem with him. In that moment, though, I didn't like the way he looked at Shannen. Didn't like that she smiled at him as she answered his question.

Was it him? Was he the one she was seeing?

You don't know she's seeing anyone. Calm down.

But jealousy and rage ripped through me in a way it never had before. There had never been any need for it. The only men I'd ever seen Shannen talking to were Guy, Scott, and her dad, and none of them were people I needed to worry about.

As if I was giving off some kind of angry prick vibe, Shannen turned to me, and her cheeks paled again as she took in whatever expression was on my face.

And he still had his hands on her.

Shannen stepped to the side towards Aiden, causing Mr Carr's hands to drop, but he touched her arm again as he walked away, offering her another grin before he left.

Good-looking son of a bitch. He was probably a bit older than me, but he was clearly fitter, and I knew he was popular with the kids because while he worked them hard, he had a good sense of humour that kept their interest and made it fun. He also had that Jack Grealish look that women seemed to love. What was most annoying was that he wasn't cocky with it. There was nothing about him to dislike, other than him laying his hands on my woman.

"Aiden," Shannen said, looking down at him, "why don't you go and show Miss Davis your medal? She's over in the corner on the toy stall."

Aiden nodded and jumped up and down before shooting across the room to where Gaby was. Once he was gone, Shannen fixed her attention on me again; I was still rigid with annoyance.

"You need to calm down," she said, keeping her distance, even though I could see in her eyes that she wanted to reach for me. They were slightly watery, and her own body was stiff too, like she was forcing herself to stay back. "This is not the place."

I'd been so focused on controlling my temper that I had forgotten how many people were in the room with us, and how many people might have seen me almost lose it. Fuck, even before that, I was so glad to be near Shannen that I hadn't considered whether anyone was watching us, trying to figure out if there was anything going on between us. I glanced around, but luckily, nobody seemed to be paying any attention to us.

"He was touching you," I said, keeping my voice low. "Does he... Are you..." I stopped, shaking my head because I didn't want to hear an answer to any of the questions I had. I would march across that goddamn hall and rip his head off his shoulders if she said she was seeing him, and screw who saw.

Letting out a long sigh, Shannen blinked away her tears. "No, Cal. He's just someone I work with, but he..." She paused, blowing out another breath. Her blue eyes dimmed then seemed to shut down, like she was blocking me out. Like she didn't owe me any kind of explanation about anything.

And even though she was right, it pissed me off more because she'd started a sentence and hadn't finished it. That was dangerous for me. It meant I would spend hours trying to fill in the gaps.

He... what? *Regularly gropes me in the supply cupboard? Wants me to suck his dick?*

I could have gone on forever trying to guess what she was going to say, and none of the endings made me feel better.

"What, Shannen?" I said, my jaw clenching as I narrowed my gaze on her. "What?"

Tears filled her eyes again, and she said, "It really doesn't matter. I have never been out with him, and I am never going to go out with him."

But going out with someone and screwing them are different things. She still hadn't given me enough information. Just because there was nothing going on between them now, it didn't mean there never was.

"Have you..."

"There hasn't been anyone else, Cal. But if there was, if I'd been with him or anyone else, you lost the right to know about it when you gave up on us."

Her words, even spoken so quietly, made me flinch. Was that how she saw it? As me giving up? She'd had a lot of time to think since the last time we had a conversation. Time to really look at what had happened, and this was where her thoughts took her.

You did give up. You talked yourself out of the best thing that ever happened to you because you were afraid she'd see you the way you see yourself.

With a shake of her head, she said, "I have to get back to work."

Before I could stop her, she was gone, walking quickly across the hall to Gaby's toy stall with her head down. I kept my eyes on her the whole way, watched as she slid behind the table beside Gaby while she was taking payments from children and passing them the things they'd bought. With an extremely weak smile, Shannen helped her, though I saw Gaby take in

Shannen's mood and lean over to whisper something to her. Shannen only nodded, continuing her tasks, and Gaby looked up then, glancing around the room until her eyes fell on me.

As our gazes met, she threw me a warm but subdued smile. And it helped. It let me know that there was something left for me to hold onto. If there wasn't, Gaby wouldn't have been smiling at me; she'd have glared at what an absolute cock I was.

Casting one more look at Shannen, who I was certain was trying hard to hold herself together, I sighed and made a move to look for Aiden.

Chapter 20

Shannen

THANK GOD WE WERE going into a three-day weekend. The May Day bank holiday could not have come at a better time because I felt totally wiped out. The May Day fair at work had been a great idea, and it had probably raised a lot of much-needed funds for the school, but by the time I got home at six, with Gaby in tow, I was exhausted.

It had far less to do with any additional exertion and more to do with seeing Cal. We'd had our longest conversation in weeks, and while it had started off well, it had disintegrated into both of us feeling awful afterwards.

And as if that wasn't enough, I had one more thing left on my task list for the day that I really didn't want to do. All I wanted was to ask Gaby to go home so I could curl up in bed and sleep.

"Do you want a cup of tea?" Gaby asked once we were inside and had settled on the sofa.

I shook my head. "Not yet. I just need a minute."

Gaby rested her hand over mine, and I looked up at her, seeing the kindness in her green eyes. She'd been super patient with me while we'd finished our tasks at the fair, not quizzing me because she knew I was close to falling apart. Now we were alone, though, it was a different story. "What happened with Cal today?"

I sighed. "It was really good to see him and talk to him at first, like nothing bad ever happened. Then David walked by and put his hands on my shoulders while he was talking to me. Cal got all possessive."

Gaby's brows rose. "Possessive how?"

"He kind of... paused," I said, seeing it again in my mind, the way Cal had gone from relaxed and chatty to murderous in an instant. "The second David's hands touched me, Cal's whole body became solid, and his eyes went dark." The memory of it caused a strange flutter in my stomach because although it had slightly scared me to see him suddenly look so intimidating, I couldn't deny that the part of me that still loved him had taken flight. I felt like he still saw me as his, and while the feminist in me hated it, the rest of me had wanted to throw myself at him. "But then I could see the questions written all over his face." Huffing out a breath, I continued, "I wanted to tell him the truth, but I didn't want him to overthink it, so I just said nothing had ever happened between me and David. I don't know if he believed me, though."

"Well, it's the truth." Gaby shrugged. "What good would it have done if you'd told him David asked you out, especially when you're never going to date him, and when Cal has to see him every Thursday at football practice?"

"Exactly. But somehow, I feel like not telling him was worse."

It wasn't even a big deal. I'd spoken to David a few times at various staff meetings, but he wasn't someone I worked with on a regular basis. However, sometimes, he sat with Gaby, Nova, and me at lunchtime, and we'd gotten along well. He was funny, but that was as far as it went for me. He'd asked me on a date about a month ago. I politely declined, and he'd accepted my answer without making things weird. That was it. And yet, keeping that tiny fact from Cal still felt like a betrayal. Maybe it was the part of me that wanted to stop him from overthinking the way he always did, but I'd realised over time that he'd do that anyway. Not telling him would make him wonder, but telling him would have probably had him stressing over whether I'd change my mind and eventually agree to go out with David. I couldn't win either way.

The fact that Cal hadn't been able to tell how much every bit of me still belonged to him blew my mind. To me, it felt like my body radiated with it, with all of the suppressed emotion I had to contain every time he was near me. It still hurt. Still felt like I was carrying around a ton of love for him that had nowhere to go because he'd turned it away. As hard as I'd tried, I couldn't just release it; it was stuck inside me, in my head and my heart, and it was getting heavier with every day.

"If it helps, Cal looked apologetic after you walked away," Gaby said.

"At this point, nothing helps, Gabs. Every time I think I'm getting somewhere, like I can start to move on, I see him and it starts again. Not that it ever really stopped, but I'm so sick of feeling like this. I'm sick of going over everything in my head and being in this constant state of wanting to see Cal and also not wanting to see him ever again so I can just get over it. I'm so, so tired." Dropping my head back against the sofa, I struggled to hold back my tears. I was stuck in a never-ending vacuum of torment, and every time I thought I might escape, I got sucked back in.

"Shannen, you know there are other factors at play here. You're not just unnecessarily wound up. We need to sort this out. Now."

That was the entire reason she was with me instead of going home. If it weren't for Nova having to go and take care of Donovan's grandma, who had been taken down by a chest infection, she would have been with us too.

Turning my head towards her, I said, "It's pretty much just a formality at this point, isn't it?"

"Yeah, I think so." Gaby took my hand again and squeezed it gently, her eyes full of understanding.

Pulling myself up from the sofa, I said, "I think I already know what I want, but... let's find out."

My hands and legs began to shake as I walked behind the sofa, where I'd dumped my handbag. Lifting it, I took out the thing we'd driven half an hour out of the city for in case someone recognised me and saw what I was buying. I said a silent prayer that I was mistaken, that this wasn't really happening, then headed for the bathroom.

Once I was inside, I removed the cellophane from around the box and turned the package over in my hands a few times.

My menstrual cycle hadn't been on top of my list of concerns when I first broke up with Cal. I was too busy tending to the constant ache in my chest. It wasn't until the end of March that it occurred to me that I hadn't had a period. I blamed the stress and carried on with my life as best as I could. After all, being overly emotional and constantly feeling drained were things that happened after a break-up too. Not any other break-up

I'd had, but Cal was different. I'd felt things for him I'd never felt before, and it had been slowly destroying me. But when another few weeks passed and my monthly visitor still hadn't shown up, it crossed my mind that my moods and my tiredness weren't right. I hadn't been sick, but my boobs were always sore, and my stomach was just a little bit more rounded than usual. I'd continued to put off finding out for sure in the hope that it really was all down to stress, but once I'd expressed my worries to Gaby and Nova, they encouraged me to get a pregnancy test so I could know one way or the other.

Like I'd said to Gaby, though, it *was a* formality now. I knew deep down that a tiny life was growing inside me. I just needed to confirm it.

Five minutes later, I did.

I'm pregnant.

I'd expected to feel something once I had the result for sure. Like a surge of emotion that would let me know how I truly felt about it, but nothing came. Just a trembling in my hands as I sat down on the closed lid of the toilet, staring at the result.

Now, along with the memories of what Cal and I had, a very real memento of our time together had made its presence known.

A baby had not been in my plans. Not for a long time yet. Not when I hadn't even been in my first teaching job for a year, and certainly not like this. With a man I wasn't in a relationship with, who had let me go, and who I now struggled to communicate with when the pain of losing him kept crashing over me, reminding me of what we'd lost. What he'd severed.

"Shannen?" Gaby's voice drifted through the closed door, and I looked up at it, knowing that once I opened it, I'd have to begin dealing with this.

"Just a sec," I said, dropping the test in the bin and washing my hands. Once I was done, I opened the door, taking in the questioning look on her face. I simply nodded, and she immediately pulled me into her arms.

Why wasn't I crying? Why didn't I feel anything beyond numbness?

Weirdly, the thought that I didn't feel anything was the thing that made my tears fall, and I held onto her for a few minutes, letting out whatever needed to leave my system. Once I was done, Gaby led me to the kitchen, and I wiped my eyes on the way. I leaned back against one of the counters while she filled the kettle and switched it on.

"Okay, so..." she began, "what are you thinking?"

She looked tense as she asked, leaning against the counter opposite me, and I said, "I don't know what I'm thinking. I don't... this... it's not what I wanted."

As I said the words, guilt rushed through me. What kind of woman found out she was pregnant and immediately said something like that? There was a baby inside me, and it was conceived with love. Even if this wasn't part of my plan, I should have been happier. Should have seen the gift that it was.

But it didn't feel like a gift. It felt like another complication in what was already a complex relationship.

Shaking my head, I said, "I don't know what to do, Gaby. I knew... I've been sure for a while that I'm pregnant, but I kept hoping I was wrong because I'm not ready for this, not now, and not with the way things are with Cal."

I could hear Jade's voice telling me what a mess I was, getting knocked up by someone I hardly knew, who I wasn't even with anymore. *What an embarrassment to be a single mother, the father of the child some random painter and decorator who probably can't even afford child support payments. God, Shannen. How will you ever dare to go out in public again with some bastard child and no ring on your finger?*

Weirdly, the sound of her judgement, even if it was only in my head, caused a reaction within me. Maybe I wasn't married, and maybe I would be a single mother, but my child would never be an embarrassment to me, and neither would Cal.

I rested a hand on my stomach, a tiny bit of warmth running through me.

"There is a lot to think about," Gaby said, her eyes dropping to the hand on my belly before looking back up at me. "But can I make a request? I know you want to look at this with logic. You want to think about how you saw your life going before this happened, but can you allow your heart in too? I don't want you to make a decision you'll regret. Take your time to think about it. And I'm here whenever you want to talk it through. Also, you should probably text Nova as she will be desperate to know."

She chuckled lightly at the last part, but I was still stuck on what she said regarding thinking with my heart.

My heart—and my libido—were what got me into this in the first place.

I could have not gone home with Cal that first night. Or I could have gone home with him and let it end with him leaving the next morning. I could have let Jade's judgements and the possibility of my family not accepting him make me stop seeing him. But aside from that first night, it *wasn't* just physical attraction that kept me with him. That was part of it, but it was always more. It was that same thing that still made everything around us disappear when our eyes met. A connection. A magnetism that had never made sense but had always worked.

My heart was what refused to let go of him.

Once the kettle boiled, Gaby made us both a cup of tea, and we sat down at the dining table. I hadn't spoken the entire time Gaby was making the drinks.

"What would you do?" I asked Gaby as I placed my hands around my cup. "If you were in this exact position, what would you do?"

Gaby held onto her own cup, her blonde hair falling slightly around her face, and said, "If I were you, in this exact position, I would be confused too. You have a good job you worked hard for, and if you have a baby, then you will have to put that on hold for a while. But then you also have to work out what to do about Cal. Whether you want to try to make things work with him, or whether the two of you can bring up a baby while staying apart. Then there's Aiden to take into consideration. But Shannen, ultimately, you are the one who has to go through a pregnancy and make decisions about your life. It's all about what you really want."

"What I want is to not have to make any decisions. I want someone else to tell me what to do."

Gaby smiled softly. "Sorry, poppet, but nobody can do that. All we can do is listen while you work it out."

With a groan, I said, "Everything is such a disaster. Even if Cal and I were still together, this would have knocked me sideways. I don't think he's ready for a baby either. God, he's only just started to really bond with Aiden. Throwing another child into the mix won't go down well."

I remembered that he'd questioned whether or not Aiden was his when Katie had told him she was pregnant, and with the way he'd looked at me earlier, after David had put his hands on my shoulders, I wondered if I would get the same treatment. Would he question me the same way?

"He didn't want Aiden," I went on. "Not at first. I know that isn't how he feels about him now, but what if he thinks that about our baby? This was not what he signed up for."

"It's not what you signed up for either, Shannen. But he'll have to deal with it."

Not if I don't tell him.

The thought flew into my head, and I immediately berated myself for considering it. Obviously, if I planned to have the baby, I would have to tell him, but what if I chose differently? If I chose to terminate the pregnancy, *could* I keep it to myself?

Sure, if I never wanted to look him in the eye again. But I wasn't that person. While Gaby was right that this was my decision to make, I wouldn't be able to live with myself if I didn't tell Cal.

"Earlier you said you thought you knew what you wanted," Gaby said. "Do you still feel the same way?"

Another surge of guilt rushed through me, and heat filled my cheeks because I was already ashamed of what I was about to say. I looked her in the eye as I confessed.

"The moment I thought I might be pregnant, I knew I didn't want to be. Having a baby right now, with the way things are with Cal, with my job only just starting, and with how stressful things have been for the last few months... it doesn't make sense to me. When I was growing up, I had friends who got pregnant, and they just made it go away because it wasn't convenient. They didn't want the single parent stigma, or the responsibility of a baby yet. It was always swept under the rug, like the pregnancy was a minor blip that could be dealt with. Everything was about appearances, and if it didn't fit into their lives, it was tossed away. It was so cold." I paused, looking away from Gaby and staring down at my cup of tea. "When being pregnant was still only a possibility, the decision seemed easy. And if I look at it from a black and white perspective, perhaps it still is. If I put emotion into it, then I have to actually feel things, and if I feel things, then the decision isn't straightforward anymore."

"Shannen, if you don't put the emotion in now, I can promise you, you will feel it later, and then it will be too late to change it. That's why you need to take your time with any decisions you make. If, when you've thought about it from every angle, you still don't think you want a baby right now, then I will back you every step of the way."

Almost without thinking, I rested a hand on my stomach again.

I'd been living in some weird case of denial for the last few weeks. Maybe even longer. After the initial pain of breaking up with Cal, I'd tried to shut off my feelings so it wouldn't hurt anymore, but it still managed to seep through, slipping into the tiniest cracks in my defences. I'd tried to do the same with the possibility of pregnancy. Told myself that it wasn't real. And if it wasn't real, even though I *knew* it was, I could deal with it. I could turn the hypothetical decision into reality if I just remained detached.

I wasn't stupid, nor was I heartless. The truth was always going to hit me in the face in the end, and I'd expected my reaction to those little lines on the pregnancy test to be bigger. Thought everything I'd been forcing down would spill over. Instead, all that had happened was the sensation of vacancy. While it was very slowly fading, I was so drained by fighting against my feelings that I couldn't think straight.

As I looked back up at Gaby, her head was lowered, and she brushed her fingers quickly across her cheek.

Is she crying?

She stiffened as if she'd felt my eyes on her, and she slowly looked up at me. Sure enough, her eyes were wet with tears, and my heart lurched.

"Gaby... what's wrong?"

She blinked a few times, then attempted a bright smile. "It's nothing, really. I'm just being an idiot."

Her voice broke, and that small catch in her throat made a shudder run through me. I'd never seen her cry. Gaby was a woman who laughed loud and loved life. She was strong and fun and wacky. Seeing tears in her eyes hurt my heart and dragged me out of my own thoughts. I stood and rounded the table, dragging my chair with me, and sat down beside her.

She winced as if she'd messed up, rubbing at her forehead, and I took the hand that still rested on the table. "Talk to me, Gabs."

Gaby let out a soft groan, shaking her head. "Shannen, this isn't about me. I'm here for you right now."

"You are always here for me. But clearly, something that was said has upset you. What is it?"

She slipped her hand out from beneath mine and stood up, pacing for a moment while taking deep breaths. After a minute, she said, "Can we go and sit on the sofa so I can hug a cushion?"

There was humour in her words, but it didn't land as well as it usually would have because there were still unshed tears sparkling in her eyes. I nodded. "Sure."

I reached over to pick up my drink, my own worries forgotten while I wondered what Gaby was going to say. What about the conversation we were having had caused this reaction in her when she was usually unflappable?

Once we were settled on the sofa, Gaby slid off her shoes then curled up with her legs tucked underneath her, picking up a cushion and holding it tight against her. Unsure where this was going, I remained silent, waiting for her to be ready to speak.

Eventually, she said, "I really am sorry, Shannen. Since you said you thought you might be pregnant, I worried this might happen, and I've tried my best not to make it about me, but... I'm just worried about you. I don't want to put my own experiences on you, but I also don't want you to regret any decisions you make."

My brows furrowed at her words. She hadn't made anything about her. All she had done this whole time was reassure me she was there for me, and she had been. Afraid anything I said might halt her words, I stayed quiet and continued to wait.

"There is a whole lot of history that would take me a really long time to go into," she began with a sigh. "But the quick version is that when I was at university, I met a guy I was crazy about. I met him in my first year, and we were together until I was twenty-six. At first, he was great. The perfect guy. Great sex, great conversation, and he couldn't do enough for me. We had maybe one whole year where things were amazing, but the decline after that was fast. I just didn't realise that until it was over."

When she paused to let out another sigh, I shuffled myself into a more comfortable position, getting the feeling that everything she was about to say was going to be decidedly *un*comfortable.

"He was abusive," Gaby went on, absently stroking the soft material of the cushion. "The kind of abusive where you don't even see it's happening because it was so subtle in the beginning. The occasional backhanded compliment, then a few more subtle digs wrapped up with affection so the sting was taken out of the insult. By the time I was twenty, I thought I was fat and not smart enough to finish my degree." Turning the cushion over and smoothing out the other side of the fabric, she said, "I lost a lot of friends. Some who didn't like him, and others who told me he was being controlling, but I didn't see it. I was pretty isolated for a while, and then in my last year of uni, I fell pregnant."

Somewhere in the back of my mind, I'd known this was where the conversation was going, yet my breath still caught in my throat. Not because of the revelation itself but because of how quickly her face had paled, and how the ghosts of horrible memories seemed to swim behind her eyes.

"At the time, I was close to graduation, and I really didn't think having a baby when my life was just about to begin was very sensible." She looked up at me, offering me a small smile of understanding because she knew it was similar to the position I was in now. "Flynn and I had talked about what we would do after uni, where we would live, and since he was also training to become a teacher, we wanted to live in a city, somewhere there were plenty of schools and lots of opportunities. Even though he had made it clear that he wanted us to be together, I felt like he'd think I was trying to trap him by getting pregnant, and I didn't want to tell him. In my mind, if I had an abortion, I didn't have to ruin things between us and everything would be as we'd planned." She took a long breath. "So, that was what I did. I told him I was going away for the weekend to see my parents, and I had an abortion and stayed at a friend's place." A tear dripped down her cheek, and she wiped it away quickly. "I felt so fucking guilty. For having an abortion and for not telling Flynn what I'd done. The thing was, even then, I was scared of him. His moods were weird and unpredictable, and my confidence had gone to shit because of all the times he'd made sly remarks about my clothes getting tight or my face getting chubby, or how he'd landed himself with me because I was the best he could do at the time, and now he felt like he had to stay loyal to me, even though he could do better."

A slithering sensation of hatred for a man I had never even met began to crawl underneath my skin. Gaby was absolutely stunning, and I didn't just think that because she was my friend. She was fit, with an amazing figure, and her smile and eyes were always so bright that it was hard not to be captivated by them. I supposed her obsession with the gym made sense now given she had perhaps been told often that she was gaining weight. That kind of mental torment does not go away easily. And yet she showed no outer signs of fighting confidence issues. She was extremely outgoing and had no problem with going against the norm; the woman had bought herself a wedding dress on a whim, for God's sake.

Unless that itself was the confidence issue. That she masked it by being exuberant so nobody would guess that, internally, she wasn't as self-assured as she appeared.

Gaby smiled softly at me. "I've worked hard to get my confidence back," she said. "And while it's mostly not faked anymore, some days are still hard."

I put my cup down on the coffee table and shuffled across the sofa to sit closer to her. Like a cat, I nudged my head under her arm, and she chuckled, letting me snuggle in beside her so I could comfort her. I wrapped an arm around her middle and held her hand, my head resting on her shoulder. I needed her to know I was there for her.

"Gaby, I'm so sorry," I began. "I-"

She shook her head. "Don't be sorry, honey. The reason I wanted to tell you was because... you're trying to make a decision based on how you feel about your life as a whole. That was what I did. I need you to consider all of the angles before you do something you can't take back."

I squeezed her hand tightly, thinking about what she'd said. Thinking about what I had just learned.

My bright, beautiful, outrageous friend had been through something awful, and I was sure there was a whole lot more to the story than she had told me. That someone had ever made her feel less than she was made me feel sick.

Of all the people in my life who I'd have suspected might have been through something, she was the last person who would have crossed my mind. It wasn't like I was particularly naive, and even less so after working in schools and hearing the stories of what went on within some families. Gaby was so full of life, so uncaring of how other people viewed her, and so... happy.

But was she really? Was all of it just to disguise how she really felt?

"Don't look at me like that," Gaby said, and she reached over, wiping away a tear I hadn't realised had fallen. "I'm good now. It's almost been ten years since it happened, and I have been through all kinds of therapy. My philosophy once I'd got my groove back was never to let anyone make me feel shitty again, to run away from any man who made me feel even slightly uncomfortable, and that the only person I ever have to answer to is myself. So, if I seem crazy sometimes when I do silly things, it's because I had to work fucking hard to feel like I've earned the right to be me. When someone drains the life out of you, once you get it back, you stop giving a shit about what other people think because their opinions of me can never be as bad as the opinions I used to have about myself."

I guessed there was some kind of freedom in that. One I might have envied if she hadn't been through so much to get there.

"Anyway," Gaby went on, "enough about me. Just promise me you'll really take your time to think about what you truly want."

I nodded. "I will."

Hearing what she had been through had certainly made me look at things in a different light.

My job would wait for me. That was probably the easiest part of the equation to deal with.

But what about me? What did I truly want?

There was no changing that I didn't want to be a single parent. Not because of what people would think but because trying to do it on my own would be hard. I had support. I had my friends and my parents and sister, but at the end of the day, when I closed my door, it would just be me and a baby.

And Cal?

Even if Cal and I were still together, this could very easily have been the thing to send him running. Aiden was the result of a fling with a woman he wasn't that into, and while I knew I was more than that to him, we had only been together for two months. It was an intense two months, and I had fallen hard and fast. I would even go so far as to say that I knew more about him than most of the other men I'd dated, but that didn't change the fact that having a child with someone I had been with for such a short time, and someone who struggled to believe he was worth anything, was risky. I didn't want more pain for any of us.

From where I was now, with Cal and me apart and barely able to talk without it descending into misery, it was almost impossible to imagine having a baby with him. I still missed him every single day, but while I wanted things back the way they were, I didn't want him to be with me because I was pregnant. He was with Katie only because she had his baby, and that had been a disaster. If he was going to be with me, I wanted him to want just that, not to be with me out of a sense of duty.

And realistically, *could* things ever go back?

Whatever was broken between Cal and me, it hadn't been fixed. He hadn't given me the opportunity to make up for hurting him, and he still—as far as I knew—had the ridiculous notion that he was no good for me.

But the baby...

Referring to 'the baby' was what kept my feelings detached. Now it was real, though, it was *my* baby. Not just an imaginary entity but a life. What would he or she look like? I imagined Cal's chocolate brown eyes and dark hair, or perhaps we'd created one of those children who would be a perfect blend of both parents.

At the idea of a tiny bundle wrapped up in a blanket, with a thick head of black hair and beautiful eyes, a wave of love crashed over me. I could see it. Me holding a baby, Cal and Aiden beside me... a family.

I hadn't seen it coming. At the beginning of the year, I was single and focused on my career.

By Christmas, I could be a mother.

Chapter 21

Cal

My interaction with Shannen earlier played on my mind for the rest of the day. It was Friday night, so I'd let Aiden stay up a little later than usual, and we'd played some video games together, which kept me distracted, but once he was in bed, my thoughts came out to play.

Seeing someone else put their hands on Shannen was something I hadn't been prepared for. In times when my imagination ran riot, I thought she might be seeing someone by now. Wondered who it would be, what kind of person. I imagined her on the arm of someone with a well-paying job. Someone her parents wouldn't mind her bringing home. Just the thoughts were enough to make me want to smash things. But actually seeing someone touching her was different. That made it real. When Shannen told me nothing had happened between them, I believed her, but it just made me see that, at any time, she *could* meet someone else. She could find someone better suited to her than me, and there was nothing I could do about it.

And then there was the call about Katie.

Why had she chosen to have me as a person to contact? The fact that she still had my number and had never used it to check on her son was crazy. I figured she'd deleted it long ago.

She'd mentioned that she had friends. People she spent time with, and even though they might have screwed her over in some way, there had to be someone more obvious than me to ask for help.

I wasn't going to pick her up. I didn't owe her anything. Not even to hear her out, really. But I also didn't think she would have the balls to ring me. It didn't make sense because she'd risked coming to find me to talk to me in person, and now she was suddenly too afraid to pick up the phone. Although, nothing she did or said made much fucking sense to me.

My thoughts went back to Shannen again. My thoughts were rarely far from her, but I'd told myself she was better without me. That she'd already lost a lot because of me. And the distance between us in that time... it didn't allow for anything to change. She'd made it clear that she needed me to stay away, and I did.

But I was so tired of it. And yet, what had changed? My opinions about myself were no different. *I* was no different, not really.

She looked so... off earlier. At first, when she'd approached me, she looked tired. It didn't look like a normal kind of tiredness, and there was a paleness to her face, but once we started talking, it had disappeared, and the Shannen I knew was back for a while.

Not for the first time, I felt an overwhelming need to hear her voice. It happened pretty regularly, and I always forced it down because I knew she didn't want to hear from me. From the way she'd walked away from me earlier, I was sure she still didn't want to, but in a moment of madness, I reached for my phone and scrolled to her number.

The worst she could do was ignore me or hang up, and I was half-expecting that anyway. I didn't know what I was going to say to her, probably more apologies, but I just needed to hear her.

I was about to hit the button to call her when my phone rang in my hand, scaring the hell out of me. The number on the screen was the rehab centre again, and I blew out a breath before answering.

"Hello?" I said.

"Cal... it's Katie."

Well, shit. I didn't think she would call me herself. I thought it'd be the woman from earlier again. Tensing at the sound of her voice, I didn't speak, waiting for her to say what she needed to say.

"I... Cal, I'm sorry for calling you," she said. Her voice shook slightly. "I know this sounds mad, and I know I'm asking a lot, but I'm stuck here. I don't know how I'm meant to get home with ten quid in my bank until my benefits get paid in. I don't have enough to stay anywhere, and no, there is nobody else I can call."

She sounded desperate, and a chink of guilt cut through my defences, but I wasn't ready to back down. "Why are you calling *me*, Katie? If you'd gone into rehab at any other time, I would never have crossed your mind, and then what would you have done?"

A bitter laugh echoed down the line. "I would never have been able to afford rehab at any other time."

"Yeah, because you got there by trying to fuck me over." The reminder made me grip my phone harder.

"Cal, please!" she begged. "I know what I did, but I came to you and explained, and I apologised! I put myself in danger by retracting my statement after Scott didn't pay me, and by telling you what I did. When I went back to Taunton, he was calling me all the time, so I did what you said and changed my number, but somehow, he managed to find it again. That's why I didn't take it to rehab with me. I just wanted some peace."

Fuck. So, he was still after her. What the hell was he planning to do when he reached her, though? He'd forced her to lie to the police, and she'd retracted her statement when he hadn't paid her fully. What could he do about that now? It was unlikely the police would take too well to her going back and saying she'd changed her mind again.

"Does he know where you live?" I asked.

"Probably, but I haven't been there. I stayed with a friend once I left Exeter in case he came for me."

I doubted Scott would go to *that* much effort. What would it achieve anyway? He'd already done what I guessed he'd wanted to do by making Shannen and me miserable, so what would be the point now? There was nothing left he could do to her, especially when he had nothing to hold over her anymore.

"And why couldn't that friend pick you up?" I asked her.

"Because she can't drive, and she doesn't have any money either. I've got to go back to my own place now. I can't keep sponging off her." She sighed. "Cal, please. I know I'm asking a lot, but I just need this one favour. I swear I will never ask you for anything again. I need to get home, so I can start rebuilding my life."

Fucking hell.

Katie *had* given me a heads-up about Scott when she could have just left the allegation hanging over me. Christ only knew what might have happened if she hadn't. But then, if she had been paid what Scott promised her, would she have still made the same decision? I doubted it.

She was the mother of my child. Not that that counted for much either since her interest in Aiden had lessened once he learned to walk.

But if I didn't go and get her, what would happen to her? She could attempt to hitchhike, but I doubted she'd get very far, or she'd get picked up by some passing maniac. At least if I took her home, I'd know she'd arrived, and I'd know where she lived if I ever needed to reach her. Although, what that might be for, I didn't know. I'd never needed her in the past. Not once I realised she wasn't coming back. When things were hard with Aiden, it wasn't her I wanted, it was someone who could tell me what to do, and she was as clueless as I was. The difference was that *I'd* stepped up.

You stepped up when Shannen came into your life. Before then, you were useless too.

Not totally useless, but it wasn't until Shannen that I realised how much I was missing out on. How much more life with Aiden could have been if I stopped being so self-centred. I'd looked after him, gave him what he needed in terms of food, clothing, a home, and sure, I took him to the park and played video games with him. But it wasn't until Shannen, with her huge heart, appeared that everything felt different. She'd made me care about things again. Made me realise that going to work and then going home to watch TV, along with the occasional night out with Guy, wasn't all there was. That having a child didn't mean I couldn't have some kind of life, and that instead of trying to separate those two things, I could have my son *and* someone in my life.

"Cal," Katie said softly, and I shook my head to pull myself out of my thoughts. "I just need to go home. I know I messed up. I know I'm a shitty mother. I wasn't ready, and I let you both down because I was selfish. I should have sorted myself out a long time ago, but I'm doing it now. I just... I need a bit of help."

As she broke down in tears, I closed my eyes. If she really was being honest, then I knew how she felt. I had been on the edge of desperation, hoping someone would tell me how to fix it, and so many times, the only thing I had to cling to was a bottle of vodka. Guy had been the one to give me a chance, and it had changed everything. I might not have owed Katie anything, but I'd been where she was more times than I could count.

"What time do you need me to be there?"

Chapter 22

Shannen

I WAS SO DAMN tired. It had been a few days since I'd been able to get a full night's sleep while waiting to take the pregnancy test. Even though I knew what the result would be, the anticipation of it had stressed me out. I had purposely waited until the end of the week, knowing there was a three-day weekend coming, so I could deal with my feelings, but I wasn't doing that very well.

After talking to Gaby, and later to Nova, I didn't sleep at all on Friday night. Both of my friends had offered decent advice, but it was Gaby's words that played on my mind.

I *wanted* to think logically, not emotionally, but I wasn't so deluded that I would actually do that.

That thought about me being a mother by Christmas continued to circle around my head. It was wild. The likelihood was as low in chance as being the sole winner of a multi-million lottery jackpot.

And yet, there I was. Pregnant.

We were five months into the year, but so many things had occurred that it felt like longer. The amount of drama in my life was usually kept at zero, and then Hurricane Cal caught me in his trajectory, and nothing had been the same since.

But I still wouldn't have changed it. Even with as confusing as everything was. As painful as it had been. I did not and would not regret my time with him because, for the first time in years, I'd actually felt alive. Not just content and cruising through life but living it. And not in a chaotic, burning-everything-to-the-ground kind of way, but in the way that I felt seen. That I felt like someone understood me, but also, when he didn't understand, he made an effort to try. As it turned out, that was all I'd ever really wanted in a partner.

The orgasms were a bonus.

And also what got me into this predicament.

Even though I'd let myself consider what could be if I had a baby, I still hadn't made a decision I was completely happy with. I swung back and forth, driving myself around in circles with my thoughts and feelings.

I had already told two people about my pregnancy before I'd told Cal, but more than anything, I wanted to tell my mum. I wanted to sit down with her and talk it out.

Without letting her know I was coming, I left my house and hopped into my car to head to Plymouth. It was raining, so I took my time, and I got to my parents' house just over an hour after I set off.

As I approached the front door, I heard the raised voice of my mother and paused with my hand in front of the doorbell.

"Annie, I know, okay? I know."

My dad's voice threw me off, even though, with it being their house and all, it should have been my first thought. He should have been at work, though, and my parents didn't argue. They got on brilliantly. While I wasn't naive enough to think they never pissed each other off, my mum had been bellowing; I just hadn't been quite close enough to hear what she was saying.

"How could you do something like this?" she yelled, and I took a couple of steps back. I didn't want to walk in on whatever was going on, so I quickly hurried back towards my car, hoping I could slip away before they noticed I was there. I'd just have to figure things out on my own or maybe call my mum later when everything in there had calmed down.

The front door opening made me pause just as my fingers curled around the driver's side door handle, and I turned to see my dad stepping over the threshold. He halted when he saw me. My mum also spotted me, and the colour drained from her face momentarily before her cheeks flushed red. I guessed she didn't want me to hear they'd been fighting.

My dad stared at me as if shellshocked, and I wondered what the hell was happening between them.

"Shannen," Dad said, a tremble to his voice.

I held my hand up. "Sorry," I said. "I shouldn't have come over without letting you know. I didn't mean to interrupt anything. I can just go."

"No," Mum said quickly, stepping outside too, and my dad moved over slightly so she could stand beside him. "It's fine. Please, come in. It's lovely to see you."

As if I were a random who'd shown up unexpectedly instead of her daughter, I could almost see her putting her 'entertaining head' on. It was a thing I'd seen her do many times when caught off-guard. She could have been elbow deep in horse shit or in the middle of dealing with a house fire, but as soon as someone came to the door, she'd smile brightly and act like everything was perfect, even if the house burned down around her.

My dad went straight to the kitchen, and I followed my mum through to the living room with trepidation. I hadn't been to my parents' house since my mum's birthday. I had to say, Mum and Dad's place was always better without the impending presence of Judith, but based on the frosty atmosphere, I wasn't sure what I'd walked into.

Mum and I sat down on the sofa, and she still had that air of forced contentment on her face. It was pointless since I could see through it, but I decided it was better not to ask. I was also rethinking telling them my news because it sounded like they had bigger concerns.

However, my mum tilted her head to the side very slightly and said, "Is everything okay, my darling? It's great to see you, of course, but you don't usually drop by without calling first."

I could probably count on one hand the times I had done so in the past. Once was when I had gone to Plymouth to collect something from a store that only had it in that branch, and another was when I was going to the theatre there to see a show. My out of the blue visit didn't necessarily mean something was wrong, but just as I could see through her facade, she could also see through mine.

Offering her a weak smile, I said, "There was something I wanted to talk to you about. I didn't think Dad would be here."

Mum cleared her throat. "No. He wouldn't usually be, as you know, but something came up and he took the day off."

Something came up?

"Must have been a big something," I said with a raised eyebrow. "You normally have to fight to get him out of the hospital."

As a surgeon, he was one hundred percent committed to his job, sometimes over his family. While it was hard, I'd always been proud of the fact that my father saved lives for a living. It didn't make sense to me to get upset over late nights or him being called in at random hours when he was needed. If he could help someone, we could do without him for a few additional hours.

"It's a long story," Mum said, refusing to elaborate.

After a minute or two, my dad came in carrying a tray holding a teapot, a jug of milk, and three teacups and saucers, which he placed on the coffee table in front of Mum and me. Instead of crowding us, he sat on the floor on the opposite side of the table and began to pour milk into each of the cups.

"Steven, would you mind leaving us?" Mum asked. "Shannen and I need a moment." She looked at me and smiled softly, having taken note of what I'd said when I sat down.

"Okay," Dad said, lifting the teapot and pouring into one of the cups. "I can get out of your hair."

However, when I glanced at him, worry lines sat deep in his forehead and there were dark circles under his eyes. My heart sped up anxiously as I wondered if maybe he was sick. But that didn't make sense. My mum had asked him how he could do such a thing, and being ill would not have been a choice.

"No, Dad," I said quickly. "You don't have to go."

I may have been in the dark about whatever my parents were arguing about, but since he was there, I needed them both to hear what I had to say.

If I was still going to say it. The mood in the room was odd. Like whatever the two of them were shouting about lingered over them. I both wanted to know and desperately wished I hadn't heard anything. Could I really drop this bombshell on them right now?

"I don't mind," he said as he finished pouring the drinks and then got to his feet. He leaned down to pick up his drink. "I can find something to do in the office."

"It's fine," I said, although I thought he would have actually preferred to get away. "Sit down."

He walked across the room and sat on the sofa under the window, sideways on to where Mum and I were sitting, his large hand wrapping around the small teacup.

Taking a deep breath, I said, "I... I have something to tell you. And I really need you both to listen and help me decide whether I'm making the right choice. And I also need you to do so without judgement." My eyes darted *almost* accidentally in my dad's direction, and he shifted slightly. I hadn't meant to make a dig at him, but although he had eventually given his blessing for me to be with Cal, he was still not going to like this.

"What is it, darling?" Mum asked, reaching over and placing her hand over mine. "Are you okay?"

I nodded, swallowing down a lump that had suddenly formed in my throat. Not just because I was about to say it out loud, but because the act of doing so was going to make it more real than ever. This was an admission. The big reveal. Once I said it, it would be out there, and I couldn't pretend it wasn't happening anymore.

And I didn't think I wanted to pretend anymore either.

Blowing out a slow breath, unable to meet my mum's eye, I said, "I'm okay. I... I've been feeling a bit tired and... weird lately. I thought it was just stress, but... I'm pregnant."

Mum's eyes widened and her hand shot up to cover her mouth. She didn't look horrified, just shocked. I didn't dare turn to see my dad's expression, but my mum's gaze darted to him momentarily before landing back on me. "How... how long have you known?"

"I found out yesterday. It's been..." I paused, swallowing again. "I've had a lot of thoughts in that time, and I just needed to go over them with someone because it's... it's a lot."

Squeezing my hand tighter, Mum said, "Of course. But... how did Cal take it?"

"He doesn't know yet. When I tell him, I need to be clear on what I want, and I can't figure that out on my own."

My mum stared at me for a moment, tears in her eyes. I couldn't read what they were for, though. It didn't look like disappointment or judgement, though, and my racing pulse slowed. Finally turning my head, I looked over at my dad, whose face was ghostly white, highlighting the black rings under his eyes more.

"Dad?" I said. "Are you all right?"

He nodded. "Yes. Just surprised is all."

With a humourless laugh, I said, "That makes two of us."

"Wh... what do... how do you feel about it?" Mum asked me, and I swung my head back to look at her.

"Confused," I admitted. "When I thought I might be pregnant, I felt like it would be a really bad thing to have a baby right now. I'd almost decided not to continue with the pregnancy before I even knew for sure." I closed my eyes and breathed through the familiar wave of guilt. My stomach twinged slightly, as if the baby was reminding me it was real, no longer a figment of my imagination. "But now... I don't know. The timing isn't good. With work, when I've only just settled into this job, it feels wrong to have to take a break from it so soon. I love teaching and I love the people I work with. And then... I... I'm on my own now." Saying the words filled me with a rush of regret and sadness, and all I could think about was how much I wished everything was different.

How I wished Cal could forgive me. Forgive himself.

"Cal... he's not going to be ready for this. *I'm* not ready for it. But I think I want to have the baby."

"Even when you're not with Cal?" Mum asked gently. "Because having a baby is hard work when there are two parents. On your own, it will be challenging."

I nodded slowly. "I know that. But, Mum..." Pausing, I rested a hand on my stomach, and my mum moved hers to cover mine again. "I just... all night I've been going over it. What's best, what I want. And the answers to each of those questions are different."

There was a short silence before my mum continued, "Have you thought about how it would work if you have the baby and Cal wants to be involved but you aren't together? Could you handle only half having him in your life?"

She'd just hit on the biggest dilemma for me. I could have the baby and be with him, and I could have the baby and be completely without him, though it wasn't my preference. But to have him want to be involved in our child's life but not want to be with me would be a special kind of torture because I'd *have* to see him regularly. There would be no escaping him. And then, one day, he'd meet someone else, and I'd have to live the rest of my life with him in it but attached to someone else.

"No," I told her. "I don't think I could handle that. But I also can't make a decision about what I want based on what *he* wants to do. I have to be sure that whatever I choose to do, it works for me."

"Does being a single mother work for you?" Mum asked gently, again, not with any judgement. More like she was coaxing me to really think about the reality of it. "Shannen, you know I will support you no matter what you decide, but you need to be certain of what you want."

Shaking my head, the bits of me I'd been holding together started to fall, along with the tears in my eyes. "I want for everything not to be such a mess. I want Cal's ex to not have made a stupid allegation against him, and I want him to have not thrown away everything we had. I... just miss him so much, and I thought it would have stopped by now, but it hasn't. I hate the way things are, but I don't know if there's a way back."

Leaning forward as the weight of everything pushed down on me, I allowed the tears to cascade down my cheeks as everything overwhelmed me again.

After a moment, I heard a crash that scared the hell out of me, and I jumped as I looked up.

My mum had got to her feet and there was a smashed bone china saucer littering the carpet close to where my dad had been sitting. Loose shards had dropped onto the arm of the sofa, though Dad was now at the other side of it, his eyes wide and his chest heaving from the shock.

"Are you happy now?" my mum yelled in his direction. "Is this what you wanted?"

Even though my tears were still falling, my brows furrowed. "Mum, what..." I began, astounded by her outburst.

She refused to look at me, her eyes still fixed on my dad, who had lowered his head. "Don't you dare try to hide from this!" she shouted, her voice louder this time. "Look at her! Look at your daughter and see what you've done, you selfish, idiotic man!"

Baffled by her words, I said, "Mum, why are you shouting at Dad? I know he wasn't happy about me being with Cal, but he got over it. I don't understand..."

When she finally looked at me, her entire body was shaking, seething with rage. Angry tears sat in her eyes before she looked around at my dad again. Now, his head was in his hands, and his shoulders were shaking.

What the hell was happening here, and why was my mum so mad at my dad? Without thinking, I stood and went across the room to sit beside him, placing my arm around his shoulders. My move only made his sobs come harder, and I held him tighter, resting my head against his. I had never seen him cry before. Never seen him even close, really. The pain he was clearly in felt like knives piercing my heart because my strong, stoic father was falling apart in front of me.

"Tell her." My mum's voice was stern, but it broke as she spoke. "Tell her the truth right now." When neither my dad nor I moved, she bellowed, "Look at her and tell her what you did!"

"Mum!" I said, looking up at her, expecting to find her glaring at him, but instead, she had dropped back onto the other sofa, her own head in her hands now.

When she refused to answer, I moved away from my dad but kept my eyes on him as an awful feeling crept through me. Whatever I had walked in on obviously had something to do with me, though I wasn't sure what or how. That Mum had been intending to make this visit as normal as possible before my revelation suggested that whatever it was, she hadn't yet processed it either, and my news had forced her hand.

I just couldn't figure out what could have caused my mother's ire and why my dad was crying beside me.

"Dad," I said softly, though my voice held trepidation and my own body was beginning to tremble too. "What's going on?"

"I'm sorry," he said. "I'm so, so sorry."

Slowly, he raised his head, his cheeks stained with tears. The second his eyes met mine, though, he shook his head and looked away.

"Steven," my mum said, and I flicked my gaze to her again.

I was stunned by the anguish in her eyes. She was staring at my dad, a mix of hate, love, and devastation written across her face. I wanted to comfort them both, but I was frozen, growing increasingly worried about what I was about to hear.

My dad looked across the room at my mum, a similar expression on his features, minus the anger. Instead, he looked completely wrecked.

My parents did not fight. They were happy. Not pretend, put on a show for their friends happy, but really happy. I'd even caught looks of contempt in their direction at parties and events because many people within their circles were just going through the motions. Married for business, money, convenience. Far fewer were in genuinely good relationships. My mum and dad were among the lucky ones, so... why did it feel like everything was falling apart?

After what felt like the longest pause that had ever existed, my dad let out a long, slow breath before standing up. He wiped his eyes, his body still shaking, but whatever he'd done, he was going to be the one to tell me about it.

"Shannen," he began, taking another deep breath. "You are my baby girl, and you know I have only ever wanted the best for you."

I nodded, my brows pulling together.

"When your mum told me you were seeing someone, I was happy for you," he went on. "And I was happy for you until that day when you told us what Cal had done."

I bristled as I remembered the conversation we'd had several months ago, when I'd explained about Cal's past violent behaviour and tried to make my parents understand that he had changed. That he wasn't the same person anymore.

"After you left, Shannen, I felt so guilty because I knew I'd hurt you, but as your father, I was more worried for your safety. All I could think about was the idea of you calling me in tears because he'd hit you, or worse. The call that he'd been so violent that he'd..." Unable to finish the sentence, he shook his head before continuing. "I was so scared that you were in danger that I called Scott."

I wasn't sure if it was possible to feel blood drain from my face, but that was how it felt. Like the shock had robbed me of colour, and coldness swept through me, making me wrap my arms around myself.

"Scott told me he had history with Cal."

"You told him, didn't you?" I interrupted. "You told him that Cal was the one who put Edward Firth in hospital and almost killed him."

Dad shook his head. "I didn't go with the intention of telling him, but it did slip out. But it doesn't matter anyway because unless the confession came directly from Cal's mouth, nothing I said could be considered evidence."

"So... then what?" I asked.

"Scott could see how much I wanted Cal out of your life..." Dad trailed off, turning his back to me and pacing the room. "I was so wound up with the thought that he might hurt you that I asked Scott if... if he could help me find a way to get Cal out of your life."

His words slowly filtered through my brain, trickling into my consciousness, but I couldn't quite make it fully sink in.

Because he was my dad. He would never knowingly try to break up my relationship. And he would never go to Scott of all people for help.

I shot a look at my mum, who was now watching my dad with coldness in her eyes, but underneath it all, I could still see her utter devastation that this was happening. This was the man she loved, the man she had been married to for over thirty years saying that he'd set out to take something from me. I'd told him. I'd sat in front of him and explained how much Cal meant to me, and his response was not to give Cal a chance but to seek help to oust him from my life.

Still refusing to look in my direction, my dad said, "Scott told me that Cal was scum. That he had no business being anywhere near you or our family. He said Cal was an angry, volatile person who was always on the edge of losing it, and based on what I'd heard from you, I had no reason to doubt his word."

I snorted out a bitter laugh. *Sure. Trust the word of a man most people can't stand just because he's an officer of the law. Because he told you what you wanted to hear.*

"I was desperate, Shannen," my dad said, finally spinning around to look at me again. "You can't understand what it's like to know your child is in danger-"

"I wasn't in danger!" I spat, my emotions finally spilling over. Standing, I shouted, "I was never in danger, and yet you refused to hear me! You know as well as I do that Scott has never liked me any more than I liked him! He's a money-hungry, power-hungry dick who likes to make anyone who threatens his perfect life suffer!"

That was what he'd done. First, he'd tried to shake things up by telling my school's principal about Cal's past, and when I'd told Jade and him to stay away from me, just because Jade was upset about something she had a hand in, he'd stepped it up a notch. I'd played right into his hands by telling my dad the truth about Cal's past.

My dad nodded, shame filling his features. "He was already trying to dig up something about Cal, and when I spoke to him, he'd found the mother of Cal's child and was trying to find out more about why they broke up.

At first, she refused to speak to him, but when I got involved, he said if we offered her money, she would be more likely to help us."

A dull ache began to form across my forehead at his words.

Money.

He and Scott *paid* her?

"Let me get this straight," I said, my limbs now practically vibrating the way my mum's had a moment ago. "You went to Scott, and he suggested paying the mother of Cal's child to report him for domestic violence?"

No verbal reply came, but my dad gave a single nod before dropping his head in his hands again.

There was a long, painful silence, while I realised the truth of his confession.

My dad. The man who, while we butted heads sometimes, was the one man I thought I would always be able to trust. Who had always been there for me. The backbone of our family. He had been a large part of the reason I was now separated from the man whose child I was carrying. A man he'd tried to banish from my life for something he hadn't even done.

"How much, Dad?" I asked, staring at the back of his head with a glare so penetrating it had to be burning through the back of his skull. "How much did you pay to mess with my life? With Cal's life? With *Aiden's* life?" I emphasised Aiden's name because Dad had liked the short time he'd spent with him. And while my life and Cal's had been damaged, Aiden had suffered the most because he couldn't truly understand what had happened.

"Five thousand pounds."

Five grand. My mind suddenly flicked back to that day Sadie and I had been in his office and I'd seen his chequebook with five thousand pounds on the stub and the word S-KY. Scott. Katie. Was the Y what her surname began with? I was sure the police had mentioned it the day Cal was taken for questioning, but I couldn't remember. Either way, the huge sum of money made sense now.

For the first time in a while, I looked across at my mum, who was still sitting in the same place, her eyes closed now, and tears dripped down her cheeks.

No wonder she'd been so angry. The man she loved had just confessed to screwing over their daughter. I couldn't even begin to understand how she must have felt, and while I wanted to go to her, I was still trying to fathom everything my dad had said.

It had to be a mistake. I was dreaming. Trapped in a nightmare where my dad was the villain, but I'd soon wake up and everything would be back as it should be.

"Shannen, I'm so sorry," he said, his voice shaky and broken. He finally turned to me, tears falling from his eyes too. "After I met Cal, I tried to stop Scott from going ahead with the plan, but it was too late. He'd already found Katie and given her the money. I told him to tell her to keep it as long as he stopped her, but he refused to, and I had no idea how to contact her. I would have paid her more to not make that report, but I didn't know where she was."

I wasn't sure if those words were supposed to help, but they didn't. He had such little trust in me that he'd tried to get Cal away from me in the most sleazy, underhanded way. Paying someone to lie to the police? It wasn't his idea, but he had gone along with it. This was a double bonus for Scott. Another step forward in his vendetta against Cal, using my father, and he didn't even have to get his own hands dirty because my dad was the one who paid her.

"It doesn't matter that you tried to stop it," I said, my voice sounding strangely unemotional. "What matters is that you thought it was okay to do something so disgusting, so messed up, to a man you had never met, and to me. You knew how much I felt for him, and you were still totally fine with interfering. With setting him up. Even now, he's still being judged by the parents at school for being taken away in handcuffs in public over an incident that didn't even happen. You allowed this to happen in front of his child, who I then had to spend the day consoling because he thought his dad was going to jail and he was worried he'd be sent to live with strangers."

I choked on those last words as I remembered Aiden sobbing into my shoulder, terrified Cal wouldn't come home. I wiped a couple of tears from my cheeks as my dad said, "I know! I wasn't thinking straight, Shannen. All I could think about was you being with a man who was violent, and I was scared of what he might do to you."

"He never did anything to me, Dad! And I told you that! I told you he wasn't the person he used to be, and you didn't listen! Instead, you went to the most untrustworthy person we know for more information!"

"But I didn't know-"

"You didn't listen!" I repeated, louder this time, standing up. "What you did is the lowest thing a father can ever do to their child. You broke my fucking heart!"

As my tears began to stream, I saw my mum was also sobbing, and I said, "I'm sorry, Mum. I'm so sorry."

"You have nothing to apologise for, my darling," she choked out, and I crossed the room and wrapped her in my arms, the two of us crying against each other as everything crashed down around us.

This perfect life we'd always had. Well, not perfect, but stable. Reliable. It was something I'd always been able to count on. Parents who were solid. Who loved each other and loved me and Sadie. Who would have done anything for us, and who had never let us down.

My dad's betrayal wasn't only against me, it was against all of us. My mum and me especially, but even Sadie because she would not be okay with this. It was a severing of trust that would tear everything apart. And all of it was because of a man I had chosen to be with. It wasn't my fault my dad had done what he did, but somehow, I still felt responsible. For going against the grain and picking someone so different than was expected of me.

At that moment, as I sat there with my mum falling apart in my embrace, I wasn't sure if I would ever be able to forgive him. And I didn't know if my mum would be able to either.

"Mum," I said softly. "I need... I have to..." I was trying to convey that I wanted to leave, but I couldn't get the words out. I didn't want to leave her, but since I'd bulldozed into the middle of their own fight, I figured they probably still had a lot to talk about.

"I know," she said, softly stroking my hair. "I know. I'll call you later."

I nodded as we released each other, and I stood up. My dad was no longer in the room, though I hadn't heard him leave the house. "Are you going to be okay?" I asked as Mum got to her feet too.

Wiping her eyes, she said, "I don't know, sweetheart. Your dad and I have a lot to talk about, but the way I feel right now... I just don't know."

The pain was still so bright in her eyes, and I was genuinely concerned in that moment that what he'd done could result in their divorce. My mother was fierce about the protection of her children, as she had shown by standing up to Judith over what Scott had done regarding Cal in the past. Keeping my name out of the mouths of gossips had been her priority, but when her own husband was responsible for hurting me... I wasn't sure what she was going to do. I just hoped she didn't make any decisions too quickly.

Ultimately, her choices were picking between her husband and one of her children. That was a black and white view of a complex situation, but I was sure that was how she saw it. And I didn't even know how I felt beyond the agony of the betrayal. I probably wasn't meant to know yet. The only thing I was certain of was that I needed to be away from him because I didn't want to see or speak to him. Not until I'd had a chance to think.

Mum walked me to the door and gave me another tight hug, words no longer necessary, before I left and ran to the car because the rain was coming down hard. It hadn't been raining when I'd arrived; it must have followed me from home. Shaking my head and pushing my already slightly frizzing curls back, I let out a long sigh. My tears had stopped for now, but there were plenty more to come; I could feel them stinging the backs of my eyes, my chest heavy and aching.

I needed to get home. Needed to put my pyjamas on, curl up on the couch, and take a couple of hours to get to grips with what I'd just heard. No doubt it would throw up a million more questions, but what did they really matter?

My dad had destroyed me, Cal, and Aiden, with no thought for the consequences.

I could understand his apprehension. Felt for him, even. Because I couldn't imagine fearing for someone so much. I could even understand, to a degree, his concerns over what people might think about me being with someone who wasn't within our usual social circles. But he'd taken action before there was even a hint that something might happen to me. And when he met Cal, he immediately knew he was wrong. That he'd made an unfair judgement.

But what I couldn't understand was taking such drastic action; action that had caused damage to ripple through several lives. It wasn't over. Even after a few months, I still hurt, and I knew Cal did too. Any chance of what might have been had been obliterated, and I wasn't sure a baby would help that.

My original reason for my visit fluttered around my consciousness. I'd had no chance to get my parents' input on that, really. I wondered what advice my mum might have offered, and what my dad might have said if the truth about what he'd done hadn't been the sole topic of conversation. There was no way to know, and I couldn't think about it when this new bombshell had just exploded.

I started the car and slowly backed out of the driveway, trying to calm the racing thoughts rushing around my head. I turned up the hill and then onto the road that led me back into the city.

As I drove, I kept hearing that shattering sound as my mum threw her cup at the wall. The panic I'd felt and the curiosity at why she was so angry at my dad who, until that day, had never done anything to provoke such a reaction from her.

Then I saw my dad, sobbing, his eyes almost begging me to understand his reasons for the choices he made.

It struck me at that moment... would I tell Cal? Would I let him know that it was my own father who had torn us apart? Shame filled me from my toes to the top of my head. I could never have guessed what lengths he would go to to 'keep me safe', but the fact remained, it was my dad who had done this. Would it help Cal to understand why Katie had come back, or would it trigger his dark side?

I slowed my car down as I approached some traffic lights, staring out at the rain lashing my windscreen while I waited for the lights to change. I let myself get mesmerised by the wipers for a second or two, wishing I didn't have to drive in this. Wishing I was already at home.

As I blinked to clear my vision, too late to brace myself, I saw a car coming up fast behind me, too fast, and although he'd slammed on his brakes, his car hurtled into the back of mine, shunting me forward.

My seatbelt locked and cut into my neck, making me cry out, and as I was thrown back against my seat as my car stopped again, I was breathing hard, stunned.

Other car horns were honking, and I noticed the lights had changed from amber to green, but I couldn't move. I placed a hand over my chest, trying to take some slow breaths as I heard a tap on the driver's side window. I wound it down slightly and saw a man standing there, a shocked and apologetic look on his face. He was probably in his mid to late thirties, and rain had already soaked his dark hair, rivulets dripping down his face.

"Oh my God, I'm so sorry. Are you okay?" he asked.

Swallowing, I nodded. "I think so. I... what happened?"

"I don't know. I think my wipers locked and I couldn't see out the windows for a second. Once they cleared and I saw the lights, I didn't have enough time to stop. I'm so sorry. The back of your car..."

As he trailed off, I shook my head, not quite able to process this next turn of events while still trying to get to grips with the last. I unclipped my seatbelt, rubbing at my neck with one hand while opening the car door with the other. My skin was sore where the seatbelt had tried to pin me, and as I got out of the car, I felt lightheaded.

The man who had crashed into me grabbed my arm, holding me up. "Jesus. Are you okay? Someone has already called the police, but do you need me to call an ambulance?"

I shook my head. "No, I'll be fine," I said, though I still felt a bit woozy. I let the man hold onto me for a moment longer as I took some deep breaths. "How bad is the damage? Is it a write-off?"

"I don't think so, but it is going to need some work. I can give you my insurance details, and-"

Whatever he said sounded like a low murmur, and I couldn't understand the words as my head swam again.

"Seriously," he said, holding onto both of my wrists now to keep me upright. "Let's get you sitting down and I'll call an ambulance."

Nodding, I said, "Yeah. That's a good idea. I'm pregnant."

The man's face paled slightly, but that was the last thing I saw as my vision faded again and I collapsed onto the soaking wet road.

Chapter 23

Cal

WHEN I ARRIVED AT the rehab facility, I didn't know what to expect. I had already told Katie I wasn't going inside to get her, that I'd wait in the car park, and at five past two, she stepped through the doors, pulling a small suitcase. Knowing I'd have to get out so she'd know which car was mine, I opened the driver's door. I'd got myself a second-hand black Nissan Qashqai a few weeks back, which was so much better than driving everywhere in my work van or asking to borrow Guy's car.

As soon as Katie saw my movement, she was across the car park, hurrying towards me, dragging her pink case behind her.

She no longer looked dirty and ill. She had some colour in her face, her hair was clean and shiny, and she wore a pair of blue jeans, a yellow top, and a blue denim jacket. It had been raining hard on my drive up to Bristol, but it had now eased to a slow drizzle. Even so, I was still getting wet, so I opened the boot and took her case from her. Once it was safely inside, we both got into the car and buckled up. She turned her head slightly, her eyes shifting to look at the back seat.

"It's just me," I said. "I didn't want to have to explain any of this to Aiden."

She nodded, smiling slightly. "I never expected you to bring him, but I..." she trailed off and shrugged.

Perhaps she had hoped he would be there, but that wasn't a step I was willing to take yet.

"Relax, Cal. I'm not going to try to take him from you. I'm sober, but I'm still a mess."

Even the fact that she had said it made me tense, and I turned my attention back to the reason I was there. "Can you give me your address and I'll put it into the Sat Nav?"

With another nod, she recited it to me, and once I'd programmed it in, I started the car and got us on the road.

"Thank you," she said after a few minutes. "For coming to get me."

"I almost didn't."

It had been a long night. I'd barely slept, wondering if I was doing the right thing. When I'd asked Guy if he could watch Aiden for a couple of hours so I could take Katie home, he'd pretty much confirmed my insanity, but he'd still agreed to help me out. I'd almost phoned the rehab facility several times overnight and that morning to say I wasn't going. The old arguments turned over and over in my head. She lied to the police about me. She left Aiden and never looked back. Never checked in. She left me to struggle with a baby I hadn't wanted, and she'd only reached out to me out of revenge to Scott for not paying her what he'd promised her. I was probably just someone she wanted to keep on side for a time like this. When she had nothing and no one else left.

Now I'd seen her, could see she had really made a go of being in rehab, I didn't completely regret my decision to pick her up. Even so, a tiny alarm bell continued to ring at the back of my mind.

"I was surprised there was no call to say you weren't coming." From the corner of my eye, I saw her head turn to look at me. "I appreciate it, Cal. I know it was a lot to ask, especially after... everything."

Keeping my eyes on the road, I said, "It's probably best not to go over that." I didn't want to turf her out on the side of the road when the reminder of the things she'd done pissed me off all over again.

"I know. I just... I wanted you to know I'm grateful."

With a nod of acknowledgement, I reached over to turn the radio up, hoping she'd take the hint that I didn't want to talk.

The hour-long drive was spent mostly in silence. The most words we exchanged were when my SatNav got confused as we got closer to her home and she'd had to direct me herself until we reached the front of her ground-floor flat.

The street she lived on was fairly close to a railway line; I heard the sound of a train whizzing by as we sat outside. It was a standard street with a long row of terraced houses—well, they looked like houses, but Katie had informed me they were flats—on both sides of the road.

Jesus Christ, I could really use a piss.

It had been bothering me since about halfway there, but I was sure I could wait until I'd dropped her off, then I'd find a service station nearby and go there. But now I'd stopped focusing on driving, I really needed to pee.

"Thank you, Cal," Katie said, still not removing her seatbelt. "I owe you."

"The only thing I want is for you to stay away from alcohol. If you can do that, we'll call it even."

She laughed lightly. "I'll do my best." She unclipped her seatbelt and I did the same before getting out to retrieve her suitcase from the boot.

Fucking hell. Now I'd moved, the need for a piss grew stronger, and I couldn't stop myself from saying, "Can I use the bathroom before I go?"

Katie smiled, chuckling. "Of course."

As she got her key out of her pocket, I locked my car and then followed her into her flat. The scent of stale booze hit me in the face, and right away, I knew that wasn't going to help her in any way. She'd need to invest in some heavy-duty air fresheners or those scented candles Helen always had dotted everywhere around Guy's place. In spite of the smell, though, the place was clean and tidy. Either she had done that before she left, or someone had been in to sort it for her.

Katie parked her suitcase in the hallway and put her keys back in her pocket. "The bathroom is just through that door at the end of the hall."

"Thanks."

I didn't waste any time rushing down the hallway, and once I was inside the bathroom and doing what I needed to do, I let out a sigh of relief. This was it. Now I could go home, and that would be the end of my time with Katie. If not forever, hopefully for a while.

After flushing the toilet and washing my hands, my eyes fell to the small, frosted window above the sink. Unable to resist, I opened it a crack and peered outside, surprised to see a decent-sized backyard with a gate at the end. *Not bad for a one-bedroom flat.* Closing it back up, I left the bathroom, not wanting to stay for too much longer. I wanted to get home, to see Aiden and pretend I hadn't gone out of my way for someone who had caused so much of a mess in my life.

As I walked back down the hall, I cast a glance to the side, where there was a door slightly open, leading to her living room. It was also pretty tidy. It was small, but from the angle I was at, I could see a large green sofa and a coffee table, and it looked comfortable enough. I could also see the back door that led out to the yard I'd just been looking at. Further down the hall, there was another open door to the kitchen, where Katie was filling up her kettle.

"Do you want a cuppa before you go?" she asked as she put the kettle down and flicked it on to boil. There was a hint of hope in her eyes, but since we'd hardly said a word to each other the whole way back to her flat, I didn't see much point in staying longer.

Shaking my head, I said, "No, thank you. I need to get back."

She nodded, wrapping her arms around herself as if she was cold. She'd taken off her jacket and it rested on the kitchen counter behind her. She took a tiny step towards me. "Cal, I really am grateful that you picked me up today. I know I don't deserve it after what I did, but I appreciate that you came for me anyway. I'm going to stay away from the drink now and I'm going to keep on getting better."

Offering her a small smile, I said, "I hope you do."

She smiled back, but then it faded. "I'm sorry. Not just for what I did recently, but for everything. When I first met you and we were spending so much time together, I... it was some of the most fun I ever had." Her smile spread slowly across her face again, as if she was remembering. "Back then, I still didn't know what I was doing with my life, neither of us did, but that was part of the fun. There was nothing to get in the way of having a good time, and... we did."

I was twenty-three when I met Katie, and just about as fucked-up as I'd ever been. I was alone, I was going nowhere, and all I wanted to do was get drunk. Katie was... edgy. She had a sharp, sarcastic sense of humour, and amongst the group of friends we spent time with, she was my favourite. I never wanted to get into a relationship with her, but we had good sex and she made me laugh.

"When I found out I was pregnant, I... I guess I hoped that you and I would be able to make a go of things," she said quietly. "That was what

I wanted, and when you said you would try... it was the happiest I'd ever been."

A sliver of guilt ran through me. I was a prick when I found out she was pregnant. Didn't believe the baby was mine. Didn't want anything to do with him or her. But once Aiden was proven to be mine, I did step up. I felt like I owed her that much. It wasn't clear to me that she was that happy to have me in her life, though, and we didn't really act like a couple either. We lived together, and we looked after Aiden together, but we didn't feel like a family. Not to me, anyway.

"The truth is," Katie went on, "neither of us were very good parents. We kept Aiden alive, but it became obvious pretty quickly that you didn't want me, and neither of us wanted Aiden the way we should have."

Her words felt like physical hits to my body, but only because they were the truth, and the sliver of guilt I'd felt intensified. I hated that I had ever been such an ungrateful piece of shit because Aiden was one of the best things to ever happen to me, and it had taken me way too long to see that. She was right. We took care of him, and when she left, I continued to do so, but it was care in the most basic form.

"Do you have a point?" I asked, my jaw tense because I wasn't enjoying her trip down memory lane. I didn't enjoy any reminder of how useless I used to be.

"I do." Katie sighed. "I know it wasn't clear, especially because I left, but I loved Aiden. I still do. And I will always regret walking out because maybe if I hadn't, everything would be different. Maybe you and I would be together. It's funny, but it wasn't until I saw you a few weeks back that I let myself remember how much you meant to me. How much I wanted you to love me."

Love. The one word that always shot terror into me because... love? Love meant pain. Love meant being let down. Love meant lives being shattered.

I didn't know she felt that way about me. She never showed it. And I didn't feel that way about her. Not even close.

Katie was never home. She was never safety. She was never anything but the mother of my child.

Shannen.

Shannen was all of those things.

She was... everything.

What the fuck are you doing, you gigantic twat. Call her. Fix it.

I'd been so close the night before. So close to calling her and talking to her and trying to sort things out, but Katie called and then... I wimped out. I got distracted. I put my focus on something else so I wouldn't have to deal with it.

"You didn't, did you?" Katie asked quietly. "You didn't love me."

Slowly, I shook my head. I didn't think I needed to confirm it with words.

"It took me a long time to accept that," Katie said. "I always hoped that maybe one day, I could come back, and we could try again, but... I didn't realise how bad things would get. For both of us. I didn't know how desperate I'd become and that I'd..." she trailed off, not needing to finish the sentence.

She didn't know she'd one day sell me out for money.

"Anyway," she said, shaking her head, "I will always regret every bad choice I made regarding Aiden, especially leaving him behind. And I would really like to be a part of his life again one day. But not for a while yet."

Nodding slowly, I said, "Let's just see how things go. You need to get *your* life back on track, and then we'll see."

She gave a soft smile. "I have your number, so... I'll check in now and again and maybe we can figure something out in time."

That was a change I didn't want, not really. I wanted Aiden to have a family, and Katie was his family, but she had a long way to go until she could prove she was reliable. I wouldn't keep Aiden from her if she really wanted to see him, but I also didn't want to put him through anything else. She did say it wouldn't be for a while, though, and I would definitely hold her to that.

"Yeah," I told her. "In time." Before an awkward silence could fall, I added, "I should go. Look after yourself, okay?"

"I will." She offered another small smile as she walked me to the door, and as I stepped outside, she said, "Drive carefully."

It had started raining again, and I nodded before running down the path to my car. Once inside, I offered Katie a wave before she shut the door, and I sighed.

I'd spent more than an hour in Katie's company, and although we hardly spoke most of the time, I learned more about her in the last five minutes than I did when we lived in the same flat. She had never shown any signs of feeling anything for me other than resentment that I'd knocked her up back then. We were friends at best, and that had felt like a stretch sometimes. For all the time we'd once spent together, I never really knew her, and she knew me even less. I was not ready to trust her; that would take a long time. But what she had done was show me the very obvious difference between what I wanted and what I didn't want.

I'd pissed away my relationship with Shannen because I panicked. Because I didn't think I deserved it.

I still wasn't completely sure I *did* deserve it, but I wanted it. I wanted back what I'd thrown away, and that relentless need to have her back in my life had never been stronger.

I'd tried a half-arsed life with someone I didn't really want, and it had failed.

And then I'd let myself care about someone, tried letting someone in, and for every bit of discomfort it caused as I fought against what I'd always done, I found something I needed. Found someone who accepted all of my shit and still wanted me.

I pulled my phone out of my jeans pocket and looked at the screen. Could I call Shannen now? Could I call her and just... tell her how I felt?

The idea shot a crippling fear through me because that was still too much. Too hard. But I could tell her I wanted to see her. That we needed to talk.

I had to.

This time, I didn't give myself a second to think myself out of it. I unlocked the phone, scrolled to her name, and hit the call button, my heart hammering against my chest. For a second, it reminded me of the first time I'd ever called her, the night after we slept together for the first time. When she didn't answer right away, I'd almost hung up, but then she did and... it was so worth it.

This time, though, she didn't answer. The phone kept ringing until her voicemail kicked in. My instinct was to hang up because she obviously didn't want to talk to me, but instead, I waited. I wasn't sure if it was the right thing to do, but I needed to tell her what was on my mind.

Once the beep sounded, I took a deep breath, and said, "Shan... I... I'm really sorry about yesterday at school. I'm sorry for acting like a dickhead. I just... I miss you, and... can we talk? Please, call me when you can. Please."

As I hung up, I felt both better and worse. I was glad I'd taken the step to speak to her, but what if she didn't call? What if I'd taken too long? What if my stupid jealousy had made her see I wasn't worth it after all?

I threw my phone onto the passenger seat, took my car keys out of my jacket pocket, and started the car. Hopefully, by the time I got back to Guy's, Shannen would have called me back.

Chapter 24

Shannen

As THE DOCTOR LEFT me to straighten up my clothes after wiping the gel off my belly, I burst into the tears I'd been holding back all afternoon. It was just after six p.m. now, and I'd been waiting around in the hospital for most of the afternoon. I'd been checked over, had my blood pressure and some bloods taken, been asked a ton of questions, and finally had an ultrasound to check the baby was okay.

Several short minutes ago, I'd been told that my baby was absolutely fine, and that I was around eleven weeks pregnant.

I'd heard its heartbeat, and the sound was the best thing I had ever heard in my whole life.

My mum had sobbed beside me, while I'd just stared at the screen, amazed and overwhelmed because I was in the middle of the strangest day I had ever had.

And I'd had a lot of strange days over the last few months.

This one had whizzed by in a blur. I'd left my parents' house feeling completely destroyed by my father's revelation, but the second that car had rammed into mine and I'd woken up in an ambulance, all I could think about was whether my baby was okay. I didn't even care whether or not I was hurt; I was still numb. I just wanted to know my baby was safe. I wasn't bleeding, and other than my neck, nothing had really hurt apart from a tiny niggle in the bottom of my back.

My mum was called, and while I was being checked over, I'd given her my phone to call Gaby and asked her to pass on Guy's number, and to tell Nova too. I knew Cal would flip out once he heard that I'd been in an accident, but I still needed him to know, and I thought it would be better coming from Guy. I'd asked for Gaby to tell him to stay calm and that I would call him as soon as I could. Weirdly, Cal had already called me earlier and left me a voicemail, but with everything that had happened, I hadn't been able to listen to it yet.

Well, I *had* had time, but I was too afraid to listen when I was sitting in a hospital, waiting to find out if our baby, that he didn't even know about yet, was okay.

I was going to listen as soon as I left the hospital, but I still needed a minute to get my head straight.

I'd been struggling to figure out how I felt about having a baby since I found out I was pregnant, but at the prospect of losing it, it became extremely clear. It was a revelation because before I knew for sure, I was almost certain I wouldn't be able to continue with the pregnancy. That being a single parent at that time was not right for me. Yet, while I waited for the ultrasound, the idea that there might no longer be a decision to make was soul-destroying. And that told me everything I needed to know.

"It's been a long day, huh?" my mum said, reaching over for my hand. She had been right beside me the whole afternoon, and neither of us had spoken about what had happened with my dad yet. It was like that subject was on hold because we were trying to deal with one trauma at a time.

I nodded, wiping my eyes as I carefully swung my legs down off the couch and faced her. "I don't know what to do. I don't.... how am I supposed to process anything right now?"

"You're not, my darling." Mum smiled warmly. "We can't. I think what we both need is something to eat and a good night's sleep."

"I don't even feel hungry, but I suppose I should have something soon." I'd had a sandwich a few hours ago as I'd missed lunch, but I hadn't wanted that either; I'd been told to eat by a nurse.

"Shannen, I'm going to have to call your dad and let him know how you are, but I'm going to ask him to spend the night somewhere else. I'm not taking you back to your place. You'll stay with me."

Her tone was gentle but firm, and I knew she was right. My car had been taken to a local garage for repairs, so I wouldn't have it back for a while, and

I didn't want my mum to have to drive me all the way home. I wasn't ready to see my dad again yet, so I was glad Mum was going to ask him to sleep elsewhere. The house was big enough that he could have stayed out of our way, but it would be easier for all of us if he wasn't there. None of us were thinking straight enough to have a serious discussion anyway.

"That's okay with me," I told her. "But what happens afterwards? What will happen tomorrow?"

She shrugged. "I don't know. But the doctor told you to rest for a week, so if you want to go home, maybe I could stay with you?"

It hurt my heart how little she wanted to be in her own home, but I understood. And actually, to spend a week with my mum would be good. It wasn't for a nice reason, but I'd enjoy having her around, even if only for a few days.

"I'd like that," I told her. "I need to speak to my headteacher and let her know what's happening too."

God, I wasn't even planning on telling her I was pregnant until I'd got my head around it, but the doctor wanted me to take it easy for the next seven days just because of the fact that my body had been jolted pretty hard in the accident. They were booking me in for a scan at my local hospital at the end of the following week with the instruction that if anything felt wrong in that time, I should go to the hospital sooner and get checked out. I'd need to tell Iris everything to explain why I needed time off when I wasn't actually hurt from the accident.

"That can wait until tomorrow, sweetheart." Mum squeezed my hand. "Right now, I think we need to get out of here."

"Can I borrow some pyjamas?" I asked with a small laugh. "I don't have anything with me."

"Of course you can." Mum got to her feet and then helped me up too. "Before we go, I'm going to ring your dad.... and I think you need to call Cal."

Wiping my eyes of the last few tears, I nodded. Mum bent down to pick my handbag up from the floor and passed it to me, then we left the examination room and went out into the corridor.

"I'll just be a few minutes," Mum said, giving me a quick hug before walking further down the corridor. I sat on one of the plastic chairs outside the room I'd just left to pull out my phone.

Cal's voicemail was still waiting for me on the screen, and taking a deep breath, I unlocked the phone and pressed the few buttons needed to get to the message.

"Shan... I... I'm really sorry about yesterday at school. I'm sorry for acting like a dickhead. I just... I miss you, and... can we talk? Please, call me when you can. Please."

Tears prickled in my eyes again at the sound of his voice. He sounded so... dejected. Like he wanted me to call him, but he didn't really believe I would.

He said he missed me. And all I had wanted since the day we broke up was to hear that from him. To know I wasn't alone in this endless cycle of misery.

He'd sent that before he knew about the accident, so he wasn't just saying it because of that. He'd been thinking about it.

Knowing I was in hospital must have been driving him crazy. It had been more than four hours since Guy had let him know, and I could only imagine how he'd be feeling.

But... would he still feel the same when he found out I was pregnant? Would that scare him more than the idea of losing me?

A wave of tiredness washed over me. I was almost positive the human brain was not designed to cope with so much mindfuckery in one day. My mum was right. I needed to eat and sleep. Anything else could be dealt with in the morning.

But I *did* need to talk to Cal first.

Taking a deep breath to steady my nerves, I hit the button to call him.

It barely rang once before he answered.

"Shannen," he said, his voice frantic. "Jesus. Are you... how are you?"

His panic made my heart lurch, and I sniffled back my tears. "I'm okay, Cal," I whispered. "I'm okay."

"Where are you? Are you still at the hospital? Do you need a ride home?"

He was talking so fast I could barely understand him, and the stress in his tone told me he was probably pacing around whatever room he was in, his hand running through his hair like he always did when he was trying to keep his cool.

"I'll be leaving the hospital shortly and I'm going to stay at my mum's house tonight."

Although the thought wasn't conscious, I realised right away that I hadn't said 'my parents' house'. A strange insight into where my head was at. Shit. That was another thing I would need to explain to Cal.

"Okay," Cal said. "Okay. Shan... I know this is sort of not important after what you've been through, but... did you get my message?"

His tone had become tenser, and knowing the speed his brain ran through thoughts, I felt even more guilty for not calling him sooner.

"I did," I told him. "I miss you too. And we do need to talk."

He let out a deep sigh. "Fuck. Shan..." He stopped, and I heard his footsteps pacing. "I can't fucking stand this. I need to... I need to see you."

Closing my eyes, a tear slipped down my cheek because I wanted to see him too. I wanted to have him beside me, to talk to him, to just be close to him because even after everything, he was still the person I wanted on the bad days. The person I wanted to share all my good news with. As desperate as I was to see him, though, I didn't know if I could handle any more talking that night.

"Shannen. Please."

His voice was the softest and most desperate I'd ever heard it. And even though he had been terrified of meeting my parents, by asking to see me, he was also offering to put that aside. As far as he knew, my dad didn't have an issue with him, but he hadn't met my mum yet. And it was a pretty big deal that he was willing to forget his worries because he wanted to come to me.

"I... I'll need to ask my mum," I said, realising I sounded like a child asking if her friend could come over to play. Under the circumstances, though, I didn't want to assume anything. My mum had had a worse day than I had in some ways, and I didn't want to blindside her any more than she already had been. "A lot has happened today and there's so much I need to talk to you about. I have to make sure it's okay with her."

"Okay," he said. "But if it's not okay for me to come tonight, please can I see you as soon as you get home?"

"Yes."

There was a long pause, but it wasn't uncomfortable. In fact, just hearing his gentle breaths down the line was comforting. It made me feel connected to him properly for the first time in months. Just then, my mum began to walk back in my direction, and I said into the phone, "Cal, give me two seconds, okay?"

"Okay."

Covering up the mouthpiece, I stood up, raising a questioning eyebrow at my mum.

"He's going to stay in a hotel," she said. "He'll be gone by the time we get home."

I nodded. "I have Cal on the phone, and he wants to know if he can come over tonight. And... I'd really like to see him."

Mum smiled. "That's fine with me, sweetheart. Find out if he's hungry and I'll order us all a takeaway. If he leaves right away, the food won't be cold when he arrives."

I wrapped my free arm around my mum and squeezed her tight. She was falling apart, but that didn't mean she was going to hide away or keep me from doing what I needed to do. "Thank you," I whispered.

As I pulled away from her, I uncovered the mouthpiece of my phone and said, "Cal? Mum said you can come, and she also wants to know what you want to eat."

He chuckled lightly. "You know what I like. I'll eat whatever you have. And thank you. Both of you."

"Shit," I said suddenly. "Will Guy be able to watch Aiden for you?"

"I already asked him earlier. The two of them have been playing board games all afternoon, and Aiden isn't in a rush to end his winning streak, so I said he could stay over."

I laughed, then added, "Does Aiden know what happened today?"

"No. I didn't want to worry him. He was having fun with Guy, and if he found out you were hurt, he'd have been as stressed out as me."

My heart swelled at his words. Not because I wanted anyone to be worried about me but because of the reassurance that the closeness the three of us had built was still intact.

"Okay," I said. "I will text you my mum's address and I'll see you in an hour or so."

"See you soon."

Chapter 25

Shannen

WHEN THE DOORBELL RANG, announcing Cal's arrival, my heart began to beat harder than it had in a long time. I'd been back at my mum's for almost an hour, and I was now rocking a pair of her pyjamas since I had none of my own with me. I hadn't dared to look in a mirror, but I was confident I looked terrible. Tiredness, stress, and a whole bunch of other emotions ran rampant through me, but I made my way to the door, the most nervous I had ever been to see him.

I'd been quiet while I waited, wondering what things he wanted to say to me, knowing I had a lot to explain to him too. If he had come all this way because he wanted to talk, I was going to have to be honest with him about my dad's role in our break-up.

Not to mention the small matter of me being pregnant.

Shaking my head to clear the thoughts for now, I opened the door.

And there he was.

My beautiful, gorgeous Cal, wearing his trademark jeans and leather jacket. His black hair was messy, letting me know I was right, and he had been running his hand through it a lot. His chocolate brown eyes softened as they fell on me, and his perfect lips quirked into a half smile; the one that had always made my legs tremble.

Tears filled my eyes, and I smiled up at him. "Hey."

Without a word, he reached out and pulled me against him. I slipped my hands inside his jacket like I had so many times before, breathing in the scent of leather and nestling against his chest. I felt his heart beating almost as hard as mine, and I held him tighter, like I couldn't get him close enough.

"Are you okay?" he asked into the top of my head.

That was a bigger question than he could possibly understand at that moment, but I knew he was asking about the accident more than anything, so I said, "Yeah. Kind of. I... I have... there are some things I need to tell you, though."

The idea of telling him everything I needed to made me feel sick, but he said, "Ssshh. It's okay. Let's eat first and then we can talk."

I figured he could smell the strong scent of the pizza wafting from inside the house. It had arrived a couple of minutes before him, and I nodded, letting go of him but taking his hand in mine. Once we were in the hallway, Cal paused to take off his shoes. It wasn't a requirement, but the cream carpets were absolutely pristine, and he had been out in the rain. I took his jacket, trying not to stare at how good he looked in the long-sleeved grey T-shirt he wore, and hung it on the rack by the door.

The smell of the food from the living room made my stomach rumble; I'd ordered Cal's favourite, Hawaiian, plus a meat feast for me, and Mum had gone for pepperoni. As I took him down the hallway to the living room, I squeezed his hand gently, knowing he must be nervous about meeting my mum for the first time.

As we entered the living room, Mum was sitting on one of the sofas, opening up the pizza boxes. I glanced at Cal, who was looking around the room. A slight frown crossed his face, and I realised he was probably expecting my dad to be there too. I hadn't specified that he wouldn't be, and I wasn't quite sure how to explain that just yet. In case he asked, though, I said, "My dad isn't here tonight. He's... I'll tell you about it later."

Cal nodded, and as I walked us around to the side of the sofa, I said, "Mum, this is Cal." I smiled up at him, hoping to ease the nerves on his face. "Cal, this is my mum, Annie."

Mum stood up and took a few steps towards us. "It's nice to finally meet you, Cal," she said. She took his free hand and squeezed it gently. Not in a handshake, almost like she already knew him and was comfortable enough to reach out to him. He seemed to relax at her calm demeanour.

"It's nice to meet you too," he said.

Mum smiled as she let go of his hand. "Come and take a seat before the food gets cold."

I threw my mum a grateful smile, and she arched an eyebrow that plainly said, 'Good choice'. I stifled a laugh by biting my lip, and we all sat down, me in the middle of her and Cal. Mum handed plates along to us and we all tucked in.

Although I'd been hungry, once I started eating, I found I wasn't as into it as I should have been considering how little food I'd had that day. I forced down three slices of pizza, enjoying how easily the conversation was flowing. Mum was asking Cal questions about how his work was, how Aiden was, and whether they were settled into their new flat. With each exchange, Cal relaxed more and more, and I loved how at ease my mum was making him feel.

Once we'd eaten as much as we could manage, Mum went to the kitchen to make us some drinks. When she returned with a coffee for Cal and a tea each for me and her, I said, "I know I'm a fully grown adult, but is it okay if Cal and I go upstairs? I really want to lie down and..." I trailed off.

Mum smiled, fully understanding that I needed to be alone with him so we could talk. "Of course," she said with a small laugh. "I'm going to sit down here and read for a while, but it won't be long until I go up too. It's been a long day."

That was for sure. Twenty-four hours ago, I was at home trying to figure out what to do about my pregnancy. Now, I was at my mum's house, my dad had been thrown out, and I was about to begin a week of rest after a minor car accident.

Most of all, though, I had Cal beside me. I wasn't sure if he would still be there once I was done telling him everything I needed to, but for the time being, he was with me, and I was going to do everything I could to enjoy the closeness.

"Okay," I said, standing up. "In that case, I will see you in the morning."

Cal stood too and said to my mum, "Thank you for letting me come over after what happened today."

She smiled again as she looked up at him. "Anyone who cares enough about my daughter to rush to her side when she needs them is welcome here anytime."

I felt my cheeks warm at her words, and I turned around to give her a hug. "Love you."

"I love you too, sweetheart. Now, go and get some rest!"

Cal and I took our drinks, and I led Cal out of the living room, into the hallway, and up the stairs to my room. Of course, it wasn't really *my* room, it was one of the guest rooms, but it was the one I was always given. It was at the very end of the hall, next to the bathroom, although it had its own en-suite. I liked it because it looked out onto the back of the house to the large garden and the surrounding fields, a couple of which also belonged to my parents. The view was relaxing, and I felt instantly calmed as I walked in. The room itself was painted a soft lilac, and the bed was enormous. Easily big enough for three or four people to sleep in it. It was covered with the snuggliest duvet, and just looking at it made me want to curl up inside it and fall asleep.

It had been a long time since Cal and I had been in a bedroom together, and tension crept over the room. It was coming from him more than me, and I could almost hear him wondering whether he should sit on the bed or take a seat on the chair by the window.

I needed him wrapped around me, and although he was the one who'd called to say he missed me, I wasn't sure if it was too soon for that.

Taking the lead, I walked around the bed and placed my cup on the bedside table, on the window side. I sat on the edge of the bed and then lifted my legs so I was propped up against the pillows. Looking over at Cal, I said, "Sit down."

His eyes flicked around the room as if still unsure. After a moment, he placed his own cup on the bedside table nearest him and then sat down on the bed too. There was a sizeable gap between the two of us, and he looked over at me. "Can I please hold you?"

I nodded. We both shuffled to the middle of the bed, where he wrapped his arm around me. Right away, I nestled against his chest the way I had earlier. Our bodies were as close as they could be without me mounting him, and I was strongly considering wrapping my leg across his like I had done so many times before. Instead, I wound my arm across his stomach, my thumb almost subconsciously moving up and down, lightly stroking over his T-shirt.

"I know there are things you want to talk about," I said quietly, "and I have things to tell you too. But right now, I want to lie here with you for a bit, just like this."

He kissed the top of my head. "I'd like that too, but I've been thinking about this... about seeing you all day. I..." He paused, pulling away from me a little. He kept his arm around me, but he shuffled very slightly back so I had to tilt my head to look at him.

His eyes were intense on mine, and I tracked my gaze across his face, taking him in. It felt like forever since I'd allowed myself to do this. To really look at him, to study his features, from his mesmerising eyes right down to the tiny scar on his chin. I still wasn't sure what he wanted to say, but it felt somehow monumental that he had been the one to reach out. That he'd done so before he even knew I'd been in an accident. He hadn't come for me because he'd felt like he could have lost me forever. He hadn't come back because I was pregnant. He'd come back for a reason I was yet to understand.

I just wasn't sure whether those reasons would hold when he heard the things I had to tell him.

He reached up and placed his palm against my cheek, his thumb stroking my skin softly. "For the last twenty-four hours, I feel like I've been in a nightmare. It started yesterday when I saw you, and then a whole load of other things happened that I need to tell you about, but before I get to any of that, I want to start from the beginning. From when I saw that teacher touch you." His jaw stiffened as if he were replaying it, and then he shook his head. "That's not really the beginning. The beginning is what happened when I got back after being arrested." I wanted to argue that he wasn't arrested, but for the purposes of this conversation, it was really just semantics. Either way, he was taken away from me in handcuffs, and when he came back, everything was different. The memory caused a shiver to ripple through me as I thought of *that* conversation, the one that led to me sobbing myself to sleep. The one that led to the end of us.

"I knew the moment I told you it was over that I'd fucked up," Cal said, dropping his hand from my cheek down to my shoulder, then rubbing slowly up and down my arm as if he'd felt my chill. "I said a lot of things that night I wish I hadn't. And every day since then, I kept thinking it'd get easier. That I'd get used to not being with you."

I nodded. "Yeah. But it didn't get easier. It got harder."

"Yeah. I spent a lot of time trying to convince myself I'd made the right decision. That us being apart would be better for you in every way, especially with work and those crazy bitches who think it's their right to know what's going on in your life. They still look at me like I'm a piece of shit."

"I'm still dealing with it too. Not from many people, but there are a few mums who I can feel watching me every time you're in the playground, or anytime I'm near Aiden, like they're checking to see if I'm showing him any favouritism." I shrugged. "But I realised it really doesn't matter what I do. They're determined to see what they want to see, and if that's how they want to live their lives, that's up to them."

Cal slid his hand down my arm, linking our fingers together. "I wanted to tell you the second you left Guy's house that day that I'd made a mistake, but I was so angry that I'd been accused of something I didn't do and that you'd considered whether or not it was possible." He lifted my hand and brought it to his lips, softly kissing the back. "You had every right to consider it."

Shaking my head, I shuffled back from him ever so slightly, sitting up straighter so I could look at him properly. "Cal, I didn't consider it. I mean... I did, but not exactly in the way you think. We hadn't been together for long, and I'd just learned about all the things you did when you were younger. Yes, for a second, I wondered if it could be true, but it was only for a second. As much as you think I was right to consider it, you were right to be angry. I just... I would have preferred if you'd been angry without letting me go. I wish you'd given it some time so we could talk about it properly. But you shut down."

His head dipped, and he sighed, the light in his eyes dimming. "That's what I do, Shan. That's what I've always done. I wanted to be different with you. But it hurt that you doubted me, and all I could think about was how, once you had one doubt, more would follow, and you'd never be able to forget that accusation. After you said you were scared about what I was capable of when I told you what I did to Edward, I thought both things would always be on your mind and it would spill over into everything."

"You didn't give me a chance."

"No. I didn't." He slowly looked up at me again. Cal had never been anything but honest with me, even though it had sometimes taken him a while to tell me the things I needed to know. However, in that moment, it was as if I could see inside his soul and read the truth in those brown eyes that had always anchored me. "I've regretted it every damn day since. I wanted to tell you I was sorry, but there's always this one thing that never fully goes away. That no matter what I do, I won't ever deserve you."

My heart clenched at his words. Why couldn't he stop doing this? Why did he put me on a pedestal I didn't deserve? I wasn't special enough to warrant the constant self-loathing he heaped on himself. It was real for him, a genuine fear that he was beneath me, but I wasn't sure what else I could do to reassure him that of all the people I'd ever dated, he was above every single one of them.

"Cal," I said, dropping my head back for a second before looking at him again, "I'm just a person. You keep focusing on where I come from, but that's irrelevant. Whether I grew up in a castle or a council flat, I'm still human, and I still make mistakes."

"I know." Letting out a long breath, he said, "The thing is, though, the whole time we've been apart, I convinced myself that after how much I hurt you, there would never be any way you could forgive me. That you'd be better off with someone who didn't cause you so much pain." He swallowed, and I watched his Adam's apple bob as he prepared himself for what he wanted to say next. "I also convinced myself that you'd probably moved on by now. That you were seeing someone else. And then yesterday happened." Running a hand through his hair, he let go of me and stood up. It was as if the recollection of David's hands on me for a few seconds had flipped a switch in him, one that made him restless and anxious in equal measure. "I know it was nothing," he said. "I know I overreacted to him touching you, but I *hated* it. I wanted to break his fingers so he couldn't do it again."

My stomach fluttered again, and I internally wondered what was wrong with me that him behaving like a Neanderthal excited me. Jealousy was a pointless emotion, an ugly one. And it wasn't as if he didn't know how to show he cared any other way. Maybe it was the protectiveness of it that affected me. That I knew nobody would ever treat me inappropriately with him around because he would rip them apart.

"He doesn't touch me regularly, Cal. He asked me if I wanted to go out with him one time, I said no, and that was the end of it."

His eyes flashed dangerously, but he gave a slow nod, accepting my words. As he calmed, he came back over to the bed and sat down again, his legs out in front of him. He stared at me for a minute, as if trying to figure out what his next words would be. Instead of letting him struggle, I moved across the bed to get closer to him.

"Cal." Unable to stop myself, I carefully lifted my leg over both of his, so I was straddling his lap; it was one of the only ways I knew to get his full attention because we were face to face and he couldn't easily slip away from me. I put my hands on his shoulders, looking right into his eyes. "I never wanted us to end. That wasn't my choice. I had to stay away from you because being near you when we aren't together hurts. Seeing you and not having you wrap me up in your arms or kiss me was like being physically tortured and I couldn't stand it. And I didn't feel like I could tell you I wanted things to go back to how they used to be because you'd made this decision. That you couldn't trust me anymore, or that you thought I didn't trust you. And I didn't... I *don't* know how to change that."

His eyes sparkled slightly. "I trust you, Shannen. And that is scary to me. I know you trust me too, and that is even fucking scarier because it means I have so much more to lose if I somehow let you down. I ended us because I didn't trust myself not to keep hurting you."

"The only way you hurt me was by telling me you didn't want us anymore." I blinked, feeling tears beginning to fall the way they inevitably did when I cast my mind back to that night. He might as well have reached into my chest and torn my heart out because that was how it had felt. And not just my heart, but my soul. The feeling of emptiness he left me with was something I still hadn't been able to shake completely. There was always something missing, and while I'd tried to fill it with ice cream, cake, chocolate, and occasionally alcohol, Cal was the only thing that fit into that space in my heart.

Cal placed his hands on my waist, one slowly sliding upwards to my shoulder, then to the back of my neck. He closed his eyes as his fingers curled gently into my hair. "I always wanted us," he said softly. "Always."

"So why did you let it go so easily?"

"It wasn't easy. It was..." He paused, opening his eyes and looking right into mine. "You scare me, Shan, because I don't have any control of anything when it comes to you. Since the night we met, you haven't been off my mind for a second. That was dangerous for me. To care about you. To *let* myself care about you. And the more I cared, and the more you wanted me, the more I wanted to run from it. Except, I *didn't* want to run from it, and that scared me more. That day, you gave me the perfect excuse. A reason to get out so I wouldn't have to deal with my shit. I made it your fault so I could keep believing that I was right. That feelings always lead to things falling apart." He took another deep breath, the hand in my hair moving back to my cheek to swipe away my tears. "The only thing that fell apart was me after I let you go." His hand on my waist pulled me closer to him, and even though I had no idea which way this would go, I wound my arms around his neck. "I didn't have a perfect family for a long time. I had a dysfunctional one for much longer than it was good. But there was just enough of the good that I remember what it feels like when something is right. What it feels like to be around people who make all of the other crap in your life fade away. And I know now that I should have trusted it. Should have told you what I wanted to when I had the chance. When I heard Gaby say that you'd been in an accident today, everything stopped. I couldn't function until I knew you were okay, and all that kept going through my head was that I should have made the call I made this afternoon so much sooner, because if anything had happened to you today, you wouldn't have known."

"Known what?" I asked, my brows pulling together.

I could almost hear his heart thudding, and his hand shook slightly against my cheek. "That I love you."

I drew in a sharp intake of breath, my eyes looking deep into his.

He'd never said that before. Not to me. I wasn't sure he'd ever said it to anyone other than his family when he was a kid.

Even though I'd felt with every single bit of me that he loved me, hearing him say it was something else because I knew his fears. I understood why he believed those words always led to disaster.

I wanted to enjoy it. To bask in the sound and let it play over and over in my head, but with all I'd learned that day... would my telling him only compound his belief?

Shit. You need to say something before he freaks out.

Blinking hard a few times to regain my focus, I rested my forehead against his. Because regardless of what happened next, he'd told me the thing I'd been waiting to hear. The thing I'd *needed* to hear. And for me, nothing had changed. Cal was still everything.

"I love you too," I whispered. "I love you so much."

Dropping his hand from my face, he put his arms around my back and pulled me as close to him as I could get, holding me tight, and I held him back just as hard.

"Fuck," he breathed, and now I was closer, I could feel how hard he was trembling. How much it had taken for him to say it.

I slipped my hand into his hair, my other still on the back of his neck, and his mouth was barely half an inch from mine. Leaning in, his lips gave the lightest brush against my cheek, then trailed agonisingly slow kisses along my jaw until, finally, his lips touched mine. It was only the softest flutter, but it made my pulse race. As his eyes met mine again, his lips slowly curved into a grin before he captured my mouth with his again, this time in a way that let me know how much he'd missed me. The way he used to kiss me every time we'd been apart, like he'd been starved and was finally given sustenance.

One of his hands moved down, gliding underneath my pyjama top, and his rough palm met the bottom of my back, making me gasp slightly because, God, I'd missed that feeling. The sensation of his hands on my skin. I wanted more. Wanted to let him undress me, touch me everywhere, and I wanted to kiss every single inch of his perfect body, but an echo of the doctor's words ran through my mind.

"Rest. No exertion for the next few days."

He didn't specify whether that included sex, but the way I wanted Cal in that moment, I knew I couldn't risk it. I'd been lucky not to have been hurt and that my baby was safe. I needed to follow the doctor's orders so as not to push my luck any further.

"Cal," I whispered against his lips. "We need to slow down."

"Mmhmm," he murmured, brushing my lips with his again. "I just... I've really missed kissing you."

I laughed lightly. "I missed that too," I told him, kissing him one more time. "But there's something I need to talk to you about."

Cal nodded. "Yeah, I have something else too." His eyes dimmed slightly again, and a ripple of dread pulsed through me.

What could he have to tell me?

Oh, God. Had there been someone else for him? He'd become fixated on the idea that I was seeing someone, but was that because he'd done the same? Had there been a fling, a one-night stand? Something more?

I hated the very possibility of it, but just as he'd had no claim over me while we'd been apart, I had none over him either.

Trying not to get carried away with my racing thoughts, I said, "Okay. Which one of us should go first?"

And which thing did I tell him first? It was all important, and he needed to know all of it, but where the hell was I supposed to start?

"You go," Cal said, pressing his lips to mine again. "It's your turn."

The baby. You need to tell him about the baby first.

Taking a deep breath, I lifted myself off Cal's lap and sat beside him again. Opening my mouth to speak, Cal and I both jumped as we heard my mum shout from downstairs. "How dare you! You don't get to come back here tonight after you promised us some space!"

Chapter 26

Cal

Shannen's face paled as she stared at her bedroom door. Until her mum had shouted, I hadn't heard a thing from downstairs. I'd been too wrapped up in Shannen. In telling her how I felt, and in being able to hold her against me, kiss her. Nothing could have interrupted the moment.

Until it did.

"Shan, what..." I began, and she shuffled to the end of the bed, then stood up as her mum shouted again.

"Get out, Steven!"

Shannen's dad hadn't been in the house when I'd arrived, so he must have come in while we'd been upstairs. Shannen had said she would explain where he was later, but we hadn't got to it yet. Was that what she'd been about to tell me?

"Cal, can you please just wait here?" she said, her face continuing to pale so much I thought she might collapse.

I jumped up and stood in front of her, my hands on her shoulders. "What's going on?" I asked, watching her with concern.

She shook her head. "I... it's... I need to help my mum to get him out of here and then I'll explain."

"Why do you need him out of here? What happened?"

She stared up at me, tears starting to fall from her eyes. "You know what? Just come with me. You'll probably hear the answer on the way, and whatever you don't hear, I'll tell you when we get down there."

She took my hand, and I followed her, confused, as she led me down the hallway to the stairs. What was strange was that it was only her mum shouting. Her dad was obviously down there, but he hadn't raised his voice.

"You have done enough for one day!" she snapped. "I asked you for one night so I could think, and you can't even give me that!"

As we neared the bottom of the stairs, I heard him reply, "I just want to see Shannen."

"She doesn't want to see you. I told you that on the phone!"

"Annie, we all need to talk. All of us."

Silence fell over the living room as Shannen and I entered, and Steven's face dropped on seeing me. He took a few steps backwards in surprise, his eyes fixed on me. The last time I'd seen him, we left things in a good place, so why was he looking at me like I was a threat?

What the fuck is going?

"Happy now?" Annie asked, rounding on him. "Shannen is supposed to be resting, and you've made her get up."

"You didn't say Cal was here," he said. "I mean, I saw a car outside, but I didn't think-"

"What else is new?" Annie snapped. The relaxed, friendly woman I'd spoken to earlier was now being borderline psychotic towards her own husband.

Beside me, Shannen was shaking, and her hand had gone cold in mine, so I let go of it and wrapped my arm around her waist, bringing her in close to me.

"Dad, please," Shannen said quietly. "I thought you weren't coming home tonight."

His eyes flicked back to me. Considering he'd said he wanted to see Shannen, he seemed to be overlooking her, even though she'd just spoken to him.

"I don't know what's happened," I said, looking at Steven, "but it seems like you aren't meant to be here tonight. Maybe you should come back in the morning."

He bristled, his eyes darkening a little as if he wanted to ask me who the hell I thought I was, because I, someone who wasn't part of his family, had just told him to leave his own house. However, his expression relaxed almost as quickly as it had angered.

"He doesn't know?" Steven asked, looking at Annie.

Annie turned to look at Shannen, who now had her arms wrapped around me, not looking at anyone. When Annie's gaze fell on me, she closed her eyes before turning back to Steven. "We've barely been home from the hospital for two hours. We ate, and they had other things to talk about."

Steven nodded, looking at Shannen and me. "Are you two back together?"

We hadn't said the words, but there was kissing, so I said, "Yeah. We are."

He gave a weak smile. "I'm pleased for you."

My eyes narrowed. It sounded like he meant it, but I still didn't know why he was enemy number one, and somehow, I was beginning to get the feeling that whatever had caused the argument had something to do with me.

"Shannen," Annie said, walking over to us. "You need to sit down, sweetheart." She gently prised Shannen from my side and led her to one of the three sofas in the room.

I knew she had had an accident, and she looked exhausted, but she hadn't been injured. Her mum had told her to rest earlier and that she'd be there if she needed her. At the time, I hadn't thought anything of it, but she was ghostly pale now. Was her father really causing her this much stress? And if so, why?

Being the only person in the room who was in the dark was putting me on edge, but I wasn't really in a position to push for answers. I was lucky Annie had been so accepting of me when Steven hadn't at first. Even though he looked worried about something, he did at least seem okay with Shannen and me being together now, and I didn't want to risk pissing him off. At the same time, though, Shannen and Annie were agitated with him in the house. I didn't like how shaky and ill Shannen had looked since his arrival, and Annie appeared ready to explode at any second.

"Since you're here," Annie said, sitting down next to Shannen but keeping her focus on Steven, "maybe you'd like to tell Cal what this is all about." Her eyes were cold, and I wondered if this was normal for them. My gut feeling told me it wasn't because if it was, Shannen would have been used to scenes like this. She looked like she was in pain. Not physical pain, but as if this whole situation was tearing her up inside.

I wasn't sure whether to sit beside her or stay on my feet for whatever Steven was about to say.

Steven was a big guy. Tall, well-built, and he clearly worked out. For his age, he was fit, and probably a bit intimidating to some people. Not to me, but to some people. He also had an intense stare, a seriousness. I imagined it would have scared the shit out of Shannen's previous boyfriends, especially when she was younger. Behind it, though, he looked as broken as the women in his life. Even so, my defences shot up because Annie had all but confirmed whatever this was, it would affect me in some way.

"Cal, can you sit down, please?" Steven said.

And have you talk down to me? I don't think so.

"I'm okay here," I told him, straightening up. "What's this all about?"

Steven's cheeks puffed out, then he huffed a breath and squared his shoulders as he faced me. "I already explained this to my wife and daughter today, so I'm going to give you the quick version. I hope... I hope you can all eventually find a way to forgive me."

In spite of his stiff, almost confrontational stance, he gave off the impression that he wished he'd never come back to the house. It was right there in the shake of his hands by his sides and the caution in his eyes as he looked at me. In my head, I was already prepared for a fight, and I guessed that was clear in the way I was staring at him.

"I'm the one who is responsible for getting you into trouble with the police," he said, his voice steady. "You know I didn't think you were good enough for Shannen before I met you, and when I found out what you'd done in the past, I was afraid you were going to hurt her. So, I spoke to Scott McCalden about you, and he was already looking to dig up some dirt on you. He found your ex, and... I paid her to make the report against you."

For a long time, I didn't move, struggling with the belief that he'd really said that. That the man in front of me, who'd said he was happy to give me a chance, had been the one to fuck with my life. I'd known about Scott's part in it for a while, but I hadn't expected there to be an extra piece to the puzzle.

223

So, Scott had been trying to dig up something about me, and he'd used Shannen's dad to put the plan into action. I knew that piece of shit wouldn't part with his own money just to get me into trouble, so it made sense that someone else had been in on it. *That* was what had been bugging me the whole time. Scott hated me, and he'd hated that I had the nerve to be with someone in his inner circle, but to spend his own money to get rid of me? Getting Shannen's dad involved was the kind of snaky thing he'd do. Even better was that he hadn't had to ask because Steven had gone to him.

Perfect Mr Morgan had gone to an officer of the law and hadn't been afraid to break it.

What other shady shit had they both been getting up to that Steven hadn't thought twice about asking Scott for help? Was this a one-off for him, or had they done things like his before? I would have put money on Scott being corrupt, but not Shannen's dad.

I moved my head from side to side a couple of times to ease the tension that had crept up my neck and across my shoulders. "You gave a woman you had never met two and a half thousand pounds to make a report about me?" I asked, my tone dangerously low.

His eyebrows dipped, and from behind me, Shannen said, "I thought you gave her five thousand?"

"I did," Steven said. "Well, I gave Scott five thousand."

I laughed out loud. "You gave Scott five grand and he only paid up half of it. This is fucking incredible." Not only had Scott screwed Katie over, he'd also gained himself a few quid at the same time, and it wasn't like he needed it.

"Cal, why did you think it was two and a half thousand?"

Shit. Shannen's question reminded me that I hadn't told her about Katie yet. I was planning to before all of this kicked off, but Steven's arrival had taken over.

Turning all the way around to face her, I said, "Because Katie told me."

Her eyes narrowed in confusion. "You've spoken to Katie?"

I hadn't told her about this for what I thought was a good reason, but the way she was looking at me told me I was wrong. I just hoped it wasn't so much that she couldn't forgive me.

"I... I've seen her," I said, sinking to my knees in front of her. "Shan..."

"You've seen her?" Her tone was a mix of snappy, hurt, and panicked, and I reached out for her hand, which she quickly snatched away. "What... when?"

Annie was also looking at me questioningly, and I felt like the worst kind of prick. Neither of them needed this today, but since it seemed to be a day of confessions, I sighed. "I saw her today."

Behind me, Steven barked out a laugh. "You were trying to take the moral high ground with me, and you've been lying to Shannen too?"

As much as I wanted to explain everything to Shannen, Steven's words had made the slightest nudge at my inner psycho. My not telling her what I knew was vastly different from paying someone off to ruin a life. For him to compare something I did for her protection to something he did to destroy me—even if he *thought* it was for her protection—had flicked a switch.

Dangerously slowly, I turned around to face him, my eyes heavy with warning. I got back to my feet again. "Making assumptions about me is what got you into this shit in the first place. Keep your mouth shut, or you're going to have a much bigger problem to deal with."

"Do not threaten me, Callum." His eyes darkened again. "I made a mistake, but you will not disrespect me in my own house."

"If that's a problem for you, I'm happy to take this outside." I took one more step towards him. "You paid someone to lie to the police about me. If it wasn't for the fact that Scott is such a two-faced dick, I could still be under investigation!"

"What do you mean?" he asked.

Shaking my head, I said, "He didn't tell you Katie retracted the statement?"

"No. As far as I knew, she made the allegation and then you and Shannen broke up. After that..."

"You didn't give a crap," I interrupted. "You got what you wanted and it was problem solved for you. The truth is, Scott took five grand of your money, kept half of it for himself, and when Katie called the police station to say she wanted to take the allegation back, Scott lost his shit and has been trying to track her down ever since. So, just to recap, your little scheme split me and Shannen up, traumatised my five-year-old son into thinking he was going to end up losing me, caused the nosy parents at school to think they were owed an explanation about who Shannen was dating and why I was arrested, something that to this day is still affecting both of us. On top of that, Scott stole two and a half grand from you, and the retraction of Katie's statement led to him being so pissed off that he has been harassing her for the past two months. So, tell me again, who gets the moral high ground here because it sure as hell doesn't seem like it's you!"

Steven rubbed at his forehead, shaking his head. "I can't believe this."

"You can't believe Scott only roped you into this for his own benefit?" Annie asked from behind me, her voice mocking. "You never liked him, Steven, and you know exactly how self-serving he's always been. Why did you think he'd be different with you?"

"Because we-" he began, then stopped abruptly, catching my eye, although he had the decency to look apologetic this time. "I thought we wanted the same thing."

"And what was Scott's reasoning for this?" Annie asked. "Why was he so hellbent on destroying Cal and our daughter?"

I was very aware Shannen was still waiting for a response from me about Katie, and I hadn't turned to look at her since I'd rounded on Steven, but I needed his answers too. I would tell her everything, I just didn't want to miss anything now he was talking.

"Like I told you earlier, he just didn't think Cal had any place in our family," Steven said, shaking his head. "And before I met him, I agreed."

"Before you met him," Annie said coldly. "That's exactly the problem. If you'd just waited..."

"Shannen made it clear she didn't want us to meet him!" Steven argued, and his words shot coldness through me. "No," he said, clearly seeing me flinch. "Not because she didn't think you belonged here but because she knew I wouldn't make it easy for you. And If I couldn't meet you, how was I meant to know what you were like?"

"Are you really blaming your actions on Shannen?" Annie snapped. "God, you really are a pathetic little man!"

"I'm not blaming her. I'm just saying, she didn't give me a chance to decide for myself."

"You'd already decided!" Shannen yelled at him. Her eyes were blazing as I turned to her. Her anger was like nothing I'd ever seen before from her, and if she ever looked at me like that, it would have killed me. "You need to get out," she said to him "I need you to get out."

"Shannen, please..."

"Get out!" she screamed, and the pain in her voice made my stomach shrink and my blood run cold again.

Annie bustled past me and grabbed Steven by the arm. "Go. You know Shannen isn't supposed to be dealing with any stress right now. Haven't you put her through enough?"

I watched as tears fell from his eyes while he looked at her. Shannen was leaning forward, her head in her hands, and I could see her shoulders shaking. Ignoring what was going on between her parents, I sat down beside her and wrapped my arm around her. She stiffened, but she didn't push me away.

"I'll go," Steven said quietly. "I'm sorry. I'm sorry to all of you. Shannen, please get some rest. If anything happened to you or the baby, I..."

I had no clue what the end of his sentence was because my brain short circuited on the word 'baby'.

What baby?

Nothing else registered with me except the tension in Shannen's body and the small sob she let out.

Baby.

I removed my arm from around her and leaned back slightly. "Shannen... are... are you..."

I couldn't bring myself to say the word because this was not happening. There was no way she was pregnant. No way she would be pregnant and not have told me about it.

There was no way I was about to become a father for a second time. Not now.

Chapter 27

Shannen

MY DAD HAD GONE from my hero to the man who continued to make my life a misery in twenty-four short hours.

He'd conspired with Scott to take Cal from me. He'd broken both me and my mother, and now he'd revealed my secret to Cal before I'd had the chance to tell him.

Today just keeps on giving...

Very slowly, I raised my head, my cheeks wet with tears. Cal was staring at me, his eyes wide and full of fear.

It was better than anger, but it still made my heart sink.

Thirty minutes ago, we were wrapped up in each other, on the verge of sorting things out. Now, we were sitting in the middle of an explosion of secrets that had rocked the foundation we'd just begun to rebuild.

Cal had learned what my dad had done, I had learned that Cal had been seeing Katie, and then my dad blurted out that I was having a baby.

So many things were unanswered for both of us, but in that moment, I knew the only thing Cal was thinking about was the fact that he was going to be a father again. It was right there in the panic that had etched into his face.

"Yes," I said quietly. "I'm pregnant."

His mouth opened and closed like he was going to speak, but nothing came out. Scrubbing his hands over his face, he said, "What... how long have you known?"

"Since yesterday evening. I was going to tell you, obviously, but..." I shrugged, not needing to finish the sentence because he knew as well as I did what a shitshow the day had been.

I didn't look around, but I was aware of movement across the room as my mum ushered my dad out. I knew he would never have mentioned the baby if he didn't think Cal already knew, but right then, it was just another thing he'd done to make my life difficult.

"Fucking hell, Shan." Cal stood up and began pacing the room, his hands running through his hair, then dropping to his sides before going back to his hair again.

If I didn't know him so well, I would have wondered what he was thinking, but I *did* know him. I could almost hear the whirl of thoughts in his head about how he'd made the same mistake twice. Got another woman pregnant. How he didn't want this baby, just like he didn't want Aiden at first. How he wouldn't be able to cope, and how he couldn't handle it. Every step he took across the carpet was like a kick to my gut because the longer he was silent, the more hurtful I was worried his words might be when he eventually spoke.

And I didn't want to speak first because I didn't know what to say.

After what felt like hours, Cal stopped pacing and turned to me. "You're absolutely sure?"

I wiped my eyes and nodded. "I did a test yesterday. At the hospital, when I told them I was pregnant, they took me for an ultrasound to make sure everything was okay. I... I'm eleven weeks pregnant. I heard the heartbeat."

The memory of it made my heart race because I still couldn't quite believe it was real, but the scan had shown me it was.

"That's why I need to rest," I added. "The doctors don't think there's anything to worry about, but they want me to take a week off work to be on the safe side. Not on bed rest, but just to take things easy. I have to have another scan at the end of the week. If everything is okay, then I can go back to work."

He stared at me, shaking his head. "I can't... Is... is everything definitely okay now? The scan... is everything..."

"Everything is good. The rest and the week off is just a precaution."

With a few long strides, he was in front of me again, and he dropped into a crouch in front of me. So close that I could see the sparkle of tears in his eyes. "I... I don't know how I feel."

"Well, that makes two of us. Although... when I thought something might be wrong, that there was a chance the accident had... I've never been so scared, Cal. And when I heard that heartbeat..." I trailed off, shaking my head as a tear dripped down my cheek. "It hasn't sunk in for me yet either, but the second I was at risk of losing the baby... I couldn't stand it."

His brown eyes hadn't left mine, and he reached out and took one of my hands with his. "Shan... I know this is a weird request, but I need a minute to get my head around this. So, can I please tell you about Katie while I process? I was going to tell you tonight anyway, but then your dad arrived."

The pace of the conversations in the last hour was enough to make anyone dizzy on a good day, but with all that I'd been through, I'd never felt so off kilter. Whatever Cal knew about Katie, that he'd not just spoken to her but seen her, scared the hell out of me because I couldn't envision any way he would have *wanted* that. She was the one who'd made the false report on him, but from what he'd said to my dad, it sounded she and Cal were now on good terms. If not, why would he know so much about her and that Scott had been trying to find her since she took back her statement?

Cal and I had been apart for a couple of months, and there were parts of his life I was totally unaware of now. I'd seen the change in both him and Aiden over those weeks because Aiden was happier, and in turn, on the days I saw Cal at school, he seemed happier too. Was Katie part of this new happiness too? Was she back in his and Aiden's life now?

Rein it in. He saw her today and yet he came here to tell you he loves you. Whatever is going on between them, it hasn't changed how he feels about you.

He said he loved me. The memory settled me slightly, and I wiped my tears away with my free hand. "Yes. Tell me."

Heaving himself up, Cal sat down beside me again and recounted how Katie had gone looking for him to let him know that Scott had been the one to set him up. He explained that she had been offered five thousand pounds but had only been paid half of it, and that she had retracted her statement when he refused to pay up. He also said she'd apologised for everything, and that while he hadn't expected to hear from her again, she'd asked him to take her home from the rehab centre she'd been checked into.

When he was done, he said, "The reason I didn't tell you Scott was involved was because I couldn't see what difference it would make. If I came to you with that information, the only thing it would have done was make you angrier, and because you will have to still see him and Jade sometimes because of your families being close, I just... I didn't want to lay that on you. You dealt with enough because of him. It wouldn't have changed the way either of us reacted the day the police came for me. It was already over. I just wanted to stop you from getting hurt again. I didn't know your dad was involved, though. And I'm not sure Katie did either, or she probably would have mentioned it."

With a deep sigh, I dropped my head against the back of the sofa, looking up at the ceiling.

Was he right to keep all that from me? Maybe. Maybe not. If he'd told me at any other time, I would have flipped out. I'd have hated that he'd kept something so important from me. But when it came down to it, and with all that had occurred that day, I knew he *was* right. If he'd told me Scott was behind it all—something I had briefly considered at the time anyway—it wouldn't have changed the outcome of that day. Knowing who caused it would merely have answered the question of how it came about, but it wouldn't have lessened Cal's resentment towards me for doubting him, and it wouldn't have lessened my hurt over him letting me go.

That my dad was involved was still the biggest kicker about it all because I didn't expect my own father to be the one who stole my happiness.

"Is Katie okay?" I asked. "I mean, is she going to be safe?"

I didn't understand why Scott would continue to look for her when she had upheld her side of their deal. Okay, so she took her statement back, but as my dad had pointed out, the damage was done. Cal was out of my life, so why did it matter to Scott what Katie did now? He'd made two and a half thousand pounds and made me miserable. What more could he want? As for her... she'd done a horrible thing, but it seemed as if she'd tried her best to fix it. Seeking out Cal to tell him she'd wrecked his life further was brave. I wasn't happy about what she'd done, but I equally didn't like the idea of Scott going after her.

"I think so. I don't... I hope she'll be okay, but she isn't my main concern. She had a big part in tearing us apart, and I do think she's trying to get herself together, but I don't plan to help her any more than I already have. She's going to want to see Aiden eventually, I know she is, but she said

231

herself she won't be ready for a while, so I will deal with that when the time comes."

My head was still tilted up to the ceiling, but I slowly turned it to the side so I could look at him. His eyes were already on me. "I'm sorry, Cal."

His lips parted for a second before he said, "Sorry for what?"

I closed my eyes. "That you had to carry this on your own. That you had to deal with Katie. Mostly, I'm sorry for ever showing any doubt in you and making you think I believed you could have hurt her. Because I never really thought that. Never." As I opened my eyes again, I swallowed the lump in my throat. I was so sick of crying, even though I could have broken down again right there. The exhaustion was taking over, but I needed him to know how much I regretted hurting him. How I would have done anything to change it if I could.

"Shannen, it wasn't you. I *was* hurt, but the truth is, I was so worried about ruining your life any more that I would have found any excuse to end it with you that night. I was so fucking embarrassed and ashamed. Being taken away in front of you, Aiden, and your friends... it was hard to even look at you. I was the one who did this to us, and I blamed you because it was easier. I'm the one who needs to say sorry. And I am. I'm so, so sorry."

Finally lifting my head, I turned all the way around to face him, tucking my legs underneath me. "No more apologies, okay? You've beat yourself up enough, and I have too." I sighed. "Maybe we need to sleep, and we can talk some more tomorrow, when we've both had some rest."

With a slow nod, Cal said, "Yeah. There's still a lot to talk about. I just.... I don't want to leave you yet."

As he pushed his hand through his hair again, his own tiredness beginning to show on his face, I said, "Then don't. Stay here with me."

He raised his eyebrows. "Really? Won't your mum mind?"

I gave him a soft smile. "I doubt it. She likes you."

"How do you know?" he asked, tilting his chin up slightly with a challenging smirk, making him look both cocky and sexy as hell all at once.

"I know my mum, and I know when she is faking politeness. She wasn't faking it with you." Reaching forward, I placed a hand on the back of his neck. "Please stay."

His lips slowly curved upwards as he leaned in towards me. "You really want me to?"

I nodded. "I just want to be close to you."

"But I don't have my pyjamas with me."

I chuckled. He was teasing me. Cal didn't wear pyjamas.

"Be a rebel, Cal. Go home with your boxers in your pocket."

He laughed out loud and brushed his thumb across my cheek. "Come on. Let's get you to bed."

There were still so many unspoken things. So much to discuss, but exhaustion was seeping into every part of me. As we went back upstairs, and as I went through a quick version of my bedtime routine, all I could think about was sleep. I had been drained of all my emotions, all my strength. When I climbed into bed beside Cal, who was stripped down to his boxers, the only thing I wanted was his closeness, to feel safe again.

As he wound his arms around me from behind, tucking me in close to him, I had to suppress a moan of absolute bliss. Every part of me ached with weariness, but his warmth surrounding me took it all away. His hand slid down my arm, lightly holding my wrist. I could feel his breath against my neck, hear his heartbeat, which was faster than I would have expected right then. His fingers slowly peeled away from my wrist, and I could feel it hovering for a moment before he placed it under my arm onto my hip, then moved it under my pyjama top and around to my stomach. The last bit of energy left in me made my heart flutter as he stroked his fingers across my skin.

"There's really a baby in there?" he asked gently, and I laughed.

"Yeah. There is."

His hand moved out from under my top and I felt the slightest tug on it. "Please can you take this off? The material is cold, and I need to feel you."

"Okay," I whispered, the fluttering in my heart moving lower, even though I knew we couldn't act on that tonight. He undid the bottom buttons, and I undid the top ones before he peeled the top off me and flung it behind him. Once it was out of the way, he pulled me against him again, his hand going back to my stomach.

He let out a soft growl against my cheek, pulling my hips back against his. "I missed you."

"I missed you too," I said, resting my hand over his on my belly.

"I want this, Shan. I want us."

"Me too."

"I've always wanted that, but today made me see... I don't want to ever be anywhere else. Only with you."

As the exhaustion washed over me again, I smiled. "Only with you."

Chapter 28

Cal

A SOUND WOKE ME, and as I blinked, I saw it was still dark. Shannen wasn't in my arms anymore, but light showed through the bottom of the door to the en-suite bathroom. The sound I'd heard was the toilet flushing, then the door opened and Shannen flicked the light off and came back to bed.

When she noticed I was awake, she snuggled into me, her arm across my stomach.

"You okay?" I asked, my voice croaky from sleep.

She nodded against my chest. "Yeah, I just... I think I'm a bit paranoid after the accident. Nothing hurts or anything. I feel like I need to keep checking to make sure I'm not bleeding."

The reminder that Shannen was pregnant helped to wake me up a bit more. The whole of the day before had been a blur of information. If I wasn't still with her, I would have been sure I'd imagined it all. Or perhaps not. I didn't think even I had *that* level of imagination.

"Have you slept at all?" I asked, entwining my fingers with hers. I had drifted off almost as soon as I'd closed my eyes, and with as tired as Shannen had been, I assumed she had done the same.

"I have," she replied. "I just woke up suddenly about fifteen minutes ago in a panic. I think I was having a bad dream, and I needed to make sure it wasn't coming true." She placed a soft kiss on my chest. "Go back to sleep."

Her body was tense against me, and I let go of her hand and slid mine up to her shoulder, my fingers landing on the strap of her bra. Now I was a bit more alert, my dick responded to the fact that Shannen's lace-covered tits were pressed against me, and I hoped she kept her hand where it was on my chest. I didn't want her to think my only thoughts right then were about having sex with her. Not that I *hadn't* thought about it, but at that moment, I was more worried about what was on her mind.

Earlier, I'd let myself move through each change of conversation as it came, never stopping to think about any part of it for too long because there had been a lot to discuss. Plus, I hadn't been ready to think about what Shannen being pregnant would mean for me.

For us.

We had already agreed we wanted to be together. I'd told her I wanted us while my hand was on her slightly swollen stomach. What I hadn't done yet was consider the reality of it. Probably because it still didn't feel real.

With that thought, I slid my hand back down her arm, resting it on her stomach like I did before. I hadn't done this with Katie. I'd never wanted that kind of closeness with her. With Shannen, though, I craved it. I had put a baby in her belly. They were both *mine*.

As my hand stroked Shannen's skin, some of the stiffness in her muscles softened. "I don't want to sleep yet," I told her, turning my head towards her. "I want to keep my hand right here and talk."

She smiled, although it didn't fully reach her eyes. "I'm sorry about the way this was dropped on you. I didn't want it to be like that."

"It wasn't your fault."

"I know, but..." she trailed off and sighed. "I guess there wouldn't have been an easy way. Ideally, I would have taken a few more days to get used to it myself, but here we are."

I felt my forehead creasing slightly into a frown. I'd been so busy thinking about how I felt about things that I hadn't considered this was new to Shannen too. She'd touched on it the night before, but we were both so tired, and the conversation had ended before we could really get into it.

Shifting my position, I turned onto my side so I could look at her properly. Even though it was still dark, my eyes had adjusted to the lack of light now, and I could see something was bothering her from the way she wasn't meeting my gaze. Her eyes were fixated on my chest, where her hand still rested.

"Hey," I said, gently tilting her chin up with my finger. "What are you thinking?"

She shrugged. "I don't know. I guess I'm just worried about a lot of things."

"Shall we start with one and then see where it takes us?" I raised an eyebrow, and this time when she smiled, her eyes brightened as she nodded.

Shannen moved her hand from my chest around to my back, and I slid mine from her face down to her hip, loving that I could touch her after so long of being deprived of it.

"One of the worries is what I just said," she began. "That something will happen to the baby. It's strange because I..." She looked into my eyes again. "This is going to make me sound like a terrible person, but when I found out I was pregnant... I didn't want to be."

She swallowed, lowering her head as if she thought I would be disappointed in her or something. I didn't speak because I knew she wasn't done.

"This is probably a product of my upbringing," she went on, "but I never thought I would be in this position. I was supposed to do things in the right order. Date, get engaged, get married, have children. And it wasn't meant to be now. It was meant to be when I'd had at least a solid few years of being in my job. I'm not naive enough to think that's really how the world works. Things happen. Things change. And it's not like I was even *that* rigid with my plans. I didn't plan to be married and start a family by a certain age. I was happy with how I was before I met you. I was happy to just wait and see how things panned out. I had faith that it would all come when I was ready."

I watched as the corners of her mouth slowly curved upwards as she looked at me, her eyes on mine. It didn't matter that there wasn't enough light in the room for me to study her properly. She was beautiful. I'd never seen her so vulnerable before. Her lower lip trembled slightly as she tried to hold herself together.

"I wasn't ready for you, Cal. You were just there. Everything I always knew I needed. I didn't expect to find all of it in you." Pushing a stray bit of hair behind her ear, she went on, "I fell in love with you faster than I've ever fallen in love before. I was in love with you way before I told you. And then... it was over."

She bit her bottom lip, and I leaned my forehead against hers, then pecked a light kiss on the tip of her nose before pulling back.

"I hadn't thought much about our future beyond knowing I wanted to be with you," she said. "For the first time in my life, I was in a relationship where I didn't care about planning each step. I just wanted to live every second of it. I wanted you and Aiden, and even if we never married or had children of our own, that would have been enough because although Aiden isn't mine, I would have taken care of him as if he were."

"You did," I said, my hand tangling into her dark curls. "You always did that. Even at the beginning, you took him on as if it was the easiest thing in the world, even though he *wasn't* easy to deal with." It was one of the reasons I'd fallen for her. She didn't look at Aiden like he was some horrible problem child. I'd started to see the possibility of us being a family because she saw through all of my bullshit to the part of me that had died the same day my mum and brother had. The part that wanted to belong somewhere again. And she'd brought it back to life. "You know... we weren't together for long. Now for how much I..." My words faltered. I'd told her I loved her now, but the words still wouldn't leave my lips easily. Years of rein-forcement that love equalled pain meant I was going to struggle with it for a while yet. However, Shannen smiled as if she understood, and I went on, "But I thought about a life with you. I wanted it. I just didn't expect to have to think about how it would work yet."

"Well," Shannen said, taking my hand and linking our fingers, "I think I still have a lot to learn about you because you have taken this way better than I expected."

I laughed. "It's the middle of the night and I'm still in shock. I can't guarantee that at some point I won't freak out, but it's..." I paused, search-ing for the right words. "I know I want to be with you, and it was only my fucked-up fears that kept me away. I'd already made the decision that I wanted you back. Even if you hadn't been in an accident today and I hadn't had to consider a world without you in it..." My breath caught as my heart rate suddenly sped up, remembering how I'd felt the second I heard Shannen might be hurt. I rolled onto my back, staring up at the ceiling.

My chest tightened the way it had while I'd waited for news during the longest afternoon of my life. While I'd been assured Shannen hadn't been badly injured, it threw up so much stuff from when my mum and Luca were killed. I hadn't been able to breathe until I heard her voice.

"Cal." Shannen placed her hand on my cheek. "It's okay."

I nodded, breathing deeply a few times until the ache eased. "Sorry." Turning my head towards her again, I said, "I haven't been that scared in a long time."

She leaned down and brushed her lips against mine. "I'm so sorry I took so long to call you. I just... I needed to know if everything..."

"I get it," I interrupted. "It doesn't matter now." Shifting onto my side again so I was facing her, I said, "What I was trying to say was that I want to be with you, and even though the timing is shit and it scares the hell out of me, a baby doesn't change that. I can't promise I'll always do everything right, and I can't promise that I won't be a prick when things get hard, but I can promise that I will work my arse off every fucking day to make sure I give you and our family everything you need. So, if any of your worries are that I will give up when it gets tough, I swear to you, I will be there every step of the way."

Shannen blinked as a couple of tears escaped from her eyes. "Thank you," she whispered. "Thank you."

Maybe that was all she needed to hear.

Maybe you promised her something you can't deliver.

Except, I could deliver. I *would*. That stupid fucking voice in my head that held me back would always be there, and some days it would probably win. But when it came to Shannen? When it came to how much I needed to be with her? I was done letting it keep me away. Done letting it tell me she could never want me the way I wanted her.

I'd come too far to give up on this.

Chapter 29

Shannen

TALKING THINGS THROUGH WITH Cal in the middle of the night, in the dark comfort of my mum's guest room, settled the ongoing war that had raged in my mind. We'd talked for hours, almost until it should have been time to wake up, at which point, we'd cuddled up together and finally gone back to sleep.

What I learned was the depth of Cal's feelings for me and how hard he'd struggled with it. I'd always understood to a degree, but I'd underestimated exactly how much it had played on his mind while we were apart. How much he'd mentally berated himself for everything he perceived he'd done wrong. I'd done it too, but Cal was almost incapable of forgiving himself for anything. I'd seen it before in the way he punished himself for not being a better dad to Aiden, for the things he did to Edward Firth, but those were things he'd been holding onto for a long time. Things that had a long-term effect on him. I understood I was important to him, but I didn't expect that he'd heap the same level of hate onto himself over me. All he'd ever had to do was come back and talk to me. And sure, I could have done the same, but all I could see happening was us going round and round in the same self-destructive circles. If we were going to get anywhere, it had to come from him.

In the time we were apart, Cal had stepped up, for Aiden if not for himself. But doing that had led to him finding a bit more of his own self-worth. Helping Katie had been another step forward, especially after what she did to him. It wasn't that he was selfish before, or that he didn't want to do things for other people, it was that he never believed he could. Never felt like he had anything to give. Somewhere along the way, he'd realised he *did* have something to give. Whether that happened with me or after didn't matter, it just mattered that he could see something good in himself, even if it was only a tiny piece.

Cal left my mum's house at nine the following morning so he could get back to take Aiden to football practice, and Mum and I left her house around lunchtime to drive to mine. She packed a bag to stay with me for a week, I called Iris to explain that I'd need to take the next few days off work, and by two o'clock on Sunday afternoon, Mum was settled in at my flat.

Cal and I had agreed that we would keep my pregnancy between us aside from those who already knew and Guy. We didn't want to tell Aiden right away because we were nervously awaiting my ultrasound on Friday. We wanted to be absolutely sure everything was okay before we let him know, and by then, we would be at the twelve-week mark.

Aiden *had* been told that Cal and I were seeing each other again, though. The decision was made so that when we did tell him about the baby, he wouldn't hear all the news at once.

Cal had brought Aiden over to see me during the week. Seeing him and not just being teacher Shannen again felt good. I asked him about his football club, and he told me about the things he'd done with Aria, Avery, and Max. He also tried to teach me about his favourite football players, but since I'd never watched football, that part went way over my head. My mum had gotten along well with Aiden too, and she'd even asked him to teach her about football too so I could have ten minutes alone with Cal.

My class had been told I'd been in a minor car accident, and although they knew I was fine, they all made me get well soon cards, which Iris delivered on Tuesday afternoon. She was super supportive of me taking the time off and pleased Cal and I were sorting things out.

As for my dad... he had been trying to reach my mum every day, and when she didn't answer the phone, he called me. It felt all kinds of wrong to reject his calls, but Mum and I had both asked for some space and he wasn't giving us that. I knew he wanted to apologise, and us staying away was breaking his heart, but Mum and I had a lot to think about, and he had broken our hearts first.

I'd spoken to my mum at length about what he did. She completely understood why I needed to keep my distance for now. We'd explained things to my sister too, and while she was enraged by his behaviour, she hadn't shut him out. She wasn't eager to see him, but she had spoken to him once or twice, mostly to ask him to give us the space we'd asked for.

My mum was struggling the most. While it was my life he had messed with, I'd been able to claw it back. My mum had to live with the knowledge that her own husband had purposely set out to destroy the man her daughter was happy with in order to split us up, and he'd done so by conspiring with someone none of our family liked. Someone with very few principals, and who would lose his job if anyone found out what he did.

There had been no confrontation with Scott. My mum hadn't told Judith—a woman who had been her best friend for almost forever—that she'd temporarily moved out of the house because to explain would mean to tell her what Scott had done. Judith thought Scott was the perfect son-in-law, and while my mum wanted her to know, she wasn't quite ready to deal with it yet. Along with figuring out what she wanted to do regarding a future with my dad, this was the biggest thing on her mind. She didn't know if any proof existed that Scott had helped to set Cal up. Since it was my dad who had paid Katie, the comeback would more likely be on him than Scott. Unless my dad had any kind of text message or email about it, there wasn't a way to link it to Scott at all. I'd asked Cal if Katie might have proof of Scott's calls to her, but we realised he wouldn't have used his actual phone to harass her, and with his job being what it was, he'd be able to find some way to hide what he'd done. So, Mum was at a loss for what to do about Judith. Scott was about to join Judith's family, which would put an ongoing strain on any future get-togethers. It certainly wouldn't be comfortable if my parents went to Jade's wedding.

I'd spent a lot of time wondering if Jade knew anything about the set-up. As much of a bitch as she could be, I wasn't convinced Scott would have let her know what he was planning. It was too much of a risk for him; the less people who knew, the better for him. I didn't think she'd have sold him out because she was so wrapped up in the idea of her wedding that she probably wouldn't risk it not happening.

I really felt for my mum because this was a horrible position for her. Depending on her decisions, she could end up cutting off both her husband and her best friend. While I understood none of this was on me, guilt ran rampant through me. I was certain Judith would also see it that way; *why couldn't I have picked someone 'respectable' to be with, and then none of this would have happened?* I could just hear her grating voice scolding me.

Respectable. That was a joke. Cal had a rough background, but he was a good father, he had started to work through his baggage to make sure our relationship worked, he had helped the ex who had left him alone with a small child, and he had been so kind and understanding to my mum that I had fallen in love with him even more. Scott? He might have been good to Jade, but he was a thief and a liar. Someone who could hold a grudge better than anyone I'd ever met.

All the things my mum was trying to figure out didn't make the week a bad one, though. In fact, having her at my place, even with the stress she was under, had been good for both of us. It had helped me because, although nothing bad had happened, knowing she was there if I needed her had made it easier for me to relax. I'd barely moved from the sofa, other than to use the bathroom or go to bed. Once or twice, I'd done simple food prep with Mum in the kitchen because doing nothing for so long was making me crazy. Mum had also driven me in to the Quay once, where we'd had a light lunch in one of the pubs there and a very short walk. I hadn't felt any pain, weird twinges, or anything averse since the accident, so I was confident I'd be able to go back to work on Monday as long as the scan went well.

As soon as the appointment came through, Cal booked the day off work so he could come with me. We asked my mum if she wanted to come, but she smiled and said this one was just for us. She'd been with me at my first scan, so she'd already experienced it, but it was a first for Cal. He had never been through this when Aiden was on the way, and as we sat in the hospital's waiting area, his foot tapped nervously against the floor.

The room was busy, with lots of other expectant parents also waiting to be seen. Our appointment was already twenty minutes late which wasn't helping matters, and I rested my hand on his leg.

"Cal, relax," I said quietly.

His foot continued to tap as he looked at me. "Are *you* relaxed?"

I twisted my lips to the side for a moment. "Hmm, not completely. Mostly because I really need to pee. But I also know that I can't change anything by worrying. So, I'm trying to stay as calm as I can. I'd rather my blood pressure didn't shoot through the roof right now."

Cal huffed out a breath, looking around the waiting room. "These posters don't help. They're all about looking for signs of illness. It doesn't make people feel very relaxed."

A man a couple of seats away, sitting next to a woman who was far more pregnant than me, snorted, and we both turned to look at him. "Sorry," he said. "I didn't mean to listen in on your conversation, but I think the same thing every time I come here. Can't they put up some pictures of a beach or something? At least then we can pretend everything is good and that there aren't unwell people all over the place."

The woman beside him smiled as she reached for his hand. Looking at me, she said, "What is it about men and hospitals?"

If I were to guess, I would say she was probably close to forty years old, and she had naturally red hair that flowed past her shoulders. Her face wasn't chubby, but she had rounded cheeks and freckles, and a smile that lit up her blue eyes. The man beside her, presumably her husband or partner, looked to be a tad older than her. His hair was brown, but there was a lot of grey streaked throughout and in his short beard.

"I can't say I'm a big fan either," I said with a laugh. Considering my dad had worked in hospitals my whole life, I wasn't keen on them, but it wasn't as if I'd ever spent time in them. Take your kid to work day was not really possible in theatre. "And I agree about the posters."

The lady chuckled. "I've been in and out of here so often that I'm used to it now. After a while, you stop paying attention."

I wondered what she meant by that, but I didn't want to pry into her medical history when I'd only known her for sixty seconds.

"I don't think I want to be here often enough for that to happen," Cal said.

"Is this your first?" the man asked us.

"First for me, second for him," I answered, looking at Cal.

"I have a five-year-old," Cal added. "He'll be six in November."

Although I knew when Aiden's birthday was, it hadn't occurred to me until then that our baby would also be due in November, according to my calculations. "I wonder if they'll share a birthday."

244

The red-haired lady said, "My sister and I were born a day apart, although she is three years older than me. Trust me when I say it's better if they are further apart because for the rest of your life, all you'll hear is family members moaning about how expensive it is to have two birthdays close together."

"I'll do my best," I said, chuckling.

"Shannen Morgan."

Cal stiffened at the sound of my name being called, and I looked up to see a nurse holding a clipboard and looking around the waiting area. I got to my feet, smiling at her in acknowledgement, and Cal stood up too. Before I followed the nurse, I turned to the couple we'd been talking to and said, "It was nice to meet you. I hope you don't have to wait too much longer."

"Nice to meet you too," they said in unison, then smiled at each other.

Gripping Cal's hand in mine, I said, "Come on then. Let's do this."

He nodded, and we walked towards the waiting nurse, who led us around a corner, down the corridor a short way, and then into a room on the left. Inside, there were two female nurses, who greeted us with big smiles as we entered. The room was set up the same way as the one I'd been in in Plymouth, though it was much smaller. There was a black examination table in the middle of the room, with the sonogram machine at the end of it. There were also a few cabinets and a sink along one wall, and a blue chair with a cushioned seat beside the examination table.

"Good morning," the blonde-haired nurse said. "I'm Delphine, and this is Stephanie." She gestured to the other nurse. "How are you doing today?"

"A bit nervous," I admitted, "but otherwise, I'm well, thank you."

"Is this Dad?" Delphine asked, nodding towards Cal, who was glancing around the room, his face paler than usual.

"Yes," I confirmed, enjoying the thrill of hearing him being referred to as the father of our child. "He is also nervous."

"Perfectly understandable. Now, if you want to hop up onto the table for me and we can have a chat before we get started."

I gestured for Cal to sit in the chair and passed him my handbag to hold while I got up onto the leather examination table, sitting on the edge for the time being. The nurses ran through some fairly standard questions about how I'd been feeling, plus a few additional ones regarding the car accident. Cal sat rigidly while I answered them, his eyes occasionally darting around the room at various pieces of equipment.

When it was time for the sonogram to begin, I carefully swung my legs up onto the table and lay back, lifting my top a bit and undoing my jeans to lower them. The dark-haired nurse, Stephanie, handed me some large paper towel type things and asked me to tuck them into my top and jeans to protect my clothes. Cal shuffled his chair closer to me as Delphine pulled the sonogram machine around to the side of the bed so we'd be able to see the screen better. She then walked across the room to pick up the gel stuff that would be rubbed onto my stomach. After warning me it would be cold, she squirted some onto my belly. As she picked up a wand-type instrument, I looked over at Cal, who now had his eyes on the screen. I took his hand, but he didn't look at me.

"Okay," Delphine said, "let's get started. Just relax."

I took in a deep breath and let it out slowly as she placed the wand on my stomach and slowly used it to spread the gel around. It seemed to take forever, but then Delphine smiled as a heartbeat sounded into the room.

"There it is," she said. "Best sound ever."

I laughed, glancing at Cal again. This time, his eyes flicked in my direction before he fully turned his head to look at me. "That's good, right?"

Both nurses smiled, and Delphine said, "That's very good."

She turned towards the screen for a moment, and since I wasn't sure what she was doing, I kept my focus on Cal. "This is really happening," I said quietly.

He nodded, his shoulders rising and falling a touch more rapidly than usual. "Yeah." His gaze held mine for a moment longer before he squeezed my hand and then tangled our fingers together, focusing back on the screen.

"Okay, so right now, your baby is measuring a bit over five centimetres," Delphine said. She zoomed the picture in and pointed. "As you can probably see, this is the head right here. And you'll see the tiny arms and legs. That is a very strong sounding heartbeat, and the heart rate is perfect. Everything is developing as it should at this stage."

I let out a tiny breath of relief, but my eyes were transfixed on the image of my baby. Seeing actual visual proof of what was happening inside my body was something I could never have imagined. It was an experience I couldn't quite describe, but it felt miraculous. I was responsible for keeping that tiny life safe inside me, and just like that, I felt... protective.

Like from then on, everything I did would be for that mini version of me and Cal.

It was crazy because I'd had the same scan the week before, after the accident. While I'd been relieved that the baby was safe and unharmed then, somehow, this felt different. Maybe because it was the twelve-week stage, where things were supposed to be less risky, or maybe it was because I was fully present this time. At the first scan, all I'd needed to know was if the baby was okay. I tuned out almost everything else after. This time... slightly less than one week later, everything was different. I had Cal back, and there was now no risk of me having to do this alone. We were together, re-building what had been damaged, and... we were going to have a baby.

"Shan."

Blinking and feeling a tear slip down my cheek, I looked at Cal, and his dark eyes shone when he smiled softly. All I could do was smile back, still stunned by how different I felt after that one pivotal moment in my life. The moment I saw my baby.

"According to the notes I have from your last appointment," Delphine said, keeping her voice gentle so as not to shatter our moment, "and to the measurements I have here, your due date is November 11th."

My eyes widened, and Cal laughed. "No fucking way," he said.

"What is it?" Delphine asked, and I tore my eyes from Cal's.

"That's the same birth date as Cal's son," I told her. "We were just talking about this in the waiting room."

"Oh, wow," she said. "Two birthdays on the same day is going to be a handful! However, first babies can be very unreliable, so while that's the date predicted, you may well find this little one will not come on the exact due date."

"I hope so," Cal said, though he was still smiling. "Aiden will not be happy about sharing his birthday."

"It would also be rubbish for him if I'm in labour on his birthday this year," I said with a small frown. "I don't want him to feel like he's being pushed aside, especially after the year he's had."

Delphine offered a sympathetic smile. "Unfortunately, we can't do much about when the baby decides to make an appearance, but you have plenty of time to prepare. Maybe you can gather some ideas just in case to make sure he feels included and doesn't think his birthday has been forgotten."

"We can do that," I said, brightening at the suggestion. It would be good to plan something in advance for any eventuality. It was only May, so we had a solid six months to come up with something.

"Great! Now, would you like me to print off some photos for you?" Delphine asked. "You get one photo for free. After that, it's five pounds for each additional, or you can get three for ten pounds."

Had I not been told about the charge for scan photos, I would have been shocked, but my sister had informed me about it when she was pregnant, so I smiled, then turned to Cal again.

"How many do you think we need?" I asked him.

"Not sure." He paused, thinking. "Maybe you and I need one each so we can both keep a copy with us. Do you think your mum would like one?"

I smiled. "Yes, I think she would. But if we're going to get two extra, we might as well get three for ten quid."

I considered asking if Guy might want to keep one of the photos since he was such a big part of our lives, and he was also going to be one of our first picks to be a godparent. However, knowing a family was something he wanted and one of the reasons he and Helen split, I wasn't sure if that would be considered insensitive. When we had told him about the baby, though, although surprised, there was no sign that he was anything but happy for us. He'd made a joke about how he'd never babysit two kids, but he'd immediately laughed, and I knew he didn't mean it. Not that we would take advantage of him. With Cal and me back together, we would have to rely on him less, even though we hadn't got into logistics yet. That would come now this scan was over.

"Okay," Cal said. "We'll do that."

"Great." Delphine smiled and turned to look at Stephanie. "Can you get the photos printed, and I'll take Shannen's blood pressure before she goes."

Stephanie nodded and got up to sort out our pictures, while Delphine turned to pick up a roll of paper towels, which was resting beside the ultrasound machine.

"Here you go," she said, tearing some off and handing them to me. "You can clean off now."

I thanked her as I took them and began carefully wiping the gel from my stomach. Once I was cleaned up and had straightened my clothes, Delphine walked across the room to pick up the blood pressure monitor. "So, what are your plans for the rest of the day?"

"Now we know the news is all good, we're going to go out to lunch," I said, smiling at Cal. That was the plan we'd made earlier as we wanted to figure out the next steps for us.

"That sounds great," Delphine answered as she came back towards me. I lifted my arm so she could secure the cuff around it. "Anywhere in mind?"

"We haven't decided yet," Cal replied. "But maybe Double Locks."

"That's a good idea," I said. "I haven't been there in ages."

Double Locks was a beautiful pub on Exeter's canal. It was a traditional pub with a large beer garden, and since the weather was nice, it would be lovely to sit outside and eat while enjoying the sunshine and watching all the other patrons wandering in and out.

"If you can just relax for a moment, Shannen," Delphine said. "We'll get this done, and then you can ask any questions you have."

I nodded as she squeezed the puffy thing and the cuff tightened around my arm. I winced ever so slightly at the point when it felt like the bottom half of my arm would pop off, but then the pressure eased slowly, and I waited silently for the result.

"Perfect," Delphine said, taking the reading and writing it down in my notes. "Your blood pressure is all good, but if you start to feel unwell at any point, don't hesitate to contact your doctor or call 111 for advice." She took the cuff from my arm and said, "Okay, you are good to go! Do you have any more questions for me today?"

"I do," I said. "Firstly, I assume it's okay for me to go back to work on Monday?"

Delphine nodded. "Yeah, you should be fine. Obviously, don't be doing anything crazy, but you don't need to rest now. Normal activities can resume."

Cal's fingers brushed the back of my hand, and without even looking at him, I knew what he was thinking. There was one very 'normal activity' we'd been deprived of.

"Erm," I began, feeling heat creeping onto my cheeks. "Last week, I was told not to do anything strenuous, but... is it okay if we... I mean... is it safe to..."

I couldn't believe I was having so much trouble asking such a simple question. I was pregnant, so it wasn't as if anyone in the room thought I was a virgin.

"Can we please have sex?" Cal finished for me, and both nurses laughed out loud, probably at the hint of desperation in his tone. It had been a challenge to keep my hands off him for the last six days. The only thing that made it easier to cope was the fact that we had barely had any time alone, but now... now we did have a bit of time to ourselves. If Delphine said we could have sex, there was every chance we might just skip lunch.

"Yes," Delphine said, still chuckling. She gave me a subtle wink, and my cheeks heated further. "Sex is absolutely fine while pregnant, but I like that you took the advice you were given for this week. Many people don't."

"If you told me not to have sex with her for nine months, I'd do as I was told if it meant keeping Shannen and our baby safe."

My lips curved into a smile as I turned to look at him, and his eyes were on me. He looked at me as if I were the most incredible thing he'd ever seen, even though there was a slightly cheeky smirk on his face. I knew he meant what he'd said, but his smile let me know he was glad that wasn't the case.

"He's a keeper," Stephanie said from across the room, and I laughed, still not taking my eyes from Cal's.

"Yeah. He's a keeper."

Chapter 30

Cal

As we left the hospital, Shannen clutching the scan photos of our baby, her other hand in mine, I felt like I was drunk. Not out of control drunk, but the kind when you've had just enough to make you feel relaxed. Everything is in focus, but it's... peaceful. We'd had the best news we could have had, that our baby was fine, and Shannen would be able to go back to work on Monday. Now, we had a few hours to ourselves before I picked Aiden up from school.

I was the luckiest motherfucker who'd ever existed.

"Before we go," Shannen said, "I'm just going to ring my mum and let her know everything went. I'll message Gaby and Nova on the way."

"Okay," I said, smiling down at her. "Do you still want to go for lunch?" My grin widened as I winked at her, and her cheeks turned red.

"Oh my God," she said, laughing and letting go of my hand to give my arm a light shove. "You could not have made it clearer to the nurses that we're going home to have sex."

Wrapping my arm around her shoulders as we approached my car, I said, "Can we?"

She snorted, her cheeks still pink. "I'm not against it, it's just... that would be the least spontaneous sex we've ever had."

"I'm not saying we'll go back to mine so I can drag you straight to bed. I'm saying we should go back to mine, relax, and we will definitely end up having sex because we haven't been completely alone together in months and you have never looked sexier than you do right now."

Internally, I was calling myself a cock for being so cheesy, but I wasn't just lying to get what I wanted. She was wearing black jeans and a white long-sleeved top, her hair back in a low ponytail, and she wore hardly any makeup—I'd never actually seen her fully made up—and I wanted her more than I ever had.

"You don't need to butter me up," she teased, her eyes sparkling. "I'm already yours."

"Yeah, you are." I stopped as we reached the car and pulled her in close to me, staring down at her and thinking about how badly I wanted to be inside her.

She grinned, and it was at that moment I knew for sure lunch was no longer on the agenda. "Give me two minutes to call my mum, and then we can go."

I kissed her again then let her go so she could make the call. She took her phone from her bag and waited while it rang. I unlocked the car and got into the driver's side but didn't shut the door. I sat sideways in the seat, my legs stretched out and my feet on the ground outside.

"Hi, Mum," Shannen said, her voice happy. "Yeah, we're all done. Everything is great. The baby is growing perfectly, and we're due on November 11th." There was a pause while her mum answered, then Shannen laughed. "I know, and also, it's Aiden's birthday, but hopefully we can dodge them both and the baby will have their own birthday." Another pause. "Yeah, we're going to go back to Cal's for a bit and I'll be home around half past two."

I smiled to myself at her words, though I wished she could come to the school with me to pick Aiden up. She couldn't yet as people had been told she was resting after the car accident, and also because I didn't want her to have to deal with the stress of the parents' gossip when they saw us together.

"Oh?" Shannen said, her voice curious. "No, of course not. I just didn't think you were ready." She began to very slowly pace the length of my car as she listened. "And you're sure you're ready to see him?"

That got my attention, and I looked over at her as she continued to walk up and down. She must have been talking about her dad.

"Yeah, I know," she went on with a sigh. "And I will have to do the same, just not yet. I still don't want to see him."

Shannen hadn't mentioned her dad to me since we left her mum's house the previous weekend. I didn't want to be the one to bring him up because she was supposed to be taking things easy, and I guessed talking about him would only make her angry again. I'd thought about him, though. About what he did and how he'd picked the most dangerous person to help him take me down. Maybe not dangerous in general, but dangerous to me. It had only been the fast pace of the conversation at the weekend that had stopped me from throwing a fist in his face. I'd felt my temper simmering, ready to explode, and I knew he'd have taken it because he deserved it. If Shannen eventually forgave him, or if her mum did, then I would cross paths with him at some point. I had forgiven Katie for her part in this... kind of. I didn't want to see her or speak to her anytime soon, but she was always going to be tied to me because of Aiden. Steven, though? I would also always have a link to him because of Shannen, but it was unexpected from him. I knew he didn't like me being with Shannen, but there was a big difference between that and setting out to destroy me. If he'd tried to unearth evidence of what I did to Edward Firth, at least when I'd been arrested, it would have been for something I'd done, but he'd tried to set me up for something I would *never* do. The thing I hated the most.

And that was harder to forgive.

"Hey," Shannen said, and I realised she was now standing in front of me, securing her phone in her bag. "Are you ready to go?"

I nodded. "You okay?"

"Yeah." Shrugging, she added, "My dad is coming to Exeter to see Mum. She's agreed to have lunch with him because she wants to ask him some questions and tell him a few things too. She thought it better for them to go out to eat so there would be less yelling. She said she hasn't made any decisions about whether she will go home soon, or whether she wants him to be there if she does, but it's harder for her to make a decision if she doesn't speak to him."

"Fair enough. He won't go to your place, though, will he?"

She shook her head. "I asked her not to bring him back. I said she can tell him about the scan, but as far as I'm concerned, that's all he deserves from me."

I don't think he even deserves that. He'd purposely done something he knew would hurt her. Even though I hadn't always been the greatest dad, at my lowest, I would never have intentionally hurt Aiden. I had done some

253

emotional damage because *I* was emotionally damaged, and I'd forgotten how to show him that I cared, but I was doing what I could to make up for it now. Maybe Shannen's dad would do the same if she let him, but the situations were very different. He had acted with intention, and I had acted because I didn't know how to be better.

Reaching for her hand, I said, "Shall we go home now?"

Smiling softly as she looked at me, she nodded. "I'd like that."

In spite of what I'd said earlier about us relaxing for a while when we got back to my flat, I realised Shannen was right. The mood had been dampened by the talk about her dad, and as much as I wanted her, it didn't feel right anymore. It wouldn't have felt like doing it because we couldn't wait anymore, it would have felt too planned.

Shannen dropped her bag by the door to the living room, and I led her to the sofa, dropping my car keys and phone on the coffee table. Sensing she needed my arms around her more than anything else, I pulled her onto my lap, and she turned sideways, lifting her legs up onto the sofa and snuggling into me.

"I was thinking," I began, unsure if this was the right time but needing to see how she felt. "As today went well, do you want to talk about what we do next?"

"In what sense?" she asked as I wrapped my arms around her and pulled her closer.

"Well, I know we didn't mean to be having a baby yet, but we are and right now, we live in different places. I'm not saying we should move in together next week, but... have you thought about where we'll live?"

She gently stroked my forearm, and even though I couldn't see her face, I felt as if she was smiling.

"I have," she said. "We both have two-bedroom flats, which is fine while the baby is tiny, but there will come a time when we'll need another room."

Shannen and I had never discussed finances in any depth. I'd seen her parents' house; they were rich as fuck. Shannen owned her flat, and it was better and bigger than mine by a long way. But it still didn't have enough bedrooms. I didn't know if Shannen had savings or could afford to buy a bigger place. I didn't want her to because it wasn't fair for her to be the one paying for everything. I had barely any spare money to save between rent, bills, food, and the extra money I was spending to keep Aiden in two football clubs and breakfast club.

"Do you have any ideas of what we should do?" I asked because I didn't want to be the first to bring up money. It was hard enough knowing I wouldn't have much to contribute to any future home we had. I didn't want to highlight that fact.

"I thought maybe, if you wanted to, you and Aiden could move in with me in the summer. Let Aiden finish the school year, let everything settle down, and then it still gives us enough time before the baby comes to be ready. Plus, there's also a good amount of time for Aiden to get to grips with the changes. Then maybe, in year or so, we could look at getting somewhere bigger. My flat will sell for a decent price and it would give us some money towards buying somewhere. We might need to look at a few different areas in the city, but we won't want to go too far because we don't want to move Aiden to a different school." She looked up at me, her cheeks flushed. "Sorry. I didn't mean to make decisions regarding Aiden. I've just been thinking about how we can find somewhere to go that won't cause him too much anxiety."

Shaking my head in amazement, I said, "Are you kidding? Shan, he isn't even yours, but you still think about what he needs whenever we do anything. I like that you include him in decisions."

"Of course," she said, leaning away slightly so she could look at me properly. "Everything we do affects him. I'm worried about us having a new baby and how he'll feel about that. I don't want him to ever feel left out or that the baby is getting all the attention. He's not mine, but I don't want him to feel any difference in the way he and the baby are treated. I will always consider him."

This woman.

I wasn't sure how I had ever got so lucky, but there was no way I was ever going to let her go.

Lowering my head, I brushed her lips with mine. "Thank you."

She smiled. "So, what do you think? Would a year living at my place be a good idea?"

Because I was so caught up in her consideration for Aiden, I hadn't thought about the question she'd asked. There was more room at her place than mine. All of the rooms were bigger, which meant it would be easier for us to fit in two children's stuff, plus my own.

"If we moved in here," I began, "how would I contribute?" Shannen's brows lowered in confusion, so I continued. "At my place, I pay rent, but you already own yours. Or do you have a mortgage I can help with?"

Shannen shook her head. "I inherited a ridiculous amount of money from my grandparents. I used it to buy this flat outright knowing it would only go up in value. I've had it since I was twenty, so it'll make me a decent profit when I sell it."

I raised my eyebrows. I knew her family was loaded, but for her to have been able to afford her flat at twenty... that was money I had never seen in my life. "Christ. Okay, so not paying rent or a mortgage would save me money. And then if we split the bills, apart from Aiden's stuff, that will mean I can save more."

Who the hell am I right now? I had never had to think much about saving money until I'd moved in on my own. Even at Guy's, while I'd paid rent, it wasn't much and we split everything else, but the only thing I saved for were things for Aiden. This was another level, though. This was me talking about saving up for a property. A place I would live, have a family.

"Cal." Shannen smiled up at me, her eyes bright. "We've got this. Between us, we'll have enough to get a good place to live. Anything extra you save from not paying rent and halving bills can go towards that and whatever we need for the baby. I also have a pretty solid savings account."

Nodding slowly, I said, "Yeah. I just never thought I'd be in a place where I could have everything I wanted."

I could hear the voice in my head getting ready to argue. Feel it crawling through to let me know it was never going to happen. That this was temporary and something was going to come along to snatch it away.

It isn't real.

But it *was* real. All the shit we'd been through. All the crap she'd put up with from me, yet there we were. We'd fixed every mess that had been made. We'd talked through disagreements, and we'd made it. I'd figured out how to be with someone, and once I let myself, it wasn't that hard. Shannen made everything easier. Everything with her was instinctive. Every time I looked at her, I just knew what to do. What she needed. I *wanted* to give her everything because she was everything to me.

My chest—that weird feeling I always got when I was around her—made itself known. It felt... bigger somehow. Stronger. My lips curved upwards as I continued to look into her blue eyes, wondering if she could feel the same thing.

Did she feel it in her chest too? Did it feel as intense? Did she know what I was trying to say?

Shannen pressed her lips against mine, then whispered, "I love you too."

I slid my hand into her hair, tangling my fingers in her thick curls. "I promise I'll get better at saying it," I told her.

She kissed me again, then trailed her lips along my jawline. "Just show me."

Chapter 31

Shannen

As CAL LED ME into his bedroom, my heart had never felt fuller. I'd watched him throughout our conversation about our future, and I could see him becoming both excited about it and terrified that it would never truly happen. Even that was a long way from the Cal I'd first met, who'd pretty much told me if I didn't leave of my own accord, he'd make me.

And he did, in the end.

But he'd also come back. He'd come back just for me and found it was no longer 'just me'. And he'd stayed.

Finally, in spite of every single thing that had tried to keep us apart, we were where we wanted to be. The full picture was far from perfect, but Cal and I... we were in the best place we'd ever been and that was enough.

Once we were in his room, I felt... vulnerable. Not in the way I had the first time we'd ever had sex, but in a brand new way. We had no more secrets between us now. Every skeleton had been released from its closet, every confession had been made. Now, the only thing left was us. Just me and Cal and whatever our relationship would become.

We were on the edge of something new. Something that would change everything again.

It was enthralling and terrifying in equal measure because this was it. We had chosen each other over and over, through every obstacle. An unspoken commitment that now, we really were moving forward.

"Only with you, Shan," Cal said softly, reminding me of the words we'd spoken at my mum's house.

Smiling up at him, I said, "Always."

As his mouth met mine, he carefully walked me backwards to his bed and lowered me onto the dark grey duvet. It was familiar, soft, and I shuffled up the bed a little, waiting for Cal to join me.

"Take off your top," he said, still standing at the end of the bed. His words were gentle, his eyes filled with heat and adoration. He watched me as I sat up to do as he asked. Once my top was off, I moved my hands to unclip my bra, but he shook his head.

"Not yet." He climbed onto the bed, lying on his side and gently pressing me back against the mattress, my head resting on the pillow. Cal shuffled down the bed a little, so his head was in line with my stomach, then he propped himself up on his elbow. He placed his free hand on my belly, so lightly I almost couldn't feel it. Slowly, his fingers spread out, and his eyes were completely transfixed there, where our baby was growing.

I knew he saw something different than I saw. I'd always hated that my stomach had forever been slightly squishy. Not in a way that affected my day to day life or caused me to work out excessively and diet to get rid of it. It was one of those minor flaws that I put up with but didn't like to draw attention to. Cal, however, had always looked at me like I was a work of art.

"That's only going to get bigger, you know," I joked with a small laugh. "It'll probably never look the same again afterwards either."

"It's already bigger, and it's fucking perfect." He moved his hand and placed a kiss on the soft flesh before turning his head to look at me.

Smiling, I said, "Oh, yeah?"

"Yeah." He pulled himself back up the bed, his eyes dark.

My body heated under his intense stare. Nobody had ever looked at me the way he did. My pussy clenched. I slowly slid the straps of my bra down my arms before undoing the front fastening and pulling it out from behind me to drop it on the floor, enjoying the flash in his eyes as his gaze fell to my chest. My breaths became heavier as I waited for him to cover my body with his, for his tongue to circle my nipples, already peaked in anticipation.

But he didn't move. As my eyes met his, he remained silent, and I realised what I'd done from the glint of mischief I saw there. He was challenging me to keep going with my strip show when all I wanted was for him to touch me. He liked it when I took control, but he equally liked to *be* in control, and it seemed that he wanted to be in the position of power right then.

Luckily, I wanted that too.

Instead of waiting for him to tell me, I trailed my hands down over my breasts to my stomach, then undid my jeans. Lifting my hips, I pushed them slowly down my legs, taking my knickers with them to save time. I could feel him watching every move I made, and my skin was flushed from the heat of his perusal. By the time I was naked, my entire body was shaking with the need to feel him. Under different circumstances, I might have continued the performance, but the only thing I wanted inside me was him. I could have touched myself, let my hands roam over my hot skin until I was ready to explode, but I needed *him*. I would have lay there forever in desperate anticipation if it meant he was the next person to run his hands over me. To awaken all the parts of me that had been dormant since our split.

"I was wrong," he said huskily. "This is the sexiest you have ever been."

Almost involuntarily, I let out a small whine, lifting my knees and parting my legs. My pussy throbbed as his gaze moved downwards.

Leaning down, his lips lazily danced with mine. It was desperate but not rushed. Urgent but so slow my limbs weakened until there was nothing left of me but a mess of neediness.

I'd asked him to show me how he felt, and that was exactly what he was doing with each delicious kiss. He remained beside me, careful not to touch any part of me other than my lips because he knew it would drive me crazy. And I knew it was doing the same to him because I could hear how hard he was breathing, like he was fighting to stay in control.

"Please," I mumbled between kisses. "Please touch me." I reached up and tugged at his T-shirt, unable to stand not having his skin against mine for a second longer.

I felt him smirk against my lips, but he didn't say anything, and I let out a frustrated moan as even that small movement made the ache in my pussy intensify. I moved my hands down to unzip his jeans then desperately pushed at his T-shirt again, trying to coax him in to giving in to me, and I scratched my nails lightly down his back.

He moaned at the contact, and the trembling in my limbs grew stronger. All I wanted was for his fingers to glide across my body, to bring me back to life.

Finally, he pulled back from me and tugged his T-shirt over his head.

The only sound in the room was our heavy breathing as everything seemed to stop when his eyes met mine again.

Then, he was on top of me, my legs wrapped around him as he covered me. He ran a hand from my hip up to my breast, and the moment his fingers closed around it, I sighed in relief, closing my eyes as I relished the sensation of him firmly exploring my body. His dick, although still inside his jeans, was rock solid, and I pushed my hips up against it.

"Cal," I begged, arching my back as his fingers teased my nipple, my legs opening wider. "Please. *Please.*"

I pushed at his unzipped jeans, shoving them down his hips then doing the same with his boxers while he moved to take my nipple into his mouth. I could no longer reach to get the rest of his clothes off, and I cried out again as my body convulsed with the pleasure he was giving me without even being inside me yet. I was so close to tipping over the edge, and the only thing I could do was close my eyes and enjoy the journey because I was so aroused that I could no longer form words.

My stomach was full of butterflies, my inner thighs were coated in my wetness, and I needed the release only he could give me.

"I could fuck you all day forever and it still wouldn't be enough," he murmured, swiping a finger through my slick folds, making me buck my hips. He pulled away from me slightly to take off the rest of his clothes and then moved back over me.

I opened my eyes when I felt him looking at me, his face close to mine, his eyes hooded, intense.

"I love you," he said.

I would never tire of hearing him say that.

"I love you too."

Lifting my leg and wrapping it around his hip, he sank inside me, and I gasped in relief. He moved inside me so, so slowly, but it was everything.

It wasn't just sex, and it wasn't fucking. He was showing me how he felt in the most intimate way. He kissed me like nothing else in the world mattered as long as he was with me, and we moved in such perfect sync that it was as if we had never been apart.

261

As my muscles clenched around him, I knew that what was coming would be epic. Transcendent.

And as I hurtled to my peak, all I could think about was him and the fact that he was mine, and we could live the rest of our lives doing this with nobody to get in our way.

Chapter 32

Cal

I DROVE SHANNEN HOME a little after two, after spending a couple of hours in bed with her doing two of my favourite things. Talking to her and making her come. Waiting for some time alone with her had made the week feel longer than it actually was, but it had been worth the wait. If there was any way I could have kept her with me for the rest of the day and night, I would have, but she couldn't come to the school with me, and I knew she wanted to see her mum to find out how the chat with her dad had gone. We had plans to see each other the next day, though. We were going to take Aiden to the cinema. I hadn't told him yet as I planned to surprise him with it in the morning. He'd been asking to see the latest animated movie doing the rounds, and I was willing to try anything if it meant he'd find a new favourite film.

While I waited until it was time to pick Aiden up, I looked around my living room, imagining my and Aiden's stuff in Shannen's place. I knew she was fully aware of how much mess kids could make, and anytime Aiden had been at hers, she hadn't been bothered by it. But that was temporary. I hoped she wouldn't mind coloured pencils and felt tip pens all over the place, toys on the coffee table or the kitchen cabinets, and additional clutter from all the things I'd bought since I'd moved out of Guy's.

Somehow, I knew she wouldn't mind at all. After what we'd been through, a bit of mess was a small price to pay.

A knock at the door made me pause in my thoughts and I looked at the clock above the TV. Everyone I knew was aware I'd be leaving to pick up Aiden in about ten minutes.

I left the living room and walked down the short hallway to the front door, opening it.

You have got to be shitting me.

"Callum Lewis?"

Two uniformed police officers stood in the corridor outside my door, serious expressions on their faces. Two others stood behind them, further back.

I nodded, my pulse racing just from the sight of them. Four men, all of them young-looking but tall. One of them was speaking, but I had already slipped into the place in my head I went to when I was cornered. I was pretty sure they were telling me their names, but I didn't hear a thing. While I would usually have been instantly angry, though, something else ran through me. Panic, and I didn't like it.

Before I knew what was happening, I was grabbed and pushed against my front door, my face sideways against the wood. A ballsy and unnecessary move since I hadn't resisted. Then again, I wasn't sure what the expression on my face was showing.

"Callum Lewis, you're being arrested on suspicion of the murder of Katie Young. You do not have to say anything, but it may harm your defence if you do not mention when questioned..."

Again, I knew one of the officers was talking to me, but the words became muffled.

You're being arrested on suspicion of the murder of Katie Young.

Katie. Who I took home less than a week ago.

My pulse, which had already sped up, was now thudding so hard I thought I was going to explode. Stiffening my shoulders, I shoved backwards, attempting to shrug the heavy-handed pricks off me, but the bigger of the two pushed back harder, and I realised my hands had been cuffed behind me. Probably a good thing as I wanted to swing for him.

"Easy," he said, although it was more of a growl. "Don't make this worse for yourself."

"What the fuck is going on?" I snapped. "Katie is dead?"

"Let's just get you to the station," the other officer said. "We have some questions for you."

"No!" I shoved backwards again, and this time the guy pinning me lost his grip slightly and I managed to turn around to face them, though I was instantly grabbed by the arms. "I can't. I need to pick my son up from school. There's only fifteen minutes before the school lets him out."

Not only did I need to collect Aiden, but I needed to not be in fucking handcuffs for the second time in four months.

There was no way this arrest could stick, was there? I hadn't seen Katie in days, so if she'd only just been found dead, I couldn't get the blame. I was either at work, with Shannen, or at home with Aiden.

But to arrest me, they must have believed they had something on me. Unless this was another one of Scott's scare tactics.

Katie is dead.

That, though, was a fact. These men didn't just rock up at my flat for a joke. They were taking me to the police station because someone had killed her.

Shit. *Shit.* It was pretty coincidental that she was dead so soon after getting out of rehab, and after she'd said Scott has been trying to contact her. Fuck! Why did she stay in Taunton when he knew she lived there? I was assuming a lot. For all I knew, she could have been randomly attacked elsewhere, and maybe Scott had nothing to do with it.

But I doubted it.

Swallowing the bile in my throat, I tried to stop myself from throwing up, but my stomach was churning so hard I was sure it would come up soon.

I'd *just* seen Katie. I had been pretty clear on how little I wanted to do with her and how afraid I was that she would one day take Aiden from me, but I didn't want her dead. I wanted her to clean herself up. That was why I'd given her a chance.

What the hell had happened?

"The quicker we get you booked in at the station, the quicker you can make your phone call and make some alternative arrangements," one of the officers said, and I shook my head.

Alternative...? By the time they got me to the station, Aiden's class would already be letting out. I needed to make the call now. I needed to focus on one thing at a time, but my head was fucked.

"Please," I said, trying not to lose my shit. "He's five years old. I can't just leave him waiting for me in the playground."

My first thought was to ring Shannen, but I immediately pushed that idea aside. She couldn't know about this, not yet. Not after the amazing day we'd had.

See. 'I love you' ruins everything. Just like it did when she said it for the first time.

Shaking my head again, irritated with the way my brain was trying to take me, I said, "Please. I just need two minutes to call my mate and we can go." Guy was at home doing some admin work, so at least once I got hold of him, he could be at the school within five minutes.

"No can do. We're under strict instructions to do this one by the book."

The taller of the two glared at the officer who'd spoken like he'd said something he shouldn't have. *This one?* Did they not have to do every arrest by the book?

This *must* have had something to do with Scott. He was the big boss in Exeter. These fuckers were probably under his thumb.

"Fine," I said. "Let's get this over with."

I need to get home to my son and my woman.

Because I was under pressure to get someone to Aiden right away, the custody sergeant ran through the same crap the two officers had told me quickly, with one additional point. I was only being booked in in Exeter. Katie was murdered in Taunton, which meant I had to wait in custody until I could be transported there for questioning. I'd stress over that later, though. I was restless and hardly listening to what they said to me until I had a phone in my hand, and I called Guy's mobile, hoping he'd answer. I was already fifteen minutes past school pick up time, and they were probably going to start calling me if someone didn't show up soon. Not that it would matter. The only thing I'd taken with me to the station was the key to my flat. I was aware my flat would be searched; that was what the third and fourth police officers were four. To make sure nobody else entered until the place had been searched. I didn't give a shit about that. There was nothing to find there anyway.

"Hello?" Guy answered, and I sighed with relief that he'd picked up.

"Guy, it's me. Listen, I don't have much time, but I need you to go and get Aiden for me," I said quickly. This was not the ideal place to have a phone call, but while I was at the police station, there was no option for privacy.

There was a short pause. "You're already late. What's going on, Cal?"

"I've been arrested. The police picked me up as I was getting ready to collect Aiden. Katie's dead and they think I did it."

Another pause. "Katie's dead? But... what?"

"I know, Guy." Sighing, I shoved a hand through my hair. "I know. I don't understand how this could have happened or why they think it has anything to do with me, but I need your help. Please just get Aiden for me."

"What about Shannen? Does she know?"

"No, and I need you to keep it quiet for now. I'm hoping I can get this sorted out and be released before she has to know. I've done nothing wrong and I'm not going down for this. So, don't tell her. She doesn't need the stress."

A sensation of nausea came over me again. What she'd been through in the week she'd found out she was pregnant, not to mention all of the drama that came with being with me, was more than enough for her to handle. She'd been lucky the day some twat had crashed into her car; I didn't want the anxiety of my arrest to put our baby at risk.

"What should I tell Aiden?"

"I don't know. Maybe tell him I'm with Shannen." I hated the lie. Hated that he was expecting me to be there and would hear Guy telling him I'd ditched him to be with Shannen. "No. Don't tell him that. Can you just tell him I had a job I wasn't expecting and that I'll be back late?"

"What if you aren't, Cal?" Guy's worried tone was a sharp reminder of how serious this was. This wasn't like before. I wasn't there for questioning over an incident that had happened in the past. I had been arrested and read my rights. For a murder. If Scott was somehow involved, then my chances of getting out were even slimmer.

"Let's cross that bridge when we come to it," I said.

On my own, with my hot head, I was screwed.

Like a lightbulb had turned on in my brain, I said, "Can you call Gaby? Do you still have her number?" Shannen had asked Gaby to call Guy last weekend so he could break the news to me about Shannen's accident, so if he didn't delete his call history, he should be able to reach her. "Ask her if her brother can help me again. I need a solicitor."

"I have it," Guy answered. "And yes, of course. But I won't be able to let you know if he's coming."

I was pretty sure I could ask the police to contact Gavin Davis for me, but I hoped if Guy went through Gaby first, it might strengthen my chances of him showing up.

"Give it a try. I need him. It has to be him."

It took approximately two hours in custody before my thoughts began to spiral. Two hours in a shitty cell with nothing but a hard bed and a toilet for company. It was another hour after that when I was removed from the cell and taken to Taunton police station, where I went through another round of being told things I already knew and then thrown into my second holding cell of the day.

By then, my temper was as close to the edge as it had ever been. The only good news I had was being told my solicitor was on his way. There was no chance this would be another freebie, but I couldn't be interviewed without his advice. I'd just have to hope it didn't take all night.

As I sat on the uncomfortable bed, my feet pulled up and my arms wrapped around my knees, I was so tense I had a headache.

If I'd thought things were a mess before, this was on another level.

I'd been arrested for murder, for fuck's sake. I couldn't take in the fact that Katie was dead. I didn't know how to feel about it. The only thing I could muster was rage that this was happening again.

I missed my boy. Couldn't stop thinking about whether he believed what Guy had told him about where I was. It was clear I wouldn't be out by the morning, and then what? I didn't want him to know the truth, but if Guy couldn't come up with another answer, Aiden might start to think I'd left him again.

My foot tapped against the bed as my eyes stared at the cell door.

Then there was Shannen. I was meant to call her later, and when I didn't, she'd wonder where I was. I didn't expect Guy to lie to her, but I didn't know how she would react. Would she doubt me again? Would she believe I'd done this? She knew I'd seen Katie at the weekend. Maybe it would cross her mind that I'd got rid of Katie to make sure she didn't come near Aiden.

That motive would make perfect sense to the police, especially since they knew she'd already reported me for domestic abuse, even if she'd taken it back. It wasn't a stretch to think someone as violent as me would permanently take her out of the picture. The only thing on my side was that I didn't have a criminal record.

Not yet, anyway.

Because if I got through this, and Scott was involved...

I was going to kill him.

Chapter 33

Shannen

IT WAS GETTING CLOSE to half past eight in the evening, and I hadn't heard from Cal since he'd dropped me home earlier. It was unusual because every other day since we'd got back together, we'd sent messages through the day and then he'd call me just after eight, once he'd put Aiden to bed. I'd text him a few hours ago, but he hadn't replied.

I wasn't worried exactly. After school, I figured Cal was probably doing stuff with Aiden, so I just waited. But now, though, it was starting to feel like something wasn't right. It wasn't helped by the fact that my mum wasn't back yet either. She had called around five to say that she and my dad were going to spend a bit more time together and not to expect her back until a bit later, but being on my own meant I had nothing to distract me. I'd tried watching TV, reading, tidying up, sorting through my emails, but none of it kept me occupied for long.

Grabbing my phone from the coffee table, I dialled Cal's number, wondering if maybe he'd just fallen asleep after putting Aiden to bed, although that didn't explain why he hadn't answered my earlier messages. Our day had been pretty intense, though. I bit back a smirk as I thought about the hours we'd spent together earlier. Nothing felt more right to me than being wrapped around him. Sex with him was something I had missed more than I'd wanted to admit, and the relief of having him right where he belonged had kept a smile on my face all day.

After six rings, the phone kicked into voicemail, and I frowned before hanging up. This was getting weird.

A knock at my door made me jump. My mum had a key, and only a couple of people knew the code to the building. Every one of them would usually have sent a text to say they were coming.

A frown still firmly on my face, I got up to see who it was. I didn't expect to find Guy standing there. His frown matched mine, and right away, my heart began to race. Guy never looked this serious.

"Can I come in?" he asked, offering me what I guessed was supposed to be a tiny reassuring smile.

My heart went from racing to plummeting to my stomach, and I nodded, moving back to let him in. Once the door was closed, I looked up at him. "Where's Cal?" I asked because there was no other reason he would drop by unannounced. Being unable to reach Cal was unheard of. Something was very wrong.

Guy gestured towards the sofa, and I felt tears forming behind my eyes as I walked ahead of him to sit down. My hands were shaking as Guy sat beside me and took one of them in his. With his other hand, he scratched at the side of his head before running his hand through his hair.

"Shannen, I... Cal asked me not to tell you where he is, but it's getting late, and there's no way I can hide it from you any longer." He fidgeted, and my heartbeat amped up again.

Where the hell was he? Cal had asked Guy to keep something from me? What could be so bad he didn't want me to know? I had never once felt like I couldn't trust Cal, so I was at a complete loss as to what was going on.

"I haven't heard from him since this afternoon," I said. "I tried to call him, but there's no answer."

Blowing out a breath, Guy said, "He doesn't have his phone with him." Shifting in his seat, he went on. "That's why I came. Because I knew if you didn't hear from him soon, you'd be worried."

"I *am* worried. Where is he, Guy?"

He sighed, looking anywhere but at me. "Fuck." When his gaze came back to mine, he said, "He called me this afternoon, just a bit after you went home, I guess. He's been arrested."

I blinked, unsure I'd heard properly. "Arrested?"

"Yeah. Shannen, Katie... she's dead. I don't know any details, other than that they've arrested Cal for her murder. I don't know what's happening beyond that. He used his one call to ask me to collect Aiden from school and I've heard nothing since then."

I stared at him, hoping desperately for any sign this was some horrible joke. Ill-timed and totally tasteless, but I had never more hoped someone was kidding.

But he wasn't. He was saying the words quickly, as if he just needed to get them out, but his face was drawn and serious. He held my hand tighter. "I'm sorry, Shannen. I wish I could tell you something more, but that is literally all I know."

The only thing in my head was a list of questions Guy clearly didn't know the answers to. When and how was Katie murdered? Cal had seen her the previous weekend, that much I knew, but how could anyone think Cal was involved in her death? The police would have needed some kind of evidence to arrest him, but what?

Cal was not capable of murder.

Well, technically, he might have been if pushed hard enough. He had almost killed someone before. But he was a different person now. Regardless of what Katie had done to him, and to us, he wouldn't have hurt her. There was no way.

So, why had he been arrested?

Another thought occurred to me then. "Wait. If you're here, where's Aiden?"

"He's at my house and he's in bed. He doesn't know I left, but Gaby's watching him."

Tilting my head to the side, I said, "Gaby? How did that happen?"

I could have sworn I saw the slightest hint of redness cross his cheeks, but he said, "You know how your mum gave her my number so she could let me know about the accident?" I nodded. "Gaby's number was still in my call history, and Cal asked me to call her and get her brother to help him out."

Before I could ask any more questions, the front door opened again, and we both turned to see my mum enter. Her eyes darted between me and Guy, who was still holding my hand, and he pulled it back sharply as if he were doing something wrong. Under normal circumstances, I would have laughed, but I looked over at Mum and said, "Cal's been arrested. For murder."

Her eyes widened. "Murder? Whose murder?"

"Katie. Aiden's mum. But we have no other information."

Flicking into 'mum' mode faster than I'd ever seen, she said, "Does he have a solicitor?"

I glanced at Guy, hoping he would confirm that Gaby's brother had gone to him.

"Yeah," Guy said. "He's worried about how much it'll cost, but he's got one for now."

"One sec," Mum said, and she dashed outside again slamming the door behind her.

Guy and I exchanged a look of confusion. Reverting to the conversation we'd been having before, I said, "Okay, so you called Gaby. How did she end up at your house?"

Every other question I had, Guy didn't have the answers to, so I asked a question he *could* answer.

He shrugged like it was no big deal. "Who else could I have asked to watch Aiden? If he wakes up, at least he knows Gaby."

His point was valid, but there was something about the way his face coloured when her name was mentioned that made me wonder if I was missing something. Had they been talking since last weekend?

Shaking my head, I said, "So, what do we do now? How do we find out what's going on?"

"Gaby's brother is going to call her when he can. When she asked him to help, he said he would get to Cal as soon as he could, but it wouldn't be for a few hours. I hope he's there by now."

If Cal had been taken in right before picking Aiden up from school, that meant he'd been in custody for close to six hours already. I knew how hard he'd found it the last time he was at the police station, so I couldn't imagine how he felt now. There was a murder charge hanging over his head and...

Like I'd been struck by lightning, I jumped, startled as something occurred to me. "Is this Scott's doing?" I asked, semi-rhetorically. "Cal said Scott had been bothering Katie. Do you think he has something to do with this?"

The idea ripped through me because, based on everything Scott had already done, this reeked of him.

"Yeah, I think he probably does. But... is he a murderer?"

Was he capable? I doubted it, but even if he was, there was no way he would get his own hands dirty. Which meant that if he *was* involved, then he'd probably paid someone else to do it for him. It was hardly the first time he'd done that. Although, *he* didn't pay Katie, my dad did...

So, even if we told the police what Scott did and could prove he was behind bribing Katie to make a false allegation in the past, if my dad was the one who actually paid her, would that mean he would be the one who would be accused of paying to have her killed off?

A chill ran through me as everything began to catch up with me.

Why, on the days when we were happiest, did things keep happening to destroy it?

We had seen our baby, found out everything was going well. We'd had time alone together and talked about our future, and now.... now we were dangerously close to losing it again.

The very real prospect that Cal could be charged for murder hurtled through me, and I shook my head. "Guy, this can't happen. I can't lose him."

As he looked at me, I could see in his eyes that he wanted to promise me it wouldn't happen, but the truth was, he couldn't promise any such thing. Especially if Scott *was* involved.

"All we can do for now is wait," he said.

Shaking my head again, I stood up. "No. I'm going to the police station to find out what's happening. "

I headed for the door to get my boots and put them on so I could get some answers, but Guy grabbed my arm and gently pulled me back. "You can't go down there," he said. "They won't tell you anything anyway."

"Oh, they'll tell me," I said, shrugging him off and starting towards the shoe rack again. "I won't leave until I find out what the hell is going on."

"Shannen, no." Guy reached for my arm again, holding it tighter this time. I glared up at him, and he said, "There is no point in you going down there. They'll just make you sit around on uncomfortable chairs waiting, and you... you shouldn't be in a place like that. You need to look after yourself."

I knew exactly what he was saying. I was pregnant, and my stress levels were elevating quickly. I couldn't afford to lose control.

But I was upset. Fuming, in fact.

More than anything, I was terrified.

My man had been taken away and locked up, once again for something he hadn't done. What if this set him back to where he was before? To the point where he believed he was worthless. What if this made him end things between us for good because he thought me and the baby were better off without him?

Unable to handle the barrage of thoughts in my head, I burst into tears, and Guy pulled me into him, his arms tightly around me.

"I've got you," he said, softly. "I've got you."

I heard the front door open, and I turned my head to the side as my mum came back in, followed closely by my dad.

My dad.

The one who had helped set this whole crazy train in motion. If he hadn't turned to Scott, there would have been nobody to pay Katie to make a false allegation. If my dad hadn't given her the money, she wouldn't have gone to rehab, and Cal wouldn't have even seen her.

She probably wouldn't be dead, and Aiden wouldn't have to find out that he'd never get a chance to meet his mum.

Almost all of this was on him.

I ripped myself from Guy's grip and flew across the room towards my dad. My mum called out to me, but it was too late. Pulling my hand back, I launched a hard slap across my father's face, so forceful that his head snapped to the side.

I had never hit anyone before in my life, but I couldn't think of anyone who deserved it more, apart from Scott himself, but he wasn't there.

God help him if I bumped into him, though.

As I stood, somewhat stunned at what I'd done but relieved to ease some of my fury, my mum took me in her arms.

"Why is he here?" I asked as my tears began to fall again. "Why did you bring him here?"

"I'm sorry," she said, stroking my hair. "When you said there would be legal bills to pay, I wanted to make sure your dad knew he was going to be paying them, no matter how much it costs. And he wanted to be the one to tell you."

The part of me that was still seething wanted to tell him it was the least he could do. I would have paid it myself, but this was down to my father, so yeah, he *was* going to pay. However, the part of me that still had a modicum of manners felt the need to acknowledge the offer. I couldn't bring myself to thank him, but I looked at him over my mum's shoulder and nodded.

He was holding his cheek, where a red mark was forming, and he still looked dazed. Not so much from the hit itself but from the shock that I'd struck him.

Maybe now he'd get it. Maybe now he'd see what a fucking disaster he'd caused. In my life, in Cal's, in my mum's, and in Aiden's. Even Guy was affected by this. My sister too.

He and Scott had demolished everything.

"Shannen," my dad said, "I will fix this. I promise you, I will fix it."

Swallowing down the lump in my throat, I looked away, resting my head on my mum's shoulder again as I sobbed. Not just for what Cal was going through, but for me. For my family. Because I knew in that moment that no matter what my dad did, I couldn't see a time when I would be able to forgive him. He had obliterated my trust. Tainted every good memory I had with him. Made my family feel like it was no longer a safe place for me.

He wasn't my dad anymore. He was merely the man who'd helped bring me into existence and nothing more.

Without a word, he left my apartment, and I stayed right where I was crying in my mum's arms until Guy came into the room with three cups of tea and placed them on the coffee table. I hadn't even realised he'd left.

I wiped my eyes, and Mum wiped hers too, as we sat down on the sofa next to each other, Guy in one of the armchairs. "Thank you," I said to him, and he smiled softly. Glancing at my mum, I said, "In case you hadn't guessed, this is Cal's friend, Guy."

She chuckled. "Yeah, I figured. Thank you for taking care of Shannen. And for the tea."

He smiled sadly. "No problem. I just wish there was something useful I could say or some information I could bring."

Mum returned his smile. "It's not your fault. I think the system was designed to make everyone on the outside feel useless." Turning her attention to me, she took my hand. "You just need to stay calm."

"Calm? Mum, the police have got Cal. Scott wants him in jail. I'm not sure if there is any way to fix this."

Closing my eyes, I dropped my head onto the back of sofa, nausea washing over me.

She was right, I did need to calm down, but there was a weird adrenaline rush pulsing through my body. Someone had placed a threat on my family, and I wanted to go out and find whoever was responsible and make them regret it. I'd never felt anything like it before. It felt alien and uncomfortable, but I wanted to borrow my mum's car, drive to Scott and Jade's house, and smash him to pieces.

Was this what people meant when they talked about maternal instincts? The desire to protect not just their child but their loved ones at any cost? Either that, or I was simply done having other people messing with my life.

Taking a deep breath, I blew it out slowly. If I began stomping around the city like Godzilla, I would book myself a place in the cell next to Cal, and that wouldn't do either of us any good. I'd already whacked my dad. My stomach churned at the thought, at the look of pain on his face. Not because of physical hurt but because it was clear I couldn't forgive him.

But my mum had been with him for hours...

Turning my head towards her, I said, "What happened today?"

She picked up her cup of tea. "We talked. A lot. Argued a bit."

"You were gone for a long time, though. It can't have been unbearable if you stayed."

She blew across the surface of her drink, steam billowing upwards as she did. "Not unbearable. But uncomfortable a lot of the time."

"So, what happens now with you two?"

Mum sighed, resting her free hand over mine. "I don't know. I thought maybe, if he worked hard to rebuild his relationship with you, then in time, there could be a way forward. But I'm still angry with him. And I don't know how he can ever regain my trust after what he did. And of course, there's you to consider."

Shaking my head, I said, "Mum, no. You have to do what's right for you. I get that you don't want to hurt me, but... this is your marriage."

"And I'm your mum. Very soon, you'll have your own little one, and you'll know how it feels to want to protect your family with everything you have."

Weirdly, I was already getting a taste of that.

"Dad's your family too," I said.

"Yeah. But he did something deliberately to hurt you, even if the intention behind it was good. We talked about it for a long time today, and I know how much he regrets what he did. Truth be told, I was close to considering going home over the weekend and making a start on trying to repair things. But now this has happened, it only reminds me of just how much damage he's done. I know he couldn't have predicted how far it would go, but he shouldn't have been anywhere near it in the first place."

"Do you think Scott is involved in this too?" I asked her. "Katie's death, I mean."

She paused to take a sip of her tea. "It seems too much of a coincidence for him not to be, but I don't know *how* he's involved. And I don't know why he would go to such lengths."

"Shannen, we can't keep guessing," Guy said. "I know it's hard to stop when we don't know what's going on, but you're going to drive yourself crazy if you keep trying to figure it out."

"I'm driving myself crazy anyway." All of a sudden, I realised how Cal must have felt waiting for me to call from the hospital. He did at least know I was okay, but he'd told me how he couldn't breathe until he'd heard from me.

That was exactly how I felt. And I couldn't even hear from him. All I'd get for now would be word from his solicitor.

I needed to hear his voice so badly it hurt. A feeling I was far too familiar with having missed him for weeks. This was worse, though. Because now he wasn't at the end of the phone. I couldn't cave and call him, and knowing that made it just as he'd said. Hard to breathe.

Standing up, I walked across the living room to the adjoined kitchen, to the fridge. I'd put my scan photos on there, under a fridge magnet from Crete that my sister had brought back for me after their holiday last year. I'd left one with Cal, and the other three were in front of me. One was for me, one was for my mum, and the other one... Cal said it was the right thing to do to give one to Guy since he was going to be the baby's uncle, albeit an unofficial one.

As I took the pictures from beneath the magnet, I stared at the image, remembering how happy we'd been that morning. Blinking, a tear slid down my cheek, and I clutched the pictures to my chest, holding the image of our baby close. After taking a few deep breaths, I went back into the living room, Mum's and Guy's eyes on me as I sat back down. I shuffled close to my mum and beckoned for Guy to come and sit at my other side. He put his drink down on the table and came to sit beside me.

I handed Mum one of the scan photos and gave another to Guy. "Meet your grandbaby, and your niece or nephew," I said quietly, placing one hand on my stomach while the other hand held the last photo.

"Wow," Guy said, his eyes transfixed. "With everything else that's happened, I didn't get a chance to ask Cal how the scan went, but I'm guessing it was good?"

I nodded. "Really good."

He laughed when I told him the baby was due on Aiden's birthday, but he kept his eyes on the picture, smiling softly.

"This is the most beautiful baby I've ever seen," my mum said, then she chuckled. "I also said that about Alexander. I was right about him too."

I smiled. "He is pretty cute. Sadie and Stefan make beautiful babies."

"The genes this kid is inheriting," Guy said, wrapping his arm around me. "There'll be modelling agencies hammering the door down from day one."

I snorted, resting my head on his shoulder. Then, with a sigh, I said, "I need him with me, Guy. I can't do this on my own."

"Shannen, if it comes to that, and that is a big if, you're not alone. Not ever."

"He's right," Mum added. "Cal didn't kill anyone, and they are going to have a hard time making it stick. But if it really did come to that, I wouldn't leave you. You're my baby, and I will do everything I can to support you."

I knew their words were meant to help. Well-intentioned and sweet. But I couldn't shake the feeling that everything was about to fall apart. That I would spend the next years of my life visiting the man I loved in prison.

Chapter 34

Shannen

AUTHORITIES HAVE LAUNCHED A *murder investigation after a body was discovered in an apartment on Willow Lane on Wednesday morning. The deceased, identified as Katie Young, 30, was found after neighbours reported their concerns for the young woman.*

Police have confirmed that the circumstances surrounding her death are being treated as suspicious. Detective Inspector Sarah Moore said in a statement:

"This is an active investigation, and we are working tirelessly to piece together what happened. We are appealing to anyone who was in or around Willow Lane between 2:00 PM on May 4th and 12:00 AM on May 5th to come forward if they saw anything unusual or have any information that might assist our enquiries."

Forensic teams have been on-site, and officers are conducting door-to-door enquiries in the surrounding area. Investigators have not yet disclosed the cause of death, but sources indicate that the victim may have sustained injuries consistent with foul play.

A local resident, who wished to remain anonymous, commented:

"It's heartbreaking to think something like this could happen here. Willow Park is usually such a safe place."

Police are urging anyone with information or CCTV recordings from the area to contact them via the non-emergency number.

Further updates are expected as the investigation progresses.

Because I knew it would be impossible to sleep, once we'd all finished our cups of tea, I went back to Guy's with him so I could be there when Gavin eventually called Gaby with an update. I didn't plan to stay all night, just until we heard something. It was getting close to ten when we got there, and once we had sat down under the dimmed lights in Guy's living room, Gaby had presented us with a news article she'd found on social media, published earlier that day.

"So," I said, handing her phone back to her, "the police found Katie's body two days ago, but they're appealing for people who were in the area last Saturday. The same day Cal took her home."

Guy, who had been reading the article from his place to my left, said, "That fits into the time he was out. He picked her up from the rehab centre at two."

Sickness churned in my stomach. Cal had been at Katie's place within the time frame they estimated her time of death to be. I still wasn't sure how anyone knew he'd been there at all, unless, as I'd guessed earlier, his fingerprints were in her flat. That would have been less of a concern without a solid timeframe, but if someone had seen him or his car there within those hours...

"In theory," Gaby said, "the timeframe the police have might be smaller than they're telling the public. But Cal being there within that ten-hour period isn't proof that he killed her. Even him going into the flat isn't proof. In ten hours, any number of people could have been in there, and they'll need to speak to everyone they can to establish who last saw her alive."

"The news report said they're questioning neighbours, so maybe one of them saw someone else around," Guy suggested.

Gaby nodded. "What I find interesting is that she's been named. That means her family has been informed of her death. If she had family, why didn't she turn to them when she needed help?"

"Cal said she wasn't close to them," I replied, thinking back on the limited information I had about Katie. "I think she only had a mum, but she threw Katie out when she was nineteen."

"It's sad," Gaby said as she leaned back on the sofa. "Sounds like Katie didn't have the best chances in life."

Her words made me pause. From what I'd heard from Cal, she was the heartless bitch who'd walked out on her child. The woman who'd spent years drinking and partying instead of facing her responsibilities. The person who had accepted money to report Cal for a crime he didn't commit. But Cal hadn't spoken of her as badly after he saw her recently. In fact, other than his concerns about what she might want regarding Aiden, he'd seemed glad she was trying to straighten herself up. To think that what she'd lacked for so long was someone to watch out for her, to be on her side, *was* sad. I didn't know what kind of person Katie had been, really, but she'd lost her life at a time when she was ready to start living it in a less destructive way, and that made it even more tragic. Thirty years old was entirely too young.

"What if no other evidence shows up?" I asked. "What if Cal's fingerprints and the timings are the only things that ever show up? Is that enough to find him guilty?" I swallowed, trying to keep the nausea down.

"It's dependent on a lot of things," Gaby said, reaching over for my hand. "The police always know more than they give away. All we can do is wait and see what happens next."

I squeezed Gaby's hand before leaning forward and resting my head in my free hand. My skull was throbbing with the weight of all the unanswered questions I had. Patience was usually one of my strong points, but under these circumstances, it was almost impossible to keep it in check. My entire life was hanging in the balance, and it was all going way too slowly.

"Cal didn't do it," Guy said firmly. "So something has to show up to prove that. Won't they need to look at every angle before they throw the book at him?"

There was a pause before Gaby said, "In theory, yes. The bigger problem is Scott's possible involvement. It depends on his influence, who he knows..." she trailed off. "I'm sorry. I know I'm not helping and I hope that isn't the case, but I can't lie and tell you I'm certain this will work out. What I can tell you is that my brother will sniff out any hint of bullshit and expose anything that doesn't add up. Cal has got the best representation he could possibly have."

Her final words were reassuring, even if the others weren't. I wasn't upset with her for telling me the truth. If I was honest with myself, she'd only put a voice to my deepest fears, ones I knew could become reality. If Scott was willing to locate someone from Cal's past in order to destroy him, there was probably nothing he would stop at.

I still didn't understand what was driving him. What he wanted. I'd never understood it fully. Cal had got away with something he had done a long time ago, but when this all started, the things Scott was doing were unethical and petty. Nothing on this level. Each time he'd been unable to punish Cal, he'd stepped it up again. Why couldn't he just let it go? It wasn't justice for Edward because he was gone now. So, what the hell was his problem?

"Do you think..." I began, sitting up slowly, "that we need to start thinking about what we'll tell Aiden?" Shaking my head, my tears began to fall because I didn't *want* to be thinking about this. I knew exactly how Aiden would respond when he found out Cal had been arrested again, and if it came to it, if Gavin was unable to get him out, where would Aiden go? When he had asked his innocent question a few months back, when Cal was in far less danger of being jailed, I'd been able to offer my reassurance, but now? I had nothing. Aiden didn't have any family left, except for maybe Cal's dad if he was still alive, and he was a stranger to him. And also a drunk.

So, what would happen to him?

Guy wrapped an arm around me and tucked me into his side, where I felt a second of safety before everything crashed over me again.

"I think we should talk to him," he said, his voice husky. "But we don't *have* any answers for him. I hope that he could stay with one of us if... you know. But I also don't want to make any false promises to him."

"He's going to want to know all the answers, Guy," I said, sobbing against his shoulder. "We need to give him as much as we can."

"Maybe you can hold off for longer," Gaby said, looking at Guy. "What if... I don't know, maybe if you take him out really early and tell him Cal went back to their place to rest. Just keep him distracted until we know which way things will go."

"That might work," Guy answered. "But we still need to consider what to say to him if Cal doesn't get out tomorrow."

Just then, the sound I'd been waiting for pierced into the room. The sound of Gaby's phone ringing. She'd left it resting on the arm of the sofa, and when I turned my head, I saw Gavin's name on the screen. The churning in my gut picked up as Gaby reached for the phone, and Guy held me tighter.

"Hello?" she said, her voice shaking slightly, and I could tell in that moment just how worried she was. For me, and for Cal, and for what her brother's words would tell us about what came next. "Yeah. I'm at Guy's, and Shannen's here. Do you want to talk to her instead of me?" There was a pause before she snorted. "Dick." She rolled her eyes. "Yes, I know. I'll hand you over."

Taking a deep breath, she passed the phone into my shaking hand, and unable to handle sitting still, I got to my feet. "Hi, this is Shannen."

"Hi, Shannen," a deep, professional-sounding voice said. "I'm Gavin. How are you doing?"

With a humourless laugh, I said, "I've been better. How's Cal? Is he..." I trailed off, not sure what the end of the sentence was because, obviously, he was not okay.

"Staying calm?" Gavin guessed. "Mostly. He's had his first interview, and it went on for about two hours, so I suggested we take a break for today. He's been taken back to his cell for now and the questions will continue tomorrow. However, because of how long everything has taken and the police believing they have enough evidence to hold him, they are going to apply to hold him for longer than twenty-four hours."

My stomach dropped. "Do you know how much longer?"

The idea of Cal being in a cell overnight broke my heart. He would lose his mind if he was left alone for that long with his self-destructive thoughts. At best, he'd let his rage build up. At worst, he'd descend far enough to let his demons convince him this was what he deserved, and then?

Then, he'd give up.

"Not yet," Gavin replied. "It could be anything from another day to ninety-six hours. When the charge is murder, they tend to try to hold people for as long as they can, so they might try for the maximum. The good news is, there is no guarantee they will get what they want. It depends on whether the evidence they have can be deemed as circumstantial. But I would say to prepare yourself for him to be here for another few days."

I'd wanted reassurance, and even though I thought I was prepared to not get it, it still hit hard to know Cal could be in custody for four days before they made a decision.

That was four more days of worrying for me. Four more days for him to let his dark thoughts take control.

"Do you know what they have on him?" I asked, starting to pace the width of Guy's living room.

"No. He's been asked why he was with Katie, where they went, what times. They've tried to, in my opinion, goad him into getting angry by asking him about why they hadn't spoken in such a long time, and how he felt about her abandoning their child, and they pushed at his worries that she wanted to take Aiden away from him. They have been really focused on what rooms he went into when he was in her flat. Every button he has has been nudged at, and this is only the beginning."

"Is he... I mean... do you think he'll get through this?"

Being confronted made Cal confrontational in return. His concerns over being charged with murder, along with missing Aiden and me and panicking over whether we were both okay had every chance of sending him over the edge. He couldn't call us himself to hear our voices, and he was being forced to answer questions designed to make him flip. It was a lot to ask for anyone to keep their cool, but for Cal...

"I think his patience is already wearing thin," Gavin said. "But I've armed him with as many tools as I can to keep it in check."

"Gavin," I said, "Gaby told me that you are the best person to help Cal. I don't care how much it costs. I need you to be with him every step of the way. Can you do that?"

"Of course," Gavin replied, his voice reassuring. "You and Cal are friends of my sister, and I do not believe for a single second Cal is guilty of murder. Something is distinctly off about this whole thing, and I will do everything I can to help him. I will represent him for as long as he needs me."

"Thank you," I said, my voice wobbling. "Thank you."

"You're welcome." He paused. "Shannen, is there a message you want me to pass along for him? Anything that might get him through the next round of questioning?"

What words could possibly help someone in the position Cal was in right then? I could hardly tell him not to worry about me or remind him to relax. It was illogical to expect either of those things from him under the circumstances. I didn't even want to tell him I loved him when I knew how that triggered his fears when he was in a bad place.

"I guess... can you just tell him that I know he didn't do this? Before, I... he thought I doubted him, and I need him to understand that I have no doubts about this. I'll be waiting for him, no matter how long this takes."

Chapter 35

Cal

THE WALLS IN THIS cell are too close.

It was late. Probably after midnight, I guessed, although time had stopped having any meaning the moment my ass was dumped in here.

I sat on the shitty excuse for a bed, my legs stretched out in front of me, staring at the stark white wall.

These places were a perfect punishment for criminals. There was nothing to look at. Nothing to do. Nowhere to go. There was barely enough room to pace around.

I wanted to sleep. If I slept, when I woke, I'd be closer to my next interrogation. My next chance to say the thing that would make these pricks let me out.

Or another step closer to letting my inner monster escape.

That was the battle. A constant fight between answering the questions and wanting to upturn the table in the interview room, destroy the recording equipment, and pummel the police officers who continued to take me around in circles until I didn't know what I was saying anymore.

Gavin helped. He'd learned to read when I was getting wound up. He'd glance at me from the corner of his eye or place a hand on my arm, and it kept me grounded.

But how long would that work? How long could I take the same cycle of questions?

My answers were never going to change because I was telling the truth. But if I had to keep going over it for another day, maybe more, what would happen? Would I somehow convince myself that they must be right? If they were so determined to get a confession out of me, would I slip into giving one by mistake? Out of exhaustion, or perhaps because somewhere deep inside me, I believed this was karma. My past finally catching up with me.

I didn't kill Katie.

But I did kill my mum and my brother.

I killed Edward Firth, in a way.

I destroyed him.

I was a piece of shit. Always had been. Just like my dad said.

My head thudded back against the cold brick wall.

Once. Twice. Three times.

Scott had been trying to put me here for a reason. And that reason was to get justice for my old crimes. Maybe this was how it was always meant to end.

You get that one taste of having everything you ever wanted, and the second you believe in it?

Boom. It's gone.

You're alone again, just how you're supposed to be.

A tear rolled down my cheek. Another thud of my head against the wall. Another.

Closing my eyes, I saw the face of my boy. My son. His smile bright as he laughed at something I said. His brown eyes sparkling.

Love.

I saw Shannen, her big blue eyes looking up at me like I was the most important thing in her world. Felt the soft press of her lips against mine.

Another tear. Another thud.

Our unborn child, sleeping safely in Shannen's warm protection. Unaware of what awaited them.

Guy. The person who had dragged me out of hell and given me a chance. I saw us in the pub, sinking beers and laughing.

Donovan, Nova, Gaby. Evie and Ash.

All of the people who made up pieces of my life.

It's funny, isn't it, what fear can do? What being alone can do.

Tear. Thud. Tear. Thud.

And Katie. I didn't kill her, but maybe I did. Maybe I fucked up her life too, and that was why she ended up dead.

"It's your past, Cal. You can't change it or hide from it."

Shannen said that to me right before I cut her out of my life. Was she better without me too?

"I wasn't ready for you, Cal. You were just there. Everything I always knew I needed."

Did she need me, though?

Was I any good to anyone?

Nah.

No good. You're no good.

Chapter 36

Shannen

I woke up entirely too early on Saturday morning considering it had been past two a.m. when I'd eventually fallen asleep. After speaking to Gavin the night before and giving him my number for further updates, I'd stayed at Guy's for another hour before Gaby drove me home.

Now, I was facing what promised to be one of the longest days of my life.

The day I waited to find out if Cal would be released, held in custody for longer, or worst of all charged, with murder.

I was surprised I'd managed any sleep at all.

Dragging myself out of bed, I made a cup of tea and a slice of toast. I wasn't hungry, but I knew if I didn't eat something, I would get a lecture from my mum about not taking care of myself properly. If it had only been me to take care of, I wouldn't have bothered. However, I had a growing baby to feed, so I sat at the dining table with my breakfast, eating and drinking on autopilot until my mum woke up and joined me. We had another cup of tea, not speaking much. I was grateful that she understood I didn't have anything to say because every single bit of my mind was preoccupied with thoughts of Cal.

Was he up yet? Had the interrogations begun? It was almost ten, so I figured they must have. I had no idea how time worked in police custody. For all I knew, he'd been up since the crack of dawn.

Did he sleep okay? What frame of mind was he in? Was he staying strong or close to breaking point? What would the police ask him today? Would it be more of the same questions, or would they change their tactics in the hopes of tripping him up?

Had he worked himself into a rage that would get him into trouble, or could Gavin truly keep him calm?

Had the decision on whether Cal would be held for longer been made already? Had any new evidence arrived? Had anyone offered information that would get Cal off the hook, or would something else emerge to make him look guilty?

Once I was dressed, for want of something to do to stop the incessant questions in my head, I took the lift downstairs to the main entrance of my apartment block to get my mail. I checked it daily, usually when I got home from work. I doubted the post person had even been yet, but I'd needed to move, to just do something.

I used my key to open my mailbox, and I gasped when an A4 brown envelope fell towards me. Reaching in, I checked to see if any normal-sized letters were in there, and when my fingers found nothing, I pulled the large envelope out and locked the box back up. As I headed for the lift, I tore the envelope open and pulled the contents out when I was safely inside.

My eyes widened.

Looking back at me was a slightly grainy black and white image. It looked like a zoomed-in still from a security camera, and as I looked closer, I let out a tiny shriek.

My gaze danced across the picture, clearly seeing the familiar storefront of the hairdresser's beneath the Bridal Loft. And right there was an image of Cal pressed against me, against the wall. My face wasn't visible, but I knew exactly what this was.

The lift doors opened, and I stepped out, stopping right in the middle of the corridor to examine the rest of the images. The next photo showed me much more clearly, my arms around Cal's neck and my face tilted up to him. In the next, I was concealed again, but Cal's jeans were down slightly, half his bare arse visible. As I flicked to the next image, my breath left me as I saw almost the same image, but this time with my leg wrapped around him, and my face in clear view. There was no mistaking what we were doing.

My blood ran cold and my knees buckled. I leaned back against the wall, the pictures wobbling in my trembling hand.

Where the hell had these come from? This had happened months ago.

And why hadn't I considered that there might be CCTV cameras down that street?

More importantly, though, why would someone go to the trouble of getting this? How would anyone have even known to look?

There was one more photo, and as much as I didn't want to see any further evidence of my little indiscretion, I needed to know what else there was.

But it wasn't a photo. It was a piece of white A4 paper with words messily scrawled across it in black ink.

I thought you might like to see a preview of the images heading to your principal. A copy of the video has also been sent to your school's board of governors. Within 24 hours, Cal will be charged with murder. You're both done.

Unable to stand any longer, I sank to the floor, shivering.

This *had* to be Scott. Nobody else so badly wanted to ruin us. But there was no way I could prove it. No way I could class this as evidence of anything other than public indecency, which would see me lose my job.

If the note was telling the truth, the *video* was being sent to the board of governors, for fuck's sake. Not just the photos. It would likely have been sent by email too, so my accidental foray into porn was probably already in their inbox.

People who held my career in their hands were going to see a video of me having sex in Exeter city centre.

I was actually going to lose everything.

I would never be allowed to teach again. Everything I had worked so hard for would go up in smoke, and I'd be left to choke on the ashes.

It was all crumbling around me. My job. Cal. My relationship with my father. What was next? What else could he ruin for me? Would it be my mum? My friends?

I had never felt less safe in my life.

Drawing in a long, slow breath, I tried to stop the tremors from wracking my body.

Scott was right about one thing.

I *was* done. Done with having my life fucked with.

Done with letting him get away with—potentially—literal murder. He had done nothing but try to get Cal into trouble, to break us apart, to put Cal behind bars.

And for what? To give his fragile ego a boost and prove how powerful he was?

Fuck him. Fuck him and fuck this.

If I'd already lost my job, my man, and my dad. I was going to protect what I had left before he took that away too.

I placed my hand on my stomach, taking another deep breath. "Hang in there, little one. Mummy is on a mission."

When the cab pulled up in Scott's driveway, I still clutched the envelope containing the photos in my hand. I'd text my mum to tell her I was going to Gaby's because if she knew where I was really going, she'd have flipped. I still wasn't completely sure about my own sanity, only that I needed answers.

I didn't waste any time rushing to Scott and Jade's front door. I usually paused to admire the beauty and sheer size of the place, but I was in no mood for their fancy architecture and foliage.

If anyone was at home, it would only be Scott. For as long as I could remember, Jade left the house early on Saturday mornings to go to the gym before relaxing in our country club's spa for a couple of hours. So, this showdown was between me and him.

I pressed the doorbell frantically before hammering my fist against the door. Within minutes, it opened, and Scott greeted me with a mocking smile.

He stood there wearing a pair of beige chinos, a pale green polo shirt, and shiny black shoes, looking every inch the pretentious shithead he was.

"Shannen. How nice to see you."

Before I could answer, he'd grabbed my wrist, covered my mouth with his hand, and dragged me inside, shutting the door behind us. His large hand was pressing so hard over my mouth and nose that I couldn't breathe, and I squirmed beneath his grip as he shoved me up against the door, my heart hammering from the shock. He pinned my body with his, then let go of my wrist and began patting me down while I tried to hit at him with my empty hand. My panic and inability to take a breath was making it hard for me to land a single shot, and I began to feel dizzy.

Once he was done with his inspection of me, he stepped back, looking me up and down while I gasped in large gulps of air. As my vision cleared, I realised he'd snatched my phone from my pocket and was looking at it carefully. When he was done examining it, he dropped it on the floor and stomped on it, the screen cracking into a spider's web of glass shards. He ground his heel into it for good measure then kicked it to the side. It slid along the entranceway carpet, landing at the bottom of the wide staircase.

The thud in my chest intensified because now it really was just me and him, and as I looked up at him, he laughed. "I'm not going to hurt you, Shannen. I just needed to make sure you weren't trying to set me up."

Smug, creepy prick. Perhaps I wasn't in any physical danger, but his eyes danced with amusement and malice, and his annoying slicked-back blonde hair made him look like a sleazy politician.

"I see you got your delivery," he went on, nodding towards the envelope in my hand.

Straightening up and taking a small step towards him, I said, "What the hell even is this? How did you get these?"

He flicked off an imaginary piece of dust from his shirt as if being so close to me had somehow sullied his perfect appearance, and I glowered. "I'm not going to answer your questions," he said. "You should speak to your father." Steepling his fingers, he added, "Didn't he call you last night?"

"Why would he call me?" I asked, trying to keep my expression neutral, even though my voice oozed with barely concealed contempt. "In case you hadn't heard, we aren't on the best terms right now."

He nodded. "Yeah, he told me. He also told me you threw a punch at him."

Unable to control the furrow in my brow this time, I stared at him. My dad had said he was going to 'fix' things, but I didn't think that meant by him going anywhere near Scott again. I'd hoped he had something concrete within his messages or emails that would prove Scott had helped to set Cal up. That alone wouldn't be enough to combat the murder charge, but it might be enough to give the police something else to look into. Especially if the investigation wasn't happening at the station Scott worked in. I wasn't stupid enough to believe he didn't have contacts, people who would cover for him, lie for him, but all we needed for now was a starting point. A way to begin to unravel it all.

"My dad was here last night?" I asked.

"Yup. He was raging, threatening me with all kinds of things, but if you're here, I guess he heeded my warning."

"What warning?" I snapped, irritated by the way he was goading me, and that I kept biting.

Scott pulled his phone from his pocket, tapped on the screen a couple of times, and then took a couple of slow steps towards me, his free hand up to show he wasn't planning to touch me. As he turned his screen towards me, he tapped it once more, and I covered my mouth with my hand, swallowing back the bile that rushed up my throat.

A video played on the screen. The live version of the photos I still clutched in my hand. It was zoomed in, less grainy-looking than the photos, and I watched as Cal stepped back from me slightly as I'd lifted my skirt and taken my knickers off. Although Cal had been mostly covering me, there was a very clear flash of my lady parts and the way the clothes on my top half were dishevelled.

I pushed Scott's arm away, leaning back against the door again as I tried to stop myself from throwing up.

He chuckled. "Yeah, your dad had the same reaction. I, on the other hand..." he trailed off, his eyes still on the screen, watching what I assumed was Cal slamming himself into me. "I just wish it had sound. Then I could have really enjoyed myself."

"You're sick," I snapped, throwing the envelope in my hand down on the floor before shoving at his arm again to stop him from looking at the video. He smirked before slipping the phone into his pocket. "You showed this to my dad? What the hell is wrong with you?"

"It's quite simple," he said, straightening his shoulders. "He came over here, threatening to make sure I pay for the terrible things I've done, which, FYI, are not terrible things, simply righting a wrong that was made in the past. So, I needed some insurance to keep him quiet, and since you've proved yourself to be a desperate little tramp since getting with that lowlife, you gave me exactly what I needed. I told your father that if he tries anything, then that video might find itself in the hands of people who can end your career. So, you see, as much as he thought he wanted to help you, once again, he chose not to."

"Because you made it impossible! The choices available to him were to ruin my career or to leave Cal to rot in jail! Either way, I lose!"

"And I win." He smiled, and I launched myself towards him, powered by all of the pain and fear that clashed over and over inside me. Just as I reached him, he gripped both of my wrists and bent them around behind my back hard, causing me to stumble into him. "Not a good idea. Not unless you want a criminal record too."

I wriggled to get free, but he held firm. "You've already sent the photos and video. I'm finished anyway!"

He shrugged, tilting his head to the side. "Unless I didn't."

I stopped struggling and glared up at him. "Why would you say you did when you didn't?"

"Because I knew you wouldn't be able to resist confronting me, just like you did last time. And seeing you like this... totally worth riling you up."

His eyes flashed in a way I didn't like, as if he was getting off on how scared I was of losing everything. How confused I was by his mixed messages. I didn't believe he hadn't sent the photos and video out, but either way, I'd allowed him to manipulate me right into his house because I wasn't thinking straight. Too caught up in my fears to take a breath and make good decisions. I wanted to burn the world down to protect what was mine, but instead, I'd thrown myself into the fire.

"Why?" I asked, trying to keep the tremor from my voice. My heart was beating dangerously fast, and my head felt close to exploding. I needed to calm down for the sake of my health and my baby, but I was struggling to catch my breath. "What did I ever do to you to make you want to ruin my life?"

"Let's see," he said, shoving me backwards and then taking a step away from me. "First, you never liked me, and I knew it. But while you weren't causing me any trouble, I was happy to let it be. But when you started seeing Cal? Come on, Shannen! I knew you'd been single for a while, but to get mixed up with someone like him? Were you desperate? He was someone I arrested, for Christ's sake, and even when warned, you still kept seeing him."

"You didn't warn me!" I snapped. "You undermined the tiny bit of friendship we had by going straight to my school with the information!

295

You weren't trying to help me, you were trying to force my hand into breaking up with him, and when it didn't work, you used my dad to help you on your fucked-up mission to get rid of Cal!"

"Your dad came to me." His tone was so calm it was making me more nervous. Anyone who could be this cool under these circumstances was dangerous. Why not shout back? Why not argue his point?

Because he didn't have to. Like he said, he'd already won.

"Jade was embarrassed for you," he went on. "She thought everyone would shun you for being with someone so different from us. Someone so obviously out of our league. She thought it would be better if we showed you who he really was."

"By lying about him?"

"Edward Firth was not a lie." His tone grew instantly cold, so much so that it made me shudder, but I refused to back down. I'd already given him enough of what he wanted by showing up and letting him see the emotions I'd struggled to contain.

"You have no proof that Cal was ever involved in that. All you have is a pathetic grudge that you couldn't get over, so you got Katie to lie for you."

"You dropped Jade and picked him!" Scott snapped. "She was devastated! Callum Lewis is nothing but a violent, worthless criminal. It's my job to keep people like him off the streets, and I will do whatever it takes to make that happen."

"Including murder?" I challenged, staring at him.

Some of the tension dropped from his shoulders, and he laughed. "Oh, I'm a lot of things, but I'm not a murderer. But if a conviction is needed, you'd better believe me when I say, I'll get it."

"Even when the person is innocent?"

"Cal isn't innocent."

"He's never killed anyone."

Scott shook his head, a sneer crossing his features. "There's more than one way to kill a person. I saw Edward after the attack. He was beaten so badly that he was barely recognisable. For a time, it seemed like he would never wake up, and when he did, he was never the same. I knew Edward a bit. He used to be a cocky little shit. Harmless, though. He would never have set out to hurt someone the way Cal did to him. That was why he never named Cal, I think. Through a misplaced sense of guilt for the accident that killed Cal's mum and brother. After Cal destroyed him,

Edward became withdrawn. He couldn't stop blaming himself for what Cal did until he eventually killed himself." He fixed his eyes on me. "You want to know why I want Cal in jail? It's because he was sick enough to plan out an entire attack on someone who'd already paid for his crime, and he did it with such precision that I have no problem believing he could do it again. I will do whatever I need to do to make sure that animal never hurts anyone again."

Saying anything to defend Cal would only have confirmed his role in Edward's attack, and I wasn't falling into that trap. I wasn't going to get sucked into his story either because true or not, it didn't mean he could set Cal up for any crime he felt like. I would never, ever condone what Cal did, but I also understood what pent-up rage could do to a person. I only had a couple of months' worth, and if I had the strength in me, I'd have beaten the hell out of Scott myself. Even more ridiculous was Scott's inability to see that by working so hard to jail Cal, he was just the same. Holding onto an old grudge and making someone pay for something they already paid for. Except he was worse. He was in a position of power. A man of intelligence, supposed integrity, who had everything he ever needed to live a good life. He didn't need to scrabble around trying to get revenge because, in truth, he didn't care about Edward Firth. He cared about getting what he wanted and nothing more.

"You're changing the subject," I said. "You can't just pin a random crime on someone based on a gut feeling."

"And yet, I did." Just like that, his smirk was back. "You won't be seeing Cal other than in a visiting room for a very long time. And unless you want everyone to know that perfect, respectable Shannen Morgan begs to get fucked in backstreets like a sleazy hooker, you'll stay away from me and from Jade."

He took a few steps towards the stairs, where my smashed phone lay. He kicked it towards me, and it stopped when it hit my toes. "Get. Out."

Aiming every single piece of my hatred at him, I spat, "I can't wait until the day you trip up. And you will."

"The only one with something to lose here is you, Shannen. I've made myself bulletproof."

There was nothing I could say to that because he was right. He'd tied this whole thing up so well that I had nowhere left to go. I had no evidence of his confession of a set-up, no way to prove what a slimy bastard he was.

And if I had anything to take him down with, he'd take me down with him.

I bent to get my now useless phone, then straightened up. Unable to even muster one more glare in his direction, I turned and walked out, the sound of his laugh following me outside.

On shaky legs, I carried myself off his property because I wanted to be as far away from him as possible. Unfortunately, I was about three miles outside the city centre with no car and no way to call a cab. Even if I stumbled across a bus stop, I couldn't pay for a ticket because I didn't have my bag with me. I'd left my flat with only my phone and the photos, which I'd left in Jade and Scott's entryway. No point keeping them when he clearly had copies anyway.

As I reached the road, I walked for a few minutes just to put some distance between me and the person who had pretty much sealed both my and Cal's fate.

There was no way out. Not for Cal. And not for me once that video was seen by the board of governors.

Stopping at a fence surrounding one of the large fields that covered a large part of this area, I leaned back against it. Clutching my arms around my stomach, holding onto the only thing I had left, I dropped to the ground and finally let out the river of sobs I'd tried so hard to hold back.

This was it.

It was over.

He won.

Chapter 37

Cal

"CAL?"

I groaned. The back of my head felt like someone had taken a baseball bat to it, and I squeezed my eyes closed before trying to open them.

"The fuck?" I mumbled as I was greeted by a window instead of the bleak white walls that were around me last night. I blinked, getting the feeling I'd actually seen that window before, maybe a few hours ago. Maybe more than once. When it was darker. Now, light came through it, and I stared at it, trying to work out where I was.

I wasn't in my flat, or Shannen's, or Guy's house. Definitely not a cell either.

"Cal, can you hear me?"

Blinking again, I tried to turn my head to my other side, where a man's voice was coming from. I hissed as the sensitive part on the back of my head brushed the pillow. When my head was turned fully towards the person speaking to me, I said, "Oh. Right."

"Cal, do you know where you are?"

My eyes drifted upwards to Gavin, who sat in the chair beside my bed. He was wearing his usual sharp suit, dark blue today, with a white shirt. However, his hair was messy and he looked tired, like he'd been sitting there for hours.

He has. He's been here every time you've woken up.

"It's not Disneyland, is it?" I asked dryly.

Shaking his head, he said, "Now's not the time. Cal, do you know why you're here?"

I nodded, the moment of amusement fading as quickly as it had appeared.

I'd got into my cell the night before, trying not to let the dark thoughts take over. It had taken approximately one hour, at a guess, for me to spiral.

The time I was in custody had been nothing but silence, enclosed space, fear, being spoken to like I was a criminal before a conviction was even made, and the ever-growing feeling that there was no way out for me.

So I'd sat, letting my demons run freely around my mind, my head gently thudding against the cold wall.

Then I woke up with someone slapping my face until I regained consciousness. I think I tried to hit them back before I passed out again, and the next time I woke up, I was lying on something slightly more comfortable. In an ambulance.

And that was when I remembered slamming the back of my head into the cell wall so hard that I blacked out.

The moment was so clear to me all of a sudden that I felt tears form in my eyes again.

I'd reached low points in my life before. Times when I wanted it all to end. I didn't want to die in a cold cell, but the only thing I could hear was the voices telling me I was never getting out.

Frustration because I felt like everything I'd said would be dismissed.

Knowledge that Scott held more power than he should have. That he could sway people to get his way.

A deep, burning rage at the unfairness.

Regret and guilt that I hadn't wanted to help Katie more, to make sure she was safe.

And more than anything? The unrelenting fear that I wouldn't see my children grow up. That I wouldn't have the life Shannen and I were planning.

Because what if she doubted me again? What if she thought I was a murderer?

I'd just needed for it all to stop.

In the ambulance, someone had told me I was going to hospital, and that they would contact my 'nominated person'. That was Guy, but the last thing I needed was for him to worry any more than he was, or to tell Shannen, so I'd asked for Gavin instead. He'd appeared sometime during the early hours as I drifted in and out of sleep, suited up like he was at the office.

He'd stayed. Not for legal advice, because I was passed out most of the time. He just sat there with me while nurses woke me up to check on me through the night.

"Thank you," I said, my voice still husky. "For coming."

Gavin nodded. "I wanted to be here. Plus, Gaby would never have forgiven me if I left you alone here. Shannen and Guy were worried sick about you yesterday."

Squeezing my eyes closed, I said, "I know. That's why I asked for you and not one of them. I didn't want them to worry anymore."

"That's not possible." He sighed. "Why did you do this, Cal? Why did you hurt yourself?"

"The noise." Opening my eyes, I said, "In my head. I've never, ever done anything to hurt myself before. Not like that anyway. I usually get drunk. But it got so loud."

Gavin leaned towards me, no judgement in his eyes. "Once the doctors have checked you over and ensured you are medically okay, there are some things we need to talk about. Also, there is an officer stationed outside your door, so don't think about making a run for it." He offered a wry grin.

"How long do I have to stay in here?" I asked. I wasn't in a rush to go back to my cell. I'd pretend to sleep for another few hours if I had to. I was in pain, and while I felt otherwise okay, my head had been battered enough. I wasn't ready for the police to have another crack at it. I wasn't up to the twenty-four hours the police could hold me yet, I guessed, but since they'd hardly had the chance to grill me, I knew they would apply to hold me for longer if they could.

"Let's just get you checked over first, then we'll know more. I'll go and find someone."

"Wait," I said as he began to stand. "You said Shannen and Guy are worried. Have you spoken to them?"

Lowering himself back into the chair, he said, "I spoke to Shannen last night. She's very protective of you." He smiled. "She wanted me to tell you that she's waiting for you, and that she has no doubts. She just wants you home, Cal."

Nodding, I scrunched my face up, trying to hold back my emotions, but they were too strong. A choked cry came out of me as I thought about how she must have been feeling. How she'd feel if she knew what I'd done to myself. "I miss her so fucking much."

"I know you do." Gavin reached over and placed his hand on my shoulder. "I'm doing everything I can for you. Just hang in there, okay? I can't fight for you if you're not here."

I hadn't wanted to die. I *didn't* want to. I'd just wanted some control over the mental torture that refused to ease. A moment of peace. What bothered me was the realisation that I couldn't handle being alone with no way to escape. When things got too much at home, I could go somewhere. Talk to someone. In my cell, there was nobody. Nothing. And even if there *was* someone I could speak to in there, I wouldn't have been able to trust them. I needed familiarity. I didn't want to be in custody for long enough that those four walls became familiar to me. They would only keep on closing in until I lost control again.

"I'm scared, Gavin," I said. "I'm scared I won't get out."

He nodded. "I wish I could promise that you will. The only thing I *can* promise is that I'll be here for you for as long as you want me to be." Getting to his feet, Gavin said, "I'll go and find a doctor. I'll be right back."

As he left the room, I closed my eyes again.

She wants me home. She'll wait for me.

Chapter 38

Shannen

I'D SAT AT THE side of the road in one of the fancier parts of Exeter, sobbing for what felt like hours. In reality, it was probably more like half an hour, but I had no idea what time it was when I'd left Scott's house.

Cars had passed me, none stopping to see if the crazy lady curled in a ball needed help. I didn't entirely blame them.

When I'd cried so hard I'd given myself a headache, I made my way tentatively in the direction of the city centre. I was desperately thirsty and I wasn't sure how far I'd get when I remembered there was a pub about half a mile from where Jade and Scott lived.

Relief filled me as I pushed through the doors of the cosy inn. It was busy since it was getting close to lunchtime, and I was glad because it meant my arrival didn't draw any attention.

I walked around to the side of the bar where it was a little quieter and sat on a barstool, waiting patiently for a member of staff to notice me. They were busy for a while, and I watched their friendly banter with the locals. It kept my mind off how decidedly lousy I felt. Head still pounding, thirsty. I kept my focus on that rather than the intensity of my fears for myself and for Cal.

Eventually, one of the bar staff, a lady I guessed to be in her late forties with blonde hair that was falling out of a bun, came towards me with a bright smile, though it faded when she took in the state of me. I must have looked horrific. No sleep, tear-stained, and dirty from sitting against a fence on the dirty ground.

"Are you all right, love?" she asked, and it took all of my strength not to start crying again.

"I broke my phone," I said, pulling it out of my pocket to show her the smashed screen. "And now I can't call a taxi to get home. I'm really sorry, but I don't have any money on me to get a drink, but if I could just use your phone, then I-"

"Oh, my darlin'," she interrupted, placing her hand on mine. "Sounds like you've had a rough morning. Let me get you some water, and then you can use the phone."

"Thank you," I said, letting out a relieved sigh. "I promise I will come back another time and buy some drinks to make up for this."

Smiling again, she said, "Sweetheart, you don't owe me anything," then walked away to get me a drink.

Looking down at my phone, I pointlessly tapped on the screen, just in case I could get any response from it, but I couldn't. Something else in my life that was broken.

It's amazing how fast you can go from having everything to it all slipping through your fingers. And almost none of it was my fault. The only thing I could have controlled about this was not having sex in public; that was on me. My one foray into total spontaneity and it was caught on camera. At the time, I hadn't been thinking about anything other than the need to not feel so fucking sad. To be with Cal once more before we went our separate ways. There was no way I could have known what it would turn into.

I was so goddamn tired. I hadn't heard from Gavin that morning, and now I wouldn't be able to, nor could I call him to find out how Cal was doing and whether he'd be held for longer, although I knew deep down he would. Scott had confirmed that. I didn't know what evidence the police had, whether Scott or someone else had gone to the effort of planting something to secure a charge, but Scott was confident that would be the end result.

The only thing I could hope for was that Gavin had given Cal my message and provided him with a tiny bit of comfort and peace of mind, even if only for a little while.

The lady behind the bar came back and placed a bottle of water in front of me. "Here you go, lovely. If you want to come with me, I'll take you through to the back so you can have a bit of privacy while you make your call."

I'd assumed I'd have to use the phone in the bar, and I offered the woman a smile. "Thank you." I slid from my seat, picking up the water bottle and opening it as she lifted the little door that led behind the bar. I followed her into a room that looked like it used to be a cupboard. It held a small desk with folders lined up on it, some blank sheets of paper, a pot of pens, and a phone.

"Take as long as you need," the woman said, ushering me to sit in the desk chair. "I'll be back to check on you in a bit."

"Thank you," I said again as she left, closing the door behind her. If I didn't use some different words soon, she was going to think I was a moron, but at least I was polite.

I gulped down some water as I thought about who I would call. I didn't know many people's numbers by heart, and I didn't have access to a way to look up the number of Guy's work phone, which he always carried with him. Even if I had, though, he was looking after Aiden. We still hadn't figured out what to tell him if Cal wasn't home in a few hours, and if Guy had to come and pick me up, Aiden would definitely have questions.

The only phone numbers I had memorised were my mum's and my dad's. They'd had the same numbers for years, and I'd remembered them in case of emergencies when I was younger. If I called my mum, she was going to kill me for being out here. For going to see Scott. She would, however, find out eventually. I could have just called a taxi company to take me home. I had cash in my flat that I could pay for it with, but I didn't want to go home yet.

"You should talk to your dad."

That was Scott's advice. While I didn't want to take anything he offered me, I had to consider it. He was the only person who might have something on Scott. Of course, that was problematic with the threat of my dirty video being exposed. If it hadn't been already.

My dad was my last hope, and as little as I wanted to see him, I needed him. And he owed me.

I swore under my breath as I lifted the phone and dialled his number. It rang three times before he answered.

"Dad. It's Shannen. I need to see you."

305

After spending most of the day before in Exeter with my mum, and after the fight with me, my dad had booked himself into a hotel in the city, so he was still pretty close by. The lady behind the bar, whose name was Glynis, was so kind to me while I waited for him. She'd left me in the small office, but she'd popped her head in a couple of times to make sure I was okay. When I knew my dad would be arriving soon, I left the office and scuttled out from behind the bar to avoid getting in the way of the staff, who were now much busier as the lunchtime rush began.

I sat on the same barstool I'd perched on when I first arrived, and Glynis offered me a wave as she saw me there. A few minutes later, my dad walked in, and I took a deep breath. He looked as terrible as I felt. He hadn't shaved, which was unusual for him, and his thinning hair hadn't been combed as it would normally have been. He was wearing the same clothes he'd had on the day before; blue jeans and a navy blue button-down shirt.

He looked around the room, and I got down from the stool and walked towards him, a strange mix of emotions coursing through me. I was exhausted; I couldn't muster the level of hatred I'd felt for him the night before. At most, I felt detached, but at the same time, desperate to throw myself into his arms and feel his protection. The kind only a father can give.

I didn't, though. The moment he saw me, he stared in my direction as I approached. His chin wobbled, but he inhaled deeply. When I was standing in front of him, I swallowed as the agony of his betrayal and the force of his love for me collided between us, creating a barrier neither of us was ready to push through.

Unsure what to say to the man before me, I waited. After a moment, he spoke. "I can take you home, or if you want to, we could have lunch together here."

We were too close to Jade and Scott's house for my liking. However, the snobbery ran deep within those two, and while we were in a perfectly lovely country pub, it was way beneath them. They wouldn't come here.

And I was hungry.

I nodded. "Okay. Let's find a table."

We weaved through the rapidly filling bar and found a table for two at the edge of the room. We both sat and plucked menus from the holder in the centre of the table. I browsed, wondering where to begin a conversation with him. I was the one who'd reached out, so I had to be the one to get it started. Once our food orders were placed and we both had a drink each, I took another deep breath.

I eyed my father across the table, still struggling with the conflicting feelings of being near him. The night before, I was sure I never wanted to see him again. A huge part of me still felt like our relationship was permanently ruined and nothing he could do could change that. But looking at his brown eyes, the shape of his face, his large frame that had always kept me safe... so many memories flicked through my mind of what he meant to me. What he'd always represented to me. Strength. Warmth. Security. I wanted it back, but I didn't want to get close to him again. Not yet.

Just focus on what you want to ask him. Nothing more, nothing less.

"You went to see Scott, didn't you?" my dad asked. "That's why you're here, at this pub."

Reaching for a napkin, needing something else to look at, I began slowly unfolding it on the table. "I did. But you went to see him too."

"Yes. After I left your apartment last night. I went to warn him that I will dig up anything I can to prove he tried to set Cal up because I have nothing left to lose now." He paused. "But he had one last card to play."

My cheeks heated, and my fingers folded the napkin in half into a triangle, carefully smoothing the crease down. "Yeah. He sent me the photos in the post this morning."

"He what?"

I flicked my gaze up to my dad for one second, unable to look him in the eye knowing he'd seen a video of me having sex, before focusing on my folding again. "He told me in a note that he sent the photos to my principal and the video to my school's board of governors. But then he told me he hadn't and was just trying to bait me into confronting him."

My dad's hands clenched into fists on the table. "That son of a bitch," he growled. "He told me he was keeping it all in case I found anything on him. That he would take you down with him."

"And so you backed down."

"Shannen," he said sharply, placing his hand over the napkin I was play-ing with to get my attention. I still didn't look at him, but I drew my hands back towards me and stopped fidgeting. "I will not let you lose your job. I was part of the reason all this happened in the first place. I don't think he's sent those things anywhere because then he'd have no leverage."

"He doesn't need leverage. He wants Cal in jail and me to have nothing. He made it pretty clear that Cal will be charged with Katie's murder, and once that's done, there'll be nothing anyone can do about it."

I reached for the napkin again, pulling it out from my dad's hand and unfolding it. An image of Cal in handcuffs. A vision of him facing a trial. Me watching while he was grilled about something he had no part in. My stomach lurched as those scenes crossed my mind for the millionth time since I'd found out about his arrest. That was what had kept me awake.

He was strong, but could he really survive that? Could Aiden? Could I?

He had to have been losing his mind by now if he hadn't already. Gavin had been able to keep him calm before, but everyone has a breaking point, and Cal's was lower than most.

"What do you know?" I asked him. "What do you know about Scott that could help Cal?"

He sighed. "Nothing I can prove. Last night, I was ready to kill him. When he showed me that video of you and Cal, I realised just how far he's gone to make sure he can make this murder charge stick."

I closed my eyes, mortification shrouding me again. My dad was fully aware that I was a grown woman who had sex, but he had not counted on seeing his daughter being ploughed up against a shop wall. He'd always viewed my sister and me as his princesses; girls who behaved well and made him proud. It wasn't that I was ashamed exactly, other than for not considering that someone might see. It was more that I didn't want my dad to think this was something I made a habit of. I was so angry with him, but it must have made him sick to see me like that.

"So, what now?" I asked.

"Until I knew he had that video, I was ready to look into some of the things he said to me in the past. I know a private investigator who can-"

"What things?" I interrupted, finally looking up at him. "And what do you mean 'in the past'?" I sincerely hoped this was the first and only dodgy deal my father had been involved in.

Adjusting himself in his seat, he placed his hands, palms down, on the table, his fingers spread wide. "When I went to Scott for help, he told me he knows people who can do things for him. He didn't say what or who, and I didn't ask. All I wanted was Cal out of your life, and I thought Katie was the way to do that. He'd found her already. All I had to do was give him the money."

"Which he stole half of," I pointed out.

"Yes. And I found out last night that he used the other half to pay someone to 'keep an eye' on Cal." Dad blew out a breath. "He was so keen to prove that Cal was a criminal, he had him followed, and he was pissed off when he got nothing from it."

At that, I laughed. "Yeah. Cal goes to work, school, football clubs, and home. Maybe occasionally to the pub, but that's it."

Dad nodded. "That's how he got that video of you, though. He was thrilled to explain that to me. Whoever he hired to follow Cal couldn't get close on a deserted street, so Scott got the CCTV footage from the building across the road, though I don't know what kind of criminal activity he thought Cal was doing with you around."

"Public indecently, apparently," I muttered, my face flaming this time as Dad's eyes met mine. "Dad..."

He held a hand up, lowering his gaze. "Look, did I need to see that? No. But looking at the bigger picture here, I am in no position to lecture you. What you did was stupid and could get you into a lot of trouble, but that wouldn't be an issue if I hadn't encouraged Scott's vendetta. There is nothing you could ever do that would make me as ashamed of you as I am of myself, so please... let's just pretend I never saw a thing." Rubbing a hand over his tired eyes, he said, "What I don't know is how Katie was murdered and who did it. My guess is that he called in a favour from someone."

"Was he still watching Cal recently?" I asked, wondering if that was how Scott knew Cal was at Katie's the day she was killed.

"I don't know. It's possible."

Shoving the napkin away in frustration, I shook my head. Nothing my dad had said was truly useful to me. They were all just things Scott had said. Still no proof of anything. "Dad, I need you to find something... anything you can because what he's doing... he can't get away with it."

My dad pressed his lips into a thin line. "Shannen, there isn't anything to find. He's made sure of that."

"You said you were planning to have Scott followed."

"Yeah, but not at the expense of you losing everything you've worked for. I won't do it."

This was what it came down to now. Cal in jail for murder, or me losing my job due to public indecency.

The humiliation of that did not bear thinking about. At worst, it could even result in me being charged and something else to add to Cal's rap sheet too.

But Cal in jail for murder? Letting him stay there at least until a trial, and for years if found guilty?

Scott must have left a trail somewhere. And he wasn't the only one with money. I had money. If I had to pay every scumbag who'd ever crossed paths with Scott to get what I needed, I would do it.

People would find out that I, a teacher, had been caught having sex in public, and I would never live it down. Neither would my family. I would never be able to get another teaching job. Even if I moved, with the wide reach of the internet, it would probably follow me for the rest of my life.

For Cal, though, to prove his innocence, there was nothing I wouldn't do. He was a father, and his children needed him with them, not behind bars where he'd be unable to see them growing up.

If the choice was lifelong humiliation or life without Cal? There was no question.

"You know what?" I said, slapping my hands down on the table. "I made a mistake. I don't need your help. I can do this on my own. You might be happy to let people suffer for your mistakes, but I'm not. I won't."

I used the pub's phone one more time, to call for a taxi home. My dad tried to talk to me, to reason with me, but something steely and determined had set itself up inside me.

After Scott informing me that Cal would be charged and my dad confirming that Scott had already gone to extreme lengths to get to Cal, I didn't have many options left. First, I was going to find something solid that confirmed Scott's involvement, and then I'd take whatever punishment he threw at me on his way down.

Aiden needed his dad, my baby needed a father, and I needed Cal.

I could live without pretty much anything else, but I would never be able to live with myself if I didn't do everything I could to make this nightmare end. If that meant I was the one who lost out, then so be it. What the hell was the point in having a great career if the only thing I really wanted was gone?

Even in the worst case, if my sacking from my job and the reason was made public—which it probably would be—then I'd take it. The hate, the judgement, because all of that? It wasn't what mattered. I'd had a quickie and it had been caught on camera. So what? If my worst crime was having sex outside on a deserted street late at night, then let people say what they wanted to.

In reality, I knew it wouldn't be that easy. It would hurt, and it would be mortifying, and giving up my career would kill me. But the alternative, to me, still seemed worse.

When I got into my flat, I was surprised to find my mum wasn't there. She'd probably gone shopping or maybe to meet a friend. Either way, I was glad I didn't have to explain what I'd done yet. I needed some solitude so I could begin my research. Although, I wasn't quite sure where to begin. Could I just Google private investigators?

I made myself a cup of tea and then curled up in my armchair, my laptop open on my lap.

Noticing it was getting close to one p.m., it occurred to me that Gavin had probably tried to call me as it was getting very close to Cal's first twenty-four hours in custody running out. Because I couldn't reach him, I did the next best thing. I opened Facebook and dropped Gaby a message. There was nothing waiting in my inbox, and I wondered then if anyone else had tried to call me. If Gavin had called and I didn't answer, he probably would have phoned Gaby to see if she knew where I was. Maybe she'd even stopped by my apartment to look for me.

Shit. I'd been so caught up that I hadn't thought that anyone might be worried about me. On the other hand, maybe they weren't. If Gavin didn't have an update yet, then maybe nobody had noticed I'd disappeared for several hours.

Hey Gabs, My phone is broken. Please can you message me here if you hear from your brother? xx

Once that was done, I yawned just as an email came through from my dad. I clicked into it, and it said: *If you're really going to do this, this is the number of the guy you need to speak to. His name is Harry George. There is nothing he can't find out. Dad x*

The number was typed underneath, and I stared at it, wondering where he knew this guy from. Did he regularly have need for a private investigator? Doubt flitted through me, a reminder of how hard he'd broken my trust. He was adamant that he wouldn't see my reputation ruined, and he had already proved what he would do to 'protect' me. Did that extend to leading me down a dead end? Letting me waste money on something that would never go anywhere?

With a weary sigh, I clicked out of the email, blinking when I saw there was also an email from Jade in my inbox.

No subject, just her name.

I highlighted it and moved the cursor to the little bin symbol. There was nothing I wanted to hear from her. My eyes stung as I stared at the screen. Yawning again, my body beginning to feel the effects of the day's turmoil, I changed my mind on the deletion and opened the email.

One line.

Stay out of my house. And keep your father out too.

Oh, for God's sake. Scott must have immediately told her that I'd been there and she'd felt the need to send this. Why, though? What the hell did he tell her because the only person under any threat after my visit was me. Unless...

The concern that she knew exactly what kind of man she was about to marry hit me again. Did she really hate me enough to let all of this go on? The lies? The blackmail?

And why an email? That would easily have fit in a text. The bonus being that I wouldn't have had to see it at all because my phone was knackered.

Her message was so blunt. I wasn't expecting kisses, but at least she could have signed off, or... something.

It wasn't like she hadn't proved how she felt about me, though. She'd chosen her side and I'd chosen mine.

My eyelids fluttered as I fought to keep them open. I didn't have the luxury of a nap just yet. I needed to stay awake until Gaby messaged me back at least. I needed to know what was happening with Cal, and I had to see if I could find someone who could help me expose Scott for the lying, disgusting pig that he was.

"Come on, Shannen," I muttered to myself. "No time to quit."

Chapter 39

Cal

THE BACK OF MY head was sore as fuck. I'd had stitches at some point during the night, apparently. That was the only thing I didn't remember, though. Everything else had come back to me once I let myself wake up fully after talking to Gavin that morning. By the time I'd been given breakfast, then waited for a doctor to speak to me and gauge how I was doing, it was twelve o'clock. When I'd proved that I was back in the land of the living, could speak in full sentences and recite my name, address, and various common knowledge facts like who the UK prime minister was, and could show I could walk around without getting dizzy, I was discharged.

The bad news was, I was going back to the police station, to my cell.

The journey was short, and on the way, I could already feel the bleakness settling over me again. Nobody had told me whether I would be released, though I doubted it, and I had no idea how much longer they were going to hold me for.

I thought about Guy and Shannen having to find a way to explain to Aiden where I was. I didn't want him to know the truth, that I was in prison, but what else was there? Either way, Aiden was going to be afraid he'd never see me again and worry about what would happen to him. The thought of him crying or getting so angry that it triggered a meltdown made me feel sick. Shannen could handle him, but she hated to see him upset too, and she would be forced to carry his hurt and hers while continuing to stress over me. All of it was dangerous to her now she was pregnant.

Guilt. Fear. Frustration.

The new cycle of thoughts in my head was as unhelpful as the rest of them. They all led me to the same place.

A few more days dicking about in custody before I was charged and awaited trial. It could be months before this went to court. My baby would already be born by then. Aiden would be six.

I would miss my first Christmas with a family. The first Christmas in a long time that would actually mean something.

The back of my head throbbed, reminding me of what I'd done to myself the night before, all because of thoughts like these. I'd been informed that I would need to speak to a mental health professional because I was now considered a danger to myself.

Ha. I'd always been a danger to myself. That was what made my arrest funny. They thought I could kill someone. Aside from that one time years ago, I was always more of a risk to myself than anyone else.

The police car pulled to a stop outside the station, and I let the officers pull me from the car, dejection taking hold quicker than ever. My chest tightened as they escorted me inside, my hands cuffed behind my back. I focused on my breathing as I was taken to the desk and my return was logged.

Home sweet fucking home.

"Is Mr Davis here?" one of the officers beside me asked the man behind the desk.

I hoped so because I wasn't answering any questions without him. He'd left the hospital about an hour or so before me, so I guessed he'd arrived by now.

"He is. You can take Mr Lewis through to the consultation room."

My arms were tugged to encourage me to move, but I planted my feet firmly. "Wait. Could someone tell me what's going on? How much longer do I have to be here?"

"Your solicitor is waiting to go over the next steps with you," the man on the other side of me answered.

I clenched my jaw to stop myself from saying something I would probably regret. My questions being disregarded and the way nobody would look me in the eye was getting really old. The only people in there who actually looked at me properly were the officers who'd interviewed me the day before. Everyone else seemed to look through me or talk to me like I was guilty.

Innocent until proven guilty was a joke.

I was taken into the consultation room, released from my handcuffs, where Gavin was sitting at the table with a Styrofoam cup full of tea in front of him. There was also a cup of tea opposite, in the place I would sit.

Once we were alone, Gavin nodded towards the chair, gesturing for me to sit down, a serious look on his face. It did nothing to ease the tightness in my chest. Everything about his expression said I had a few more days of this shit to get through at least.

Slumping down into the chair, I picked up the cup and took a sip of the tea. It tasted like shit, but I raised it slightly in a gesture of thanks.

"How are you feeling?" Gavin asked, his eyes studying me.

"I'm not sure you're ready for the answer to that," I told him, putting the cup down. "Any word on how much longer I'll be stuck in here?"

Gavin nodded, sitting up straighter with a sigh. "I'm sorry this is taking so long, Cal. If you hadn't done what you did last night, we could be a lot further along by now than we are."

I lowered my head. He wasn't wrong. I'd have been through a lot more questioning already if I hadn't been in hospital, but I didn't think it would have made that much difference overall. Even Gavin knew they wouldn't be done with me after twenty-four hours.

"I'm sorry," I said. "I fucked up." When he didn't answer, I looked up at him. "So, how much longer?"

"About an hour, max."

An hour?

I stared at him. "What?"

The corners of his lips twitched into a smile. "It's been an eventful morning."

"Gavin... what?" My knocking myself out must have affected my hearing and my ability to understand because I thought he said I only had an hour left in that hellhole. But... how? I'd barely been interviewed and they were letting me go? "Are you fucking with me?"

He shook his head, then reached into the inside pocket of his jacket and pulled out an envelope, which he slid across the table to me. Shannen's name was written on the front. My brows furrowed. "You'll need to deliver that when you get home," he said.

"Okay, look." I pinched the bridge of my nose. "I've got a head injury, so I'm going to need you to tell me exactly what is going on. What is that letter, and am I really getting out of here?"

"Yes." Gavin laughed. "I'm sorry. I've just been waiting for this for so fucking long." Taking a deep breath, he said, "First thing this morning, while you were in hospital, someone came here with some new evidence. I was trying to find out whether you were going to be held for longer, and I figured you would be because hardly any interviews had been done, but I was told any application to keep you here was on hold due to some new information. When I left the hospital and came back here, I asked to speak to someone about what was going on with your case, and while I was waiting, a young lady approached me. She'd just come out of an interview room with a couple of officers, and she overheard me saying your name." He nodded to the envelope. "She realised I was working for you, and she gave me that and asked me to get it to Shannen. She also told me to tell you not to waste your chance with Shannen because you would never do any better."

My eyes widened.

No. There was no way.

I was shaking my head quickly, unable to believe what Gavin was saying, and he laughed again. "Jade," I said. "Her name was Jade, wasn't it?"

"Ding, ding, ding. We have a winner!" Gavin slapped his hands on the table, grinning. "I'm not sure what evidence she brought with her yet, but what I do know is that it clears you of all charges and that means you can go home. With her being McCalden's fiancé, I'm pretty confident that means he's done screwing with you now. She wouldn't have come here if she didn't have something damning."

My mouth opened and closed a couple of times before I said, "How did you know who she was?"

Gavin's smile widened. "Let's just say Scott McCalden's name has come up more than once amongst my clients over the years, and while I've never been able to nail him for any wrongdoing, I have done my research on him. I knew who she was as soon as I saw her."

Maybe I died last night...

Things like this didn't happen to me. I was the guy who was accused, blamed. The guy who had to fight for every single thing I had. I'd gone back to that police station expecting a fight. Expecting disappointment. And I hadn't got any fight left to give. All I could see ahead of me was a prison sentence because I *had* been in Katie's house and now she was dead. And when someone as high up in the ranks as Scott McCalden wants you jailed, that's where you stay.

God. Katie. Because of the aftermath of finding out she was dead and how quickly everything had changed, I still hadn't fully accepted that she was gone. That was something I would need time to process when I was certain this was all over.

I was still shaking my head in stunned silence, when Gavin said, "Cal, this is real. When you're ready, someone will come and speak to you, and then you'll be released. I can take you home."

Home. I didn't want to go home. Not to my flat. That was a building. I wanted Shannen and Aiden and Guy. They were home. Wherever they were, that was where I wanted to go.

"Wait," I said. "Does anyone know I'm being released?"

Gavin winced slightly. "I've tried to reach Shannen a few times today just to let her know where things were at in terms of whether you would be kept here, but I couldn't get through. I called Gaby about an hour ago to see if she knows where Shannen is, but she couldn't reach her either."

My tiny flicker of happiness died in an instant and panic filled me again. "She doesn't usually go for this long without checking her phone. Especially not if she was waiting for you to call her. Where the fuck is she?"

"Cal," Gavin said calmly, "take it easy."

"Take it easy? What if something's happened to her?"

Or the baby. What if something happened to the baby? Or what if she was with Aiden and something happened to him? I stood up quickly, knocking the chair over.

"Get me out of here. I need to find her."

Chapter 40

Shannen

"SHAN."

I groaned, the sound of Cal's voice in my mind making me squeeze my eyes closed. *Stay with me, Cal.*

But he wasn't with me. I had to stay in the dream for longer. Hear his voice again. I shivered, curling up tighter in the ball I was in, willing him back to me.

"Baby, wake up."

Fingers lightly brushed against my cheek, and I groaned again, needing whoever was disturbing me to back off.

Reality was not my friend.

"Shan. Open your eyes."

A kiss on my cheek. The lightest flutter of familiar lips.

You're dreaming. You need more rest.

I felt fingers in my hair, gently teasing at the curls, and then a hand on my cheek, the thumb stroking gently.

Cal?

I slowly forced my eyelids to open.

And there he was.

A slow half smile spread across his face, his hand still on my cheek as he crouched at the side of the chair I was in.

I blinked a couple of times, certain I was still asleep until I heard a laugh from behind me, and I turned towards it and saw my mum grinning as she stood at the other side of the chair.

Flicking my head back to look at Cal to make sure he was still there, I said, "I... how?"

This was too weird. The last thing I remembered was reading the email from Jade, and then I must have fallen asleep. Now, Cal was in front of me and my mum was back, and I had no idea how any of it had happened.

I reached forward to touch Cal's hand that rested on the arm of the chair as if checking he was real. When his fingers curled around mine, I jumped up and flung myself at him, knocking him onto his ass. I wrapped myself around him, my arms around his neck and my legs around his waist, just holding him tightly. He pulled me in as close as he could get me and held me just as hard.

"Cal, what happened? How did you get here? I don't..." I trailed off as confused and relieved tears began to fall.

"Shhh," he whispered into my hair. "It's all over, Shan. It's over now. I'm home. Are you okay? Nobody could get hold of you and we were worried."

Nodding, I said, "I'm fine. I... I was so tired, and my phone got broken. But... I saw Scott, and he said..."

He said Cal would be charged. In the next twenty-four hours.

Cal loosened his hold on me and leaned back slightly to look at me. He looked exhausted, his stubble thicker than usual, but his brown eyes, the ones that had always anchored me, held me captive. "Scott won't be a problem anymore. He's been taken into police custody, and he has a lot of explaining to do."

"But he's... he's got...." I couldn't bring myself to tell him about the video and photos he had of us with my mum in the room. I'd already blurted out that I'd seen Scott without meaning to.

"Shannen, I've spoken to your dad," my mum said, and I turned my head to look at her again. "He told me everything. Including what you were willing to do." She gave me a smile that was prouder than I would have expected given I'd planned to let Scott expose what was essentially a sex tape if it meant getting Cal out of jail.

My heart sank as I remembered I wasn't out of the woods yet. If Scott had sent the photos and videos out like he said, I was still at risk of losing my job and seeing my reputation disappear down the toilet.

"What are you talking about?" Cal asked, a frown on his face. If he didn't know, that must have meant he hadn't been here for long, or surely my mum would have told him about the video.

"Scott was following you," I said. "That night we... you know... outside the Bridal Loft?" He nodded. "There are security cameras out there, and Scott has the footage. He told me he's sent it to important people at the school. So, he might still get the last laugh."

Cal tensed in my arms, shaking his head. "I hope that fucker spends the rest of his life in jail."

"Me too," I said, though people like Scott always seemed to get through everything unscathed. I just hoped whatever the police had on him was enough to keep him away from us for a very long time.

I still stood by what I'd said to my dad, though. I didn't want my career to be over. It terrified me to think I could lose it, but Cal being by my side was the only thing that mattered for now. Wrapping my arms tighter around him again, I breathed in deeply. "I can't believe you're here."

"Neither can I," he said with a small laugh. As I wound my hand into his hair, he winced, and I moved it away quickly because something didn't feel right. His hair was matted, and it felt... bumpy.

"What happened to your head?" I asked.

He lowered his gaze, his smile disappearing. "Can we talk about that later? Right now, I just want to enjoy being next to you."

I nodded but waited for him to look at me again before saying, "Are you okay?"

He shook his head. "I wasn't. And I think I'm going to need you while I get my shit together, but I'll be all right now I'm out of there." He smiled softly, and I knew he probably had a lot to tell me when we were alone. I could take a guess at what was wrong with his head, and I was going to hate hearing about it.

Over the last few months, we had both been through a lot, but Cal had had nothing but constant changes. In fact, for him, those changes had been going on for a lot longer. While not everything we'd experienced lately had been terrible, Cal had dug deep into himself and faced things he'd been hiding from for years. Dealing with that on top of learning to connect with Aiden, figuring out a relationship, moving, the drama with Guy and Helen, and Scott's bullshit too. I wasn't sure he had quite dealt with the knowledge that Katie was dead yet either. He may not have ever been in love with her, and she did some horrible things, but she was the mother of his child. He had cared about her in some capacity for a time, and he had recently witnessed her pulling herself out of her issues, only for someone to take her life.

When I laid it out like that, it was no wonder he'd been so confused about who he was sometimes.

I, however, always knew.

He was my person.

Since we had, once again, cycled through conversations so quickly, I realised I still had a whole bunch of questions for him, mostly about exactly what had enabled him to be released.

"Cal, what happened today?" I asked. "You said Scott wouldn't be a problem anymore. But... how?" I'd been so busy freaking out that I hadn't understood *why* Scott wouldn't be a problem.

Shifting his position slightly, Cal let go of me with one hand to reach into his pocket. He took out an envelope that had been folded in half and offered it to me. "I don't know all the details, but this was given to Gavin for you. I hope it will give you some of the answers."

I frowned as I unfolded it and instantly recognised Jade's handwriting on the front.

For her to have given this to Gavin, that meant she would have had to be at the police station herself. The one in Taunton, where Cal was detained.

She had driven from one county to another to speak to the police?

Did she know Cal had a lawyer, or was it just luck that she'd stumbled across him?

Shaking my head because the logistics were not important, my fingers almost burned with the need to see what she'd written to me. *Hopefully, it's more in-depth than the email.*

My eyes narrowed at the reminder. Why the hell did she warn me and my dad to stay away from her house earlier?

If I didn't open the envelope, I was never going to know a thing.

I let go of Cal with both hands so I could get into it, though I kept my legs wrapped around him. I had no plans to break contact with him unless someone physically prised me off him.

I pulled the letter from the envelope and unfolded it, taking a deep breath before reading.

Shannen,

This is quite the cliche because this actually is the hardest letter I've ever written.

Cal should be back with you by now, depending on when you get this. If not, he will be soon.

I'm unable to reveal all of the details you probably want because I don't know everything. The less I know, the less I have to feel guilty about.

I loved Scott, and I truly thought he was a good man. I know you didn't like him, but he was good to me. Some weeks ago, though, I found a stash of money in the house. Ten thousand pounds in cash, hidden in the wine cellar. I was curious about why he would hide that much money there and not tell me about it. I didn't immediately assume the worst, I believed he had his reasons, but one day I came home from shopping and he was in his office, shouting at someone about why they hadn't 'found her yet'.

It could have been about work, but in work calls, he always remains professional, and in this call, he was angry. As you know, he never locks his office door when he's out, only the drawers. So, I ordered one of those tiny spy camera things and hid it on top of one of the cabinets. I set it up to alert me when there was movement in the room, so I could see and hear what he was doing. I saw him changing SIM cards in mobile phones and then throwing them in the bin. Heard him speaking to people about looking for people. One of them was Katie Young, Cal's ex. He also talked a lot about following 'Lewis'. He said a lot of things, and I gathered them up. Last night, though, your dad came to our house, and he was furious. Scott confessed to having Katie killed, by whoever was following Cal, I presume.

I was also made aware from that conversation that Scott had a video of you and Cal having sex. That explains what he was masturbating over in his office.

So, anyway, it became clear to me that the man I expected to spend my life with was not the man I thought he was. Perhaps I'd just moulded him into what I wanted him to be in my head. I believed him to be a man of morals. A man who wanted to uphold the law, and that was why he was so pissed off about Cal getting away with half-killing someone.

I can put up with a lot of things. I did put up with a lot of things. But I couldn't chain myself to a man who claimed to be proud to serve his community when all he was really doing was paying people to do awful things, and also things that earned him money on the side. If I married him and he got caught, I would have lost everything. By doing this, I've lost most things *anyway, but at least I can be satisfied knowing I got out before he took me down with him.*

I'm leaving the UK and I'll be spending a long time away. I'll be fine as I have the funds to take care of myself. I will miss my family and friends, but I'm sure they will understand that what I did was for the best. I did the right thing.

You chose Cal, and while I will never understand it, I hope he makes you happy. He's certainly never going to make you rich.

For what it's worth, I am sorry about what Scott did to you both, but it's time for me to move on now.

Love Jade x

I had to read the letter over a few times before it all sank in. I wasn't sure what the purpose was. It was an explanation, but it didn't seem like a real apology. It was all about her. Almost like I should be grateful that she sacrificed her life by giving the evidence of what a bastard Scott was to the police.

I *was* grateful, but I'd hoped for a little more... something. To feel like she regretted some of her actions, but that wasn't evident. It did occur to me then, though, that her earlier email wasn't a warning to protect Scott and herself, but to protect me and maybe my dad when the police swarmed in. It was far better that we weren't there when it happened.

"Wow," I said, dropping the piece of paper to the floor.

"What does it say?" Mum asked. I'd almost forgotten she was there. She'd moved around to sit in the armchair I'd been asleep in and she was peering over at the letter.

"That she suspected Scott was doing something shady, so she set up a camera in his office and saw and heard a lot of things, which she has now given to the police. And she's leaving the country."

"Boo hoo," Cal said sarcastically as he picked up the piece of paper and scanned his eyes over it. Shaking his head, he handed it to my mum, and I put my arms around him again, letting the information she'd given me filter into my brain.

"God, she really is the most self-involved bitch," Mum mumbled. "Her, her, her. I appreciate that she gave up a lot to do this, but she still can't resist sticking the boot in with her nasty little digs."

"They're not digs to me," I said. "That's why she and I never agreed on things. I would have given up my career, my money, my everything to get

Cal out of jail. She gave up a wedding and a house. She's still rich and can swan around all over the world. I believe she's upset about Scott, but she still cares more about stuff than people. The only thing I want is my family."

Mum smiled at me. "And that is why you make me proud."

Cal tightened his arms around me, and I snuggled into his shoulder. "Speaking of family," he said. "Guy and Aiden should be here soon."

I glanced up at him. "How do you know that? You don't have a phone."

He smiled. "When we were all looking for you earlier, Gavin called Gaby, and she called Guy, and then Gaby reached out to your mum, who came back here and found you. Anyway, Gaby told me that Guy and Aiden will come over in a little while. As far as Aiden knows, I was not in jail. I had to do a job late last night and then slept in. Which he will probably believe looking at the state of me."

Laughing, I said, "You look good to me."

The best ever because he was where he was supposed to be.

Cal smiled, pressing his forehead against mine, then sighed. "I missed you so much."

"I missed you too." Turning his head towards my mum slightly, he said, "Annie, could you give us a minute? I need to kiss your daughter in a way that might make you uncomfortable."

My mum laughed out loud at his words and stood up as I felt my face heating. "Go ahead. I'll go and make some tea." As she passed us, she lightly placed a hand on Cal's shoulder. "Welcome back."

He smiled up at her before turning his attention back to me. His eyes sparkled, even though his exhaustion was clear. "I really thought this was over, Shan. I didn't think I'd ever get out of there."

I nodded. "Me too."

Cal moved his hand into my hair again, looking at me just as he always did; like I was the most amazing thing he'd ever seen. "I was always scared that falling in love with you would be dangerous. Because when you have something to lose, you're always afraid. But I was looking at it backwards. Yes, there is something to lose, and I couldn't handle it if something took you away from me. But it was always me. I was the one throwing the obstacles in the way. I spent a lot of time making things harder than they needed to be when all you ever wanted was this. Us, together. I felt so out of control yesterday when I couldn't see you or speak to you. I thought about you being on the outside, and Aiden and our baby growing up without me, and how much I'd miss." He swiped away a tear from his cheek. "Now, I'm not going to miss anything. I don't want to wait until the summer to live with you, Shan. I want to do it now. Can we?"

Smiling up at him as tears fell down my cheeks too, I said, "I would like that. We've spent long enough apart. It was all I could think about while you were gone, and I was worried I would never get you back, but... even though I was afraid, I never wanted to stop loving you. I *never* stopped loving you."

The smile Cal gave me wrapped me in warmth, and comfort, and safety. The smile he gave only to me. "I loved you too, Shan. From the first time I felt that weird feeling in my chest when you looked at me like I was something special. I didn't know what it was then, though. Now, I know."

He leaned in close to me and captured my lips with his, each soft brush showing me how much he meant his words. How much he was done being afraid.

We had come a long way. Fought through a lot. We had new challenges to face and more obstacles to overcome.

The difference was, now Cal believed in us as much as I always had. We were ready to take the next step. Together. Only with each other.

Epilogue

Eleven weeks later

Cal

Most of the time, Shannen was happy with the simpler things. She loved where we lived, loved how we were becoming a family, and she never wanted much more than to spend time with Aiden and me.

Sometimes, though, the middle-class woman she really was craved a bit of the fancy shit she was used to, and that was why I was standing on the balcony of a harbourside hotel in St. Ives, Cornwall, looking out over the sea in the hot sun.

I'd never been anywhere as expensive or classy as this, and even though I'd been sceptical about whether they'd let someone like me through the doors, I loved it.

Shannen and I hadn't had much time on our own since we'd moved into her place together. Between work for both of us and all the plans for the baby, and then getting ready to move house again soon, there had been no way for us to be on our own for long. With three months until the baby was due and the summer holidays just beginning, this was going to be one

327

of our only chances to have some time to ourselves, so Shannen said we were going to do so in style.

We had driven down to Cornwall the day before and met Guy, Nova, Donovan, and Gaby. We were all staying in Penzance for a group holiday, courtesy of Donovan, and Gaby had offered to watch Aiden for us so Shannen and I could 'regroup' after the last couple of months. The two of us were staying at the hotel for the night, and while I was going to miss my boy like crazy, Shannen and I *needed* this.

"Hey," she said as she stepped out onto the balcony, a bottle of water in each of her hands. She passed one to me, then opened her bottle and leaned one arm on the railing, looking out at the view. She turned her head to look at me and smiled, her dark curls moving slightly around her face in the breeze.

A rush of something I still wasn't used to washed through me.

Happiness.

This woman was mine. The baby growing inside her, underneath her long black summer dress, was mine. We'd bought a house. Well, technically, Shannen had bought most of it, but it was going to our home. Mine and hers and Aiden's and our baby's.

It didn't unsettle me the way it used to. Now, it was more a tiny feeling of uneasiness instead of a loud roar of, 'You cannot have this forever' that kept me always ready to run.

"You okay?" she asked, her eyes even brighter than usual as they almost sparkled in the sunlight.

I nodded slowly, my eyes not leaving hers. "Yeah. Just glad we've got a whole day and night together so we can process... everything."

"Thank God for early check-ins," Shannen said with another smile. In the heat, she didn't want to be walking around all day in a busy town. Plus, we just wanted to sit together somewhere quiet, and Shannen had mentioned there was nowhere quiet in St. Ives in August. From what I could see of the beach below me, she wasn't kidding.

I turned to put my water bottle down then straightened up and wrapped my arm around her waist to pull her in closer to my side. In response, she rested her head on my shoulder.

"It's beautiful here," she said, her focus once again on the sparkling waves. There were so many people out on the beach, and loads in the water too, swimming or surfing. Being close to it but having a decent distance made me feel so fucking lucky. A bit of calm from the noise.

"It is. This was a good idea." I dropped a kiss on the top of her head then drew in a deep breath. "I can't believe we're here, Shan. Not just *here*, but with everything going well. Two whole months with nobody trying to mess things up for us."

Two months of me learning how not to mess things up for us.

Shannen looked up at me again. "It's really over, Cal. Scott is out of the way, and he won't see the light of day for a long time."

That fact made a small smile play on my lips. Nothing bigger, though, because any thoughts of him, even ones about him suffering, would never be something to laugh about. Not because he didn't deserve to suffer. That fucker deserved every bit of misery headed his way. It was more that the reason he was suffering was because of the pain he'd caused Shannen and me, and neither of us was anywhere near all the way over it yet.

Shannen's headmistress had received a copy of the photos of me and her outside The Bridal Loft, and the stress of that had almost landed Shannen in hospital because if Scott had followed through on that, then he'd probably also sent the video footage to the school's governors. As it turned out, though, he hadn't acted on the second part of the plan. I wasn't sure if it was because he was trying to mess with Shannen's head or that he'd been arrested before he could do it. Shannen's headteacher, although she was an older lady, had been more than understanding about the situation. She didn't want to see photos of one of her staff members having sex, but she was aware of Scott and everything he'd put us through, and she refused to end Shannen's career over a public quickie. She'd given Shannen back the photos, and we'd ripped them into tiny pieces and dropped them in the outside bin just before they were emptied by the refuse collectors so nobody could have a chance to get near them.

After I was released from custody and Scott was taken in, life had got better. In that time, the extent of Scott's corruption had been exposed, and he really had lost everything. His posh house had been swapped for a shitty cell, and it would stay that way until he eventually went on trial, but as he'd not only been proven to have set me up and blackmailed Shannen, he'd also taken payments to ensure arrests back before his promotion to superintendent, and the higher he climbed, the more fucked up he'd got, including possible involvement in sex trafficking.

I wasn't sure how that dickhead was surviving. Probably on the arrogance that his money could buy his way out of this, but I doubted it would. Even if he did somehow get away with it, he'd never be able to live the life he had. There aren't many things people hate more than a corrupt police officer. He wouldn't be welcomed back to his social circles with open arms. He'd be an outcast, so either way, he was fucked.

"It's weird," I said. "In a good way," I added quickly. "It's just... it's hard to remember I don't have to look over my shoulder all the time."

Not even just from the time I'd been with Shannen. It was as if Scott's arrest had stripped away everything I'd been afraid of. Things I'd done in the past, things I felt like I was being judged for. Even though I didn't see McCalden for years, never even thought about him, in the back of my mind, I always felt like I didn't deserve the life I had—even though it wasn't always so great—and I was waiting for it all to fall apart.

Not living with that constant noise should have been a relief—and it was—but it was also fucking scary. I didn't know who I was without it. And having someone who knew the worst of me and still wanted me? That was even scarier.

It was all too much, so Shannen gently suggested therapy.

I was so messed up after being arrested that I didn't even fight the idea. I just wanted a way to get used to the silence in my head and to learn how to have a relationship that wasn't full of fear and feeling undeserving.

It was going to be a long, long road. But I was on it, and it was helping.

"I know," Shannen said, winding her arm around my waist. "It's taken time for me to relax too. We never had a fair shot when we got together. Everything was a series of hurdles and things jumping out at us. But the monsters are gone. The dragons have been slayed." She smiled, and I chuckled.

"Well, I'm pretty sure that's all because of you. Nobody has ever fought so hard for me."

She shrugged a shoulder. "Likewise. You could have left me behind too, Cal. But you kept coming back for me."

As her gaze met mine, I smiled at her, and her blue eyes twinkled. "I always will."

Shannen

Cal's arm around me, the gentle hum of the noise below, and the warmth of the sun combined with the peace of it being just the two of us, filling me with a joy I hadn't experienced in a long time.

The last couple of months had been the best we'd had, and at last, I felt like there were only good things in front of us. Before, it felt like things would never settle, that we'd always be living on the edge of the next nightmare, but it had finally ended.

This summer felt like the start of something. A new beginning. I wasn't just on a summer break, I'd begun maternity leave, which meant a year off work. The next big thing on our list would be moving house, but that was a task I would worry about once we got back to Exeter. Being given a chance to disconnect from everything was rare, and that was what I planned to do this week. No thinking ahead, just living one minute at a time.

"So, what shall we do with all this free time we've got?" Cal asked. "I know we still have a lot we want to talk about, but maybe we should go out for a walk and eat pasties and ice cream while we're here."

The idea caused a grin to form on my lips. There was nothing better than a proper Cornish pasty. "Yeah, we can. I thought we could have lunch here in the hotel, maybe use the pool or even just sit out here on the balcony, then go out later this afternoon when it's a bit cooler. I don't really care what we do, I just want to be with you and enjoy having no distractions."

While the thing I loved the most was being with Cal and Aiden, Cal and I hadn't been alone in a while. Guy had Aiden for a night sometimes, and we were so grateful for that, but everything was always one hundred miles an hour. Even a night to ourselves wasn't always enough.

"I've never been here before, so I don't know what's around other than what I can see from here," Cal said, and we both peered down over the balcony to see mostly water, sand, boats, and lots of people.

"The shops here are great. Nothing much in the way of the usual high street stuff. It's a lot of gift shops and art galleries." I straightened up as excitement hit me. "There used to be some galleries that had the artists in them, and you could watch them work."

My parents had taken my sister and me to St. Ives a few times when were kids, and I'd loved looking at the artwork in the galleries, watching people work and talking to visitors. I would have taken home an entire car full of paintings I loved if I'd been able to, but it would have cost a fortune to get everything I'd wanted.

I wasn't against treating myself to a couple of things now, though. Especially as we were about to move from a two-bedroom flat to a three-bedroom house.

Cal grinned. "You know I'm not an art gallery kind of guy, don't you?" he asked as he turned towards me and pulled me against him again. "In fact, I would rather do almost anything other than look at paintings."

"Trust me when I say, you will enjoy it," I told him. "It's not a fancy art gallery like you're probably thinking of. It's really just a place where local artists can display their work. I promise you'll like it. There are also a ton or arcades around so we can go and play games after."

Aiden loved going to amusement arcades whenever he could, and Cal and I had developed a pretty serious rivalry over who was best at air hockey. Now, neither of us were able to walk past an arcade without going in to play.

"That sounds good. We'll pretend it's a first date and I'll try to win you something."

Lifting up onto my tiptoes, I pressed a soft kiss against his lips. "I'll hold you to that."

As I began to pull back, he moved a hand from my waist to the back of my head and gently kept me close, kissing me again.

Oh my God.

The feeling his kisses brought out in me never changed. They were addictive, soft, but still full of so much passion that my stomach swarmed with butterflies and any thoughts in my head and surrounding sounds disappeared.

It never failed to blow my mind that we'd been together for no time at all, yet we'd been through enough trauma for a lifetime. Everything had been on a fast track from the start. I didn't fall in love with him the moment I set eyes on him. Love isn't instant. But I did know after one night with him that he was going to change everything for me. I just didn't know how much.

Being with him had highlighted things I was missing, things I was clinging onto for no good reason, and shown people for who they truly were. I'd lost a lot, risked a lot, but I wouldn't have made any different choices.

When Cal slowly pulled back from the kiss, he gave me that smile that made my insides turn to mush. He was so goddamn good-looking that I still couldn't believe he was mine.

"You know what I was thinking about today?" he asked, his face turning slightly serious again.

"What?" I asked, my eyes on his.

"That it was only a couple of months ago that I was sitting in a cell, losing my mind and thinking that I could never have this. You. A life."

Instinctively, I held him tighter because I had a feeling I knew where this was going, and aside from therapy, he hadn't talked about it much because I knew it scared him to think back on it. Scared him that he'd been so out of control. I shivered slightly as a warm breeze fluttered over me, making my hair tickle my cheeks.

"When we went to the hospital and we saw our baby at the scan, Shan, I didn't think life could get any better. I thought I had it all." His eyes moved from mine to look out at the view over my head. "And in a few hours, I was locked up. I knew I hadn't done anything wrong, but I was treated and spoken to like I had, and the second I was on my own in that cell, the fear kicked in. All of the bad, dark thoughts. It had been such a long time since I'd felt that low. Since I'd let the volume turn up on everything that's wrong with me." He paused. "On everything I *thought* was wrong with me," he corrected.

My heart fluttered a little because I had waited what felt like forever for him to be able to admit he wasn't the total screw-up he'd always believed. He still had a lot of work to do, but therapy was working wonders for him; a 'gift' from my father because as much as I didn't want to take anything from him, my mum had insisted he was going to pay for whatever Cal needed because waiting on an NHS list was not an option when his mental health was close to breaking point.

"I hadn't wanted to end my life since I was a teenager," Cal went on. "I thought about it a lot back then. But that day, when I was sure there was no way out for me, it was the only thing I could think of to do. And I'm

333

not even sure I really wanted my life to be over. I just let all of the fear and my own self-hatred take control. I could have died, Shan," he said, finally looking back down at me. "I could have died that night, not knowing that the next day, I'd be free. I'd have left you and Aiden and our baby just because I couldn't handle everything I thought about myself anymore."

A lump formed in my throat at his words. It was something that had tormented me over the last few months. If he'd just hit his head a bit harder, or maybe in a different place. If he hadn't been found so quickly. I could have been on my own, waiting to give birth to a baby Cal would never have seen. Sometimes, I had nightmares that saw me at a funeral, surrounded by my friends, as Cal's coffin was lowered into the ground. Each time I woke up from it, I'd been sobbing, sweat covering my forehead, my hair plastered to my face. Those nightmares only showed me what an impact everything had had on me too. I had also seen a therapist for six weeks, and that had been enough to help me, but I never forgot how dangerously close I'd come to losing Cal forever.

"Why were you thinking about that?" I asked, my voice croaking slightly.

"Because when I woke up today, surrounded by the best people, I realised I could have missed out on this. I could have died not seeing how good life was about to get. I'm here with you, and Aiden is being taken care of by our best friends. When we get back to the others tomorrow, we've got so much else planned. We have a whole summer, and we're moving house, and everything is so fucking good. I'm not going to pretend that I'm not still afraid it could all end, but I'm also not afraid to think about looking forward. I can do that now, and I can see something there that isn't just me fucking everything up."

A slow smile spread across my face at his words. "That's all I've ever hoped to hear from you, Cal. I don't expect you to fully let go of the things that scare you, at least not right away. But if you can stop it from controlling you, you can be happy."

"I am happy. And I wasn't sure I'd ever let that happen."

A contented sigh slipped from my lips. "I'm happy too. The happiest I've ever been."

He opened his mouth as if to speak when I heard my phone ringing from the bedroom. My brows furrowed because everyone important to me knew not to call today unless something major happened. We couldn't go completely off the grid because of Aiden, so if someone was calling, it would have to be important.

I reached up and pressed a kiss to his lips. "I'll be two minutes."

Cal nodded as I let go of him and walked back into the suite. The bedroom was directly behind the sliding glass doors that led to the balcony, and I retrieved my still ringing phone from my handbag, which I'd left on the bed. My mum's name was on the screen, and I frowned as I unlocked the phone to answer it.

"Hello?"

"Hello, sweetheart," she said, her voice steady. "I'm sorry to ring you today. Are you able to talk?"

Sinking back to sit on the large bed, I said, "Yeah, I can talk. Are you okay?"

There was a pause as she let out a breath. "I am. I just... Shannen, you know things between your dad and me have been hard since... you know."

I nodded, even though she couldn't see me. I knew. Because things between my dad and me had been difficult for the exact same amount of time. Since we both found out that he'd had a hand in setting Cal up. My mum had gone back to her own house a few days after Cal had been released from custody, but she didn't want my dad there yet. She needed time to think about what she wanted to do after her husband had so spectacularly shattered their daughter's life. He'd been living in a nearby AirBnB since she went home, and they'd met up a lot of times to talk, to see if they could salvage something from the wreckage of their marriage.

"Did something happen?" I asked quietly.

"Yeah. And I'm still not sure telling you over the phone instead of waiting until you get home is a good idea, but I figured your dad might also try to call you, so I wanted to tell you before he does."

I waited, braced for what was to come. The truth was, I didn't know what I wanted or expected to hear. I'd said to my mum from the start that she needed to do what was right for her and for her marriage, outside of what I might want or how I might feel. My issues with my dad were my own, but for my mum, he was the man she'd married. The man she'd built a life with, had children with. I didn't want any decisions she made to be swayed by me.

"I told him I don't want him to come home."

My mum's voice remained mostly steady, but I heard the tiniest tremor at the end of her words, and my heart clenched. No matter the reasons for her decision, this had to be unbearably painful. This was her putting an end to the life she'd lived for so long. Making a choice to no longer be with the man she'd loved for more than thirty years.

"Mum," I whispered, then swallowed. "Are you sure about this?"

"I'm sure, sweetheart. I think I've known the whole time, but I didn't want to make any fast decisions. But I also didn't want to give your father hope when there's none to be had now. I told him this morning that it's over. We'll probably have to see each other while we figure out selling the house because it's not fair for me to keep it. I don't want a long, drawn-out divorce. I just want us to take what we have, split what we bought together, and go our separate ways."

I blew out a long breath. "Sounds like you've thought it all through."

"I have. Like I said, I thought this was how it would end up, so I wanted to be ready to tell him exactly what I want and what I expect."

"How did he take it?" I asked quietly.

I had barely spoken to my dad since the day he'd met me in the pub near to where Jade and Scott used to live. The day he'd told me he wouldn't help Cal if it put me at risk, and I'd decided to go it alone. He'd been in touch to arrange payments for Cal's therapy. Although it was my mum's suggestion—or insistence—he had been happy to pay, and not just because he thought it would go some way to repairing some of the damage he'd caused. He truly did want to do something to help Cal, and I appreciated it. But it didn't change the fact that he had been involved in the reason he *needed* therapy. He was far from the worst villain in the story, but the fact that he'd had any kind of role made it hard for me to want to see him or speak to him. Deep down, I'd hoped that maybe one day we could rebuild the trust. That I could have my dad back, and our family would be whole again, but he had ripped it into too many pieces. I had sort of expected this to be the eventual outcome, but a small part of me wished it wasn't so.

"Not well," Mum said, and her voice cracked again. "He begged me to reconsider, said he'd give me more time, but it's been more than three months. If I still feel the same way now as I did the day I found out what he did, I don't think it'll ever change. I'm so sorry, Shannen."

A tear slid down my cheek as the enormity of it all began to hit me just as Cal came in through the glass doors. "You don't have anything to be sorry for."

"I wanted you and Sadie to always have a solid home with two parents who would always be there for you. Together. But no matter what I do, Shannen, I can't get over that level of betrayal. This wasn't just some stupid little secret. He paid someone to get Cal out of your life and he hurt you both so much. I cannot remain married to a man who could do that to his own daughter. It doesn't matter that he thought he was helping you. He wasn't, and he nearly ruined your lives."

Cal sat down on the bed beside me as my tears fell harder. It was a lot to take in. The finality of it. He wrapped an arm around my shoulders, and I leaned in closer, taking his comfort. I put my mum on speakerphone so he could understand what was going on.

"I'm sorry too," I said. "I'm sorry any of this happened."

"It is not your fault either," my mum said firmly. "This is all your father's doing. He is the only person to blame for this."

"He is, but I just... I wish it had never come to this. And I don't... I don't know if I can forgive him either."

"I don't expect you to," my mum said gently, and I could tell that my crying had set her off too. "Your father did something he knew would hurt you. But also... just because I can't get over it, that doesn't mean you have to feel the same way. I won't be upset with you if you want him in your life."

"I know that, Mum. But I don't think I can. I mean... I don't know if I can cut him out completely, but I also don't want to be meeting up for lunches and spending time with him regularly. I just... I don't know."

"You don't have to make those decisions now, sweetheart. In fact, you don't have to make them at all. Your father, in spite of what he did, loves you so much. He'll wait as long as it takes."

With a sigh, I thought about her words. She was right. My dad did love me, but I'd seen a side to him that had made me question if there had always been a part of him that needed to get his own way. That didn't respect my choices or trust me. No matter how many times I tried to see it from his side, that he was trying to protect me, I could never fully accept that. I understood his concerns about me being involved with someone who had so much violence in his past; any parent would have felt that way. But it was the fact that he'd made a rash decision, and that wasn't something he was known for. It was a shock and a stab to the heart all at once.

"Listen," Mum said, "I want you to go and get on with your day. Try to put this out of your head for the week and we can meet when you get back."

She was right because if I spent too long thinking on all the things my dad had done, the things he'd said, I would never be able to enjoy the day. The point of being with Cal, just the two of us, was that we could not focus on all of the bad and look towards the good things coming to us.

"Yeah," I said with another sigh, lifting my head from Cal's shoulder and wiping my eyes. "That sounds like a good idea. Cal and I are going to get lunch soon and then maybe go for a walk. Are you going to be okay?"

My mum didn't really have a lot of close friends anymore. After the truth had come out about Scott, and Jade had hopped on a plane out of the country, Judith had turned on my mother in the most horrific way. In spite of them being friends for their whole lives, she had somehow reached the conclusion that our family was to blame for hers falling apart. Not Scott for being a morally corrupt arsehole. Not Jade for being a horrible friend who cared more about appearances than people. Us. The Morgans because I'd dared to go against the grain by being with Cal.

As if having a lying, manipulative, potential sex trafficker as a son-in-law was something to be proud of. What she meant, of course, was that without my meeting Cal, Scott might not have been exposed, but he still would have been a disgusting human. If anything, we did her a favour before such a terrible person became a part of their family.

My mum did have some other friends, but not too many she was as close to as she had been to Judith. In my opinion, Judith was no great loss, but I did understand the pain of letting go of someone who had been a part of her life for so long. Now, my mum had to deal with losing my dad on top. Even though it was her choice, it had to have been crushing at her insides, and I wasn't even there to go and hug her.

"I'll be fine, Shannen," Mum said. "Really. I'm going to see Sadie later and I might just stay at her place for a couple of nights. It'll be good to spend time there, and then we can all meet when you're home."

Knowing she had already planned to see Sadie helped relax me a little. At least she wouldn't be alone.

"Okay," I said. "Well, I'll ring you in a couple of days to see how you are, but you can call me if you want to. I don't mind."

"I know, my darling. But don't worry about me. You go and have a good time with Cal and I'll see you very soon, okay?"

"Okay. I love you, Mum."

"I love you too."

As we hung up, I huffed out a deep breath, dropping my phone onto the bed. I gave Cal a brief rundown of the things my mum had said before he had come into the room, and he didn't seem surprised by my mum's decision. I knew he never wanted to speak to my dad again, but he also accepted that even if my dad and I were no longer close, there would be times when they'd probably need to be around each other. Cal's intention was to be polite, but he never wanted any kind of relationship with him, and I was fine with that. Maybe it wasn't a good thing for him to hold onto resentment, but that wasn't really what it was. He was learning to let that go, but like my mum, he would never be able to comprehend how a father could do something so awful to his child, and there was no coming back from it for him.

"Shan," Cal said, as I'd gotten lost in my thoughts. I turned my head to look at him. With his deep brown eyes on mine, he said, "About your dad. You know how I feel about him, but if you want to see him, I'm not going to be upset about it."

I nodded. "I know. But it's also..." I paused, placing a hand on my stomach. "Whatever I decide to do myself is one thing, but what about the baby? This is his grandchild. If I decide to see him, would you be okay with him getting to know our baby?"

He raised his eyebrows as if that hadn't crossed his mind before. "Would *you* be okay with him getting to know our baby?"

"I'm not sure," I said honestly. I hadn't thought a whole lot about it myself. "But I don't want to use our child as some kind of punishment for him either by keeping him away."

"That's not what it would be," Cal said, reaching for my hand. "Any decisions we make would be because we think it's best for all of us." Linking his fingers through mine, he added, "Come on. We need to get out of here and have some of that fun we've been talking about before we ruin this day before it's started."

He leaned forward and placed a soft kiss on my lips, making me smile, and some of the tension eased from my shoulders. "Okay. Let's do this!"

Cal

We had a long, relaxed lunch in the hotel restaurant, taking our time while we ate and chatted. Looking at Shannen across the table, seeing her slowly loosen up after the conversation with her mum, I began to relax again too. We'd already had some pretty heavy conversations, and even though I'd expected it, I also knew we needed a break.

After lunch, we left the hotel and took a walk along the busy beach, hand in hand, both of us taking in the sights around us. I wasn't really the kind of guy who took much notice of views and scenery, but even I could see St. Ives was beautiful. It was old-fashioned, and even though there were a lot of people engaging in swimming, surfing, playing games together, or eating a picnic, something about it felt calm. The pace felt slower, and I guessed that was one of the reasons Shannen wanted to come here. Over lunch, she'd told me more about how she and her family visited the town and had spent a lot of time on these beaches. Maybe we'd bring our kids here sometime, as a family.

I loved the idea of having more kids with Shannen. Even though our first wasn't born yet, I wanted more. For someone who had feared being a father the first time around, the change Shannen had made to my life was huge. It wasn't just Shannen; I'd had to do a lot of work on myself, and there was way more still to do, but I could see a future. And it had a lot of children in it.

I should probably run this by Shannen at some point.

The thought made me laugh. If she only ever wanted one with me, I'd have been okay with it, but she'd said herself that she liked the idea of a big family. We'd just need to agree on a number.

Shannen and I had the best time looking around the shops, playing in the arcades... I even liked the galleries. I couldn't remember the last time both of us had been so completely chilled out, neither of us needing to support the other. We were just us. Who we'd always wanted to be without all of the shit that had followed us around.

When we eventually made it back to the hotel, Shannen was tired, so we decided we'd order room service instead of going back down to the restaurant. Before we did that, though, Shannen and I collapsed onto the bed, and she curled herself around me while I called Guy so I could speak to Aiden.

"Hey, bud," Guy said, and I heard laughter in the background. I wasn't sure whose, but it was followed by a loud female shriek, and then I heard Aiden cackling afterwards.

"What's going on over there?" I asked, laughing. The phone was on speaker so Shannen could speak to Aiden too, and she burst out laughing as Donovan yelped, "Fuck off!" even though he was also laughing, quickly adding an apology for swearing, which made Aiden laugh more.

"Erm," Guy said, pausing for a second, "Water balloon fight. It's dangerous over here. Aiden is tormenting Gaby, and Nova and Gaby are ganging up on Donovan. I'm only safe right now because I have a phone in my hand."

"Bad luck, mate!" I heard Donovan say, followed by a loud splash, and Guy threw out a string of curse words while everyone else taunted him for thinking he could avoid getting hit.

"Just wait until I'm finished here," Guy shouted to them, but there was amusement in his voice. "Fuckers just soaked my legs!" he said to me. "How's your day been?"

"Good," I said, grinning at Shannen, but I couldn't help feeling slightly gutted that we weren't there with them. It sounded like they were having a blast. "How was Aiden today?"

"He was good," Guy said. "Gaby and I took Aiden to Godrevy for most of the day, and we made a gigantic sandcastle. He really enjoyed seeing Gaby in a swimming costume."

The background noise was getting quieter, and I guessed Guy had gone back inside the lodge we were staying in for the week.

I also think Guy probably liked seeing Gaby in a swimming costume... Not that she was dressed in a way that was inappropriate around my son. I saw her before we left; her swimming costume wasn't low cut, and she had a skirt covering her bottom half.

Shannen laughed beside me, fully aware of Aiden's crush on Gaby. He had been besotted with her since the day we'd gone to Dawlish Warren together, so we knew he'd enjoy spending the day with her. We'd only found out that morning that Guy was going with them, and I was pretty sure Aiden wasn't the only one who was into Shannen's friend. "Will Aiden come to the phone?" Shannen asked. "Or is he having too much fun to stop?"

Laughing, Guy said, "Nah, I'll go get him." Within a few seconds, Guy called out to him and told him we wanted to talk to him, and in another few seconds, Aiden's voice came down the line.

"Hi, Dad!" he said brightly.

"Hey, buddy," I answered, the feeling of missing him getting stronger just hearing him. "You okay?"

"Yeah. I went to the beach and then when we came back here, Gaby said I needed a nap, but I didn't want one, so we watched a movie and then Nova and Donovan came in and gave me water balloons!"

"Make sure you save some for when we get back," Shannen said. "I think your dad wants to play too!"

"Can you play as well?" he asked, and Shannen's lower lip pouted out slightly, knowing she wouldn't be able to join in.

"Probably not, sweetheart," she told him. "I have to be careful and I can't run very fast. But it'll be fun to watch!"

"Okay," Aiden said. "I miss you."

"We miss you too," I told him, my chest aching slightly with the truth of it, "but we'll be home early in the morning, and then all of us are going out together for the day."

"Yay! I can't wait!"

"Will you promise to be good for Gaby and go to bed when she tells you?" I asked him, knowing he wanted to wrap this call up so he could go and play again.

"I promise," Aiden said. "I love you!"

That never got old. Neither did him calling me Dad. The ache in my chest intensified as I thought about how fucking gut-wrenching it was to be away from him. I hadn't been apart from him for this long in a while, and though I knew he was safe and enjoying himself, I would have given anything to just give him a quick hug. I never took for granted how fortunate I was to have him now.

"I love you too," I told him, the words coming easily. It had taken way too long for me to be able to say it, but now I could and it didn't give me palpitations, I said it to him every day.

"Me too," Shannen added, and Aiden giggled.

"Love you!" he told her, then hung up the phone before I'd had a chance to say goodbye to Guy. I stared at the phone for a moment before placing it down on the bedside table beside me.

Shannen held me tighter, and as I turned back to her, I shuffled closer; more and more challenging as her baby bump grew. I loved the feel of it close to me, though.

"We are so lucky," she said softly, her breath tickling my neck as she moved her hand lightly up and down my back. "We've got so much."

Nodding, I said, "Yeah, we have." I rested a hand on her cheek, and she turned her head to place a kiss on my palm before snuggling into me again.

"You know what I really want right now?" she asked, a mischievous glint in her eyes.

"What do you want, Shan?"

"A nap."

I snorted out a laugh. "That wasn't what I was hoping you'd say." I ran my hands down her back, resting them on her ass, and she laughed.

"I want to do lots of that later," she promised, looking up at me. "But first, I just want to lie next to you and rest because this might be the last chance we have to do that in a long time. Everything has been so... loud lately."

Loud. That was a pretty good way to describe the chaos we'd been living in for so long. The volume had been going down slowly, and while we hadn't reached full silence yet, we were getting there. We were close enough that we could afford to do just what she wanted. To lie together in peace and know everything we'd been building was safe.

We were safe.

**

You can read about the group's summer holiday and see what happens next in Over You, Oakwood Lane Book 3 here!

343

Acknowledgements

Coffee.
That is all.

I jest, although I do thank the caffeine gods for the energy bursts.

My most gigantic thank yous go to Clare Dugmore and Clare Bentley for helping me to tidy up this book. Also for the squeals of delight and the messages of rage at each new twist and turn; it kept me amused throughout! Love you both!

The members of the Write Here, Write Now Community for cheering me on through those last few chapters - the support is unmatched and so appreciated!

Sophie Mitchell - the queen of marketing campaigns. Thank you for your constant support as a marketing genius, but most importantly, for your friendship and hours of entertaining conversations!

Richard - my long-suffering fiance. Thanks for allowing me to play the same songs on a loop for three months at a time while I write. Sorry I ruined some of your favourites. :p

And of course, my incredible readers. Thank you for your love for Shannen and Cal. They have been in my heart since I was a teenager, and I am humbled that you have taken them into your hearts too.

Other Books by Kyra Lennon

You can find free content for the Oakwood Lane Series here!

Razes Hell Series
Nobody Knows
Everybody Knows
Chaos and Consent Series
Hear What You Want
Say What You Feel
Take What You Need
Oakwood Lane Prequel
Re-Writing Christmas
Oakwood Lane Series
All Of You
Only With You
Over You
Standalones
Reasonable Doubts
Picture (Im)Perfect
Unintended

About the Author

Kyra Lennon is a British romance author who has published several books in the contemporary romance genre. She began her writing career in 2012 with her debut novel "Game On" and has since published several other books, including "Unintended," and the Chaos and Consent trilogy.

Lennon's writing is known for its relatable characters, emotional depth, and compelling storylines. Her books often explore themes of love, loss, and self-discovery, and are generally well-received by readers for their heartwarming and engaging nature.

In addition to her writing, Lennon is also an avid reader and blogger, and has been involved in the online book community for several years. She is active on social media and maintains an active presence on platforms like Twitter and Facebook, where she interacts with her readers and fellow authors.

If you would like to keep up to date with all of Kyra's latest news, you can follow her on Facebookor, sign up to her newsletter for news, book recs, and freebies!

www.ingramcontent.com/pod-product-compliance
Lightning Source LLC
Chambersburg PA
CBHW020528020726
47494CB00006B/1674

* 9 7 8 1 7 3 8 4 8 0 6 2 3 *